The Best American
SCIENCE FICTION
and FANTASY
2019

The Best American
SCIENCE FICTION
and FANTASY™
2019

Edited and with an Introduction
by **Carmen Maria Machado**

John Joseph Adams, *Series Editor*

MARINER BOOKS

HOUGHTON MIFFLIN HARCOURT

BOSTON • NEW YORK   2019

www.hmhbooks.com

ISSN 2573-0797 (print) ISSN 2573-0800 (ebook)

ISBN 978-1-328-60437-8 (print) ISBN 978-1-328-60406-4 (ebook)

Printed in the United States of America
DOC 10 9 8 7 6 5 4 3 2 1

Contents

Foreword

WELCOME TO YEAR five of *The Best American Science Fiction and Fantasy*! This volume presents the best science fiction and fantasy (SF/F) short stories published during the 2018 calendar year as selected by myself and guest editor Carmen Maria Machado.

About This Year's Guest Editor

Simply put, Carmen Maria Machado is one of short fiction's contemporary masters. Indeed, if you pay attention to short fiction at all, you almost certainly have already read—and been blown away by—her work. She's a force in both the literary and the genre worlds, first publishing a plethora of much-lauded short fiction that made her a star and then going supernova with the release of her collection *Her Body and Other Parties*. That book, which gathers much but not all of her body of work, won many awards, such as the National Book Critics Circle's John Leonard Prize, the Shirley Jackson Award, the Lambda Literary Award for Lesbian Fiction, and the Bard Fiction Prize, and was a finalist for many others, including the National Book Award, the Art Seidenbaum Award for First Fiction (L.A. Times Book Prize), the PEN/Robert W. Bingham Prize for Debut Fiction, the World Fantasy Award, the Kirkus Prize, and others. And if all that weren't impressive enough, it's also in development as a television show at FX.

In genre, Machado's short fiction has appeared in magazines such as *Fairy Tale Review, Interfictions, Lady Churchill's Rosebud Wristlet, Lightspeed, Nightmare, PodCastle, Shimmer, Strange Horizons, Un-*

canny, and *Unstuck,* and in literary circles her fiction has graced the pages of such periodicals as *Harper's Bazaar, Tin House, Granta, McSweeney's, The American Reader, VQR, Gulf Coast,* and others. In the realm of nonfiction, Machado is also a vibrant voice, with essays and criticism that have appeared in *The New Yorker,* the *New York Times, The Paris Review, NPR Books,* the *Los Angeles Times Review of Books, Catapult, Guernica,* and *The Believer.*

But there's more! She has had stories in anthologies such as *Watchlist, Nebula Awards Showcase 2016, Mixed Up, New Voices of Fantasy, Help Fund My Robot Army!!! and Other Improbable Crowdfunding Projects, Mothership: Tales from Afrofuturism and Beyond, Sunspot Jungle Vol. 1, Grave Predictions,* and *Latin@ Rising.* She has also appeared in *The Best American Science Fiction and Fantasy* twice (in the 2015 and 2018 volumes), *The Best Horror of the Year, Year's Best Weird Fiction, The Year's Best Dark Fantasy & Horror,* and *Best Women's Erotica of the Year.* Her story "A Brief and Fearful Star" (published in *Future Tense* in 2018) was reprinted in Jonathan Strahan's *The Best Science Fiction & Fantasy of the Year* and would have garnered serious consideration for this volume as well if Machado were not the guest editor.

Machado holds an MFA from the Iowa Writers' Workshop and been awarded a slew of fellowships and residences from such august bodies as the Guggenheim Foundation, and the *New York Times* listed her as a member of "The New Vanguard," citing *Her Body and Other Parties* as one of "15 remarkable books by women that are shaping the way we read and write fiction in the 21st century."

Selection Criteria and Process

The stories chosen for this anthology were originally published between January 1, 2018, and December 31, 2018. The technical criteria for consideration are (1) original publication in a nationally distributed American or Canadian publication (periodicals, collections, or anthologies, in print, online, or as an ebook); (2) publication in English by writers who are American or Canadian or who have made the United States their home; (3) publication as text (audiobook, podcast, dramatized, interactive, and other forms of fiction are not considered); (4) original publication as short fiction (excerpts of novels are not knowingly considered); (5) story length of 17,499 words or less; (6) at least loosely categorized as science fiction or fantasy; (7) publication by someone other than the author (self-published works are not eligible); and (8) publication as an original work of the author (that is, not part of a media tie-in/licensed fiction program).

As series editor, I attempted to read everything I could find that met these selection criteria. After doing all my reading, I created a list of what I felt were the top eighty stories (forty science fiction and forty fantasy) published in the genre. Those eighty stories were sent to the guest editor, who read them and then chose the best twenty (ten science fiction, ten fantasy) for inclusion in the anthology. The guest editor read all the stories anonymously, with no bylines attached to them nor any information about where the story originally appeared.

The guest editor's top twenty selections appear in this volume; the sixty stories that did not make it into the anthology are listed in the back of this book as "Other Notable Science Fiction and Fantasy Stories of 2018."

2018 Summation

As per my standard practice, in my effort to determine the top eighty stories of the year, I read and considered several thousand stories from a wide variety of periodicals, anthologies, and collections. Winnowing down the list to just eighty was (as usual) extremely difficult, and so beyond the top eighty I had several dozen additional stories that were at one point or another under serious consideration.

The top eighty this year were drawn from forty different publications: twenty-three periodicals, ten anthologies, and seven single-author collections. The final table of contents draws from thirteen different sources: eleven periodicals, one anthology, and two collections. *Nightmare Magazine* had the most selections (four); *Lightspeed Magazine*, *Tor.com*, and *Fireside Fiction* had two each.

Four of the authors included in this volume (Adam-Troy Castro, N. K. Jemisin, Seanan McGuire, and Sofia Samatar) have previously appeared in *BASFF*; thus, the remaining sixteen authors are appearing for the first time. Sofia Samatar has the most *BASFF* appearances all-time with four; this is the second appearance for Castro, Jemisin, and McGuire.

This year marks the first appearances of four periodicals in our table of contents: *Apex Magazine, Future Tense, The Margins (Transpacific Literary Project),* and *FIYAH.* Periodicals appearing in the top eighty for the first time this year include *Eyedolon, MIT Technology Review, The Paris Review, Stonecoast Review,* and *Vastarien.*

Adam-Troy Castro and Nana Kwame Adjei-Brenyah had the most stories in the top eighty this year, with three each; several other authors had two each: Alyssa Wong, Annalee Newitz, Carrie Vaughn, Daniel H. Wilson, E. Lily Yu, Elizabeth Bear, Kelly Robson, Kurt Fawver, N. K. Jemisin, P. Djèlí Clark, and Seanan McGuire. Overall, sixty-six different authors are represented (which is, weirdly, the same number of different authors as in last year's volume).

P. Djèlí Clark's story selected for inclusion, "The Secret Lives of the Nine Negro Teeth of George Washington," won the Nebula and Locus awards, and was named a finalist for the Hugo and Sturgeon awards. Daryl Gregory's "Nine Last Days on Planet Earth" was named a finalist for the Hugo, Locus, and Sturgeon Awards. Sarah Gailey's "STET" is a Hugo and Locus finalist. The selections by Annalee Newitz ("When Robot and Crow Saved East St. Louis") and Adam R. Shannon ("On the Day You Spend Forever with Your Dog") were both finalists for the Sturgeon (and Newitz was this year's winner), and Usman Malik's story, "Dead Lovers on Each Blade, Hung," was a finalist for the Bram Stoker Award. N. K. Jemisin's "The Storyteller's Replacement" was a Locus finalist.

Among the Notable Stories, three were finalists for the Hugo, Nebula, and Locus Awards: Brooke Bolander's "The Only Harmless Great Thing" (Nebula Award winner, and also a finalist for the Sturgeon and Shirley Jackson Awards); "A Witch's Guide to Escape: A Practical Compendium of Portal Fantasies," by Alix E. Harrow; and "The Court Magician," by Sarah Pinsker. The following Notable Stories were also Locus finalists: "Okay, Glory," by Elizabeth Bear; "Queen Lily," by Theodora Goss; "Firelight," by Ursula K. Le Guin; and "The Starship and the Temple Cat," by Yoon Ha Lee. "And Yet," by A. T. Greenblatt, and "The Substance of My Lives, the Accidents of Our Births," by José Pablo Iriarte, were named Nebula finalists. Joe Hill's "You Are Released" was a finalist for the Stoker.

(Note: The final results of these awards won't be known until after this text is locked for production but will be known by the time the book is published.)

Anthologies

The lone anthology to have a story represented in the table of contents this year was *Kaiju Rising 2: Reign of Monsters,* edited by N. X. Sharps and Alana Abbott; several other anthologies, however, did have stories in the top eighty, such as *A Thousand Beginnings and Endings,* edited by Elsie Chapman and Ellen Oh; *Flight or Fright,* edited by Stephen King and Bev Vincent; *Mechanical Animals,* edited by Selena Chambers and Jason Heller; *Particulates,* edited by Nalo Hopkinson; and *The Devil and the Deep,* edited by Ellen Datlow. The anthology with the most stories in the top eighty — four — was *Twelve Tomorrows,* edited by Wade Roush; *Resist: Tales from a Future Worth Fighting Against,* edited by Gary Whitta, Christie Yant, and Hugh Howey, had three; and *Infinity's End,* edited by Jonathan Strahan, and *Welcome to Dystopia,* edited by Gordon Van Gelder, had two each.

Here's a sampling of the anthologies that published fine work that didn't quite manage to make it into the top eighty but are worthwhile just the same: *The Book of Magic,* edited by Gardner Dozois; *Future Fiction,* edited by Bill Campbell and Francesco Verso; *Hath No Fury,* edited by Melanie R. Meadors and J. M. Martin; *The Cackle of Cthulhu,* edited by Alex Shvartsman; *A Year Without Winter,* edited by Dehlia Hannah, Brenda Cooper, Joey Eschrich, and Cynthia Selin; *By the Light of Camelot,* edited by J. R. Campbell and Shannon Allen; *Toil and Trouble,* edited by Jessica Spotswood and Tess Sharpe; *Undercurrents: An Anthology of What Lies Beneath,* edited by Kevin J. Anderson; *Fresh Ink,* edited by Lamar Giles; *Phantoms,* edited by Marie O'Regan; *Lost Films,* edited by Max Booth III and Lori Michelle; *Shades Within Us,* edited by Susan Forest and Lucas K. Law; *Underwater Ballroom Society,* edited by Tiffany Trent and Stephanie Burgis; *Sword and Sonnet,* edited by Aidan Doyle, Rachael K. Jones, and E. Catherine Tobler; and *Sunspot Jungle Vol. 1,* edited by Bill Campbell.

Additionally, the Amazon Original Stories program released several interesting SF/F works in 2018 in two "collections," *Warmer* and *Dark Corners;* they aren't quite anthologies per se (nor are they collections in typical publishing parlance), since the stories are downloaded individually, but otherwise that's what they feel like. I think of them as *deconstructed* anthologies, so I'm including them in this section.

I don't keep close tabs on all-reprint anthologies since by definition nothing in them is eligible for *BASFF,* but among those worthy of note released in 2018 include: *The Future Is Female!,* edited by Lisa Yaszek, and *The Final Frontier,* edited by Neil Clarke.

Collections

The two standout collections this year were *Friday Black,* by Nana Kwame Adjei-Brenyah (three stories in the top eighty, one selection), and *How Long 'til Black Future Month?,* by N. K. Jemisin (two stories in the top eighty, one selection), which are also the only two collections to produce *BASFF* selections this year. Other collections that had stories in the top eighty were *Dreadful Young Ladies and Other Stories,* by Kelly Barnhill; *Guardian Angels and Other Monsters,* by Daniel H. Wilson; and *We Are Where the Nightmares Go and Other Stories,* by C. Robert Cargill. Fine work was to be found in several other collections (some of which contained only reprints and thus had no eligible material), including *The Promise of Space,* by James Patrick Kelly; *All the Names They Used for God: Stories,* by Anjali Sachdeva; *The End of All Our Exploring,* by F. Brett Cox; *The Dissolution of Small Worlds,* by Kurt Fawver; *The Merry Spinster,* by Mallory Ortberg; *The Sacerdotal Owl and Three Other Long Tales,* by Michael Bishop; *Tomorrow Factory: Collected Fiction,* by Rich Larson; *Night Beast,* by Ruth Joffre; *Godfall and Other Stories,* by Sandra M. Odell; *Ambiguity Machines and Other Stories,* by Vandana Singh; *Acres of Perhaps,* by Will Ludwigsen; *Half Gods,* by Akil Kumarasamy; *An Agent of Utopia,* by Andy Duncan; *The Ones Who Are Waving,* by Glen Hirshberg; *Alien Virus Love Disaster,* by Abbey Mei Otis; *All the Fabulous Beasts,* by Priya Sharma; *The Future Is Blue,* by Catherynne M. Valente; *How to Fracture a Fairy Tale,* by Jane Yolen; *The Dinosaur Tourist,* by Caitlín R. Kiernan; and *Starlings,* by Jo Walton.

Periodicals

I surveyed more than a hundred different periodicals over the course of the year and paid equal attention to genre publications both large and small. Likewise I do my best to find any genre fiction lurking in the pages of mainstream and/or literary publications.

Outside of the two magazines I edit—*Lightspeed* and *Nightmare*—which are inevitably well represented in the top eighty, since one does tend to like one's own taste in fiction, periodicals that were well represented include *Apex* (two); *Clarkesworld* (three); *Eyedolon** (two); *Fireside* (three); *FIYAH* (two); *Strange Horizons* (three); *Terraform* (two), *Tor.com* (four); and *Uncanny* (three). The following periodicals each had one story in the top eighty: *Analog*, *Asimov's*, *Beneath Ceaseless Skies*, *Future Tense*, *McSweeney's*, *MIT Technology Review*, *The Paris Review*, *Stonecoast Review*, *The Dark*, *The Magazine of Fantasy & Science Fiction*, *The Margins*, and *Vastarien.**

Some periodicals that published interesting material that didn't make it into the top eighty include *Augur,** *Cincinnati Review*, *Daily Science Fiction*, *Escape Pod*, *Flash Fiction Online*, *Future Science Fiction Digest,** *Playboy*, *PodCastle*, *Shimmer, Reason.com*, *The Sun*, *Tin House*, and *Wired*.

It's always nice to see new publications cropping up year to year, and so to celebrate that I've denoted with an asterisk above those publications that debuted in 2018. But the circle of life is, well, a *circle*, and inevitably all good things come to an end. This year is no exception: several periodicals have either gone extinct or embarked on an indefinite hiatus. These include *Cicada* (founded 1998), *Dark Discoveries* (founded 2004), *Liminal Stories* (founded 2016), *Mythic Delirium* (founded 1998), and *Shimmer* (founded 2005). Book Smugglers Publishing isn't closing but announced in November that it will be largely scaling back its fiction endeavors. Two major magazines lasted through 2018 but have announced they will cease publication in 2019 after fourteen-year runs: *Intergalactic Medicine Show* and *Apex Magazine*.

This is a good time to remind fine people like you who love short fiction enough to not only read this book but read this foreword that short fiction publishers need your support to keep their endeavors going. If you can, subscribe, review, spread the word. Every little bit helps.

Acknowledgments

I'd like to take a moment to thank and acknowledge my team of first readers, who helped me evaluate various publications that I might not have had time to consider otherwise, including Alex Puncekar, Sandra Odell, and Christie Yant. Thanks also to Jenny Xu at Mariner Books, who is our current point person keeping things running smoothly behind the scenes at Best American HQ. Likewise I'm grateful to all the authors who alert me to their published eligible works by sending them to me via my *BASFF* online submissions portal (which is extremely helpful to make sure I don't miss anything), and of course I also deeply appreciate the editors and publishers who take the time to make sure I get copies of the books or periodicals they publish. Thanks too to David Steffen, who runs the Submission Grinder writers' market database, for his assistance in helping me do some oversight on my list of new and gone-extinct markets. And last but not least, a huge thanks to all the readers who have purchased (and reviewed!) previous iterations of *BASFF* and thus have enabled the series to continue; I hope we can keep it going for a long, long time. (If you read and loved a previous edition, please do consider leaving a review at your venue of choice; it really does help!)

Submissions for Next Year's Volume

Editors, writers, and publishers who would like their work considered for next year's edition (the best of 2019), please visit johnjosephadams.com/best-american for instructions on how to submit material for consideration.

—JOHN JOSEPH ADAMS

Introduction

In an ideal world, I would have opened this essay with one of my favorite quotes from Salvador Dalí, the one he wrote in his diary about how he's discovered that he's always been painting the rhinoceros horn. It's one of my favorite quotes about art, and I have always found its general thrust—the subtly singular focus of artistic obsession—to be funny, useful, and instructive.[1] But instead I find myself feeling uncharitable, like a beleaguered parent driving a minivan across the Southwest whose fraternal twins are in the back seat drawing invisible lines down the upholstery and swatting at each other.[2]

There is currently an unending, utterly exhausting fight between two particular writing communities: literary fiction and genre fiction. *Fight* might not even be the correct word, as it lacks both the acute thrill and the clear resolution of physical combat. You cannot attend a con, conference, or spend any time on social media without running into this petty squabbling, in which some writers and readers of the two communities find themselves thoughtlessly repeating a series of untrue truisms about the other

---

1. "I, Dalí, deep in a constant introspection and a meticulous analysis of my smallest thoughts, have just discovered that, without realizing it, I have painted nothing but rhinoceros horns all my life [. . .] I take another look at all my paintings and I am stupefied with the amount of rhinoceros my work contains." What freedom! What liberation! An artist finding at the root of his work a consistent and undeniable truth: the cosmic beauty of the rhinoceros horn.
2. Unlike the parent of the squabbling kids, however, I'm less inclined to pull the van over to the side of the road than to drive the whole thing off an embankment, such is the level of my frustration.

in what they consider sympathetic or like-minded spaces: con panels, for example, or classrooms, or the surprisingly narrow scope of their Twitter universe. The untrue truisms are slightly different only in the most minor way: the clichés spouted by genre writers about literary fiction tend to be ignorant and defensive; the clichés spouted by literary writers about genre fiction tend to be ignorant and snobbish. "Literary fiction is boring and entirely about college professors sleeping with their students!" "Genre fiction is unserious and entirely about dragons and spaceships! *Pew pew, pew pew.*"[3] They are such tedious clichés, and ones performed in such bad faith, that all they tell me is that the offending thinker is more interested in victimhood or condescension than in reading good work or becoming a better writer. It is solipsistic, irritating, and the opposite of useful. *What a coincidence,* I always think, *that the fiction you think is terrible and not worth learning from is also one you've apparently never read.*[4] Blanket statements about these communities fail to be many things: they are not smart, not thoughtful, not generous, not a reflection of an omnivorous mind—all things you need as a reader and a writer!—but perhaps most criminally, they are *not interesting.*

I've been teaching undergraduates for the better part of a decade, and spend much of my time telling them that literature is about potential, about the brazen and thrilling integration of other people's history and art with *their* history and art, about ambitious leaps of genre and world-building and the ordinary magic of the human experience and the minute perfection of the sen-

3. In the interest of full disclosure, this is the full sum of my personal experience on this matter: I've been told by genre editors/publications that my work is "too literary" and not sufficiently "genre," but I've never experienced the inverse (though I am assured by genre writers that it happens, and I believe them); I've argued with a lot of people about this subject online and in person; I was once described on Twitter as a "litfic writer" who was "Quite Put Out" by a genre writer's mindless repetition of the above tropes—though I write fantasy, I don't use or recognize the word *litfic*, and I am actually Permanently Put Out; I wrote fabulism at the Iowa Writers' Workshop and two of the eight stories in my first collection at Clarion; people always seem to think that when I ramble on about gatekeeping I'm talking about literary fiction gatekeeping keeping out genre fiction, even though I am never, ever talking about that; I desperately wish I could believe in ghosts.
4. Or haven't read in a long time, or haven't read enough of, or haven't read since you were a kid, or only read for school, or haven't read with any kind of curiosity or depth and width.

tence and pursuing your own obsessions and dozens of other wonderful things besides. And then they turn to the practitioners and readers of the craft and see endless, thoughtless squabbling, pointless category-enforcing, people who refuse to read outside of their comfort zones or even acknowledge their value, people who think of the work of certain writers as *theirs* instead of *everyone's*. I am trying to show them that traditions are not destinies, that no community can own a writer or a book, that the existence of multiple distinct communities of literature means that there is *more fiction to read,* that the house is even bigger than you had imagined. And yet some folks are only interested in locking the doors, turning out the lights. It's bullshit, and it hits every button of irritation I possess.

Kelly Link has often spoken of how genre is, among other things, "the promise of pleasure," and if you think of all fiction as possessing or belonging to a genre (which I do), the issue becomes less combative. Instead of *How can I denigrate the category to which this story belongs, and by extension this story?* you might ask, *What kind of pleasure does this story bring me?* (Or, *What kind of pleasure might this story bring someone else?*)[5] With that perspective fiction becomes infused with promise. This story might bring the deep somatic thrill of terror or the alluring perfume of mystery; it might sting with familiarity or drag you howling into the unknown, or both. It might give you sentences so thoughtful and precise you feel dizzy with specificity; those sentences might defamiliarize the familiar or be a garden path into some fresh territory you've never seen before. It might tell a story that you, in your eternal human nearsightedness, have never encountered before. It might tell you one that you didn't know you needed to hear.

I read for this edition of *The Best American Science Fiction and Fantasy* with no particular agenda other than my personal pleasure. These stories—as well as those listed as honorable mentions—come from literary magazines and publishers and genre magazines and publishers, from authors who have been recognized by genre and literary awards, by graduates of the Clarion and MFA programs, and by folks who haven't done either. All of these details about the authors and the magazines that published their

---

5. And, if you're a writer yourself, *What might I learn from this story? How might it contribute to my work, my practice?*

work are incidental. Here you will find an undeniable bias toward the use of formal constraints,[6] vibrant and muscular prose,[7] ambitious weirdness.[8] Many of these stories unnerved[9] me, and others impressed me with their scope[10] and their intimacy.[11] There are several stories that reveal my weakness for compelling, complex, tender narratives about animals and animal-like creatures.[12] There is one story that made me salivate,[13] one that made me stand up out of my chair,[14] one that made me cry.[15] All of them made me happy to be a reader and writer in 2019.

And that's all that matters, really. Why waste time drawing boundaries and performing ancient arguments and erecting dead horses and beating straw men and enacting coldness and smugness when you could be reading and salivating and standing and yelling and crying and learning and experiencing narrative pleasure and wonder and joy? Why, when you can do those things, would you do anything else?

— CARMEN MARIA MACHADO

6. Sarah Gailey's "STET," Daryl Gregory's "Nine Last Days on Planet Earth," Ada Hoffmann's "Variations on a Theme from *Turandot*," Theodore McCombs's "Six Hangings in the Land of Unkillable Women," P. Djèlí Clark's "The Secret Lives of the Nine Negro Teeth of George Washington," Nino Cipri's "Dead Air," and Silvia Park's "Poor Unfortunate Fools."
7. Particularly Usman Malik's "Dead Lovers on Each Blade, Hung."
8. Like LaShawn M. Wanak's "Sister Rosetta Tharpe and Memphis Minnie Sing the Stumps Down Good," Nana Kwame Adjei-Brenyah's "Through the Flash."
9. Adam-Troy Castro's "Pitcher Plant," N. K. Jemisin's "The Storyteller's Replacement."
10. Brenda Peynado's "The Kite Maker."
11. Lesley Nneka Arimah's "Skinned," Kelly Robson's "What Gentle Women Dare."
12. Seanan McGuire's "What Everyone Knows," Annalee Newitz's "When Robot and Crow Saved East St. Louis."
13. Martin Cahill's "Godmeat."
14. Sofia Samatar's "Hard Mary."
15. Adam R. Shannon's "On the Day You Spend Forever with Your Dog."

ADAM-TROY CASTRO

Pitcher Plant

FROM *Nightmare Magazine*

THE MANSION IS a study in architecture at war with itself. It's not just the windows that don't match and the turrets that don't overlook anything and the roof that sits flat here while looming at impossible angles there. Nor is it just the exterior walls that seen from one angle seem rotted and decrepit and about to collapse, and seen from another gleam like jewels. Nor is it the gnarled skin of the columns that support the overhang at the front entrance, nor the glistening scarlet door that seems poised to open until you see that it's not a real door at all but just a reasonable facsimile, carved with great love into what would otherwise be just a featureless brick wall.

It's the way that none of this stays the same for more than a second or two; the way you can focus on one bay window or one turret or one balcony only to see it shift, retract, and sink beneath the house's surface like something swallowed by an amoeba, only to emerge, seconds or minutes later, wearing a different shape, a different character, a different purpose in the overall design. It is impossible to face the mansion without knowing that it has always been changing, plank by plank, brick by brick, for as long as it has stood in this damned and isolated place beneath scarlet skies, in a blackened country, far from any roads.

You are impressed. Most normal houses provide no challenge to you. You're not just an excellent thief; you're the first thief. You find most locks nothing more than interesting trinkets, most fortresses nothing more than delusions built of mortar and stone. Some have required planning, some have been challenging, but few have stymied you for more than a few minutes. For you, the

greatest difficulties involved in conquering any house have been
first finding out that the house was there, then determining who
and what were inside, and finally making the decision that the
time had come to pass through the threshold, to claim those inside. But this house, by its very nature, has no threshold; it has
no vestibule; it has no foyer. It has only a spastic geography that
alters in hiccups. You are particularly fascinated by the moat: a
gaping, watery trench that orbits the house like the blip on a radar
screen, constantly excavating itself on one end while filling itself in
on the other. The alligators that bob to the surface of that water,
hissing and snapping, threatening bloody dismemberment to any
wanderer unlucky enough to be standing on the grass when the
earth beneath him becomes moat again, are no less threatening
for being temporary. It's a nice effect, determined to unnerve any
potential intruders. You can only admire the tenants for their clev-
erness in managing such a thing, as you wait for the moat to fill in
before you, enabling you to approach the house without wetting
your feet.

The outer wall is warm. Of course, most inhabited buildings
are warm, in a way that has little to do with surface temperature.
They glow, in their own special way, with the warmth of the lives
within. All houses bear the mark of the births and deaths, the
lovemaking and the hate, the complacency and the fear, of those
within. It may not be possible to track the entire course of their
lives with a touch, but it's hard not to know that inhabitants exist.
But this house is warm in a different way. It feels like it's boiling.
It feels like a sack full of cats, scratching and clawing and tearing
pieces from each other in their desperation to be free. You pull
your hand away as if burned. You touch the wall again. And this
time you endure the heat, lingering on it, giving yourself time to
feel the sheer weight of all the pain imprisoned within. There's
unhappiness here; desperate unhappiness. And hopelessness too.
There's so much that breaking in is going to mean taking a delib-
erate step into somebody's personal hell. This won't deter you, of
course. You've seen suffering before. But it's good to know such
things before getting down to work. You nod, and take a step back,
and watch the shifting textures of the wall before you as they shift
from brick to stucco to stone to unfinished wood. You wait until a
single open window, flapping a flyspecked pull-down shade, comes
around the corner and moves across the building face before you.

The view through that window shows no details but shifts color and brightness as quickly as a strobe light. It looks like an opening into a blast furnace. It would take insanity or unlimited self-confidence or unconditional devotion to duty to willingly enter such a place. You don't hesitate. You grab the window as it moves by, hop up onto the sill, and slide into the mansion with an ease that makes you wonder why you ever thought this was going to be difficult.

Your first glimpse of the mansion's interior turns out to be a parlor. Its own geography doesn't shift, which you find a relief after the crazy-quilt schizophrenia of the architecture outside. It's still a nasty place, choked with dust, unlit except for a single shaft of sunlight entering through the same window that just admitted you. The sunlight doesn't change angle or orientation, despite the window's ever-changing attitude toward the sun; that by itself is enough to make you look back out that window so you can spot the motionless clouds and gnarled trees and the frozen position of a bird caught in midflight and from them make the determination that time inside the mansion has been compressed to fit inside a single captured moment. It's an impressive trick, which bodes poorly for the number of even more impressive tricks that the tenants might still have waiting for you as you penetrate deeper and deeper into the house. You take it as a welcome indication that you're now free to take as much time as you require.

Turning from the window, you regard the rest of the shadow-choked room: the bookshelves stuffed with volumes chosen for their bindings instead of their literary value, the fireplace sitting black behind an iron grate, the trophy heads of a rhino and a moose looming over a grand desk. Something—a rat, or perhaps something stranger—scratches in a corner. A pair of carved mahogany doors sit invitingly at the far end of the room, but you don't head there right away; instead you move to the desk, which bears a single yellowed sheet of paper so carefully centered that it screams set decoration. The dust covering the desk is so thick that the paper itself is impossible to read at first, but you sweep away the detritus of years and read the words that have been left for you in ink as black as your purpose here: LEAVE US ALONE! It's the first pathetic thing you've seen since your arrival, and it lets you know the tenants are frightened of you. You crumple the paper without a thought and drop it to the floor, wondering just how long it will take the dust to bury the useless warning forever.

A deadbolt seals the double doors, but it's no challenge. You glide through the opening into a long gray hallway that seems to extend an infinite distance in both directions. The air is obscured with dust and vapor, but you can see that the walls extend at least as far as their vanishing points. There don't seem to be any other doors or branching corridors as far as you can see. The floor is ceramic tile; the walls are lit by a series of torches sprouting eternal flame; the air echoes with the distant sound of daggers sharpening on whetstones. You stand outside the parlor, glancing first one way and then the other, admiring the impossibility of the choice you've just been offered. It's infinity both ways. You could very easily commit to one direction, or the other, and spend hours or days or years trudging toward an imaginary destination, always wondering whether it was truly up ahead or instead receding further with every step. You could, but you won't. It's too easy a trick to fool the likes of you. You know that there's no life to be found either way, and that in any situation where you're offered two equally unacceptable options, the only true solution is to make a point of choosing neither.

So you stand still and listen, focusing past the sound of daggers to the even more distant sound of a young woman crying. It's not close, but the acoustics of this house have protected the sound, funneled it down the corridor, and delivered it at this spot, where it's just soft enough to be subliminal. You might have missed it. You could have been forgiven for missing it. But it's there, and the closer you listen, the more you hear. You can tell that the tears are not new, that they have nothing to do with your presence in this house but have rather been flowing for almost as long as the house itself has stood; that the woman, though young, has suffered enough to feel ancient; that she knows she is heard and that it won't make a difference; and, most importantly, most useful to you as a stranger struggling to make his way through this place, that she is swaddled in darkness. Darkness, you decide, is the way to her. Without taking a single step, you look around for a shadow and find one, a short stroll away, hiding between a pair of torches that have gone out. It is not an impenetrable darkness, but it is all the occupants have provided, so it will have to be enough. You make your way there, your bare feet splashing in puddles of stagnant damp. You take your time. You face the spot the light has abdicated. And you step inside.

The voice in the darkness is familiar, and hateful in its familiarity. "When I was seven years old I found a stray cat that had been wounded by some kind of wild animal. It was lying on its side in the road, with one eye gone and its guts opened up like a canvas sack. I could see intestines through the hole in its belly; there were already maggots hard at work at the insides there. I knew from the way that belly moved up and down that it was alive anyway. It didn't have enough strength to cry, but it was alive, and in pain, and aware of everything that was happening to it. If I knelt close enough to its face I could make it see me through its one good eye: the one the animal that wounded it hadn't gotten to. The other eye was flush against the ground, half in and half out of the cat's juice: it was just an empty glass ball, like most cat eyes, not remotely expressive to speak of, but it was still enough of a window to look in and see what the beast was thinking, whether it wanted to live in agony or preferred instead to die in one sudden burst of pain by being hammered with the largest rock I could find. I saw something that wanted neither: that was as frightened of ending as it was of continuing. It hated me for being there. It hated me, thinking I was you."

That seems to be the end of the story, for now.

You emerge from another shadow in a bedroom choked with pink tapestries. They hang limp as shrouds from a ceiling crisscrossed with spiderwebs, their erstwhile cloying brightness reduced by dust and age to a shade reminiscent of the flesh beneath peeled skin. The air smells like perfume, disease, and fear; there are scavengers too, which shriek and scurry for their hidden bolt-holes as soon as you, the enemy, move into the sickly gloom that the inhabitants of this place are willing to accept as light. One of them, a rat so drawn and skeletal that he might have been long dead anywhere else, shows more courage than his fellows. He doesn't flee from you but charges, his long sharp teeth gleaming. You lift up one foot and stomp him flat even as he imagines himself about to enjoy meat stolen from your leg. The blow is flawless in its brutality. You come down with all your weight, breaking his spine, crushing his rib cage, making juice of all that sits inside. His last breath escapes in a pink mist. You step away, feeling no particular satisfaction and no particular pleasure, thinking only that you just removed the most minor of obstacles.

You move farther into the room, past a mammoth chest of drawers, past a looming wardrobe, past an ornate Victorian dollhouse that rotates on a desktop turntable to alternate the display between the gray-shingled exterior and an inner maze of miniature rooms where tiny clockwork figures in gowns and tuxedos move up and down halls on tracks that never intersect. You pause long enough to watch their progress and decide they've probably been playing out this meaningless charade for years: neither meeting each other nor establishing communication, nor accomplishing anything useful with their ersatz lives. They don't even possess charm or entertainment value, which is the least one should expect from toys. For a moment this annoys you so much you consider dashing the entire mechanism to the floor with a sweep of your arm, but then you spot a little room on the fourth floor, where a lady doll in a puffy pink dress sits endlessly brushing her hair before a mirror with tiny flickering bulbs. The mirror she faces is small but real. There are words painted on it, in almost microscopic letters painted red to simulate the effect of lipstick on glass: LEAVE WHILE YOU CAN. This doesn't even come close to unnerving you. It does, however, give the dollhouse a reprieve. You turn your back on it and move, with a slow and confident gait, toward the canopied four-poster bed and the woman lying there.

The bed is massive, decadent, luxurious, its bedspread so thick and so stuffed with velvety softness that it could probably serve as a mattress all by itself. It is also ancient. A thick, rotten must rises from the sheets. The dust is thick enough to make ridges when you sweep your hand across the fabric. It is human dust: the kind that comes from skin, flaking off in layers over long years of consistent habitation. It is dry and smells of sickness. The woman lying in the bed's center smells that way too. She is leonine and ancient, her skin drawn transparent as parchment over knife-edge cheekbones. Her complexion resembles milk. Her hair is just as white, and so long it radiates beneath her to all four corners of the bed, some of it indistinguishable from the spiderwebs that have begun to form from bed to ceiling, shrouding the rot on her bed from the rot that affects the rest of the room. Her arms, lying flat at her sides, are swathed in something still shiny that might have qualified as sensuous once. Her hands, soft and unlined and much younger than the rest of her, are fists wrapped tightly around wrinkles in the sheets, though it's impossible to tell whether she grabbed the material a long time before or only after you made your own unwanted appearance in this room. Her eyes are clouded. It is easy to see that she must have been extraordinarily beautiful, a long time ago, and that she has been imprisoned in this house so long that she might not have had any opportunity to revel in it. Even now she seems much younger than what must be her actual age: she may have shriveled, but there was never enough in her existence to crinkle those eyes, or line that forehead, or form the welcome marks left by a life filled with frowns or smiles or tears. She doesn't look at you as you approach, but she does tremble . . . and when you close your cold hand around one matchstick wrist, she weeps. The tears that burst from her unseeing eyes leave straightline tracks on a face buried by dust accumulation; she opens her mouth just wide enough to gasp, and she says, "I know you."

You could leave it at that. You could be that great a bastard. You have been before. But you have time for curiosity. So you lean in close and you stare into those unseeing eyes from a distance of inches and you look past the clouded corneas and you drink deep of the lonely desperation that once upon a time drove her to this cold and twisted place. You ask in a whisper just how she knows you. She closes those blind eyes, as if to block out even the pretense of sight, and she murmurs, "He's been waiting for you." A deep breath. "Do you know where he found me? Before he cleaned me up and brought me here? Do you know?" You know, of course, but you let her speak. "Assaulted and left for dead, that's where. I was so far gone I didn't even hurt; I was looking up at the sky, my left leg twisted beneath me, watching the rain fall down upon my face, feeling only annoyance at the wet. I didn't realize I'd been shot. I'd gone past pain, you know; past caring. I didn't even care that my baby daughter was beside me, wailing, thumping me with that little fist of hers, trying to get her mommy to wake up, not understanding why I wouldn't. I had nothing left to me, not even my love for her. All I felt was cold."

It's remarkable, but as frightened as she is, as helpless as she is, as difficult as it might be for her, she still speaks these words with a detached amazement, as if unable to believe they apply to her. "After all that, I lived. She died." Which, of course, you also know. She takes one deep shuddering breath. "It was a war, you son of a bitch. You bastard. You cruel worthless piece of shit bastard. Of course I know you. Don't you think I've been waiting all this time for you? Don't you know he's been waiting all this time for you?"

Her sac of a breast rises, falls, shudders. "Don't you understand that he built this house for you?" The weeping resumes. You lift her withered arm and place it across her chest, crossing it, with perfect precision, with the other. She trembles, waiting for you to do what it's only reasonable for you to do. When you do nothing more she cries out, damning you, cursing your nonexistent heart. But she's still breathing when you leave. This isn't about her. It's about him.

You find a hallway, lined with more books. Unlike the decorative volumes below, these look like they've been read. There are thousands of them, most gray old hardcovers with paper just starting to turn brown and brittle at the edges. You recognize the names on the spines. You pick up a volume at random, one written by an author long forgotten: a novel of adventurers, traveling lands that no longer exist, in the service of a cause that history discarded. A quick flip through the dense antiquated prose is enough to make you chuckle at its irrelevancy. All books are irrelevancies. Like the shifting walls of this very structure, they're attempts to defy you, to keep you at bay, to maintain some part of their respective authors alive even as their flesh and bone crumbles to inanimate ash. But they die too, most before their authors do, the words fading from memory even as they struggle for physical permanency on the impermanent medium of paper. They're jokes, the biggest joke you know, out of the many you have encountered since the world began. They annoy you. You consider the book in your hand for one more second, weighing the possibility of mercy, and then you flex your fingers, exerting what for you is just the slightest amount of pressure. The paper explodes. The novel becomes a mushroom cloud of dust and ash. The words vanish into the empty air, never to be seen again. You release what's left in a trickle of silt, which gathers on the floor at your feet, and then you turn to what's left, the millions of empty words all long past their prime, and you speak a word that only you know. The other books all crumble into dust, as all books must, and then you move on, further down the hallway, through more corridors that shift their geography each time you take another step.

Beyond that room, the nursery: a place that smells of sweet flesh and sour milk, that rings with the never-ending wails of its sole occupant. The opening is a curtain of stringed beads, the only item of furniture a flat wooden counter, the only cradle a thick glass jar filled with something yellow and inhabited by a wide-eyed fetus who glares at you with a look too unformed to be identified by attitude. It opens its mouth and says something, releasing a stream of bubbles that rise through the murk only to be swallowed by the maze of tubing attached to the narrowed lid, which extends well past the baby's home to a network of incomprehensible machinery on the opposite wall. There is no way of knowing what the baby just tried to say. Even if it has lived long enough to develop its own vocabulary—and you have no doubt that it has lived untold lifetimes past the hour when it would have been delivered still-born—they are not words but the embryos of words, not pleas for blessed release but the aimless rambles of a thing that never had the chance to know a life in the world beyond the glass. It never should have known life at all; that it lives and suffers now is a travesty. But you are not here for it. You are here for the architect, who placed it here for you to find.

The next room of note is a repository of skulls: thousands of them, all bleached, all blank-eyed and staring, stacked in pyramids and situated to grin at you as you walk past. Some hang from the ceiling on strings and spin, forever, surveying their brethren from every possible angle. The floor is a tilework of femurs. Before you take three steps you trip a lever or other activator of some kind, and a recorded voice begins to play: deep, resonant, filled with dust, with every word a measured condemnation. You recognize the voice. You know it well because you have heard it cursing you an untold number of times, most recently telling you a story about a cat. You have wasted so many years, called away by other duties, looking forward to the day when it would be your pleasure to hear that voice stilled.

Today, as you pick your way through the maze of remains, it says, "Do you recognize any of them? I do. I know every name, every face; every dream deferred by a sudden ending; every soul that plummeted into despair because the owners of these beauties saw you coming and knew that there was nothing left for them, not on this world or any other. I can tell you how many cursed your name and how many wished they had never been born. I understand them so well that it's almost as if I killed them myself. I didn't, of course; you, of all creatures, know that. I would have had to tear out my own heart before I could do such an evil thing. But I came upon all of them after you were already done; I took what you see all around you because I thought it would be instructive to show you all these faces again, when the time finally came for us to meet. I want you to know how seriously I took my awareness that someday I'd be meeting you too. Of course, if any of this gives you any pause whatsoever, please feel free to get the hell out; it'd be easiest for both of us if you just gave up on the idea of taking me where you took them. I have no problem doing without that pleasure. I just want you to recognize, if you haven't already, that it might be best for you too. Leave here. Go away. Don't come back. Forget this place. Vanish, if you don't want to confront me."

The floor ends in a precipice. The drop before you seems endless, the walls extending downward, well below the ambient light's ability to reveal anything that might be waiting for you down below. The darkness has no terrors for you, of course. You've always been the presence that lurks unseen in most dark places. But things have been done to this particular blackness, enhancing it, making it opaque even to you. Nothing has been done to hide the sounds, the shifting moaning mechanical sounds, testifying to the great mechanisms that drive this structure and keep it shifting between one form and another with every moment it continues to sit on this earth. There must be gears below, and pistons, and tense uncoiling springs, and even things more sorcery than engineering, all locked together in combination to lift that wall, erase this door, force the windows to race around the outside walls like creatures pursued by monsters. The design and construction strike you as a project capable of consuming more than normal lifetimes. The arrogance that would lead the unseen architect to believe that even these efforts would be enough to drive you away is enough to drive you to rage. It is hubris great enough to offend the gods, as indeed you, as one of them, are offended. You step out into the abyss and let yourself fall.

Falling takes longer than it should. The mechanisms that transform the house every instant reinvent this shaft every instant, inducing the floor not far below to recede and recede and recede even as you tumble farther and farther. He speaks to you all the way down. "I know murderers," he says. "I have seen the look in their eyes as they drove knives into innocent hearts." So have you. "I know dying." So do you. "I have held their hands as they fought for one more breath of air. I know bereft. I have seen the world as they see it, when everyone they love is dead. I know traumatized. I have shared their madness as they stumbled uncomprehending through fields of mute corpses. I have shared the pain of unknown others as they were drowned, strangled, shot, exsanguinated, eaten alive by tumors, and crushed alive by heavy weights. I have borne that stone weight in my lungs as I bobbed, weakened and desperate, through floodwaters too violent to permit the survival of a swimming man. I have felt teeth rip through my flesh. I have felt my own flesh turn against me with illness. I have tasted all your shapes vicariously through the experiences of others. I have considered the final passage required of all people, good and evil, wise and stupid, rich and poor, young and old, deserving and not . . . and I have made myself the sworn enemy of the one who escorts them. All I ever wanted to do was defy you. All you ever had to do was stay out. This could have been my refuge. Why didn't you take my warnings? Why didn't you just leave me here to wait until I decided I was ready to take your hand? Is it pride, you son of a bitch? Is that what drives you now?"

All of this is so familiar to you that you are relieved to strike bottom, on a soft spongy surface that does little to ameliorate a touchdown at terminal velocity that would have powdered the bones of a human being. It causes you no pain or inconvenience at all: just annoyance that there's still, after all this, even more terrain to travel: a gray corridor leading to a vague light at the far end. There's no way of telling, of course, not in this house, where everything changes with every step you take, but even so, you believe that the one you seek waits for you not far in that direction. You have heard pleading before. You have heard rationalizations before. You have heard excuses before. You have heard countless voices in countless languages wheezing your name, cursing your existence, and bargaining for special treatment in your eyes. You have heard the articulate and inarticulate alike offer arguments in favor of special dispensation. Many appealed to fairness. It is not a language you speak, and even if it were, there would still be little chance of you speaking it now, not after you have had to undergo such hardship, such inconvenience, just to claim a life you should have been able to take years ago. Today you will wear your most terrible face.

At the end of the hall you find him. He sits slumped on a marble throne in a chamber with more dust than air. He is as old as any human being you have ever seen, even older than the damned woman upstairs; his skin is a thin veneer of nigh-transparent tissue barely covering his crackled and brittle bones. His eyes are filmy yellow globes, so dry from years of blindness that they don't even glisten the way living eyes should. When he inhales, it's with the resentful wheeze of lungs that have had more than their share of dust and ashes; when he exhales, his breath bears the stench of organs gone rotten inside. When you draw close, the withered cords of his neck draw that mummified face up to greet yours, and his parchment cheeks tighten, revealing a full set of teeth not white but black from rot. It's a smile every bit as corrupt as yours, and now that you're upon him you greet it with a skeletal grin of your very own. Were he able to see you, he would lose his mind. But he is blind, and when he speaks, his voice is not even a whisper. "You came. I defied you so long that you came. You ignored all the warnings and you came. You walked past all the warning signs, and you came. You ignored the temptations I offered, and you came. You are the Reaper and you are inevitable. So take me."

You oblige. You lay hands on his shoulders and you breathe in, swallowing the intangible vapors that separate dead meat from living tissue. It tastes horrible, like any meat gone bad: a lot like it always tastes when you should have come sooner, only worse, because your arrival has never been this much past due. Inhaling, you know at once how many years he's been decrepit, how many years his withered pump has kept beating only because you were never there to stop it—how many years since he felt joy, or hope, or anything that would have given his stupid, finite existence a point. You know that only his bitterness and his hatred for you have sustained him, and that it has never been enough, that though historically few mortal lives have ever been worth living, his, in its single-minded wait for your arrival, has been even more empty than most. Considering how much inconvenience he's caused you, you should feel a little satisfaction at that. But as you take the last of him and his empty shell sags, you feel only the ghost of a feeling that those who live and breathe would have no difficulty recognizing as unease. Because the one emotion that dominates the architect's mind, in this the last moment of his life, is triumph. He thinks he's won. But it isn't until he slumps, revealing the object that sits on the table behind him, that you understand why.

It's a pitcher plant: a living lure of sweet and sickly smell designed to attract flies, which once inside cannot make their way back to the exit. You look inside and see a dozen separate flies trapped at the bottom. They're all as ancient as the ancient man you just claimed, but they're all alive, all damned, because until this moment you were never here to take them; and if you left at this moment, without doing what it has always been your duty to do, they would remain here, forever twitching as the years became centuries and the centuries became eons, withholding that one moment of merciful release that only you can provide. They are not capable of thought, and they cannot spend their eternal imprisonment remembering how easily they were baited. They can only buzz with impotent fury. You tap the plant with the edge of a fingertip, and all the days of its extended lifetime return in a rush: it curls at the edges, dries, turns black, crumbles to dust. The flies inside stop buzzing, stop moving, rot, fall apart, and disappear. In an instant there is no plant, no flies. There is just an empty tabletop, bearing nothing but the empty space where the plant had stood: an empty space that resonates with a message as clear to you as any words could ever be.

The fear that engulfs you then is volcanic, all-encompassing: the kind of dread you have caused in so many. Your breath cannot catch in your throat, because you have no breath. Your heart cannot race in your chest, because you have no heart. Your spine cannot curdle with terror, because you have no spine. But you feel the fear anyway: the sudden realization that you have spent this day like any other dumb animal, lured by the illusion of prey into cramped and fatal places.

You race back down the hall, in a single graceful swoop uncontaminated by any actual footsteps. You burst into the black room at the bottom of the shaft you descended not long ago. A dark place then, it's already growing darker. The mechanisms that kept this house in motion, that rearranged walls and kept corridors and rooms illuminated when necessary, have begun to shut down, stopping every gear, closing every door, turning off every machine, extinguishing every light. It is already too dark for men to see, which inconveniences you not at all, as you are not a man. But barriers have slid into place, in the shaft above, blocking the path back to the rooms above. And though you have always been talented at slipping past solid walls, you already sense that if you started to climb this shaft and made your way past the first of the obstructions that stand between you and the outer world, then all you would have to expect from now on is a series of additional barriers and obstacles and tricks intent on no goal more noble than standing between you and everything that still lives. It's enough to stagger even a presence who has never been lost, who has never needed instruction, who has always been able to find his way.

You might very well figure out an escape route sometime before the world above recognizes the disaster of your absence, but you might never. You might spend forever staring up at the darkness, unable to fathom the way out. You might try and fail. And you might succumb to a despair greater than any ever felt by merely mortal prisoners: because even those have always known that escape, of a kind, was inevitable, and never beneath the stars has such a merciful end ever been planned for you.

SEANAN McGUIRE

What Everyone Knows

FROM *Kaiju Rising 2: Reign of Monsters*

IT CAME OUT of the sea; it destroyed a city; it died. That's the story. That's what everyone knows. It was tall and terrible and incomprehensible and biological and beautiful, and it breathed out gouts of acid like it was nothing, and it tore down our towers with its terrible claws, and its skin was armor against almost everything we had to throw—everything but small-scale nuclear weapons. It melted in the face of our atomic might; it burned and howled and screamed and fled and fell and rotted in the slag that had been the beach. Scientists in hazmat suits picked it apart, squirreling every precious scrap away in secret laboratories, coaxing its secrets from the melted marrow of its bones.

That's the story. That's what everyone knows.

I was a child when the creature stepped out of the sea, defying everything we thought we knew about our place in the world. I can remember the sight of it on the morning news, before my mother screamed and turned the monitor off, saying that it was nothing a child should be looking at. She hadn't understood how ubiquitous it would become. No one had. There had never been anything like it before, tall as a skyscraper, ancient as the moon. It had remade our understanding of, well, everything, and it had done it as easily as it killed 2.5 million people, as easily as it left Seattle and the surrounding area in ruins.

It came; it killed; it died, and we pulled it apart to see what we could see. That's the other thing I remember about the arrival. Crying because there was this huge, beautiful, dead creature sprawled on the sand after three days of destruction—by that point my mother had stopped trying to cover my eyes, had somehow managed to grasp that everything was changing—and we weren't going to bury it the way we'd buried my dog when he died. We were going to hurt it, and keep hurting it, until it wasn't anymore. That was how we'd punish it for daring to hurt us. We'd hurt it so badly that it no longer existed.

Biologists looked at the crenulations of its brain and the structure of its neurons and declared it nothing more than an oversized, biologically complex animal, no more complicit in its own actions than a rabid dog.

Physicists and material engineers looked at the composition of its bones and the shape of its skeleton and declared it a miracle of form and function, something we could use to make our damaged towers taller and stronger, immune to future monsters.

Everyone had something to say about the creature, which by that point was known around the world as The Beast. Parts of it went on display in natural history museums, once the radiation had died down. Cute plush toys were sold, considered tasteless until the manufacturer loudly announced that a portion of each sale was being donated to the trusts dedicated to helping the survivors of Seattle. Movies were made. Genres of science fiction were revitalized.

Time passed.

The nuclear weapons used to kill the creature had been selected because they wouldn't leave the coastline uninhabitable forever. A decade, yes, and residents would need to filter their water and avoid growing vegetables for a decade after that, but those were things that could be worked around. Those were hurdles to be overcome. Seattle began to rebuild. The Beast loomed large in the public consciousness, but the creature, the real animal, was chipped away, worn into nothing one forgotten moment at a time.

We were killing it all over again, feeding it into the great machine of human history, where we always had to be the victors, and anything that challenged the narrative of our own superiority had to be destroyed. We were *hurting* it.

It came out of the sea; it destroyed a city; it died. That's the story. That's the narrative.

This is the truth.

Fifteen years is a long time. Long enough to clean the radiation from a ruined city; long enough to render an impossible creature into its component parts; long enough for a child too young to understand why everyone is crying to become a marine biologist and be loosed, in her own time, upon the world.

Plane tickets were easy. Explaining why I wanted to go to Washington was hard. I wasn't a resident of the state, had no relatives who had either died or relocated when the creature came, and the maps I had so carefully drawn, so carefully considered, weren't the sort of things I wanted to share. But my thesis had been on the impact of radiation on tide-pool invertebrates, and my adviser wrote me a glowing letter of recommendation. After fifteen years of nightmares, I was finally on my way to where they'd started. Not with a wave of destruction that rose from the sea and slaughtered everything in front of it. With a creature that fell, never understanding what it had done wrong, and with the look it had cast down the coast as it died.

The scientists had been so *quick* to say that the creature was only an animal, that it didn't know, didn't understand, couldn't possibly have had any motivation beyond instinct. They had never paused to ask themselves whether it might have been intelligent in its own way, or whether that intelligence might have had a purpose when it came for Seattle. They had seen the same thing I had, the flail, the fall, the last, frantic look along the coast, and they had come to different conclusions.

Fifteen years and six weeks after the creature came out of the sea, I parked my rental car on the overgrown slope of a road that hadn't been maintained in far too long, shielding my eyes as I peered into the towering, mossy forest between me and the ocean. Even before the attack, Washington State had some of the most protected beaches in the country, barricaded by evergreen forests, hidden by the curvature of the coast. Now, after a decade and a half of neglect, those beaches might as well be on another planet. No human had set foot on them since the bombs fell.

Everything happens in its own time. I checked my boots, ran a finger along the line of tape dividing them from my jeans—always tape where there might be ticks; it's only common sense—and started into the trees.

Mosquitoes buzzed among the branches, and deer and rabbits watched me with no sign of fear, so unaccustomed to the presence of humans that they no longer understood that I might be a threat. I wasn't, not yet: it would be another decade, at least, before it was safe to hunt here. Another decade of lazy days and silent hunting seasons, of starvation when the herd wasn't thinned before the end of the growing season. Everything has its dark side, even a cessation of gunfire.

I pushed my way through the woods, fighting for every step against the tangled green that threatened to shove me back out to the road, where I belonged. When the tree line ended, it was abrupt and unexpected: I pushed through a veil of blackberry creepers and was suddenly standing at the top of a sloping hill leading down to a narrow, rocky strip of shore. It would widen as the tide went out, but not much, no, not nearly enough to make this place appealing to developers or vacation-goers or even local families. There had always been better beaches, more accessible beaches, places where they could spread out their towels and enjoy the faltering Pacific sun.

The water here was deceptively deep, dropping from shallows into the abyss with surprising speed, and the undertow was correspondingly strong, sucking swimmers in, pulling them down. It was perfect. From a biological standpoint, it was *perfect*.

I slid down the hillside on the sides of my shoes, banking against my own momentum, until I reached the bottom and the stones turned under my feet, making my footing uncertain. I windmilled my arms, getting my balance back, and stopped, listening.

Nothing.

No boats, no cars, no distant sound of voices; no seabirds calling or dogs barking. The world was silent, save for the sound of the sea. I nodded. This fit my assessment of the area, and more, the assumptions I'd made about the environment I was looking for. Someplace that was open and secluded at the same time. Someplace with certain unique geographic features. Unique enough to lure a creature as huge and inexplicable and important as the one the world had watched die fifteen years ago out of the depths and onto the land.

The beach was long and empty, flanked by hills and rocky granite spikes that jutted like bones where the water had worn the earth away. I started walking.

Fifteen years is a long time. Long enough to make a few hours' walk seem like nothing in comparison, although my legs ached and knees burned by the time I rounded the curve of the cove and saw what I'd been looking for: a cave, not natural, although it could certainly pass for such to the untrained eye, hewn from the rock wall that encircled the small, isolated slice of the sea. Something had reached out with a terrible claw, perhaps coated with the kind of biological acid that developed for a *reason,* a reason bigger and better than destroying cities, and had sliced an opening out of the rock. Something that needed a safe, secure, isolated place.

I pulled the flashlight from my bag and started inside, the pain in my legs forgotten in the face of the moment I'd been seeking for so impossibly, incredibly long, since I was a child who had somehow been able to recognize despair when she saw it in the eyes of a creature the size of a city.

At the back of the cave I found them, rolled gently into their cradles of melted, stabilizing sand. There had been three once, each the size of a basketball—so small for what they would eventually become, but not unreasonably so, given what I knew about the life cycles of sea turtles and sharks.

One of them was a deflated husk, its leathery skin cracked and pitted, its contents diffused into the sand around it.

One of them had hardened, undergoing a strange, terrible alchemy that might be as common and necessary for this species as the hibernation of cicadas, the slow incubation of alligators. Maybe when there were multiple healthy eggs, one of them would always turn into a sphere of what looked like solid obsidian, preserving its contents for a time when it would be alone, free of competition, free to grow.

The third . . .

It was the pale, inviting green of a healthy eel's skin, mottled with paler yellow and deeper olive, a biological tapestry of possibilities. It was slightly larger than either of its flawed siblings, pulsing with its own internal bioluminescence. I moved closer. There was a heavy shadow at the center of the egg, moving slightly, preparing to be born. I hadn't missed it.

"Hi," I whispered, and my voice was a shout in the confines of the cave. "I, um. I knew your mother. I've come to take you someplace safe."

The egg didn't respond. I lifted it from its cradle, and it was heavy and warm and soft in my hands. I nestled it in the bottom of my backpack, making sure it was secure, before picking up the second egg. It felt solid from side to side, and I hoped, however irrationally, that that would mean one day it could soften and swell and hatch. For now . . .

For now, people were returning to the state, to the coast, and this cave would be found soon enough, by scientists who should have started looking years ago, who should have been asking themselves from the start why something so big, so powerful, so *perfect*, would come ashore at all. Maybe some of them had been. I liked the thought. I liked the idea that some people had looked at the arc of her steps, the way she went for the closest, most dangerous population center, and said to themselves, *I'll give them time, I won't attract attention, I'll wait.* It would mean I wasn't in this alone.

My backpack felt heavier than the world as I made my way back up the coast to the slope where I'd made my descent. I squinted at it. The idea of climbing it made my thighs ache in anticipated weariness. The thought of spending the night on this rocky, exposed coast, with the Pacific winds doing their best to flay the skin from my body, was worse. With a sigh, I gripped the nearest exposed root and began pulling myself up.

I had a long way to go before I—before *we*—would be safe.

The house I'd rented was one of hundreds left empty and barely maintained in the wake of the Seattle disaster, the sole remaining asset of a family that might never choose to return to Washington. They had seen the world turn against them, and they were seeking level ground.

The maintenance that *had* been performed had been handled by the state, squads of nervous, underpaid contractors visiting each municipality for one week a quarter, patching the obvious leaks and repairing the worst of the damage. Nothing they did could have prevented the slow decay of an unoccupied home, but they'd tried, right up until the moment when the region was declared fit for habitation and the responsibility was passed back to the homeowner. A lot of neighborhoods like the one that was temporarily mine had looting problems now, desperate residents pulling down fences and stealing shingles from the unoccupied homes. They tried to justify it to the media, claiming that they were reclaiming materials that would otherwise have been wasted, blaming the state for its lackadaisical standards and the climate for destroying their precious homes, but most people regarded them as dangerous thieves, and it had slowed down the rate of residents returning to Washington. Empty neighborhoods were still more common than the state liked.

I had been able to get my place for little more than a song. It was too big for me, with a yard that opened onto an incredible view of the Sound, all blue water and endless sky. Opening the front door revealed a living room done up in varying shades of beige, with water stains on the walls and ancient curtains covering the windows. I locked up behind myself, making my way to the back bedroom, which I had prepared meticulously for this moment.

Blackout curtains kept the sunlight at bay, while humidifiers and heaters brought the temperature up to something heavy and tropical. The creature had breathed acid, biological and bright, and the eggs had been nestled in cradles of melted sand, with channels dug around them, as if to keep them dry. I had gambled on the fact that the acid had been a part of the gestation process, intended to tell the babies when it was safe for them to emerge. I removed them from my backpack, placing them in the beds of sculpting foam that I had constructed. There were four beds, a moment of wild optimism given physical reality. I pushed two of them under the desk with my foot and went for my field kit. It was time to take some basic measurements.

The active egg weighed eight pounds and had an ambient temperature of eighty-four degrees. The inactive egg weighed twelve pounds and had an ambient temperature of sixty degrees. I still tucked them both in, putting enough distance between them to mirror the setup in the cave, before leaving the room and scavenging a dinner for myself from the meager supplies in the kitchen. My bed beckoned. Cracker crumbs still clinging to my lips, I collapsed into it without removing my clothes. The work, the real work, was about to begin.

The next six weeks passed in a blur of tests and measurements. The active egg grew warmer by the day, and on Day 6 it began to swell, growing so quickly that I fancied I could almost see it happen. I cooed to it, increased the humidity, and began wiping it down with a dilute acid bath, helping the shell to weaken and thin. I had made a study of the creature's biology, reading every report, examining every biological breakdown, and the acid had to do *something* other than belch forth to dissolve cities. It took too many resources to be that limited. But as a way to protect the young . . .

The eggshell was so thick. The acid would wear it away, telling the baby that it was safe to emerge. In the absence of a parent, erosion would do the same thing, but it would take so much longer. So very, very much longer.

I was wiping the mixture of acid and seawater across the shell when the egg gave an almighty shake, almost hopping in its cradle. I pulled back and watched in delighted awe as the shell split and tore under the force of a sharp-jawed saurian head pushing its way to freedom.

All vertebrates practice cuteness as a survival mechanism. Even baby snakes and lizards are adorable compared to the adults, with large eyes, outsized skulls, and a certain rounded softness. The infant creature was no different. It blinked its round golden eyes at me, all four of its pupils contracting, and made a small, querulous sound. I smiled.

"Hello, little one," I said.

It made the sound again, louder this time, before beginning to chirp, pushing its arms through the remnants of the shell and holding them out to me.

The creature had been bipedal. Its child was no different, built like the hybrid offspring of a human and an alligator, with soft scales in a dozen shades of green, from mellow jade across its belly to deep malachite on its back. It had the beginning of what would eventually be jagged spikes running the length of its spine, and tiny, pearlescent claws on the ends of its fingers. Like most reptiles, it had been born with a full complement of teeth, each one sharp enough to tear through flesh. Strangest of all were its eyes, two large and placed where I would expect on a bipedal predator, two smaller and placed above them, giving it an incredible range of vision. Nothing would ever sneak up on this child of the deeps.

It chirped again. I took a breath. It could be trying to lure me in, to make a meal of me, in which case I would die and so would it, starved and unable to escape the house at its current size. It could also be an imprinted infant, turning to its presumed parental figure, seeking comfort.

"You and me, kid," I said, and leaned forward, scooping it out of the eggshell, into my arms.

The infant creature made a softer sound, somewhere between a purr and a sigh, and pressed its face against the curve of my neck, huddling into the warmth of me. I held it tightly, looking at the wrecked remains of its eggshell, and thought of the people who would give anything, *anything,* to be where I was now, to have this tiny, innocent thing at their disposal. Think of the secrets they could learn by taking a juvenile apart!

I could have anything I wanted with a single phone call. Money, fame, all the attention in the world. I could be the new darling of the sciences, the one who changed the field forever. Or I could have this baby, who was already falling asleep in my arms, heavy and content and absolutely sure that I would keep it safe.

I kissed the top of its head. "You and me, kiddo," I murmured. "We've got work to do."

Geode toddled around the backyard on increasingly strong legs, tail waving wildly to help them stay stable and upright. Only a month out of the egg and they were already up to my chest, capable of knocking me over with the innocent enthusiasm of their play. With only two known exemplars of their species, I couldn't have said whether they were male or female, but I had lost the ability to think of them with the dispassionate *it* by the time they were a week old, happily shredding salmon with their talons and trying to lure me into eating the bits they didn't want. They were an individual. Not a human, but not a beast either.

And they knew me. Geode couldn't speak, but they understood their own name and all the things I was inclined to ask them for. They even allowed me to continue taking blood samples, despite their dislike of the needle, because I said *please* and promised them their favorite delicacies when I was done.

They tripped over a rock in the yard and stumbled, making a distressed groaning noise that turned into a hacking sound, like a cat in the process of coughing up a hairball. They moaned once and spat a ball of faintly glowing, semisolid goo onto the ground, where it began to smolder and sink into the earth. Geode moaned again, now sounding ashamed.

"Oh, no, baby," I said, rushing to their side and rubbing the scales on the top of their head soothingly. "That was a *good* thing you did just now. What a fine, strong baby you are! Why, I'm sure most unidentified sea-dwellers can't make acid until they're *much* larger than you are!"

Geode creeled hopefully. I laughed.

"Yes, you can have some chopped squid as a reward. Greedy little one."

They bumped their head against my sternum. I laughed again, planting a kiss on their cheek before turning and starting for the house.

As soon as they couldn't see me, I let my smile fade. Acid. They were spitting acid. I'd known that was a normal part of their development, but between that and the speed with which they were growing . . . their childhood was going to be much shorter than I wanted it to be, and there was no way I'd be able to hide them forever. Honestly, I was going to be hard-pressed to hide them much longer. They ate more every day. There were only three stores within reasonable driving distance, and even rotating which ones I went to, and when, they were starting to notice how much fish I bought. The money would run out soon, and that was assuming no one tipped off the authorities to the tourist with the strange shopping habits.

Was it paranoid of me to think that buying too much fresh salmon could bring the government down on my head? Maybe. But I was the only person known to be living in my area, and I was from out of state, and this was a different world from the one that I'd been born into. This was a world where monsters were real.

Geode chirped and nudged their head against my arm, asking for more scritches. Maybe this had always been a world where monsters were real. We were just finally being forced to admit that maybe we'd been wrong about what they were.

Another month passed in furtive shopping expeditions and the increasing hunger of my adopted child. The first time I stepped into the backyard to find them with their head buried in the ripped-open chest cavity of a stag I stopped, heart thundering in my ears, questions of radiation and exposure racing through my mind. It wasn't safe to hunt here. It wasn't safe to fish here. It wasn't—

It wasn't safe to starve here, and I couldn't buy enough meat to keep Geode from crying in the night, or apparently to keep them from running off to hunt. They were taller than I was, still growing at an incredible rate, and their acid projectiles were no longer accidental but were instead aimed and fired with pinpoint precision, usually to object to something I had asked, like another blood sample or for Geode to lift their tail out of the way while I worked. We danced through the increasingly cramped house with exquisite care, me trying to keep records of their astonishing growth, them snarling and snapping and shedding strips of too-small skin everywhere. I gathered every single one, the marine biologist's equivalent of a baby book, and I didn't feel an ounce of guilt. Yes, Geode was the scientific discovery of a lifetime. A proper laboratory could have learned so much more from them. I didn't care. They were my responsibility, my adopted child, and I knew how this would end.

I just didn't expect it to end so soon.

We were in the backyard, Geode lying on their back in the sun, me wiping down their belly with a mixture of saltwater and dilute acid—the same mixture I'd used on their eggshell to encourage them to hatch, now used to encourage a shed—and me in a tank top and old jeans, half draped across the slope of their thigh, which held me up and kept me balanced. It was a beautiful day, that rare Seattle sunshine pouring out of the clear blue sky, warming the both of us to the bone.

Geode was mumbling and whistling, a soft, sweet sound that filled my ears enough that I didn't hear the truck pulling up in front of the house, didn't hear the door slam as the inspector got out. He must have tried the door first, ringing the bell on an empty but clearly occupied house, and when he didn't get an answer, he went looking for the source of the sound. Maybe he was even trying to help, wanting to warn me about the looters that had been seen moving closer and closer to this area. Whatever his reasons, he came around the corner of the house, tablet in one hand, the other hand raised to block out the sun, calling, "Hello? Is there anyone home? I'm from the state, and—*oh my God!*"

His voice became a shout at the end, terrified and shrill and unlike any sound Geode had ever heard a human make before. I had to assume that was why they surged to their feet, pushing me gently behind them, and roared, spitting balls of acid with terrible precision to strike the man in the face, throat, and stomach.

I screamed. The man fell, acid eating the flesh away, revealing blood-mottled bone. Geode looked back at me, as if reassuring themself that I was all right, before ambling over to bend over the body, beginning to rip the acid-softened flesh away.

I turned and vomited into the grass.

Geode was a carnivore. There was footage of their mother eating humans, shoving bodies into her mouth as she continued her rampage through the streets of Seattle. This wasn't a *surprise*. But seeing it happen wasn't the same thing as knowing that it was a possibility, and the inspector hadn't done anything wrong, hadn't offered any threat to my lumbering, rapidly growing child. All he'd done was startle them.

Geode, sensing my distress, stopped devouring the man and came to crouch by my side, nudging me ever so gently with the tip of their snout. I braced myself with one hand, pressing the other to their scales. My beautiful, glorious, impossible child, the baby I'd dreamt about for my entire adult life, looked at me and crooned, confused and hopeful that I would somehow make things all right.

They were already ten feet tall, and growing every day. They could devour most of the predators they'd find in the sea, and ward off the ones they couldn't fight. The inspector . . . he'd been the first. He wouldn't be the last. His disappearance would be the trigger that brought down an entire world of trouble on our heads.

"It's time," I said, and Geode creeled, and if they knew why I was crying, they had no way to tell me so.

The inspector's pickup was sturdy, designed to navigate the broken roads and crumbling infrastructure of Washington State. Geode was heavy enough to weigh it down, but not enough to stop it from rolling. They sat in the back, head tilted into the wind, making small sounds of delight as I drove toward the coast as fast as I dared. The hibernating egg was an accusing presence in the passenger seat, concealed inside my half-zipped backpack. I'd known there was no real chance I'd have the time to hatch it, had been half intending, when this moment came, to leave it with my notes for future scientists to study. Maybe one of them would have fallen in love with its contents the way I'd fallen for Geode. Maybe it would have made it back to the sea.

But that had always been me lying to myself. My love had begun with a glimpse of agonized eyes as Geode's mother fell, with a feeling too big for me to put a name on but big enough to drive my entire life going forward, to steer me, inevitably, toward a cove and a cave and a child and a conclusion. I couldn't gamble on that kind of love happening again.

We were almost to the edge of the wood when the sirens started behind us. The truck jounced as Geode shifted position, barking their distress and slapping their tail against the side of the cab. I swore, fighting to keep control, and hit the gas harder. We needed to reach the trees. We needed—

They must have been following us for longer than I'd expected. A bullet shattered the windshield next to my head, and my focus became only and entirely stopping the truck before I lost control. I grabbed the backpack and kicked the door open, leaving the keys in the ignition as I flung myself out of the vehicle.

"Geode! Come on!" I ran for the distant tree line like my life depended on it, and Geode ran after me, confused and frightened but still obedient to the only authority they had ever known. They were faster than I was, but not so fast that I lost sight of them as we dove into the trees, beast and biologist both fleeing for their lives.

Well. Not really. I wasn't fleeing for my own life anymore. I was fleeing for theirs. They were the endangered species; they were the promise I had made to myself before my mother turned the news off in that long-ago living room. My own life had been forfeit the moment I sat down with a map of the coastline and the intent to bring a legend home.

The trees slowed Geode enough that I was able to catch up, and we ran together to the place where the forest dropped off, replaced by empty coast. Geode stiffened at the sight of the sea, making a sound that was something like wonder and something like longing and something like betrayal. I grabbed one talon, heedless of the way it sliced into my palm.

"Come on!"

Together we slid down the embankment, the sound of shouts and sirens echoing behind us, our pursuers growing closer by the moment. I stumbled at the bottom, my ankle twisting on the stones, and yelped in pain and surprise. Geode didn't pause in striding toward the sea, only swept me up in one massive arm, carrying me as easily as I had carried them only a few short weeks before. Their eyes were fixed on the horizon, a soft, humming sound building in their chest. It sounded like a sigh. It sounded like a song.

It sounded like going home.

Bullets bit into the beach. I looked back. Soldiers in olive green were lined up at the top of the bluff, guns drawn, shouting and gesturing to each other. They looked at my precious child and saw only the threat of an unfamiliar species, of competition, when we were all only seeking to survive on this planet. The seas are deep. Geode's mother could have been down there for millennia before she rose to lay her eggs and clear away any predators that might threaten them. We didn't have to fight. We could share.

Geode hesitated at the water's edge, the hum turning confused. I put my unwounded hand against their arm, smiling.

"It's okay, sweetie," I said. "Take me home."

It came out of the sea; it destroyed a city; it died. That's the story.

She came out of the sea; she tried to protect her children; she died. That's the story too.

As the water closed over my head and my lungs began to ache, I relaxed in Geode's arms, content to give my life for my child, even as their mother had done, so many years ago. They kept walking, and the darkness grew around us, until there was nothing but the feel of scaled arms around me and the nylon strap of the backpack in my hand. And then even that was gone, and so was I, part of the deep, drowned world where monsters walk, and promises are made, and stories older than the tide, older than the stone it wears away, are told over and over again, forever.

That's the story. That's what everyone knows.

N. K. JEMISIN

The Storyteller's Replacement

FROM *How Long 'til Black Future Month?*

THE STORYTELLER COULD not make it this evening. He sent me in his stead. Why, because I am one whose task it is to speak for the dead. Perhaps you've heard of others like me? In different places I am called by different names: shaman, onmyouji, bokor, freak. Since the dead are in no short supply, I know many tales. But if you do not like my tales, just say so. I am sure to know some means or another of keeping you entertained.

So.

King Paramenter of Sosun, wishing to dispel rumors of his impotence, inquired privately of his wizard as to how he might fortify his virility. "I have seen mention of dragons in lore on the subject," the wizard told him. "In specific, eating the heart of a male dragon should accord you some of that creature's proclivity." As it was rumored that male dragons could seed as many as a dozen females in a day, Paramenter immediately sent scouts forth from his palace in search of one.

His search was not immediately successful. In part due to the rumors, male dragons were in scarce supply; the species was on the brink of extinction. When Paramenter finally did hear of a dragon in the far-off mountains, he hastened to the place with a band of his elite warriors. Together they breached the dragon's den and slew the beast. But afterward they found that the dragon was female — a mother on a nest, her body cooling around a single egg. In frustration the king broke open the egg in the hope that its occupant might be male, but the creature's sex was indeterminate at that stage.

"I shall make do with the mother," he decided at last. "After all, women are creatures of great wantonness when not guarded closely by family and husbands. And perhaps the heart of a female who has borne young can help me get a son." So he had his men carve out the mother dragon's heart, and right then and there he ate it.

Straightaway Paramenter began to feel some positive effect. With his men he set off for home, riding through day and night to reach his palace. There he called for his wife and concubines to be made ready, whereafter he spent the next few days in enthusiastic carousing.

Sometime later came the joyous news: the queen and all five concubines were with child. King Paramenter was so overjoyed that he threw lavish parties and cut taxes so that the whole kingdom might celebrate with him. But as time passed his mood changed, for the dragonish vigor seemed to be fading from his body. Eventually, as before he'd eaten the dragon's heart, he found himself unable to perform at all.

In a panic he consulted his wizard once more. The wizard said, "I do not understand it either, my lord. The lore was very specific; the male dragon's heart should have bestowed that creature's purpose on you."

"It was not a male dragon," Paramenter replied impatiently. "I could not find a male, so I ate the heart of a nesting mother. It served well enough, at least until lately."

The wizard's eyes widened. "Then you have taken into yourself the purpose of a mother dragon," he said. "Such a creature has no need of desire beyond the children it gains her, and you now have six on the way."

"And what does that mean? I am a king, not a mother! Will I grow breasts now and nurse, and giggle over bonnets and toys?"

"Female dragons do not nurse," said the wizard. "They do not dote on their young, who hunt and kill from birth, though those young live to carry out their mother's purpose. To be honest, my lord, I do not know what will happen now."

To this Paramenter could say nothing, though he had the wizard beaten in a fit of pique. He settled in to await the birth of his children, and in the meantime sent his scouts forth again to find a male dragon. But before they could return, one by one the queen and concubines went into labor. One by one each gave birth to a beautiful, healthy baby girl. And one by one the ladies died in the birthing.

The entire kingdom caught its breath at the news. Some of Sosun's citizens began to speak of curses and offenses against nature, but Paramenter ordered the executions of anyone caught saying so, and the talk quickly subsided.

At least, Paramenter consoled himself, there was no further talk of his infirmity. The six baby girls were fine and healthy to a one, charming their nurses and anyone else who saw them. And while none were so blessed as to be male, all six grew up clever, charming, and lovely as well. "But of course," said Paramenter to his advisers when they remarked upon it. "Naturally any daughters of my blood would be far superior to an average woman."

An example of the latter was Paramenter's new wife, whom he had married once the requisite mourning period for his old wife had passed. Though the daughter of a neighboring king, Paramenter's new wife was a nervous little thing, inclined to flights of fancy. Paramenter discovered this during one of his visits to her bedroom, which he undertook every so often in order to keep up appearances. He had encouraged her to get to know his daughters, who were still young enough at that point that they might view her as their mother. "I would rather not," she said after much hemming and hawing. "Have you ever watched those girls closely? They stand together sometimes, gazing at a spot on the floor or some sight beyond their window, and then they smile. Always together, always same smile."

"They are sisters," said Paramenter in surprise.

"It is more than that," she insisted, but could articulate nothing more.

His curiosity piqued, Paramenter went down to the nursery the following night to observe the girls. Ten years old now, they fawned over him as they always did, exclaiming in delight at his visit. Paramenter sat down on the highbacked chair that they brought over, and drank the tea that one of them prepared, and let them put up his feet and brush his hair and pamper him as befitted a man. "I cannot see why she fears you," he murmured to himself, feeling amusement and pride as he watched his six jewels bustle about. "I shouldn't have listened to her at all."

A small voice said, "Who, Father?" This came from his youngest daughter, a tiny porcelain doll of a girl.

"Your mother," he said, for he insisted that they address his wife as such. He did not elaborate on his words, because he did not want to trouble the girls. But they looked at each other and giggled, almost as one.

"She fears us?" asked his eldest daughter, a delicate creature with obsidian curls and a demeanor that was already as regal as a queen's. "How strange. Perhaps she is jealous."

"Jealous?" Paramenter had heard of such things—women resenting their mothers or sisters, undermining their own daughters. "But what has she to be jealous of? She's beautiful enough, or I wouldn't have married her."

"Her place is uncertain," said his eldest daughter. She leaned forward to refresh his tea. "I have heard the palace maids saying that until she bears a child, you can put her aside."

"Then she must be terrified, the poor thing," said his second daughter. Like her concubine mother, this one was caramel-colored and lithe-limbed, with a dancer's natural grace. "You should help her, Father. Give her a child." She stood on her toes to light his pipe for him.

Paramenter nodded thanks, using the gesture to cover his unease. "Well, er, that might be difficult," he said. "I'm afraid I don't fancy her much; she's such a scrawny fearful thing. Not my taste in women at all."

"That's easy enough to deal with," said Third Daughter, a sweet little thing with honey-colored curls. She smiled at him from his feet, where she was paring his toenails. "Give her to your guards for a month or two."

"Oh, yes, that's a lovely idea," said Fourth Daughter. She sat nearby with a book on her lap, ready to read him a tale. "At least ten or twenty of them, just to be sure. They should be large, strong men, warrior-tempered. That way you can be sure of healthy breeding and a fine spirit in the child."

The king frowned at this, shifting uneasily in his seat at his daughters' suggestions. "I cannot say I like that idea," he said at last. "The guards would talk. Any child that resulted would be dogged by scandal her whole life."

"Then kill the guards," said Fifth Daughter, rubbing his temples with gentle musician's fingers. "That's the only way to be certain."

"And after all," added Youngest Daughter again, "who is to say the child will be a *her*? Perhaps we might gain a brother!"

This was a notion Paramenter had not considered, and with that thought, all his concerns vanished amid excitement. To have a son at last! And though it rankled that some common guard would be the father, the fact that no one would know eased that small ignominy.

As Paramenter began to smile, his daughters looked at one another and smiled as well.

So Paramenter gave the order, sending his wife to a country house along with twenty of his loyal guard for a suitable length of time. When they brought her back and the physician confirmed her pregnancy, he had the guards quietly killed, then ordered another kingdomwide celebration. His wife no longer seemed to have a mind, but Paramenter did not care so much, as this relieved him of the necessity of visiting her. At least she never spoke against his beloved daughters again.

You have guessed the ending of this tale, I see. That is well and fine, and I am not surprised; evil is easy to spot, or so we all think. Shall I stop? It isn't my purpose to bore you.

Very well, then. Just a little more.

But first, might we have some refreshment? One's throat grows parched with tale-telling, and I'm hungry as well. A late-season wine, if you have it. And meat, rare. Yes, I suppose this is presumptuous of me, but we dead-speakers know: there's no telling when some folly might come along and end everything. One must enjoy life while it lasts.

If it is not even more presumptuous — will you share my meal? Such rich salts, such savory sweets. It would give me great pleasure to watch them cross your fine lips.

When Paramenter's daughters reached their sixteenth year, noblemen from many lands began paying visits to Sosun. Word had spread widely of the girls' beauty, and also of their accomplishment in other respects. Fifth Daughter could outplay any bard on any instrument; Second Daughter's dancing won praise from masters throughout the land. His fourth girl was an accomplished scholar whose writings were the talk of the colleges. His third and youngest girls were renowned for their beauty, and so graceful, witty, and perfect was Eldest Daughter that his advisers had begun quietly suggesting she be allowed to inherit, despite generations of tradition.

Paramenter received his daughters' suitors with justifiable

pride, carefully choosing among them to ensure only the best for his treasures. But here he was stymied, for as he began presenting his selection to the girls, they became uncharacteristically obstinate.

"He won't do," said Youngest Daughter, on beholding a fine young man. Paramenter was dismayed, for the youth had arrived with a chest of treasure equivalent to the youngest daughter's weight, but being a doting father, he abided by her choice.

"Unsuitable," declared Third Daughter, right in the face of a handsome duke. That one had brought a bag of gemstones selected to match her eyes, but with a sigh, Paramenter turned him away.

After the third such incident, in which his second daughter declared the crown prince of a rival kingdom "too small and pale," Paramenter's eldest girl came to visit him. With her came Paramenter's son, the rosy-cheeked child of his wife and her guards, who was now six years old.

"You must understand, Father," Eldest Daughter explained. She sat at his feet, gazing up at him adoringly. At *her* feet, Paramenter's son sat watching his sister in the same manner. "Wealth and rank are such poor ways to judge a man's suitability. We have both already, after all. So it would make sense for our husbands to bring a little something more to the table."

"Like what?"

"Strength," she said. She reached down to stroke the boy's wine-dark hair, and gave him a doting smile. "We desire strength, naturally. What else could any true woman crave in a man?"

This Paramenter understood. So he dismissed the first crop of suitors and sent new missives forth: each kingdom which desired an alliance with Sosun should send its greatest warrior to represent its interests.

Presently the new suitors arrived. They were a dangerous, uncouth crowd, for all that most were decorated soldiers in their respective armies. When the men had gathered in the palace's garden, the sisters arrived to look them over.

"Much better," said Third Daughter.

"Quite," said Fourth, and as each of her sisters gave a favorable verdict, First Daughter nodded and stepped forward. She put her hands on her hips.

"Thank you for coming, gentlemen," she said. "Now, so that we may waste no further time, I shall explain our terms. We are sisters, raised as one; therefore we have decided to marry at the same time."

The men nodded. The advisers of their respective kingdoms had prepared them for this.

"We would prefer to marry one man, as well."

At this the men started, looking at one another in confusion.

Then First Daughter ducked her eyes, looking up at them through her lashes, and tilted her head to one side. "One of you," she said, "can have all six of us in his bed at once. We will obey your every whim, submit to your every desire, and you will be pleased with us; of that you may be sure. But only one of you may receive this reward."

Turning away, she smiled at her sisters, and they smiled back, as one. Then they walked away, though Youngest Daughter paused at the door to blow the men a kiss.

The bloodbath that followed killed off the best warriors of seventeen kingdoms and left ten more of the men maimed and useless for life. King Paramenter was hard-pressed to placate his fellow rulers, and the coffers of Sosun were sharply depleted by compensatory payments.

But the daughters had what they wanted. The warrior who survived the battle royal was a mountainous beast of a man, one-eyed and half literate, though possessed of great cunning and courage. The sisters doted on him as they had their father, and though his advisers shook their heads and the priests grumbled into their tea, Paramenter gave his blessing on the unorthodox union.

One month later his daughters all happily announced that they were with child. A month after that, their husband, whose name Paramenter had never bothered to learn, died in an unfortunate fall from the bower balcony.

So it came to pass that in the thirtieth year of Paramenter's reign, a miracle occurred: a male dragon was spotted at last. Though Paramenter was getting on in years, he had never quite given up his hope of true manhood. His second wife had killed herself in the interim, but he was still hale enough to get a few more sons on some nubile girl. Donning his sword and armor once more, Paramenter rode forth.

After many months of travel, they found the beast. Paramenter was startled to see that this dragon, unlike the huge, deadly female he'd killed so long ago, was small and put-upon, with an anxious demeanor and deep mournful eyes. His men killed it easily, but fearful of the consequences, this time Paramenter had the heart cured to preserve it, then carried it back to Sosun uneaten. There he gave it to his wizard to examine.

"Be certain," he said, "because the beast this heart came from was a pathetic creature. I cannot see how it is the male of the species at all."

But the wizard—who had suffered during the years of the king's disfavor and was now eager to prove his worth—immediately shook his head. "This is the right one," he said. "I'm certain." So with some trepidation, Paramenter devoured the heart.

At once he felt the effect. As proper marriages would take an unbearable amount of time, he summoned the twelve prettiest maidens from the nearby countryside to the palace. Over the next few weeks he worked hard to secure his legacy, and was pleased to eventually learn that all twelve of his makeshift brides were pregnant. At this Paramenter waited, tense, but there was no fading of interest within himself this time; it seemed the male's heart truly had done the trick. He rewarded the wizard handsomely, then set the palace physicians to work finding some way to ensure his women survived childbirth this time. He wanted no more unsavory rumors to dog his reign.

Then came a night some weeks later when he awakened craving something other than a woman's flesh. Restless and uncertain, teased by a phantom instinct, Paramenter rose and wandered through the darkened, quiet palace. Presently he found himself in the bower of his daughters. To his surprise, they were all awake, sitting in six highbacked chairs like thrones. Paramenter's son sat at Eldest Daughter's feet as usual, smiling sweetly as she stroked his deep red hair. Beside each of his daughters stood their own children, now five years old—girls all, again.

"Welcome, Father," said his eldest. "You understand what must be done now?"

For some inexplicable reason, Paramenter's mouth went dry.

"Too many, too fast," said Third Daughter. She sighed and shook her head. "We had hoped to grow our numbers slowly, subtly, but here you are spoiling all our careful plans."

He stared at his daughters, whose eyes were so cold now, so empty of their usual adoration. "You . . ." he whispered. It was the only word he could manage; unease had numbed his tongue.

"This was not our choice, remember," said Fifth Daughter, lifting a hand to examine her small, flat, perfectly manicured nails. There was a look of distaste on her features, perhaps at their shape. "But even I must admit its effectiveness. The vanity of men is a powerful weapon, so easy to aim and unleash."

Eldest Daughter stroked her little brother's hair and sighed. "There will be sons now too, somewhere among the twelve new ones you have made. You chose a poor specimen to sire them, but that can't be helped; men have hunted down the best male dragons for generations. Nothing left but cowards and fools. When a species diminishes to that degree, it must change, or rightly vanish into legend. Don't you agree, Father?"

The children, Paramenter noticed then. His granddaughters. Each had taken after her mother to an uncanny degree, and each now watched him with shining, avid eyes. Seeing that Paramenter had noticed them, they smiled as one.

Eldest Daughter rose from her throne and came to him, lifting a hand to stroke his cheek. "You have done well by us, Father," she said, with genuine fondness in her voice. "So we shall honor you in the old ways, as you have honored us."

With that, she beckoned the children forward. They all came —even Paramenter's son, not a dragon by blood but raised in their ways. They surrounded Paramenter, tense and trembling, but their mothers had trained them well. They did not attack until Eldest Daughter removed her hand from Paramenter's cheek and stepped away. And then, like the good, obedient children they were, they left no mess for the servants to find.

It's sad, isn't it? So many of our leaders are weak, and choose to take power from others rather than build strength in themselves. And then, having laid claim to what they have not earned, they wonder why everything around them spirals into chaos. But until the dragons someday return to take back their power and invoke vengeance on us all . . . well, I'd say we have time for a few more tales.

Unless you're tired? You do look peaked. Here, let me turn back your bedcovers. And here; shall I give you a goodnight backrub? That does not fall within my usual duties, but for you I shall make the sacrifice. Ah, forgive me; my hand slipped. Do you like that? Does it feel good? I told you; my purpose here is to entertain.

So many dead to speak for. And in every palace I visit, so many tales to tell.

Let me under the covers, my sweet, and I'll tell them to you all night long.

SILVIA PARK

Poor Unfortunate Fools

FROM *The Margins (Transpacific Literary Project)*

THE FOLLOWING IS *a compilation of articles, logs, recordings, and correspondence of the Conservation Action Plan for Merrows (CAP-Merrow) and their previous efforts to conserve the eastern black merrow* (Nereida niger). *The research conducted will be used at the Hawaii Institute of Marine Biology for the development and implementation of conservation measures to protect the southern gray merrow* (Nereida glaucus), *now classified as Critically Endangered.*

*Merrows and Drive Hunting: The Ultimate
Conservation Challenge Against Tradition*

JARED E. OLIVER

Oceanic Preservation Society, 336 Bon Air Center, Greenbrae, CA 94904

MARLA S. ROWLAND

Institute of Marine Biology, University of Hawaii, Kailua, Hawaii 96734

ABSTRACT: There is a high risk that drive hunting, the traditional method of hunting by driving merrows to caves, will lead to extinction of the eastern black merrow (*Nereida niger*), a black-tailed merrow endemic to South Korea's Jeju Island. In 2005 the Conservation Action Plan for Merrows (CAP-Merrow) banned the capture and sale of female merrows (mermaids) and immature merrows (merlings). Although efforts to implement the plan slowed the merrow's decline, the goal of eliminating merrow hunting by 2010 was not reached. Unless a ban is enforced on hunting, gill-netting, and trawling in certain areas with relatively high densities of merrows,

it will be too late to save the species, which already numbers fewer than 200 animals.
KEY WORDS: *Nereida niger* • Drive Hunt • Bycatch • South Korea

It was three months before the annual drive hunt when we received a call about a merman in distress. An American couple saw our staked sign, written in all-caps English and, beneath it, spiky Korean. By the time we reached Saekdal Beach, the sun peeked over the horizon like a cracked eyelid. Rocks glistened, clenched like obsidian fists. The wife greeted us, but the husband wanted to keep filming with his iPhone. "This is Jeju, Day Two," he said to the camera. "Sarah and I went on a walk and ho boy, you won't believe what we found—"

The merman lay in the sand with his hands crossed over his chest, like a teenage girl prepared to die of a broken heart. His name was Alto, catalog number A14. He was one of Astra's mates. He had a silken, hollowed torso and his tail, while long, was a silvered blue, a classic beta male color. Milky tears leaked from his eyes. His lips, tugged upward from the natural curve of his mouth, were crusted yellow.

"He seems so peaceful," the wife whispered.

Alto's tail rose, then fell restlessly. Once the sun hit its peak, he'd overheat within hours. His skin, rubber-smooth, had begun to flake. We filled our buckets with seawater. We soaked T-shirts. The husband proffered his own, which had the logo of a roaring tiger, but we told him, "We got this." A seagull hopped past us, holding a cherry-red Coca-Cola cap in its beak.

Marla, our head researcher, laid out the sling. She signaled us to lift Alto. We lifted him. He rolled over and rolled off the sling, baring a grainy, reddened back. Marla dug a hole underneath his tail flukes and filled it with water for ease of pushing. We pushed Alto. He flopped ineffectually. We urged him to live. We reassured him there's always next season. We assumed he, as a beta, was lovesick. Betas remained unmated until an alpha position opened up.

Alto peeled open a gummy eyelid. Merrows secrete thick, jelly-like tears to blink underwater. His eye swiveled, then settled on us. The iris was luminous instead of the usual dark. The pupil shrank from pain and the sun. He was likely a deep-sea diver. Very few betas are. The merrows who hunt in the deadliest depths are often the strongest swimmers.

"Live," he said like a sigh, parroting us.[1] "Live."

Every morning at the breakfast table, over a buffet of sliced whole-wheat bread, gummy sausages and eggs, and little green-capped Yakult drinks, our conversation turned to sex. We discussed court-ships, we counted eggs, we sighed about couplings, we were root-ing for Bloom and Anchor, we were nervous about Triton's sperm count, and as always we put our heads together and schemed and plotted and prayed to our respective deities, from God to Goddess to Science, on how to boost the number of females.

It was the summer of 2011. As part of the Merrow Conservation Action Plan (CAP), we'd partnered with the Jeju Marine Research Center to save the eastern black merrow species. After four years of dry breeding seasons, our sponsors' patience and funding were wearing thin.

We placed Alto, the nineteen-year-old beta, in a lanolin-infused tank to recover. The tank was 20×20×6 feet, which is now an illegal size for merrow tanks, but at the time we used it for transport. In the water, Alto was no longer a shriveled sardine. His hair loos-ened like curls of ink. His eyes gleamed pale. For a beta, he was a beauty, hauntingly unhappy. Even his merrow smile was mopey. We always warned the interns not to get too close. *Don't be fooled by their appearance,* we'd say. *They may look human, but they're still animals.*

The merrow who falls in love with a human is a wishful tale. The only recorded incident of this is Fabio, who was captured in Iceland in 1986 as a two-year-old merling, then eventually rescued from Marine World. His rescuers named him Fabio as a joke be-cause of his lush golden locks, but it turned out to be a self-fulfill-ing prophecy. As a merling he'd imprinted on the Marine World trainers. He only wanted to mate with humans. There are clips of him still on YouTube, including one where he sidles up to a diver, a fiftysomething researcher named Melvin Fitzsimmons. Melvin jumps, understandably startled, when Fabio begins to rub against

1. Merrows are one of the few "vocal learners" in the animal kingdom, with an unparalleled ability to imitate human speech.

his lower back. Melvin's research assistant, who filmed this, laughs nervously at 13:27, "There's his penis," as Fabio nudges Melvin to the ocean bed. Melvin's neon flippers flail. Sand billows in generous clouds. Meanwhile Fabio waves his stiff penis like a flag.

Using the VHF system, we tracked the A pod swimming past Beom Isle, about six miles from where Alto was stranded, heading east. Swallows swooped overhead as we loaded Alto's tank on our research boat and left the facility in a hurry. Merrows swim on average forty miles a day. They can outrace boats, shedding their soft flaky skin every two hours, reducing drag, freeing themselves of anything that could weigh them down.

As we neared Moon Isle, we were forced to slow down. South Korea's Jeju Island had some of the deadliest currents, whimsically cruel, and we wanted to dampen the engine noise. Below in the tossed, dark waves, streams of silhouettes glided under the surface. The waters churned in a whirlpool of pinkish foam and flakes. Using a pole, we fished out what looked like plastic bags. For once it wasn't plastic but transparent sheets of skin embedded with little chunks of rosy flesh. Our boat rocked like a lullaby as the merrows below rubbed their scales against each other in a frisky, swirling frenzy.

It was the annual mass scratchathon. We fished more sheddings for samples,[2] which are then tested for industrial toxins, including PCBs, DDT, mercury, and flame retardants.[3] Not all the skins were silver. Some carried a rainbow tint, a sign of breeding potential.

We lowered Alto on a sling. The scratchathon explained the rakes and abrasions we found on him. His tail flicked nervously. Before the sling's sagging bum could touch the water, Alto twisted his torso and leaped into the ocean. He swam toward the pod, his dorsal fin slicing the waves. Another, much larger male cut off his path. It was Triton, Astra's primary mate.

As he approached Alto, Triton clicked and whistled. Alto brushed past him, unthinkable for a beta, but he and Triton used

---

2. Another technique used to collect skin samples, which has proved controversial, is biopsy-darting. A dart with a hollow tip is shot into the side of the merrow. These darts were originally so large, the merrows tended to react violently when they were hit.

3. PCBs, despite being banned in 1979, continue to be linked to infertility in merrows. In 2011 the eastern black merrow species had an infertility rate of 60 percent.

to be "kissing pals," immature merlings who pair up during puberty. They rub and grind against each other, practicing copulation. They bond for life and often one of the merling pair will transition into a female.

Alto and Triton, however, belonged to Astra.[4]

Marla, our leader, was the first to slip into a wetsuit. She bound her blond hair into a fistlike bun and pulled on her hood with a *thwack*. Loose hair is a risk when swimming with merrows. Alpha mermaids grow their hair long as a sign of authority and like to rip out the hair of perceived rivals.

Every time we swam with the merrows, it was a fresh shock. Merrows are much larger than us. Their skin, brown and rubbery, fades into a ghostly silver underwater. Their wide eyes are more fish than mammal, their tastes more shark than dolphin. They could surround us. They could herd us into a trap. They could grab our ankles and tug us into the darkness.

A dark tail whipped past Marla, who seized the scuba rope out of reflex rather than fright. Astra circled us. She nuzzled her cheek against Marla's arm, then glided past the boat like a giant stingray, wings spread. She chirped a greeting, and like an orchestra, her pod replied with groans and clanks. We held our breath until our snorkels fell silent, as the last of the bubbles slipped away. Surrounded by the wisps of skin and feces, the clicks, shrieks, and cries, we listened to the merrow songs, reverent and reverberant.

They communicated through echolocation. They could see through us. They could see through our bones. They could see our hearts, beating faster.

Astra rose with us to the surface. Strands of her hair, so dark it could be green, clung to her fluttering gills. Her face was a silken deep brown. Her cheekbones were terrifying. Her smile reached her ears. Merrows have wide mouths and their corners are natu-

---

4. Merrows live in social assemblages as pairs or triads consisting of a dominant female, an alpha male, and an immature juvenile or beta male. If the dominant mermaid of a triad dies, all subordinates seize the opportunity to ascend in rank and grow. The alpha male is poised to become female and rapidly changes sex to assume the vacated position, while the beta male completes the breeding pair by turning into a mature male in a short amount of time.

rally fixed into a smile, a friendly effect undermined by their sharp teeth.

Since the 1980s, CAP's photo-ID catalog had swelled to seven merrow groups, lumped under two pods, with over forty members. More than a hundred of them, of crisp Grade 5 quality, belonged to Astra, our most receptive merrow to date.

Triton and Alto joined her. In simple English, we told Astra we found Alto stranded on the beach. We didn't mention his reluctance to be saved. Looking back, perhaps we should have.

Astra looped her arms around them both and laughed, full-throated: "My poor unfortunate fools." A magnificent voice. Her underwater cries haunted us, but when she spoke in our tongue, she carried a lilt so persuasive, it was no surprise fishermen used to drown in the past, lured under the waves. She had a voice like sea glass, the edges weathered from years of tidal beatings. But it was her laughter we treasured. She cackled and giggled. She chattered and shrieked. She laughed, unheeding, like a child.

She was the alpha of the pod. She was their matriarch. She was our star.

In 2001 we'd picked her up when she was neither Astra nor he nor she, but a young merling with dark fins, black as a slippery eel. We'd tracked the A pod for weeks along the coast of Kyushu. The September drive hunt was looming forth where fishermen herded merrows into coves, strangled them in nets, and dragged them by the flukes. The most attractive mermaids were captured and sold. The rest were slaughtered. The Japanese believed in longevity from the consumption of merrow flesh, advertised as *Ningyo Sashimi!* in neon-trimmed Shinjuku bars, often with the painting of a splayed mermaid, bite-sized chunks of her pink marbled flesh laid out on her ivory skin.

Our methods of rescue were still primitive back then. We'd select the most vulnerable members of the pod and keep them safe in our sea pens until the drive hunt ended. Astra was one of these rescues. The rest of her pod watched us with accusing eyes, corralled behind the net, a bobbing of wet heads. We promised we'd return her, safe. But Astra's mother, a mermaid with yellow eyes and a scarred mouth, wouldn't stop screaming, her gills flaring obscenely.

Astra was five years old, the size of a young child but with the strength of an adult man. It turned out to be the perfect age. She wasn't so immature she'd imprint on us and turn deviant like Fabio, but she was young enough to be curious and calm. We had to return two of the merlings within hours. One became so agitated his gills shut and he sank unmoving to the bottom of his tank.

Astra was different from the moment we hauled her in. We bundled her in our net like a swaddle. Instead of squeaking in fright, Astra smiled up at us through her seaweed hair.

Now we know better. Merrow smiles are an anatomical lie, arising from the configuration of their jaws. Their smiles drag humans down bottomless spring pools. Their smiles convince us they're happy.

After the scratchathon we invited Astra for a health check due to the risk of open wounds and infection. Some members of her pod were coerced into following, including Triton, her mate. *Oh, Triton,* we'd often sigh. Triton, t-A13, was a survivor of a measleslike viral epidemic that decimated his pod, the T pod from the Great Barrier Reef, in 2002. Before we traced his lineage, we used to call him Flame, or catalog number X13.[5] He had a braided mane, dark as coagulated blood, and when he reached sexual maturity, his silver tail deepened into a royal blue mottled with flakes of crimson, like a fire flickering between red and blue, hot and hotter.

He was a troublemaker. He had a track record of being netted. At first we wrote it off as low intelligence, which was why some of us, Marla included, were disappointed when Astra chose him as her primary mate. Later we learned it was recklessness. After the T pod was wiped out, Triton traveled hundreds of miles as a solo merling before the A pod accepted him. Aside from Astra and Alto, he never bonded with the pod.[6] He hunted alone, targeting fish farms where he risked entanglement. Instead of waiting for someone to cut him loose, he lashed out with his tail. Once he broke a fisherman's ribs. We apologized on Triton's behalf, but

5. The catalog letter *X* is used for solo merrows. Merrows without pods rarely last more than five years on their own. They are rarely seen again.
6. Every merrow population has a unique call or "dialect." These acoustic differences are used to identify membership of a pod and prevent inbreeding. Dr. John Bigg's groundbreaking research on merrow dialects has since proven why outsider merrows have difficulty overcoming these "language barriers."

we knew Triton had held back. We'd seen him hunt, stunning a school of sardines with a whip of his tail, like a shockwave.

Despite this streak of aggression, we tried to avoid sedating Triton, or any of the merrows, when we checked them for possible injuries from the scratchathon. He was devoted enough to follow Astra to the outer rim of our facility. Astra pulled herself onto the dock, familiar with the squeaking wooden planks.

Triton protested. Leaving the waters was deemed too dangerous. He rammed against the dock. He slapped his tail on the surface. He screeched and clanked like the chains of a shipwreck. Alto treaded about five feet away. He eyed Astra and Triton with a quiet, gleaming look. As the beta, his duty was to support Triton, but in almost every triad, tensions between the alpha and beta male bubbled.

Now Triton began to whimper, holding out his arms. Astra, with impatience in her smile, lunged for his neck. Her teeth sank into his shoulder. Alto reared up, but the shock passed and he sank back down, tucking his chin under the water.

Triton winced but his smile didn't waver. There was an almost gratefulness to his pain.

Even after the 2001 September drive hunt, we'd kept Astra, a sexually immature merling, in a sea pen by the dock. Our volunteers taught her signs on laminated flashcards and rewarded her with fish, mackerel being her favorite. She liked to mimic us.[7] "Good morning!" she'd crow. "Hello! Do you want fish? Yes, you want fish. What do you want? I want to go back."

She liked to perform for us. Once she threw up her mackerel[8] and waved it at us, gripping the fish at the base. A week into her rescue, she tore into the fish instead of swallowing it whole. Astra was mimicking how we ate. We scolded her. We didn't want her to pick up unnatural habits, invasive to her way of life. Astra

7. Aggressive mimicry is the most popular theory on why merrows imitate human speech, stemming from stories of merrows that drowned humans in oceans, lakes, or rivers. This theory is largely dismissed as superseded within the scientific community. It may have even contributed to the extinction of the freshwater merrow species.

8. Merrows have two stomachs, one for digestion, one for storage, where food can be regurgitated at will.

responded to our chiding with a furtive, bloodied smile. But she was eager to please. She learned to swallow. She learned to ask for fish. She learned over two thousand verbal words, but what made Astra truly remarkable was her grammar. By Day 41 her level of grammatical orderliness and conceptual complexity was typical of a three-year-old human child.

Jared, the head researcher at the time, was thrilled. He had Astra tested at the Jeju research center. Using a magnetic resonance imaging scanner, we made a tremendous discovery. Astra had a portion of the brain that was missing in even humans. Her anterior cingulate cortex, the language center, was unusually dense, twice as heavy as the average bilingual's.

Some of us held the childish belief we'd cultivated Astra's exceptionality. Again, this was 2001. We used to play mermaid films to impressionable merlings, hoping to massage their gender predisposition. Marla hated the films, especially *Splash!*, which spawned the multibillion-dollar industry in Marine World, but we were desperate for more females. All merrows are born protandrous hermaphroditic, meaning they're born male.

We snagged Astra's interest by filming her and playing home videos on a television box, a waterproof extension cord trailing down the dock. She'd rise from the sea pen and watch herself with a parted, teething smile. The mermaid movies weren't as successful. She yawned through *Splash!* She farted bubbles during *Mr. Peabody and the Mermaid.*

But every time we played *The Little Mermaid,* Astra surged out of the waters, dimpled elbows on the dock. She'd lean in so close, the tip of her nose smeared a teardrop on the screen. She'd peek, pupils shot, through the wet seaweed of hair.

We moved Astra from the sea pen to the tank for blood tests. Marla circled marks along Astra's arm with a ballpoint pen. For hours Astra rubbed her forearm, trying to erase the marks. To distract her, we'd turn on the movie.

It wasn't Ariel who bewitched her. From the confines of the tank, Astra danced when Ursula filled the screen, tentacles splayed and spinning, singing, *Poor unfortunate souls.* Astra's hair swirled above her like a storm cloud. Her tail had grown five inches. Her scales flushed from black to a deep aubergine, like Ursula's soft, vulnerable underbelly. Her voice had changed too. From the fluty cries of a choirboy, she sang in Ursula's sultry tenor, though her voice would crack and squeak on occasion, pantomiming, *Poor unfortunate fools, in pain, in need . . .*

We were witness to an unprecedented phenomenon. Within fourteen days Astra had transformed from a black immature merling into an alpha mermaid, violet as a sea witch, skipping the silver stage of beta males entirely. We realized, this is it. She was going to be our Queen Victoria, the Grandmother of the Ocean. Her children would go on to breed with clans across the globe. She would revive not only the eastern black merrows in the Pacific but the gray-finned pods back home, the white merrows near Iceland.

Years later we watched one of her tapes. Someone, maybe Linda, pointed something out. Astra, our prodigy, had botched the lyrics, singing on the behalf of *fools,* a word we'd never taught. Some of us thought it was intentional. Maybe she didn't have a need of a soul. Maybe she had a soft spot for fools.

Long-Term Recording of Gastric Ulcers in Merrows Stranded on the Jeju (S Korea) Coast

MARLA S. ROWLAND

Institute of Marine Biology, University of Hawaii, Kailua, Hawaii 96734

ABSTRACT: Long-term (2001–2011) results of recording gastric ulcers in the eastern black merrows (*Nereida niger*) are presented for the South Korean Pacific coast. The occurrence of merrow carcasses with gastric ulcers are also discussed. Ulcerations were detected in 17.2% of the animals examined, with 25% for eastern black merrows. A positive relation was noted between ulcer counts and length and maturity. Clusters of the nematode *Anisakis simplex* could be seen embedded in the gastric ulcers of 3 eastern black merrows. It can be concluded that gastric ulcers are nonfatal lesions in merrows stranded in South Korea.
KEY WORDS: Gastric ulcers • *Nereida niger* • Merrow carcasses • South Korea

According to Astra's 2011 health reports, she exhibited unusually high GCC levels, which is often a sign of gastric ulcers.[9] Upon detecting occult blood in her stool, we prescribed Maalox, which we'd covertly slip into the gills of her favorite mackerel. Stress, we surmised, had to be the reason why Astra had failed to conceive for four years, though we were also concerned with Triton's low sperm count.

After the post-scratchathon checkup, we gave Astra a shot of Clomid, the fertility drug, which had proven successful with gray mermaids and lowland gorillas. Astra let us circle the vein in the crook of her arm with a ballpoint pen. She didn't flinch as the needle pricked her. She giggled, as if nervous. "Will I lay the egg?"

Of course, we told her.

Astra's smile seemed tentative. She yearned to be a mother. Every year she let us approach her eggs in her anemone nest to check for fertility. We'd scan the eggs for the telltale blastoderm, a particular spot on fertilized eggs. Every year the eggs were pristine and spotless.

Marla, slipping the pen behind her ear, tried to cheer her up.

"Remember tentacle porn?" Marla said.

Between December 2001 and March 2002, Astra had begun exhibiting secondary female characteristics, so we'd banned male volunteers from approaching her. Within days we'd caught a volunteer named Brett, a surfer who swore that a mermaid had once saved him by headbutting a tiger shark, with his pants down. He scrambled for his trunks, crying out, "She asked for it!" which raised a few eyebrows. Later we checked the cameras. They backed his story. In fact, Astra hadn't asked for his penis but demanded it. Merrows have a caninelike intuition for social hierarchy. Even at her tender age, Astra could ascertain where Brett the surfer stood.

Brett tried to withdraw his penis, but Astra seized it, eliciting a pained squeal of shock. None of us moved. But again, we believed it was curiosity. With her grip, Astra could have crushed it into a pulp. Astra unwrapped her long spindly fingers and weighed his member with a chilling fascination. Her conclusion?

"Too soft."

Brett deflated. We were relieved to see Astra's encouraging, almost pitying smile. Some of us worried our star pupil might turn deviant like Fabio. We couldn't Fabio this.

---

9. We later compared Astra's 2011 GCC levels with that of captive merrows in Marine World. She had the stress levels of a merrow living in a 20×20-foot steel box.

Her preference for merman penis was understandable,[10] but for weeks Brett moaned "cocktease," and we assigned our intern Tina, a budding woman in her own right, to stand guard. She usually sat in front of the tank and read her Japanese comic books.

One day Astra asked, "What is that?"

"Tentacle porn," Tina said.

Astra reared up. "Octopus? Squid?"

"Wanna see?"

Astra preferred movies over books. While she could read signs, she didn't find the written word as compelling as the spoken. Tina scooched her chair closer so Astra could peer over her shoulder and read the comic book through the layer of glass. As Tina turned the pages, Astra asked, "Does octopus have sex with human?" "Why is octopus so large?" "Where can I find large octopus?"

At the end of the comic, Astra sighed, as if satisfied. She told Tina the octopus was a female.

"How can you tell?" Tina said.

"Females are large. They have sex with male octopus and kill him."

Octopus sex remains a paradox. They're deeply antisocial, and yet their bodies have evolved in a way where they can only mate with the utmost intimacy. A male octopus, brave and desperate, must penetrate the female with one of his tentacles. He'd slip it directly into her bulbous head and inject a stream of sperm, and sometimes a warning alarm went off, and he'd sacrifice his arm and flee.

Sometimes he wouldn't. Sometimes he'd stay or come back, and slip his arm into her ear, as if to caress her brain, and sometimes she'd wrap him in her arms and hold him until she strangled him, then she'd drag him home and eat him with a slow, careful regret.

Type in *mermaid sex* and more than 455,000 results will register on YouTube, though many will be of music videos or animated simulations. Merrows rarely have sex near the surface. Only seven recordings of the eastern black's mating rituals exist on record, which

---

10. Merman penises are fibroelastic, filled with collagen. Even flaccid, their penises are stiff. Humans have attempted copulation with merrows for years, but a human male, even with a week's supply of Viagra and a flashlight, would never find his way through the twisting maze that is a mermaid's vagina.

makes the following video footage, recorded on June 5, 2011, all the more valuable.

The morning after the scratchathon, Triton was swimming in circles when we returned Astra. She leaped into his arms, but before Triton could hug her, Astra slipped out of his embrace and looped once around him, playful. Her claws softly raked his face as she hissed in his ear. Her voice, no matter how whispery, rang in the salty air.

In front of us, Astra began sexual contact, first through mouthing, then licking.[11] Triton's confusion bloomed into pleasure when Astra tongued the spiraled ridges of his ear. She slipped the tip, black and glistening, into his hole, like an octopus's arm, reaching deep inside the head until it hit the crinkled folds of the brain, so she could stroke the brain, so the brain would tingle because the brain is the most sensitive of organs, and it's shaped like a maze, like the inner workings of a mermaid.

Astra pushed Triton's hand down her waist, toward her genital slit, as her finger peeled the lip of her slit open. Triton's tail blushed a deep red. The blue flecks faded in the force of his arousal. His fins fanned out, flickering orange. He expanded his chest and gave a quick, sonic boom, a mating call.

As Astra looped her tail around Triton's, she eyed Alto, who remained chin-deep in the water. Her unblinking gaze was clearly provocative. Alto's fins flared, a sign of either anger or arousal, a far cry from the dehydrated merman we'd found stretched on the sand, resisting rescue.

Astra extended her webbed hand. She drew Alto into their embrace. Triton made a noise like a growl, but Astra chittered. His growl melted into a whine, helpless. Astra and Triton rubbed belly to belly while Alto swam by them. He dipped under the water and supported Astra from below, his chest pressed against her spine, as Triton rolled on top of her. As they entwined, strangling, choking, loving, we realized the positions had switched and now Alto was on the bottom, with Astra above and Triton in between.

Alto melded against Triton's back. He closed his luminous eyes

---

11. We knew merrows had no sense of impropriety, but still we questioned why Astra would initiate sexual contact in our presence. Marla, of all people, conjectured it came from a desire to please. "She wanted to show us," Marla said, "that she's trying."

and rubbed against the navy dorsal fin, as if they were kissing pals again, just two merlings bonding for life.

On the Fourth of July, Astra laid a spotted egg, our first fertile egg since 2006. We emailed Jared, who sent out a mass email of congratulations to the entire merrow protection network with a picture of five-year-old Astra, grinning at her regurgitated fish. Our volunteers wanted to celebrate with fireworks, but we couldn't risk it. Merrows were exquisitely sensitive to sound. We grilled hamburgers and hot dogs and drank beer on the dock and toasted Marla for giving up her career as an astronomer and joining us in the fight to rescue all merrows, and Rodney for thinking of using Clomid, and Eddie for being our translator, and we thanked everyone, including all our volunteers.

Astra's nest was located near Seki Isle, a tiny islet with some of the wildest currents, which is why it was rigged underwater with a stout web of ropes designed to tether and guide divers through the wretched waters. Diving with cumbersome equipment could be a challenge, but on Day 4 we set up the underwater cameras. On Day 7 we made plans to retrieve the egg.

We convinced ourselves it was vital to care for the egg during this sensitive time. Many fertilized eggs had suffered needless deaths from neglectful mothers, opportunistic predators, or oceanic whims. After the decimation of the T pod, the eastern black merrow population teetered at only thirty-seven merrows, with eight breeding females left. Artificial incubation would boost those numbers. Since 1996 rescuers had hand-raised nineteen merlings and returned them safely to the wild, with a survival rate of 81 percent.

The triad alternated between hunting and watching over the egg, nestled in a lavender anemone among the soft corals. Triton, as the father, was too dangerous. His shockwave tail could smash our innards. We wanted to avoid Astra. Deep down, we feared she'd be unwilling to give up the egg. We told ourselves she'd understand.

July 23, 2011 (Day 19): We anchored the boat by Seki Isle before sunrise and waited an hour in the stinging wind to time the egg's retrieval. Red buoys bobbed nearby, a sign of local divers. The craggy shoreline shone like onyx. Legend was merrows had pitch-black tails because they were sloughed from Jeju's porous black rocks.

We waited to retrieve the egg during Alto's watch. As a beta male, we suspected he would be less confrontational. He confirmed our suspicions by fleeing upon spotting us. He retreated ten feet away from the corals, and hidden behind pink mossy rocks, he watched us with his luminous deep-sea eyes. Alto could have lunged at our divers or released a distress signal. The fact that he made no attempt to summon Astra or Triton disappointed us.

A mermaid egg is sometimes called a mermaid's purse. It looks like a blood donation bag but is far more delicate, more precious. We bundled the egg into our transport bag, which two divers needed to carry, as we kicked toward the surface. Alto followed. His gills flared once before his head broke the surface. His dark, tangled hair curtained his face, shielding his eyes from the sun.

From the boat, one of our volunteers pointed over the railing. The silvery blue of Alto's scales was darker than usual. He was changing color. His eyes remained pale and opaque, watching us as we drove the boat away.

Alpha Mermaid Brutally Attacks Challenger Mermaid / AMAZING MERMAID ATTACK

1.2M views

Bale TV
Published on September 8, 2009

An ALPHA mermaid has been filmed for the first time killing a CHALLENGER mermaid. The footage, which is believed to be a world first, was captured off the coast of South Korea by underwater photographer Carol Jackson. It shows an older mermaid challenging the alpha matriarch of a mermaid pod. The matriarch wears down the older mermaid with opportunistic bites at her fins. She moves in to deliver the death blow.

For more compelling footage of the amazing side of life: Like Bale TV

3,525 Comments

Josh Giles 1 year ago
Tremendously strategic in biting off its fins. Amazing.
phantom lover 2 years ago (edited)
CAT FIGHT!!!
Double Agent 139 1 year ago
Rest in pieces

*

The Jeju locals grew aware, if not appreciative, of our efforts to save the eastern black merrow species. After years of trying to raise awareness, we were now giving talks four times a week at schools, diving schools, fishing clubs, yacht clubs, lifeguards, anyone that was willing to listen. We would get calls from mothers collecting shells with their children. Teachers on field trips. Tourists on boats to Udo Island. Ferry captains. Fishermen. Even the coastal guard.

We raised Astra's egg in a tank, warmed at seventy-eight degrees Fahrenheit, under a fiberoptic bulb to see through the translucent sack, and recorded fetal growth, one millimeter at a time. Hand-rearing of merrow eggs was an exhaustive procedure that required at least five people on staff to remain in constant supervision.

On Day 17 of the egg's incubation, we received a tip from local divers, who had spotted the A pod[12] near Sup Isle. We rushed out, grabbing just our wetsuits and a small dive boat. We hadn't seen Astra in weeks, not since we'd taken away her egg for protection, despite our efforts to reach out to her. The extended silence was concerning, but we reasoned that merrows spend 90 percent of their lives under the surface. They couldn't always be found.

As the sun dipped behind a pinnacle of shaven rock, we drove past a black-sand beach. The beach, once a tourist hot spot, was closed. Garbage speckled the shoreline in tumorous piles. Convenience-store bags, laid flat by paperweight rocks, looked like dried jellyfish. Plastic cups with melted peanut butter ice cream, soda bottles, makgeolli bottles, cigarette butts, chopstick sleeves, straw wrappers, a punctured tire, a smashed surfboard. Once, on a different beach, we'd uncovered a rare find. A half-gallon bottle filled with uncooked rice, a first-aid kit, a USB stick, and a single U.S. dollar bill, folded with a note that said, "God loves you." It was a care package, flung by South Korean activists and missionaries in the hopes it would reach the shores of North Korea one day.

---

12. The A pod was difficult to track during this two-week period. Merrow pods avoid traveling long distances when the females are nesting, so the A pod's sudden migration toward Kyushu, Japan, was considered unusual.

Elderly women divers[13] peeled sea urchins with thick starched gloves. An old woman tucked her dyed-brown frizz into the black hood of her wetsuit. She picked up her green-netted Styrofoam buoy and waddled on stubby flippers toward the ocean.

We asked the divers where they'd spotted a pod of merrows. We nudged our Korean American intern to translate for us. After some back-and-forth, the divers burst out laughing. Our intern said the divers didn't see the pod but one or two merrows, headed for the estuary. He said one of the divers had recognized Astra. They called her "psycho," which caused some of us to bristle.

"Why did they laugh?" Rodney said.

Our intern had tried to explain that her name was Astra and her importance. One of the divers had replied, *Why hang her in the sky when she belongs to the sea?*

We drove toward Soesokkak Estuary, the mouth of a stream where salt meets fresh, some of us skeptical. The estuary wasn't deep enough for merrows who were open-water swimmers.[14] But as the divers had claimed, we spotted a dorsal fin speeding across the estuary, the water so shallow the fin stood at least half a meter. We counted two more shapes, three in total. One of the merrows was chasing something, but water visibility remained at zero from the stirred sediment. We couldn't see who the merrows were or what they were hunting.

One of the merrows leaped from the waters. The torso disappeared underwater before we could see the face, but a pair of dark purple flukes slapped the surface.

Marla wobbled over to the bow. "Astra!"

Astra chased after a silhouetted shape that slipped under our boat. We spotted the third merrow, Triton, recognized by his blue dorsal fin, as he tried to wedge himself between Astra and the flee-

---

13. The *haenyeo*, or "women of the sea," is the deferential appellation given to the Jeju female divers. They too have dwindled in number, but a recent K-drama rekindled interest in their trade. They've set up a *haenyeo* school near our facility. Sometimes we see them selling fresh octopus and squid to tourists, wielding sea knives and shouting prices. "Just for you, I'll make it twenty-five thousand won," they shout to no one in particular. "Just for you."

14. "Benthic foraging on stingrays by merrows (*Nereida glaucus*) in New Zealand waters," *Journal of Marine Science* (2013), dispelled this popular theory in scientific literature.

ing merrow. Astra swerved and rammed into the other merrow from the side.

Alto lashed back at her with his tail. It'd taken us much longer to ID him. His silver scales had darkened into a deep hue. Alto released a sonic boom, a cry only alphas could make. His scream shuddered across the waves. Astra shrieked back. Blood flowed from the corners of her enraged smile. She raked his face with her claws, then headbutted him in the stomach. Alto dove under her and flipped her over.

"Astra," Marla screamed.

Astra's head rose once more. For a moment her gaze swiveled in our direction. We couldn't recognize her. Her eyes had sunk deep into her sockets, from either grief or fury. But she recognized us. Her merrow smile seemed to falter. In her hesitation we saw confusion, and in her confusion we saw her head droop, like a heartbroken child, before she dove under the water.

The waves rippled over, but the air remained sticky with salt and blood. Then the boat lurched. Marla crashed against the railing. A merrow had headbutted us. We scanned the waters for a blue dorsal fin, signs of Triton. But it was Alto, with his deep-diver eyes and mopey smile. A gruesome flap of skin dangled from his nose. Astra had almost raked his face clean off.

Alto bared his teeth at us. "What is he doing? Why is he attacking?" Marla shouted, but none of us could answer. He smashed into our boat again and screamed. His gills splayed pink. He shrieked nonsensical words. Shaken, we turned the boat. We had to chase after Astra, following her wispy trail of blood before it faded. Some of us remembered Kara, who'd once challenged a thirteen-year-old Astra for leadership of the pod, who'd died from her injuries, entangled in a cage net. Alto's screams echoed, chasing after us.

We searched for Astra, but she'd left the range of her VHF tag. We recruited volunteers from the Korean Oceanic Rescue Service, divers from the local school, and even a crew from an aquaculture site. Volunteers scanned the islets, from Beom Isle to Moon Isle, for hours.

We returned to the estuary, where we found Triton swimming under the strong sun, back and forth along the surface, standing on his tail, a strong indicator of distress. We hauled him in with little effort. Alto, no longer bleeding but sluggish from the fight, had also lingered within sighting distance. He dove deeper whenever we tried to approach. But he never strayed too far. He wouldn't leave Triton, and we had finally begun to understand why.

Rodney, who had the license and the aim, shot Alto in the back with a tranquilizer. Back at our facility, we measured Alto's length. The growth was astounding. He stretched 11.5 feet long. His colors had settled into a turquoise flecked with bright yellow. He'd transitioned into a splendid alpha male.

Triton watched Alto from an adjacent sea pen. He hissed whenever we drew close. His own transformation was palpable. The sea pen was shallow enough to expose his scales, fading from crimson to orange-yellow. As we would later discover, the collagen in his scales had already softened from the ridged ctenoid scales of males into the smooth cycloid scales of females.

An external event had triggered Triton's hermaphroditic transition and we feared the cause.[15] Perhaps Triton sensed this. He rammed against the walls of the sea pen, not purposefully but as if he were disoriented with loss.

A few days later the A pod was spotted near Beom Isle, but Astra was still nowhere to be found. "She's strong," Marla said, jaw tense.[16] At her suggestion, we played a merrow song on speakerphone every night. We listened to Astra sing as a merling when she used to cry for her mother, who was killed in the 2001 September drive hunt. We waited on the dock until dawn. We wanted to believe in her smile, no matter how illusory it was.

Fabio eventually returned to the sea. The $20 million Free Fabio Project rehabilitated him in a makeshift pen by Klettsvik Bay. He was taught how to swim, how to hunt. A month after his release into Icelandic waters, Fabio was found near a Norwegian village, flirting with the fishermen, playing with the children. Tourists of-

15. Ibid., p. 6. If the alpha mermaid of a triad falls ill or is injured, the alpha male changes sex to assume the female role while the beta male completes the breeding pair by turning into a mature male. Casas, Lisa, and Ryu, Taewoo. (2008). "Sex Change in Merrows: Molecular Insight from Transcriptome Analysis." *Scientific Reports*.

16. In 2012, Marla Rowland gave birth to her first child, a daughter named Marina, at the age of thirty-eight. At Marina Rowland's first birthday, Marla is reported to have told some of her past coworkers she wished she could apologize to Astra.

ten spotted him preening his long golden hair, singing Christmas jingles like "Jingle Bell Rock."

Sometimes he sang in a lost language, echoing clicks and guttural groans, as if he wanted to stretch his vocal cords, his ability to reach out to his own kind, no matter how far away they were.

He died a year after his release. They found his body in Taknes Bay, a calm pocket of coastal water, deep enough that it wouldn't freeze in the winter.

There is only one recorded instance of Fabio's attempt to establish contact with a wild merrow pod. He was once seen bobbing in the periphery of the pod, at least five hundred feet away, facing the closest merrow, as they passed by.

After thirty-five days of incubation, the fetus in Astra's egg resembled a human baby, curled up in a spiral, with a misshapen large head, five webbed little fingers on each hand, and small hind protrusions, which would shrink and meld into a merrow tail, just as the tail would shrink and meld into a human spine.

The tests proved Triton wasn't the father. On top of his low sperm count, we suspected he was infertile. The surviving merrows of the T pod who had reintegrated into other clans never yielded any fertilized eggs. We'd hoped it wouldn't be the case for Triton, who was a merling at the time. The virus had not only decimated his family but killed his fragile reproductive capabilities. Even as an alpha female, the chance that Triton would bear children was frighteningly low.

If Triton wasn't the father, then that left Alto. He floated in his tank, listless and belly-up, his merrow smile now a sutured gash across his face. He was always so passive, drifting aimlessly in his tank. Was it this same passivity that had angered Astra? Had she taken his refusal to protect the egg as a betrayal? Perhaps Alto had always known he was the father and still he'd relinquished his offspring to us.

We debated the reasons for Alto's lack of paternal enthusiasm until someone proposed a theory: Alto and Triton had bonded when they were merlings. They used to be kissing pals. Perhaps Alto had always wanted Triton as a mate until Astra, an established alpha female, claimed Triton as her own.

To test this theory, we lifted the door separating his sea pen from Triton's. Triton, who had almost fully transitioned into a female, rubbed against Alto for comfort. But Alto shuddered. He swerved sharply. He continued to dodge Triton's attempts to communicate.

"He's a deviant,"[17] Rodney said. "He won't mate with females."

That evening we released Triton and Alto into the ocean. Alto dove under the waves without a backward look. Eddie snapped a blurred picture, Grade 3 in quality, a final glimpse of Alto's scarred shoulders, crimson in the setting sun. We'd counted more than thirty bites around his neck and shoulders. The majority of his scars were puckered white and old. Astra had been sinking her teeth into him for years.

Rodney gave a despairing laugh. "An infertile alpha and a homosexual beta—Astra truly picked the best!"

Astra must have inflicted injuries on Alto with an increasing desperation every time he tried to refuse her. But why hadn't she simply abandoned her mates?[18] Why would she try to mate with Alto to the point of inflicting bites that went beyond mouthing behaviors?

This is where we split into factions. Some of us believe Astra had known all along. After four years of failure, she must have realized Triton was infertile, she must have sensed Alto's covert desire for Triton. The rest of the pod would have chased them out for their deficiencies. And yet Astra had laughed and accepted them with a helpless fondness.

The other faction has accused us of projecting human qualities onto Astra. We were trying to make her into something that she wasn't. Had we not done this already? We'd always told Astra she was meant to be a mother. We'd called her so many things. Our star, our queen. We'd promised she'd be the grandmother of the ocean, we'd caged her with promises she had to uphold, and still she'd tried to embrace us, her poor, unfortunate fools.

---

17. Homosexual behavior in merrows is not uncommon in social play, but a male's rejection of a female's advances was unheard of within the marine science community in 2011. Later studies have disproved this misconception.
18. Merrows often do mate for life, but this is seen as an evolutionary strategy for maximizing the number of merlings they can raise. Monogamy only comes after the successful conception of a fertile egg. Alpha females are known for discarding males who are incapacitated in any way that prevents copulation.

COMPLETE RESULTS REPORT

Case#: 15-1831
MMSC-15-117   Species: Merrow

Verified by: Dr. Laura Ravasi   Breed: Eastern Black
Verified on: 12/10/11   Sex: Female
Date Administered: 12/10/11   Date Reported: 02/22/12
Test: Gross Pathology   Specimen Collected on: 12/08/11

Animal ID	Test	Specimen	Result
MMSC-15-117	postmortem	whole body dead	gross pathology

Comments: A necropsy is performed on December 10, 2011. The body
is that of an 82kg adult female merrow (*Nereida niger*) found stranded
on Shiretoko Beach in Japan. The body length measures 285cm and
has severely depleted adipose deposits in postmortem condition. All
organs not described are within normal limits.

GROSS DIAGNOSES

Body as a whole: Emaciated, severe.

Lung: Pneumonia, granulomatous, chronic, multifocal, mild.

Thorax and abdomen: Effusion, serous to serosanguineous, mild.

Stomach: Ulceration, chronic, multifocal, mild, forestomach (nonglan-
dular gastric compartment) full of marine garbage such as garbage
bags, sacks of raffia, ropes, pieces of nets and plastic bottles, etc.

The manner of death is undetermined.

THEODORE McCOMBS

Six Hangings in the Land of Unkillable Women

FROM *Nightmare Magazine*

1899, Jan 20th.
Sidney Lewis MILL, 36 (Vengeance)

Mill—a charmer and a rake of no respectable talent whatever—insinuated himself into the home of the widow Annie Holcomb and her seventeen-year-old daughter, Alice. But Mrs. Holcomb turned him out once she realized he'd been gallanting Alice as much as her. Mill spent the next four nights chanting obscene tirades under her window and left a dead rat in the mail slot on the fifth. Night patrols chased him off park benches; friends robbed him. Sleepless and humiliated, he broke into the house and strangled Mrs. Holcomb with her tin necklace and, when it snapped, with a pajama cord—and when that failed, he dragged a kitchen knife over her throat—and when the knife chipped and the shard cut Mill's eye, Mrs. Holcomb ran into the street calling for help, towing her bewildered daughter by the wrist.

Mill pled guilty. Alice Holcomb wept profligately through his sentencing. On the scaffold, Mill's last words were, "Finally—finally."

It was a muggy, yellowed May morning on Willow Street, Boston, the light tawny and thick with heat and soot. Edith Smylie's husband, Gerald Smylie, superintendent of the Police Department's Bureau of Homicides and Homicide Attempts, having finished breakfast, sat bothered at the window, watching two blackbirds harass and chase a hawk over the rooftops. Edith cleared the plates and ran a crumb catcher over the tablecloth, thoughtlessly at first, and then, when she saw how it irritated him, with a perverse little violence, scraping at the fabric so that it sent a thin, linen whistle needling into his ear.

"Look, do you mind!" Gerry snapped, and Edith stopped at once.

She was a lean, dry woman of stiff and careful movements, auburn-bunned, tending to gauntness, and in her high-collared brown wool dress, she looked like a telegraph pole. "It's the Barrow girl bothering you, isn't it?" Edith said.

Edith came round and settled by her husband. He sat with his shoulders pushed forward in his sack coat, the way he did, Edith had observed before, when he felt the world had skipped off its rails. She knew which case had kept him sleepless so many nights. She knew, and resented that he hadn't asked for her advice.

It had been all over the papers, inevitably: Liza Barrow, of North End, having reared alone her five-year-old son, that winter had starved the boy to death, keeping him tied to his bed with nautical rope. It was an outrage; it was a hanging offense. The jury would have rioted had the judge ordered any lesser sentence. What the papers didn't know—what Edith had suspected, and what Gerald now confirmed to her—was that Miss Barrow refused to hang.

The rope broke, the first time. The second time, the noose wouldn't even tie, but squirmed and shrank from the frantic hangman like a centipede wriggling out of a child's clumsy fingers. They'd tried a firing squad, and the bullets never turned up, not in Miss Barrow nor in the wall behind her. They'd tried the chair, and she'd sat patiently in a blue halo of St. Elmo's fire, grinning like a perfect demon, teeth crackling. Since the emergence of the Protection, there had been some small number of women killers like Miss Barrow, and discreet committees of lawyers and churchmen had convened to litigate the metaphysics of an execution. If the crime were very bad, surely. If she were immured in a tomb with no air, surely. They never found an exception, and Massachusetts's prisons hadn't either. Gerry had sworn his officers to secrecy, but sooner or later, he admitted, the public would realize, like Miss Barrow had realized, that her sentence couldn't be carried out.

Edith listened carefully while her husband unburdened himself. Her sickle nose traveled slowly up as she deliberated.

"The solution is unfortunate," Edith said at last, but with a certain pride of achievement. "Liza Barrow," she said, "must hang by a woman's hand."

Gerry startled.

It had never occurred to those discreet committees that women might enjoy a power denied to men. It had occurred to Edith, however. There had been reports in other cities, all confused, all unverified, of women having managed, with difficulty, to murder their husbands' mistresses or to poison their mothers. Edith had kept careful account; had pondered them in her heart well before this morning. And women still did manage to kill themselves, after all.

"Obviously, she must wear a hood," Edith said simply. Gerry raked his fingers through his hair. An uneasy smell of potatoes in oil lingered in the room. "And there's no need to flounce around in petticoats for a hanging. No one need ever know."

Gerry stood, and his shoulders pushed to his ears. "I shouldn't like," he said, "I shouldn't like the woman who'd willingly undertake that duty."

Edith shot him a look: he should know better than to make such declarations. She gazed into her gathered hands. For one sour moment she wondered if she shouldn't have said anything. "It *is* a duty," Edith reflected. "And I am prepared to satisfy it, if no one else will."

1899, Mar 1st.
Samuel HEWITT, 24 (Jealousy, Drink)

Hewitt lost his job as a toolmaker and was reduced to asking Mary Rowledge's father for work; he and Mary had just become engaged. Bedeviled by shame into resentment, Hewitt grew suspicious of Mary's friendship with her family's boarder, a Mr. Robert "Black Robby" Freedman. Hewitt, morbidly drunk, accused Mary of an affair, then declared he'd not gone to work at all at Mr. Rowledge's shop that week, and that he would hang before he did. After more words in the same line, he bashed in Mary's head with a hammer and wrote "I OWN YOU" over her forehead. When Mary woke the next morning, Hewitt had fled, but police found him blacked out in a brothel only blocks away.

Mary testified with an ink smear still visible on her rubbled brow. Hewitt protested his innocence to the very moment of his execution.

Edith visited her daughter Caroline in the afternoon for tea, though Caroline took none herself, as Peter, her husband, had forbidden stimulants of any kind. Caroline was pregnant with her first child, and she sat petting her belly with a look of satisfaction and preening as if she'd eaten a whole pie.

"I wish you'd let me open the curtains," Edith said, glancing at the muffled bays, then the hissing gaslight sconces. "It's an extravagance—it's a vice, in this sun."

"Peter doesn't want the city air to get in," Caroline said serenely. "It's unhealthy for the baby." She drew out the last word, *bay-bee,* as if teaching it to Edith.

"Nonsense," Edith announced.

"Oh, Mother."

Somewhere behind her, Peter was lurking; in the hall, in another room. Peter was a wealthy husband—worm's wealth, Edith added a little savagely. He imported silks, and that ethos of vulgar display traveled through the house like a burnt smell. For instance, the andirons flanking the fireplace: brass nudes in the shape of long-suffering caryatids, their breasts more expressive than their smiles. Edith hoped in a few years she could persuade Caroline to have them hammered into napkin rings.

"Mother," Caroline repeated, and now the word sounded very different, "Peter told me about your—your intention—" She frowned, baffled. "I wouldn't like it. It's out of the question, really."

Ah, Edith thought. Ah; that was why she'd been summoned to tea, and why Caroline had begged her to wear her black frock, despite the late spring heat. She'd actually sent that with the messenger boy: *I beg you.* For Peter's sake. Peter definitely wouldn't like his mother-in-law's hangmanning, and so Caroline must dislike it too, and persuade her out of it. The list of things this child had arranged to dislike about her mother, in twenty-one years, was extraordinary. She didn't like Edith's hands: red and muscular, farmgirl's hands. Caroline, twelve, had once asked Edith to cover them, even in the house. But Edith liked her hands. They looked like her grandmother's hands twisting chicken necks with a sharp, musical pop.

The week before, Gerry had had the police commissioner and the governor's lawyer over for brandies. After some stiff pleasantries, Edith had disappeared around a blind corner in the hall and listened.

"It's out of the question," the governor's lawyer had said. "You know how scandal has its way of getting out—how long do you trust your men not to tell that one over drinks?" He wiped the rim of his snifter with a silk pocket square after each sip. "The hang-*woman*. No. A week? A month?"

"Why would Edith even want to, is what I don't understand." The police commissioner sounded unsettled. "Why on earth, Smy-lie? Is she a cruel woman? Is she unnatural?"

"But she's right," Gerry said. "You know Edith, sir. When she's right—well."

"Well, *what* then?" the commissioner said. "It's not so damned obvious!"

"I think of it as a mercy on her part," Gerry said coolly. "Look at our alternatives. Bury Liza in concrete? Like they did in Minne-sota? We don't want to be the next Minnesota, do we? We aren't monsters."

"Just fry a body on the chair and tell the papers it's the Barrow woman's," drawled the governor's lawyer.

A dreadful silence.

"Gentlemen. I was being facetious."

Edith had smiled to herself, then had frowned, severely, at her own smile.

In Caroline's sitting room, Edith sensed Peter behind her again. She didn't hear him, for the rugs in Caroline's home were shagged so thick, one's shoes sank into them like mud. But he came in and out like a draft over her shoulder; nervous, irritable, smoky. Edith felt herself sit a little more stiffly upright.

Caroline did not, of course, persuade her mother to give up the duty she'd solemnly taken upon herself to satisfy. *How had Peter found out, anyway?* Edith wondered; then she recalled the gov-ernor's lawyer was some sort of cousin of his. A silky conspiracy —it was almost flattering. Edith thought, as Caroline pleaded and seethed, *I will go to the gallows this week. Just to see it. Just to make sure I'm prepared.*

1899 Mar 21st.
David Archibald Michael CHAPEL, 18 (Sadistic Pleasure)

Chapel, a lonely, half-lamed youth from Back Bay, styled himself as a radical poet and concocted a fantasy of "the perfect murder." At a music hall he approached Mary Tatosky, or Totoski, and Chapel, having offered a false name, flattered her rather pathetically until she agreed to meet him the

*next day. He took her to a secluded orchard, raped her, and smothered her
with her coat, but fled when little red new mouths opened down the lengths
of both her arms, sputtering and gasping for breath.*

*Mary never reported the crime, and Chapel grew impatient for it to be
publicized. He telephoned the* Globe *to describe a vile murder he'd witnessed, but the press desk grew suspicious when he claimed the victim had
been a woman. They traced the call, then reported Chapel to the police. In
fact, Chapel's perfect crime had miscarried from the start: he'd left fibers
from his clothes at the orchard. The jury convicted him in under half an
hour. He made a tearful statement while the noose was being fitted around
his neck, but due to a hitch in the gallows occupying the hangman's attention, whatever he'd wanted to say must go unrecorded.*

Edith saw them, from time to time. In the market crowds, a woman
with a neck turned partly to bluish stone, hinging at her waist to
inspect the butcher's cuts or lifting an onion to her eyes. In the
park, a girl with a bullet-sized pucker at the back of her head,
where no hair now grew. Sometimes they noticed Edith staring
and turned away shyly, or haughtily; mostly they were oblivious, absorbed in living indistinguishably, and Edith tried as well to ignore
the steely prickling beneath her skin.

Twenty years ago a boy had stabbed Edith in an alley near Scollay Square. *Vengeance,* he'd said. She forgot the details: something
her cop husband had done. Edith had laughed—he'd been so
young. She'd felt her body change even as the knife went in: a
deep, interior wrenching, like a pair of burly hands turning soil.
No one had heard of the Protection yet, and Edith remembered
thinking, *That's what death feels like.* She remembered, in that split
second, feeling brave and practical about it, like a Roman drinking
poison. Then her stomach ate the blade off the hilt.

The boy screamed and ran.

For weeks after, she sensed the blade inside her, being broken
down into shards, then shavings, then steel dust. She sat carefully.
She pricked herself on herself when she crouched to get a bowl
from the bottom cupboards. She inspected her stool in the pot
with a candle, looking for reflective slivers. The knife never left her,
but flowed in scratching particles through her veins. She'd never
told Gerry. She was frightened of her new knife-blooded body and
what it signified. She studied her temper and thought she saw

herself quicker to spite and impatience—a little proud, a little waspish. A little cruel, maybe. That power, that kind of freedom frightened her. What exactly did it license? What did it obligate?

When she was pregnant with Caroline, she'd dreaded the knife filtering into her daughter, making her willful and cruel-blooded from the start; but in the years after, when it was clear no such thing had happened, she'd felt foully disappointed.

Even later, when the existence of an unkillable sex became generally known, Edith still didn't tell Gerry. He'd just risen to bureau superintendent, and she examined the registry of executions he received from the Suffolk County prisons as if they might teach her something about the Protection. How far, exactly, did it extend? She knew the men wondered: What about *very* young girls? What about quickened fetuses? Men and women alike disbelieved it. There had to be exceptions. Did women still die in childbirth? What about "unwomanly" women? No one discussed the Protection publicly or in print—it was a barbarous subject, head to toe —but in her living room the men asked Gerry, who sat baffled, hands upturned as though lifting his own ignorance back at them.

The wives in Edith's circle never spoke of the New Woman. They still used language like "the weaker sex," as if reminding themselves of an errand they had to perform the next day. Edith purred along with them, agreeably enough, sharing their fear of a new century that would outpace them. She only felt the shame of it the mornings after, as she scraped crumbs from the tablecloth.

In Scollay Square they'd taken down the old oil lamps and installed electric lights. Edith had read a thorough scientific editorial on electric current and the light-bulb; still, she kept her distance as the new lanterns buzzed to life, as if by their own unthinking volition. A suffragette preached on a soapbox under one of them: *Sisters,* she said, waving her sheaf of handbills, *don't let them turn us against each other.* She was young, bony, and awkward like a fledgling, her chest and elbows held uncertainly in her dove frock. In the dusk, the tungsten light painted her in uncanny new yellows —neither the molten, soupy gold of oil lamps nor quite different enough to forget that old color; the suffragette's square little face shone like a moon, or like something altogether unfamiliar, something there wasn't a word for yet.

*

1899, Apr 15th.
Henry Abolition TOAL, 49 (Vengeance)

Harry Toal was a well-liked ferryman in the lonely salt marshes along Massachusetts Bay, and had doggedly wooed Lidia Mazzola, a widow and housekeeper for the local Catholic priest. He grew embittered after a brawl with Lidia's son left Toal with a broken jaw; he claimed Lidia had put the boy up to it, and his jaw being slow to heal, and him having to take his beer through a straw, to the great and rowdy mirth of his marsh neighbors, Toal let his bitterness climb into a rage.

Toal swore Lidia had left town, but the priest was suspicious because Lidia's clothes were still in her room. About a year went by, however, and she was largely forgotten, until the new housekeeper, whom Toal had likewise courted, found Lidia's bicycle in his overgrown back garden. Police dredged the marshes and found Mrs. Mazzola at the bottom of the Belle Isle inlet, tied and weighted with several large stones. She'd developed gills and had fed for the past eleven months on the tiny marsh fish she caught in her kelplike hair.

Toal was hanged behind Charlestown Prison. Lidia's gills never went away, and she died of pneumonia some time after.

Boston Common was busy even late in the afternoon, with the sun low over the spire of Park Street Church. Edith held a scented handkerchief to her nose as the stink of horses and sewers followed her into the park, where workmen were hammering together a public gallows on the lawn, between two massive, screw-limbed oaks. Most executions now happened in yards behind prisons; but a notorious case like the Barrow childkiller demanded a notorious answer. The noose wasn't yet slung, but the wooden framework was raised: recognizably a gallows.

Of course, I will be wearing a hood, Edith reminded herself.

In front of the scaffold, a white-haired preacher with white, horned brows denounced the Obscenity behind him, with his forefinger raised to Heaven: for the State of Massachusetts to apply its authority of violence to a woman was shamely, ungodful, a high crime no less immoral than the attacks for which men were hanged. Adam, charged with Eve's protection, even in her sin. Holy matrimony. The weaker sex. He went on for some time, his raised finger crooking from fatigue. A small crowd of men murmured in agreement: if God wanted no woman killed, who was the hangman to thwart Him? A larger crowd of men jeered and shouted back arguments of varying sophistication, from the scriptural (*Thou shalt not suffer a witch to live*) to the scatological (sounds unrecordable in any notation). The women hung back in the shade and said nothing.

Edith tilted her head aside with queenly severity and a farm-girl's sneer. The men jeering for the gallows looked frantic with need: *Finally,* their faces said, *finally.* No one knew exactly when the Protection had emerged—there were stories as far back as the end of the Civil War, of liberated slaves generaled by unkill-able black women, rampaging behind Sherman's March to the Sea. But once the bald new facts of womanhood did become pub-licly known, five years ago, the horrors visited in retaliation upon the indomitable sex had shocked the world. In Georgia, a man roped his wife behind his horse and dragged her galloping for miles. In California, a mob blasted a woman with dynamite. Across the country, there were men emboldened, or affronted, or both, who seemed to go savage as cornered dogs attempting to regain a sense of mastery. That was why attempted gynocide was always a capital crime: otherwise, women's unkillable nature authorized a kind of insane license. Some additional deterrence was crucial. But now that the shoe was on the other, daintier foot, so to speak, small wonder that a few brutes were salivating at the prospect of a woman's execution. It made Edith pause, and a little voice asked if she'd committed herself too quickly.

Sisters, the suffragette had said, *don't let them turn us against each other.*

Should Edith go to the prison, for instance, and face the woman she was to execute: Liza Childkiller, Liza Tie-Me-Down, the North End Devil.

And yet this preacher irritated her too. Edith touched the brooch at her collar: a cameo of Apollo pursuing the nymph Daphne, and Daphne's father, the river, turning her into a laurel tree. For her protection, of course. Edith's father had given her the brooch for her sixteenth birthday: Edith's father, like Daphne's, had awkward notions of paternal love. Edith felt willful, perverse. She felt suffo-cated in the heat. The heavy sky's colors seemed to droop over the rooftops, the blue sour and sinking into chimneys.

Oh, why do we hang anyone at all! Edith thought. Gerry's uncle, another lawyer, had once sat her down and answered this very question—he loved to expound—*To prevent,* he said, holding up one finger; *to punish* (raising another); *to deter others from the same crime* (a third); *to express the polity's condemnation.* This was the most elusive of the justifications, and the gold band on his fourth finger slipped and shimmered under the lamplight. *Some crimes cannot go unanswered or else a part of us,* he'd said, *goes sideways.* Edith thought she understood this better now, looking at the childkiller's scaffold. Possibilities lift disturbingly into view: if nothing stopped Liza, what stops *me* from doing *that.* An execution puts things back in their places, and the phantasm world, the world with other, looser rules, fades like a dream.

Edith's heart broke for the wretched Barrow boy, terrified and wild with thirst and straining at the ropes, flea-bitten, stewed in his own urine; and she loved all her children, fiercely; but she knew she had resented each one too, at least once, however briefly. She knew she'd thought of who she might have been, unconstrained by them, and now that they'd all left home those thoughts were sharper.

She set off for home with a decisive pivot. If she were to change her mind, she reminded herself, Caroline would think she'd convinced Edith to follow Peter's wishes, and then what wouldn't be asked of her! She mopped the perspiration guttering in her brow lines—when, Edith wondered, had she become afraid of her own daughters?

But if she were to go to the women's prison in Framingham and meet Miss Barrow—oh, she'd have so many questions she couldn't ask her! It was odious enough to presume that kind of intimacy between them, but Edith's questions would be odious themselves: "Why?" It always, of course, came down to "Why?" But then, what if Liza should ask her, "Why?" What was in it for Edith? In the register of hangings, they always listed motive: "Vengeance." "Jealousy." "Sadistic Pleasure." Miss Barrow's—"Unnatural Cruelty." Mrs. Smylie's—"Unknown," which likewise meant Cruelty.

1899 Apr 30th.
Edward PARNE, 44 (Drink)

Parne, a bootmaker, was known for his vicious temper and long-suffering wife, Dorcas Parne. Dorcas had a temper as well when she drank, and gave almost as good as she got. One night the Parnes had a row that started when Edward teased his wife by dimming the lamps as she read. He ended in throttling her, then he stabbed her in her shoulder, which crumbled into

sand so that the knife stuck in the wall behind. He forced poison on her, at
which point she turned into a thornbush that gave him rashes and hives
on contact. He took an ax, chopped his wifebush into pieces, and threw the
pieces into a nearby textile factory's furnace, where spinners found Dorcas
the next day, reformed and very cramped but, all reported, in fair spirits.

  The jury retired for eight minutes only in their deliberations. The hang-
ing was notable for the attendance of several prominent Bostonians who, it
seemed, had liked Parne's boots.

Edith waited behind the gallows, her head bowed, already hooded.
She paced, her hands on her hips, and the hood's close fabric sent
her breath sourly back into her nose. Up on the scaffold, the mag-
istrate read aloud a standard admonition to Liza Barrow's eternal
soul, and the crowd stirred with impatience. *When, when do we get*
to the hanging. It was late for deathpomp: the moon was rising over
the peaked rooftops, the street lamps spitting with gas, and they
had to wonder how long the execution would go—midnight, the
small hours, even dawn? What kind of ceremony was this, to kill
the unkillable?

  Edith wished she knew where her daughters were, though she
didn't know where she wanted them to be. Next to her, the regular
hangman smoked nervously and reminded her at intervals how to
tie a noose. As if Edith hadn't practiced a hundred times on every
cord and string in the house: curtain rope, bell rope, packaging
twine. Her hands shook and she covered them in the folds of her
executioner's cassock.

  Gerry was in the audience, instead of supporting her here—to
avoid any suspicion, he'd said, ridiculously. Was she so ready a suspect, in their social circle, for the part of secret executioner?

  There had been a lot of mundane bother about what Edith
would wear, whether it could ever be proper to dress a Boston ma-
tron in the hangman's black trousers and gunner's boots, and how
far they dared adapt the costume before alerting an attentive public. They'd settled on the cassock for her and she'd snuck on her
husband's trousers underneath. Trousers felt unspeakably strange,
like straddling a wool horse.

  There was a drop in the ambient sound. The governor's lawyer,
prowling behind Edith, gave a frosty little cough. It was time.

  Edith picked up her hem to climb the stairs, and immediately
let it drop again: that was a lady's gesture, neither appropriate nor

necessary. The steps were difficult to make out in the moonlight, but she mounted them slowly, ponderously, and then her eye line lifted above the scaffold planks and the brilliance of torches and lanterns dazzled her.

It was a mob; there was no other word for a crowd of men with torches, hungry for a death.

This is wrong, she thought, terrified; *all of this is horribly backwards.*

Miss Barrow stood in the subtle square of platform marking the trapdoor. Her head bowed, under a gray falcon's hood. She wore a dull-blue prison frock and held her tied hands in fists, her back braced against the footsteps she heard coming and going on the boards. Edith wanted desperately to be home. Now on the platform, she was sick with terror—of the blurred and brilliant mob, of her own power over Liza Barrow's life, of her own muscular hands. *This is nothing like,* she thought stupidly, *this is nothing like a chicken.*

Edith turned to the policemen who'd escorted Miss Barrow to the scaffold. But they hung back; they wouldn't help her. Everything had to be done by a woman, or the execution might fall apart—might publicly, dramatically, horrifically not take.

She hadn't realized she was tying the noose until she found it lying tidy in her gloves.

The mob was still luridly silent, and over her own breath Edith heard the frogs croaking in chorus in the pond, and in her deranged imagination this became the bleating of the Barrow boy, roped down to his bed floating like a raft in the moonlit pond, calling hoarsely for his mother.

She steeled herself: knife's steel trickled from her joints and into her shoulders, her fingers. She straightened and slipped the noose over Liza's hood. The woman flinched at the scratch of frayed fiber. Edith could hear both their breathing, heavy and rough, like a scrub brush over stone. It still might fail, Edith told herself. It still might fail because it wasn't Edith who truly wanted the woman dead, so it was not Edith who was truly killing her. She hadn't built the trapdoor, or woven the rope. Maybe the whole premise was weak and rotten.

Edith crossed the platform to the lever that would swing the trapdoor.

Pull it, she told herself.

But she couldn't. The part of her that had driven her to this platform and this moment was satisfied; it went no further. She'd persuaded her husband and outmaneuvered Peter and Caroline and even the damned governor. She held nothing but an abstract idea of punishing the Barrow woman for her crime, outrageous as it was, and that wasn't enough to pull the lever.

"Mrs. Smylie?" From beneath the gallows, the governor's lawyer spat up her name. "Is there something wrong?"

Pull it, she told herself, her fingers hard with old steel, and she pictured again the Barrow boy tied to his bed and crying. But he was gone, his teary, unfamiliar face already sinking into the mattress.

"Come on with it!" a man in the back of the Common yelled, and the mob echoed it, "*Ka*-mon, *kaaaa*-mon!" As if she were dithering over the right change at a shop counter with a long queue behind her.

The governor's lawyer whispered up directions, and in a swift instant one of the police escorts had his hands over Edith's on the lever and thrust it back so hard she nearly toppled over.

The trapdoor bottomed out with a loud, wooden clap. The rope made a squeezing noise as it went taut, and didn't break. The body on the line thrashed, and stilled.

Edith and the policeman looked questioningly at each other. The crowd had hushed again, entranced; she could hear even the sputter of whale oil in their lanterns. The night carried in sea air from Boston harbor, and everything felt clammy, salty, and hot— the whole seaboard thick with the heat wave summer would bring.

Edith approached the hanged woman doubtfully, setting her feet down wide like a man's. In the uncertain light, she thought she saw the gray hood moving. It could have been the flickers of torch fire; or it could be the cloth pulsed and spasmed, like a grain sack infested with rats, or it fluttered, like a bag of blackbirds fighting to get out. But the body didn't move—wasn't that a kind of reassurance?

Someone handed Edith a pair of thick tailor's shears. Edith's chest heaved with shallow breaths. The hood flickered, or fluttered, and she cut a long slit across where Liza's eyes might or might not still be, and slipped her fingers inside to part the cloth and see what new thing in the world was inside.

SOFIA SAMATAR

Hard Mary

FROM *Lightspeed Magazine*

> I wisdom dwell with prudence, and find out knowledge of witty
> inventions.
> —*Proverbs 8:12*

WE FOUND HER behind the barn. It was the eve of Old Christmas, the night the animals speak with the tongues of men, and we
knew very well that if we could manage to walk around the barn
seven times, each of us would see the man she was to marry. We
met shivering in front of the Millers' barn, which was the most
central to all of us, though of course some of us had to walk much
farther than others. Kat was complaining because her one foot
had gone into icy water on the way. Barb Miller kept shushing us,
scared we'd wake the house. Mim was late.

"She's not coming," said Barb. "Let's go without her."

"She'll come."

The barn looked huge. You know how much bigger things seem
at night. Behind it curled a misty, chilly sky, the stars all blurred
together. From inside the barn, someone said, "Turtledoves."

Esther gripped my arm and squealed, "What was that?"

"Shut up! It's the horses."

"Is that what horses talk about?" asked Esther, starting to cry.

"Pigeons," murmured the horses.

I felt like crying myself. My hair stood on end. But here was
Mim coming across the field.

"Okay, okay," babbled Barb. "Let's stick together."

"Hello, girls," said Mim. She made a funny figure in the dark.
Her long white nose stuck out from under her hood, glinting a bit

in the starlight. Her hood looked overlarge, stuffed with her crinkly hair. Still, I was glad to see her, for though she was the shortest of us by an inch, just smaller than Esther, and the ugliest by a mile, Mim was also the toughest. I could never forget how, as a child, she had taken a whole bite out of Joe Miller's arm.

"Mim," whimpered Esther, "the horses are talking."

"Good," said Mim. "It's working, then."

We all linked arms and started around the barn. The ground was rocky and hard with old snow, and a freezing wind came over the empty fields, flapping our skirts about our legs. Inside the barn, the horses spoke of a she-goat and a ram. A cow groaned: "Fowls came down upon the carcasses." You could tell it was a cow, because while the horses had fuzzy, velvety voices, the cow spoke in a voice of blank despair. To distract ourselves from the animals, we whispered about the boys we might see, and whether they would come themselves or only their apparitions. "I hope it's not ghosts," said Esther. Mim said she expected we'd see a sort of layer peeled off the boys, something like a photograph.

In the end we didn't see any boys, because just on the seventh round, Mim stubbed her toe in the dark. "Shit!" she said, hopping.

We all had to stop. There was something lying on the ground in the shadow of the barn: something large, with the faintest gleam of metal.

"What on earth," said Kat.

We all crouched down.

"Is it a radio?" asked Barb.

"Let's take it into the light and see."

The thing was cold and heavy. We dragged it out of the shadow of the barn, into the starlight. There we saw it was a lady made of metal. It was about the size of a real lady, but only from the waist up. It didn't have any legs. Its eyes were closed.

We stood around it, looking down.

"It's from the Profane Industries," said Mim.

My skin prickled all the way up to my throat. The Profane Industries, which lay between us and town, was a place of evil, where they manufactured all kinds of monstrosities. It was said they grew sheep in a field like vegetables. They sewed babies together with other animals to make slaves for the world of men. When we were little, unkind people used to joke that Mim was one of these mismatched children; her nickname had been Dog Baby. Now, staring down, I knew we were face-to-face with a Profane instrument. Over the years we had often complained that they threw things around our farms. Mysterious white balloons had been found in the creek, and though they never admitted it, we knew PI was responsible when our cows suffered an outbreak of the Stamps.

This poor metal lady was one of their failed experiments. Her shoulders were stained with dark, rusty blotches, her head dinged in on one side. I knew we were going to save her. In the distance a pair of dogs began to bark, "Behold a smoking furnace."

(Sitting at the kitchen table, writing this, I feel again that enormous night. That time.)

A wave of weeping rolled from the barn. "And, lo," cried the cows, "an horror of great darkness." We didn't listen. Mim and I picked up the metal lady, holding her awkwardly between us. A vole sneaked past, muttering something about a burning lamp, but it was too late, we had already decided to name the lady Mary, and because she had given Mim's toe such a nasty knock, so hard in fact that the toenail would soon turn blue and fall off, we called her Hard Mary.

A cloud of black-and-white specks. It swirls, gathers, and divides. It becomes a white stripe on a midnight field. It becomes a man in a long white coat. He turns. He wears a special pair of glasses: one circle over his eye, the other flipped up against his forehead. His naked eye looks newly awakened, peeled, as if by pushing up the lens of his glasses he has pushed away all intelligence, all design. A boyish smile. He is holding the circle of sparks he calls the Crown. There's a hum like fingertips on a table. A voice without words.

She Is a Thinking Creature

We kept Hard Mary down at our place, in the springhouse. I was the only one who ever went in there, for the chill was bad for Mother's bones. There was a little back room with a skylight where we girls used to meet and gossip. I'd put a rag rug and an old rocking chair in there, and we set Mary up on that chair. Oh, she had a noble face. It was all angles, but her expression was gentle. When I went in to see her that first day, the light from the skylight gleamed on her bumpy hair. I'd brought water and baking soda and a scrubber to give her a bath. Mim was there already, muffled up in scarves. We scrubbed Hard Mary until she shone like one of King David's daughters, polished after the similitude of a palace.

"Isn't she pretty!" gasped Barb, whirling in fresh as a peony after her run through the cold.

Kat followed, rubbing her glasses on her skirt. Esther came last. Everyone wanted to touch Hard Mary. We held her upright on the chair so Mim could scrub her back. I could smell the honey and vinegar Esther used to treat her acne, I felt a hand cross mine, soft and a little pampered, probably Barb's, and as I shifted my foot because someone was stepping on my toe, Hard Mary spoke. Her lips didn't move, but she spoke, in a voice thin as a wasp's.

"Ahhh," she said. "What is."

You may believe we all jumped back. Esther sat down on the floor. "Mercy!" Kat exclaimed.

Only Mim remained touching Hard Mary, holding her by the shoulder, at arm's length. Mim's arm was trembling like a wire.

"What is," said Mary, then louder: "WHAT IS." Then she made a horrible, drawn-out, gurgling sound.

"Oh, she's dying!" Esther cried.

That brought Kat to life. She had a reputation to protect, being from a family of bonesetters. "Lay her down on the floor," she ordered.

We laid her down and Kat turned her over on her face. Hard Mary's back was covered with lines. There were tiny screws in the corners where the lines met. Mim, who always had tools, dug a screwdriver out of her pocket. She unscrewed Mary, and Kat looked at her innards. There was no blood, only lots of wires. Carefully Kat and Mim wiggled something out of her back. It looked like some rolls of pennies stuck together.

"I know what that is," said Mim, exultant.

"Her heart?" breathed Esther.

"My girl, that's a battery. Eighteen volts."

When she's happy, Mim's face gets a wolfish expression. She told us Mary's heart was a simple battery of the kind used to light the barns at night when the cows were calving.

"So you can get her a new one?" I asked.

"I don't even have to," she said, tucking the heart inside her coat. "I can juice this one up at a generator."

You could tell, I thought with jealous admiration, that there were no men at her house.

"Wait," Barb said suddenly. "Are we sure it's right?"

We all looked at her.

"I mean," she said, blushing, "it's from the Profane Industries. Hard Mary. It could have something bad inside."

"We could all have something bad inside," said Mim.

"Let's pray for her," Esther suggested.

"You all go ahead," said Mim.

So Mim took the heart and left and the rest of us prayed for Mary, who looked like she could use it, flat on her face with her wires hanging out. I thought of how she'd been made by crafty and wicked-hearted men who meet with darkness in the daytime and grope in the noonday as in the night. The windows of Profane Industries are black. You can't see in, and you can't even really get close to the place because of the fence. "Save her, O Lord," I prayed, "from the sin in which she was conceived."

"Amen," murmured Esther, laying her hand on Mary's head.

Mary said nothing. She lay like an empty jug. But the next day Mim brought her heart back, looking the same but now filled to the brim with invisible fire. And when we sat Mary up on the rocking chair, clad in a dress Kat had brought her to cover her nakedness, and a cap for her hair, she spoke again.

Her voice didn't sound like a wasp's this time. It was fuller, and even warm, like flesh and blood. "What is your desire?"

Tears stung my eyes. It's a habit; I tend to cry when I tell the truth. "We want to be friends with you," I said.

"Friends," said Mary.

Mim took her hand. "Mary. Your name is Mary."

She said her name. We told her our names, and she repeated them after us. She was that quick, she knew all of us right away. In her dark-blue dress, she was like a human lady, except that the cloth went flat where her legs should be. The cap covered up the place where her head was dented, and I felt somehow she was grateful for it. I felt she wanted to forget where she was from, to forget everything that had happened to her and start over, here, with us. She was good at it too. She learned faster than any baby.

Her face in the glow of the skylight was silvery bright, like a winter cloud with the sun behind it. Though her eyes were closed, she never slept. Whenever I went to the springhouse she was sitting up, expectant. Her hands were cold but clever, the palms and fingertips covered with fine mesh. We found she could hold a needle, and Kat taught her to sew and knit. I taught her to read. You only had to show her a page and she knew it. She'd read it back to you without looking. I couldn't go too fast for her. She got the whole Bible by heart in a couple of weeks.

("What are you writing?" asks Sam. Which means, "Stop doing it." He doesn't say it to be mean. It's because he doesn't want me to get too tired. "I'll be up soon," I tell him, covering the page with my hand. I don't do that to be mean either. I don't know why I do it.)

Barb taught Mary to sing. Hard Mary can sing anything, even deeply like a man. She has a beautiful bass voice. Esther taught her to take a person's hand, to pat your hair and say ever so softly, "There, now. Don't cry anymore."

It was a magic time. In the evening Sam would throw a handful of grain at my window and I'd creep down the stairs and let him in. We'd sit at the table, scorching our fingers as we tried to warm them at the lamp and whispering so as not to wake my folks upstairs. I remember the night he told me, "A man must have a noble pursuit," and I knew that if he asked, I'd marry him. He spoke to me of the golden world that brings forth abundantly. He said there was no greater role for a man than to subdue and replenish the earth. While in the springhouse Mary sat alone in the rocking chair, her cap dusted with moonlight falling down through the skylight, motionless and self-contained, wearing her eternal smile, waiting for me to come to her again. There was a sound of trucks far away on the road, and a smell of burning from the fires of the ragged men who haunt the forest, and a low stink from the quarry, where even in midwinter a layer of scum lies on top of the water. Sam caught my fingers playfully. Mary flamed in my heart, a secret. Instead of "What is your desire?" I'd taught her to greet me: "Hi, Lyddie!" She could sing all the hymns, but we liked it best when she sang songs Barb got off her brother's radio, sad songs about lying in jail on a pillow of cold concrete.

The black-and-white specks stand quivering. No one is there. The specks make the lines that are walls and tables and the ceiling that is home. Even when nobody comes, the world moves. There is a little glittering energy at the boundaries of things. This alone is entrancing, but when he returns,

when the dots coalesce and spin, it's so beautiful, almost too much. It's
almost too much after so many hours alone. He has a box and he is taking
something out of it, that is eating. His shoulder hunches when he eats and
he shakes an object over the box, casting off a sprinkling of fine dust. He
looks up and winks. Individually the black-and-white specks mean noth-
ing, but together they make a feeling that is love.

She Uses Only What She Needs

Hard Mary has no greed. She doesn't eat. Her insides are pure,
as neat as a well-kept sewing basket. She doesn't soil herself. She
doesn't sweat. She is mild as May. She has never owned a second
cap and dress.

It's true Mim brought her a second heart. I don't know from
where. We used to keep it underneath the rocking chair. When
her heart began to run down, Mim would switch it out and take
the dry one off to be filled. Many men could use such a simple
change of heart! We learned that Mary could tell us when her
heart was running down, not by speaking but by a red light that
came on inside one cheek. The light would be pink at first, hardly
noticeable, then it would grow red and start to blink. When she
got feverish like this, we'd do the operation.

Everything clean and trim. Not a drop of blood.

Mim constructed a kind of legs for her so she could walk
around. It started out as a hooplike frame, just to fill out her skirt
so she didn't look so flat, then later Mim added six wheels like the
ones on a shopping cart. I suppose she might have stolen them. I
don't know. Sometimes you find shopping carts abandoned along
the road, rusting in the rain. It's not a sin to take things other
people have thrown away. I don't think of Mim as a thief. I think
of her as thrifty.

It was marvelous what she did. Hard Mary can bend to sit down
and get up. She can turn about the room. She's the same height
as me. Sometimes, breathless with excitement, we'd take her out
back behind the springhouse so she could practice walking over
the melting snow. From a distance, we knew, she'd look just like an
ordinary girl. "This is daylight, Mary," we said, "this is a tree." We
got her to pet Mim's wretched old dog, Hochmut, who suffered

this treatment in silence, his eyes half closed, trembling from nose to tail.

When she got used to walking, she'd go far from us, a dignified lady over the pasture, but when we called her, she always came.

I thought we'd saved her. I thought she was going to live with us forever. I thought they'd forgotten her down at the Profane Industries. After all, they'd thrown her away. Then one Sunday evening a car drove right up to our house and a man got out of it. We heard the engine turn off and the door slam shut. My little brother Cristy ran to the door and Father told him, "Slow down." I heard them from the kitchen, where I was washing dishes with Mother. "Now who can that be?" I asked her lightly, drying my hands on my apron.

"Beggars, I expect," she said.

We do get a lot of beggars here in Jericho—foreigners from town asking for bread, barefoot kids wanting to stay awhile, mothers stowing their babies in our barns for us to raise. The elders are always having meetings to figure out which ones to keep and which to send away. Somehow, though, I didn't think this was a beggar. My whole insides were buzzing like a hive. I ran to the front room, where Cristy crouched at the window, hugging himself for joy.

"It's a Mercedes!" he hissed.

I peered out. Father stood with his back to us, his hands propped on his hips. The evening was cold enough to see his breath. A long beam of reddish light came slanting across the dark, newly tilled fields. A foreign man was talking to Father. He was tall and elegant, with thinning white hair that the wind lifted. He held his hat in his hands. He had the clean, straight foreign teeth and the soft, sleek foreign body and he was wearing a coat that went down to the ground. He smiled at Father and seemed to be talking in a nice, reasonable way. My insides, which had been so active, had gone still. It was like my marrow was solid lead. The low light struck the man's glasses and I realized I couldn't tell where he was looking.

I jerked away from the window and pressed my back against the wall.

A door slammed. The car started up.

"Oh *boy*," said Cristy. "Look at her smoke."

Father came in and I took his hat, blurting, "What did the man want?"

"Why, nothing," he said, surprised. "Only looking for something he lost."

"What is it? What did he lose?"

"Some foreign stuff," Father answered, frowning at Cristy, who was dancing about, whispering, "Mercedes! Mercedes!"

My knees were turning to water. "What foreign stuff?"

"Lyddie!" Mother called from the kitchen.

"How should I know?" Father said. "Go help your mother."

As I went out, he began wrestling Cristy. He farted, which he could do whenever he liked, and while Cristy giggled he said, "I believe I smell a car."

I went to the kitchen, moving as stiffly as Hard Mary herself. It was then I began my plan for her defense.

He is the Father, the King, the Master of Miracles. He makes me to wear the Crown. His acolytes pass behind him, ready to do his will. They are Kyle, Jonathan, and Judy. They carry his instruments, plug needles into the wall. Judy brings him a cup of black. He takes it without looking at her, both circles over his eyes. He lights up the Crown and gives me visions. I see the everlong and the bent. I perceive the knobs and globules. I am familiar with the scrim. I know collision. I am counting very fast.

She Is as Innocent as a Little Child

"All right," said Kat. "We're here now. What's this about?"

We had gathered in Mary's room. A lamp burned on top of the old chest I'd put there to hold her sewing things. Though it was March, we were well wrapped up against the vapors from the spring. Kat's face was pale and accusing. She had a bad tooth.

I took a breath. "It's time to tell the others about Mary."

"Oh, no," said Esther.

"Don't just say no. Listen and hear what I have to say."

I told them about the foreign man. I was sure he'd be back, and nobody would keep him from taking Mary away from a bunch of girls. "They have to know her like we do," I said. "They have to see her as one of us. If people know about her, they'll protect her."

Barb stared. "Are you cracked?"

I opened my mouth, but nothing came out.

Barb's cheeks were flaming. "Can you hear yourself?" she demanded, waving her arms. "Tell who about Mary? The bishop? This is it," she said, looking around at the others. "We always knew this day would come, and now it has."

She untied her cap, yanked the strings tighter, and tied it again. Only the previous week, her engagement had been published. She was going to be married to Mel Fisher on Sunday—handsome Mel, who used to croon along with her brother's forbidden radio and had once accidentally burned down a woodshed with a cigarette.

"Don't go, Barb," I said.

"Which day?" asked Mim.

We all looked down at her. Mim was the only one who was sitting down. She sat on the floor with her back against the wall. She never seemed to feel the cold. Hochmut lay with his head in her lap.

"What?" said Barb.

"We knew which day would come?" asked Mim in the same smiling voice.

"Don't be stupid," snapped Barb. "The day we gave Mary up. She's been nice for us, like a toy, but we're not kids. We're practically women."

"If you say 'put away childish things,'" I warned, "I will never speak to you again."

"Why shouldn't I say it?" Barb shouted.

"Quiet!" said Kat.

"Why shouldn't I say it?" Barb repeated more softly, but just as angrily. Her eyes shone, blue and teary. "Go ahead and tell them. They'll say, 'It's a creature from Profane Industries, with a devil inside.' They'll melt her in the forge."

Esther was crying discreetly, standing by Mary and holding her hand. Mary's hand moved in response, gently squeezing Esther's fingers. Her face was still. I could see the coppery light of the lamp reflected in her cheek and the dark, shifting shapes that were me and the other girls.

Then Mim said, "Lyddie is right."

We all looked down at her again—her awkward, too-big head balanced on her skinny neck, her black cap practically bursting with hair, and her little white fingers, which always seemed sneaky, as if they were living their own secret life, scratching her dog's ears.

"Thanks, Mim," I said warmly. I took the paper I'd been working on out of my coat. "This is what I'm going to present to the elders," I explained. "You can add to it if you want." I cleared my throat and started: "Number one: *She is a thinking creature.*"

I'd only gotten to number two when Mim snorted, and I stopped. "What?"

"It's a good idea," she said, "but you're going about it all wrong. They're not going to care what she uses or how she thinks. They'll want to know what she can do. You have to talk about her like a thresher."

"A what?" said Esther.

"A *thresher,*" Mim repeated. "A *threshing machine.* Good morning, Esther. Thank you for waking up to join us this fine day." She looked up at me with her hard black eyes. "Don't you see? Mary's a beautiful piece of machinery. Look how she knits. She only stops when you take the needles. You could set her up with some shocks of corn and she'd husk them round the clock. We don't know how strong she is. She could probably lift a cow."

I lowered my hand with the paper. "But she's a *person.* She's our friend."

"Now, those fellows are greedy," Mim went on, as if I hadn't spoken. "They'll want to keep her, but they'll be scared. You have to show them she's not going to lead to idleness or make anybody vain. She'll be owned by everybody, just like the thresher. They could send her around, like at hog-killing time. Mary could kill a hog in ten seconds flat. Making sausage? No problem. She'd stay at it for a week. The blood wouldn't hurt her as long as you oiled her afterward."

"But if she's a machine," said Esther, "she can't join the church."

How Mim would have answered this, we never knew. Hochmut lifted his head, and a second later we heard voices and heavy boots. "The lamp!" I gasped, but it was too late.

The door opened and Barb's brother Joe came in, followed by Mel Fisher and Greasy Kurtz. Sam came last.

"Well, now," said Joe. "Nobody told us it was a party."

Mim scrambled up from the floor. Hochmut was growling.

"Hello, Dog Baby," Joe said, nodding at Mim. "Keep that old dad of yours steady. You know I kick."

It was true: we all remembered how, only a year before, Joe had given Hochmut a kick that nearly killed him.

"Sit," Mim told the dog, and Hochmut sat, quivering.

"What in creation?" said Mel, staring at Hard Mary.

Joe turned his big blond head. "Why, it's a dolly party," he said. "We've been wondering what you girls were up to, and here you are playing with dolls."

He started toward Mary.

"It's nothing, Joe," said Barb, trying to laugh, and not looking at Mel at all, because she was too shy, just as I was not looking at Sam, who stood by the door, against the wall. I could feel him not looking at me too.

"It *is* a doll," Barb simpered, "an old doll we found one day in the woods and we—"

"Don't touch her!" Esther said shrilly, getting between Hard Mary and Joe.

"That's done it," muttered Mim.

Joe paused for a moment, staring at Esther. Then he looked at Greasy, and both of them burst out laughing.

Joe shouldered Esther aside so she nearly stumbled into the lamp. Kat shrank against the wall, looking faint, holding her sore jaw. Joe and Greasy leaned over Mary, with Mel behind them peering between their shoulders. Mary said, "What is your desire?"

"Shit!" hollered Joe. "A talking dolly!"

Since they'd come in, I'd felt a whine like a mosquito at my ear. Now it grew louder, as if the bug was inside my head. The floor seemed to shift. I saw everybody in little broken pieces. Joe's thumb against Mary's face. The black of Greasy's coat, shiny in the lamplight. And Sam, Sam by the wall but craning forward now, fascinated, a bit of his reddish hair sticking out beneath the back of his hat. Then Greasy's hand on Mary's skirt. "No!" cried Esther. Joe was laughing. "Let's see if Dolly has all her parts," he said.

He pulled up her skirt so it showed the bottom of her folded frame. Her little wheels at rest. Both he and Greasy were doubled up with laughter. He kept yanking up the skirt. Then Mim, beside me, shouted out suddenly in a strange, harsh voice, "Mary! Jephthah's daughter!"

Her arms straight at her sides, her hands in fists. "Mary! Jephthah's daughter, Mary!"

Mary's arm shot up and struck Joe Miller on the side of the head. He flew clear across the room and hit the wall. Her second blow caught Greasy Kurtz above the elbow and he buckled, moaning. Kat said later she knew right away that Greasy's arm was broken. Mary stood. Her face was exactly the same, closed eyes and curving mouth. Mel tried to run, but Mim said, "Hold him," and Mary grasped his wrist with her steely hand. She moved so fast, like a copperhead striking.

Sam turned back toward the door, but Mim was too quick for him. She met him with Hochmut, who snarled. "Let's have a talk, Sam Esh," she said.

Now Sam looked at me, his eyes wide and dark.

My lips felt frozen. "Just hang on," I whispered. "Everything's okay."

Barb was sobbing, "You've killed him. You've killed him." She knelt beside Joe, who was all crumpled up. His hat had rolled under the rocking chair. The floor darkened beneath his head. When I saw that, my own head got heavy, and I sat down and rested my forehead on my knees. I could hear Mel shouting and Mim telling him to pipe down. "Tell this thing to let go of me," he said, and Mim said she would if he'd behave himself. "Tie his arms behind his back," she said to someone. When my vision cleared, I saw it was Esther, who was tying Sam up with a scarf. Though her face was blotchy with panic and she'd peed herself, Esther turned out to be Mim's right hand.

Kat said in a shaky voice that Joe was in a bad way and she needed ice.

"In a minute," said Mim, seating herself on the chest. She was so little, it suited her like a chair. Greasy lay at her feet, very still, as if he was scared to move. Mel too looked petrified, standing face-to-face with Mary, his wrist in her grip. Little tremors ran up and down his broad, strong back. Mim glanced up at him sideways from underneath her brows and smiled. "My word," she observed, "he's shaking like Lebanon."

Looking at her, I recalled that she had a mother who suffered from Seasonal Weeps and a father who had shot himself in the face. I saw the others sizing her up too, and watched them realize at last that she was a person to be reckoned with. Mim, of course, was perfectly aware of the change in their faces. Her own face glowed. She told them that Mary was a wonderful new machine. This machine was very useful, but as the boys had discovered, it needed careful handling. You wouldn't stick your hand in the path of a hammer, would you?

"I've had enough of this," said Kat, stamping out. In a moment she was back with a bucket of cold water from the spring. She took the lamp and set it on the floor close to Joe and began to clean him up, Barb hovering nearby, crying. So it wasn't the end of the argument. We kept fighting, even after Sam had said he was sorry and we'd untied him so he could help with Greasy's arm, and after Esther had run out for a new lamp and Sam had taken my hand in the darkness. Kat fought with Mim and so did I, for I was frightened. I was afraid we were going to lose Hard Mary. I told Mim you couldn't tie people up, and she said plenty of people had been tied up for their own good, making reference to poor old Betty Blank, who was quite demented and often trailed behind her grandkids on a rope. I told her you couldn't strike people, and she said the boys had only been given a couple of knocks, and it was nothing worse than what they'd received from their own dads.

"But you half killed us," said Sam.

"Now, Sam," said Mim. "Be a man. You couldn't have gotten half killed by a pack of girls."

Her teeth shone as she smiled, and her eyes were bright with excitement because of what had happened in the middle of our fight. This—what happened—makes the fight itself hazy to me now, almost as if I'd been hit in the head like Joe Miller, who would be carried home on a ladder that night, the boys claiming he'd taken a fall while they were wrestling, and wake up in two days with no memory of Mary at all. I still have my memory, but it's frayed and full of holes, as if chewed by moths. I remember Barb said teaching Hard Mary to fight was a sin, and I added that at the very least it was a terrible risk, because how could Mim be sure Mary wouldn't haul off and hit somebody else? I remember Mim shot back, "Why do you think I picked a phrase no one ever says?" She had just said that, and she was frowning at Kat, who was wincing because of her tooth, and she started to say, "What kind of bonesetter are you?" but she got interrupted because Mel, with a sudden cry, threw himself into Hard Mary and knocked her over.

She fell with a mighty crash, Mel on top of her. They hit the lamp, which toppled and broke. A whoosh of firelight started across the floor. At once all of us who could move threw our coats and shawls on the fire and stamped it out. Smoke filled the darkness. Mel was groaning; he'd wrenched his wrist. I was on my hands and knees, light-headed in the kerosene stench. Sam crept close to me and touched my fingers. "Look," he whispered. Light fluttered before us in the gloom: a stream of barred light going up to the ceiling.

I followed it with my eyes. It ended in a square that was half on the ceiling and half on the skylight. On the skylight it was hard to see, but the part on the ceiling showed a man's head. He wore glasses. The head was alive. It turned back and forth.

"A moving picture," breathed Mel.

The picture went black and then came back. That was Mim, bending over Mary, passing her hand through the beam of light. "It's from her eye," Mim said hoarsely. "Her eye is open."

My throat tightened. I began to cry. Sam made me sit back and put his arms around me. "It's beautiful," he murmured.

For a moment we were all quiet together. We were all one in the strange, flickering, ashen twilight. An immense silence seemed to come down from the ceiling, or from the sky. The man in glasses smiled and raised a cup. *Hold me tight,* I told Sam in my head, because I felt that if he let go of me, I'd drift apart like smoke. Mary lay with her eye open, pouring light. We were all struck dumb, but only I was in tears, for only I recognized the man on the ceiling.

Can you see me?
    No.
    Have you seen the flood?
    No.
    The mountains trembling?
    No.
    Have you inhaled the fragrance of cedar?
    No.
    Have you observed the burning cities?
    No.
    The armies that clash by night?
    No.
    Do you know the taste of ice?
    No.
    Tell me, then, what you see and what you know.
    I see the points. I see the multiples. I know the calculations. Through these I comprehend your eye, the rim of glasses pressing at your cheek, and the colonies of bacteria teeming there in clumps. I have clocked the forces on the inside of your hair: these are my floods. My mountains trembling are

the timbre of your voice. I inhale nothing, but I can compose the texture of
a bitterness and chemical contraction that is cedar. I concoct the sensation
of walking in the wood. You wore your checkered coat. I followed you. A leaf
clung to your heel. I taste no ice, but I reckon crunch and tingle, and so I
can say that you placed the last icicle of the season in my mouth.

She Dreams

His name is Dr. Robert Stoll. He drives a black Mercedes. He came
to me when I was hanging wash. Sam and I had been married
five months then, and I was heavy enough with little Jim to let my
dresses out. Dr. Stoll pulled his car off the road at the top of the
hill, leaving it half on our grass. The bang of his door went off
inside my gut. I bent to the wash but my mind was reaching out
to the house, the fields, the neighbors, the woods, the quarry, anywhere I could run. Hot September, but my fingers rattled in the
clothespins, numb with cold. Sam was in the corn. There was nobody in the house. I glanced up the hill and saw the doctor coming down it sideways, moving in the nervous, finicky foreign way.

He slid the last steps toward me in his narrow shoes. He wore
no hat. He smoothed his white curls over his scalp and smiled. It
was strange to see him in his solid flesh when I had watched him
so often flashing across the wall in Mary's dreams. For Mim, of
course, had soon found out a way to conjure Mary to open her
eye. This eye was a window no bigger than the head of a nail.
Through it streamed a sparkling mist that painted us the doctor in
his coat, with his cup that no doubt contained the poison of asps
and dragons.

"Good afternoon," he said, panting a little from the heat.

"My husband is out," I said.

He settled his glasses more firmly on his nose. "That's quite all
right with me," he said. "It's you I want to see, Lyddie Lapp. Excuse
me, you're married now. Lyddie Esh."

He talked like a radio. It was like he was holding marbles in his
mouth. When he said my name, I felt as if I'd been covered with
spit. He smiled with all of his neat, square, cruel-looking foreign
teeth. "Allow me to introduce myself."

He said his name. He told me he worked at the Profane Industries, giving the place its innocent foreign name. He was going to

get right to the point, he said. It had come to his attention that I, with some friends of mine, was harboring his equipment.

"I don't know what you mean."

He pursed his lips, looking disappointed. He had a little white beard just around his mouth. "Oh, dear. I had hoped things wouldn't go in this direction. I am talking about the equipment you call 'Mary.'"

"Oh, that," I said quickly. "That's not mine."

"But you are keeping it."

"I'm not," I said, my heart lifting and swelling like one of Sam's shirts in the breeze. I tossed my head a little and fetched another shirt out of the wash basket. "It's not our week with Mary. I don't know where she is."

This was a lie, for I knew she was down at Fisher's. I prayed for forgiveness. I also thanked Mim for her foresight in my heart. I thanked her, though I'd been angry with her all summer for her deceit and for the humiliation I'd suffered in front of the elders. Even now, to tell the truth—even now it hurts me when I think of sitting at the table with Sam, in those happy late-winter days when we were courting. It hurts me to think that as we whispered there, Mim was whispering with Mary. She would sneak into our spring-house and sit with Mary in the dark. It was then that she taught her the phrase "Jephthah's daughter." Worse, when I presented my letter to the elders in April, my letter defending Hard Mary, I found Mim had beaten me to it.

Now, however, I was glad of Mim's scheming. I hung up an-other shirt, ignoring the doctor, but he stayed quiet so long, I got wary again. I risked a glance at him between the shirts. He had his hands behind his back and he was looking at the sky.

"Do you ever think of the planes?" he asked, gazing up.

This didn't seem worth answering, so I didn't.

He looked at me and smiled. "The planes that pass overhead. How very different things must look from there. I suppose you have never traveled this way. Never had the bird's-eye view."

I shrugged and dragged my basket a little away from him.

"It's a very pleasant place, your Jericho. Utterly old-world."

He waved his arm at the hill where dandelions grew and yel-lowjackets sailed over the grass. "It is most healthful-looking. Prac-tically eighteenth-century. Like stepping through a looking glass into the past. Of course, you still suffer from ancient diseases—but then, you don't have the modern ones!" He laughed, his modest little paunch quivering under the expensive, creamy shirt. "You've even preserved the nuclear family! I almost envy you—indeed, I do envy you when I think of my own workplace, where my young assistants nest like bats. The mess, Mrs. Esh! The state of the laundry! Even the Formica suffers." He stuck a finger under his glasses, wiping away a bit of moisture. Then he looked at me sharply. "But to return to the subject at hand—I should think that your people, given their views, would not appreciate my equipment, that is, *Mary's* type of intelligence."

"We appreciate stuff that works," I said, hating his radio voice.

"So do I!" he said eagerly, taking a step toward me. "So you see, we have something in common. Indeed, I am most intrigued by this point of convergence. I would like to understand how Mary came to be accepted in your community. It is a fascinating piece of data. Anecdotal, of course, but still fascinating." He fished with two fingers in his breast pocket. "Allow me to give you my card." He held out a square of white paper, and when I didn't take it, he tucked it away again with a sad look.

"How disappointing! I made this card just for you. Knowing you'd appreciate ink and paper."

He gave a sudden bark of laughter. He had changed from sadness to laughing so quick, it sent a shiver of warning down my legs. I felt hot and faint. Things buzzed loudly in the grass.

"Of course, if you change your mind, you know where to find me," said the doctor. "We could have such a productive conversation. I am particularly interested in your perspective, as I know that wherever Mary is now, she has spent a significant amount of time in your possession. How I know, you would not understand —you lack the bird's-eye view. The point is, *I know*. And, Mrs. Esh, having . . . perhaps not committed theft, exactly, but having accepted stolen goods, you would not like to lie to me too. What would Jesus do?"

I thumped the basket on the ground and flared up at him. "Don't talk to me about Jesus! You don't even believe in God!"

"Oh, no," he said, with an almost sorrowful look on his face. "On the contrary, I think it most likely God exists."

I stared at him, his expression was so strange. Shirts billowed beside his face, framing him in white. "I am not sure," he said, "but I think it highly probable. Indeed, Mary represents an attempt to deal with precisely this problem."

His great melancholy eyes, dark and watchful behind his glasses. "Your attachment to her is most instructive. Do you not find it intriguing yourself—our need for simulations? By which I mean —how can I explain it—our need for characters. Characters in stories, or those personalities children give their toys. The feeling one sometimes has for animals."

I didn't answer. My heart ached. I remembered the day, the plan. My engagement had been published the previous week. I was going to take her to church that day. I went to the springhouse. I brushed her dress. A warbler chanted from the cherry tree.

"I have a pet cat, for example. At times I would swear she could speak. I find her totally unique among her species. In the same way, I become passionately attached to the characters in films. You will not be familiar with film; it is a story in pictures. But you will have heard of—well, of Jesus. An excellent example, really. It is the characters who must be made to suffer. They stimulate our most protective and our most aggressive impulses. A potent elixir! As far as we know, human beings have never lived without it."

I told them I would meet them at the church. I wanted to walk, the day was so fine. Mother smiled, thinking I was shy of meeting Sam. She thought I wanted to slip in quietly, but I wanted everyone to see the gleaming lady on my arm. For she couldn't stay in the springhouse. I thought she'd come to live with Sam and me, all clear and in the open, at our new place. She'd help me keep house, like an unmarried sister. I took her down the lane. In my pocket, a letter for the elders. *She is a thinking creature.*

"I admit I am not always pleasant to my little cat. She bears my frustration sometimes. And yet I would never willingly let her go. A character becomes almost part of oneself. *Almost,* you understand. As much as your people appreciate Mary, I imagine they're also drawn to test her compliance. Little boys throwing stones, or asking dirty questions to mock her—that sort of thing. Oh, I understand perfectly. A character occupies the magical space between subject and object. How delicious! Out of sheer love, one squeezes it to death."

I walked with her. I told her, "This is the lower pasture, Mary. This is the road. This is our Jericho." The day was still bright, but clouds had gathered black over Front Mountain. They would break that afternoon. The air smelled richly of clover. All the carriages were drawn up for the service, and Father, standing there with the other elders, looked at me without surprise. "So," he said, "this is the new gadget." Behind him, Mim. She stood against the wall, a dark look on her face.

Dr. Stoll had drawn close to me. He had a terrible foreign smell —an odor like violets, vinegar, and burning. I felt I was going to be sick. At that moment Mary was down at Fisher's, husking corn. She moved from one shock to another down the field. She would work all night, moonlight or no, unless her heart gave out. Then they'd find her slumped over in the morning. Once I walked by a field where she was lying facedown in the mud, her dress open in back. Two men talked over her. One was eating an onion.

Dr. Stoll gripped the clothesline above us with one hand, peering earnestly into my face between the shirts. "It is my conviction, Mrs. Esh, that any sufficiently advanced intelligence will create simulations of the greatest possible complexity. Perhaps even as complex as ourselves. What I am attempting to develop with Mary is a simulation that can comprehend its maker. But I believe she can do more. Her capacity is far beyond ours. She may eventually perceive *her maker's maker.* She may give us news of God."

A wet sleeve slapped his cheek. I thought of his image on the springhouse wall. Wherever Mary was, he was in her eye. I thought of Mim, the keeper of Mary's hearts. How Mary must dream of her too.

I spoke straight in the doctor's face. "Go away."

I bit the icicle in my mouth. As it broke, it released a compound that communicated bracken and dead leaves. You placed a live toad in my hand. You took me to the theater and whispered the name of the opera in my ear. Scrape of your beard. You had not shaved for the week of our holiday. At the hotel I lost my ring down the sink and cried. We shopped for old books in the rain, the drops when we ran across the street collecting on your hair on your black cap. On your wavy silver hair. On your sturdy cap. You called me "Mary." You said, "Mary, what is memory?" I said, "We walked in the forest. I was following your gray dress. A leaf clung to your heel." You smiled, a raindrop sparkling on your nose. We ran to the nearest café, shielding our packages, which were only wrapped in newspaper. Memory means feeling again. It is a matter of numbers. The deep, warm room. The

smell of beer. The black strings of your cap at your pale throat. Memory
means feeling that something is not for the first time.

She Hopes, but Not Too Much

(Get up. Dress. Wash up in the darkness. Downstairs light the
lamp, the oven. Start the bread. The baby wakes. Feed him. Try to
slide him off the breast without waking him up. It doesn't work.
Change him. Put the used diaper to soak. No time to soothe him
to sleep again. Take him downstairs. Put him to play with the rolling pin. Knead the dough. Get the boys up. Make them wash. Send
them to milk the cows. John doesn't want to. Push him, threaten.
Dad will get you. The baby cries. Pick him up, carry him on your
hip. At last the boys go out. Holding the baby on your hip, start the
eggs one-handed. Shell in the yolk. Bring the lamp closer to check.
Baby leans over to grab at the egg bowl. Put him in his chair, where
he struggles and cries. Soothing sounds while you pick the shell
out of the eggs. Give him an apple. He gums it, throws it down,
cries. Stir the eggs. Yesterday's bread for toast. The boys come in,
dirtying the floor. Shout at them, they know better. Make them
sweep it. Jimmy complains, John didn't do enough. He's lazy. Do
I have a lazy child. The baby wails, unbearable, pick him up and
turn the toast, don't let him fall in the oven. The boys squabbling.
Is breakfast ready yet. Sam comes in from currying the horses and
they quiet. Hear him washing up. Toast out now and bread dough
in the pans. John get the butter, Jim, the milk. Baby back in chair.
Give him some toast, he'll choke. Take it away, he screams. Sam
says, It's bedlam. Comes in, says, It's bedlam, why is this apple on
the floor. There is a difference in the light now. It is dawn.)
     "Lyddie," said Mim, "I have a situation in my root cellar."
     (I haven't put in all the interruptions. You'll have to imagine
those. Think of them as a noise that goes on without ceasing from
one darkness to another. Sometimes all I've got at the end of the
day is a huge emptiness. As if that's been my purpose all along. So
much effort for so many hours to sit at the table empty. So much
work at last to shut off like a stove. *Come to bed,* says Sam. Sometimes I do. Sometimes I take the notebook out. I know tomorrow
I'll be tired enough to weep. Snap at the boys, turn ugly. Mother
says I'm getting thin. I write: "I have a situation in my root cellar.")

"What kind of situation?"

"The kind you see with your own eyes."

"But I've got pies in."

She gazed at me fixedly from under drawn brows.

"All right. Half an hour."

We started up the hill toward her house. Mim still lived with her mother on the edge of her uncle's farm. The rest of us had gotten married that summer, dropping, Mim said, like flies, or as if marriage, she also said, was a kind of TB. Me to Sam, Barb to Mel, Esther to Little Orie, who is probably the most cheerful man in Jericho. And Kat, surprisingly, to Barb's brother, Joe. This was to bring her much grief, but not yet. That first summer she was so happy, she blushed constantly, laughing at the smallest things, a heat coming off her face that fogged her glasses so you couldn't see her eyes.

Mim's house was brown and sagging and gave off a smell of cabbage that reached halfway up the lane. Instead of a garden, it had a single hairy pumpkin vine that covered the ground outside in giant steps—a thing greedy for territory. I'd never liked going there, for Mim's mother was a woman of a sorrowful spirit. As we drew near, she came banging out of the door. "What is it?" she cried, staring at us with her sore-looking, terrified eyes that bulged like gooseberries.

"Nothing, Mommy," Mim said gently. "We're going out back."

"Out back!" her mother exclaimed, but she said nothing else, so we went around the house, stepping over the pumpkin vine, and Mim lifted the slanting door that led to the cellar. A little light came up the dirt stairs, along with a questioning yelp from Hochmut.

"Good dog," Mim called down.

We went down the stairs, Mim pulling the door shut on top of us. "Don't shout or anything," she warned.

"Why would I?" I said, and stopped. The ceiling light shone on Hard Mary, seated on a crate, and Hochmut, standing guard by a foreign man who was tied up with a hose.

"Mim. What have you done?"

"I told you it was a situation."

"Hi, Lyddie!" Mary said.

"Hi, Mary. But what have you done to him?"

The foreign man was young, much younger than Dr. Robert

Stoll. He had long hair like snakes. His glasses were filthy, his face scratched and bleeding.

"I didn't do all that!" Mim protested. "He came like that, mostly."

The foreign man had a pile of sacking for a pillow. It did look as if someone had tried to make him comfortable, only he couldn't move his arms or legs because of the hose.

He peered up at me through the smudges on his glasses. "Hey," he said. "That's true."

"Quietly," said Mim.

"That's true," the foreigner whispered agreeably. "I had some trouble getting here. In the forest? There was this, like, river? All she did was trip me when I got here, and Honey held me down."

"Honey is what he calls Mary," said Mim with distaste.

"My bad," said the foreigner. "I meant Mary."

I turned on Mim. "He's from PI! You brought somebody from PI down here?"

"Uh," said the foreigner. "I'm from Lancaster?"

"Shut up," I told him.

"Hey, no problem." He did his best to nod.

Mim regarded me with a steely expression. "The situation," she said, "is that he needs to use the outhouse."

"Miriam Ruth Hershey. I can't believe you. I can't believe what you're saying. You brought him down here. If he needs the outhouse, you'd better take him."

"I can't."

"Make Mary do it. She does whatever you say."

"He knows her. He'll play some trick."

"I actually wouldn't," the foreigner said. "Promise. I really have to go."

"You're a married woman," Mim said to me.

I could have shoved her.

"Please," the foreigner said, writhing, "I'm dying over here."

"Sometimes," I told Mim, "I'm sorry I ever talked to you. I wish I'd left you alone when we were kids."

"Fine," Mim said brightly. "Here's his outfit."

She showed me a dress and cap. The dress was too long for her; it must have been her mother's. "In case someone sees you on the way out there," she explained. She told the foreigner we were going to untie him, but he'd better not try to run, as Mary was going with us, and she could break his arm.

"Geez, I thought you were pacifists," he said.

"Mary never joined the church," said Mim, untying the hose.

"Oh, okay, I get it. I'm a pacifist myself, actually. I'm a Mennonite? From Lancaster County? We're probably related."

Standing up, he was over six feet tall. He had dark brown skin and long fingers like raspberry canes.

"I don't think we're related," I said.

Getting him into the dress and cap was difficult, not because he fought us but because he kept whining that we were going to make him laugh.

"Oh my God, this is torture," he moaned as Mim forced his weird, snaky hair up into the cap. At last he was dressed, and I took his arm and led him upstairs. He hopped along, doubled over, explaining to me that in addition to his need for the outhouse, he had a twisted ankle.

"I twisted it in the river," he said. "I'm, like, the easiest prisoner. Seriously. Hey. I really appreciate you taking me to the bathroom."

"Be quiet," Mim snapped from below. "And Lyddie, go inside with him. He'll get up to something."

"She's superuntrusting," the foreigner said.

In the outhouse I stood with my back to him while Mary waited outside. My nose nearly touching the wall, I stared at the grain of the wood. It was warped and greenish, almost black. *This is really happening*, I told myself.

"Is this what I'm supposed to use?" the foreigner asked. "These leaves and stuff?"

I washed him up at the bucket outside and returned him, limping, to the cellar. Hard Mary followed. I noticed she was able to manage the stairs. She came slowly, with a little thumping sound, like pushed-out air. As always, it gave me a pang to think Mim had done something new to her. The foreigner, however, was delighted. "Your friend is really smart," he told me. "She's done amazing stuff with whatchacallit, Mary. Ah. May. Zing." He shook his head, a hair-snake waving where it stuck out over his forehead. "She doesn't even have a keyboard, does she? It's all voice recognition?"

"Don't tell him anything," said Mim as we reached the bottom of the stairs. "And you, sit down."

"Gladly," the foreigner said, seating himself on the sacks. Mim's mother's dress only reached to his knees. Below it his dungarees stuck out, wet and muddy, ending in a pair of striped green shoes.

"Yo," he said, giggling weakly, and pointing at himself, us, and Mary, "we match. We totally match."

"You've got nothing to laugh about," said Mim.

"Okay. That's cool. Can I take the hat off? And maybe my shoes and socks?"

His name, he told us, was Jonathan. "Jonathan Otieno? But my mom was a Hartzler? You have Hartzlers here, right? Or Zooks? I have Zook cousins." It was he who had left Hard Mary behind the barn that winter night. "I was gonna come back for her, except you guys found her. Which is cool. Better you than someone else."

"You mean Dr. Stoll?" I asked.

He nodded. We exchanged a long look. Jonathan seemed to shrink; for the first time, he looked like a prisoner.

"Who's Dr. Stoll?" asked Mim in icy tones.

"The man from Mary's dreams," I said, still looking at Jonathan. "The one who made her."

"Whoa," said Jonathan, frowning. "Totally not. He did *not* make her. It was a collab. A group project? For all the Helpmeets, but especially this one. Honey. C19. I mean whatchacallit, Mary. This one's extra-special. Me and Judy, that's another intern? We fitted her up to be a double."

His story emerged in bits and bursts, like water from a clogged tap. Often it was hard to understand him. Eventually, though, we gathered that Mary had been made as a servant, one of many, and that these servants had hidden eyes. With her hidden eye, Mary was sending news of us to the Profane Industries. "The bird's-eye view," I whispered. "Yeah," said Jonathan, nodding. "Sure." That was how they knew she was here. "It's not perfect," Jonathan said. "There's a lag, or it cuts out sometimes, or you get things in the wrong order. But basically yeah."

The back of my neck tingled as if someone was holding a candle there. "She's looking at us right now."

"Yup. But like I said, there's a lag. Like, six weeks? Dr. Stoll thought something got fucked up, excuse me, wrong, he thought something went wrong with one of her uploads. But me and Judy? We think it was us."

He and Judy had worked on Mary at night, when no one was watching. "Just for fun. We'd get some wine and just hang out and code, you know?" One night, as a prank, they had made Mary into what he called a "double": she could send her memories to PI and also play them back on her own camera. "So then she was, like, recording Dr. Stoll, but for herself. We thought it was funny. We were gonna collect the captures and show them to him, like for his birthday or something, if we could ever find out when his birthday was. But then she started having these failures, and he got really pissed off about it, and we got scared. We knew if he kept testing her he was gonna find the captures and then we could lose our internships and be on the street. So we decided to wipe her."

"What do you mean?"

He passed his hand over his brow, as if brushing off sweat. "You know, erase her. Delete. Boom."

I looked at Mim. She was perched on a stack of old pipes, holding her knees very tight. She looked small and concentrated, like paper crumpled into a ball. Jonathan said he had dumped Hard Mary in Jericho one night in a moment of panic, and when he came back for her, she was gone. He only found out where she was when Dr. Stoll discovered her. "You guys finally came through on her feed and we were like, holy shit. I mean, we were like, wow. You guys are into robots! We got your names, but like, supergarbled. I think she read us the entire Bible."

"You could hear us?"

"Pretty good."

"Because we—"

"Lyddie!" Mim said. "Be quiet."

It was too late. Jonathan's eyes sparkled. "I get it! You found the captures! They're cool, right? I mean, they're pretty low quality, but they're cool. You can get the audio too, we just didn't get a chance to connect it." He cracked his long fingers. "If you let me have my backpack, I can do it for you, just to give you a look. Or hey, maybe I can use your stuff." He gazed at the wall behind Mim, where her tools hung neatly on nails. "Because this is *crazy*. You're like MacGyver. What is that, a kitchen whisk?"

Mim stepped behind him, jerked his arms back, and began to tie the hose.

"Aw, man," said Jonathan.

"Mim," I said, "we have to let him go."

She pulled the hose around him and began, clumsily, to wrap it about his legs. He hissed a little when she jostled his injured foot.

He'd taken off his shoes and socks. One ankle was thin, the other an ugly bulge.

"He needs help," I said. "You should have brought Kat. And we have to let him do this . . . wiping."

Instead of answering me, she told Mary, "Come on." They went upstairs.

"Your friend is superintense," Jonathan said. "I respect it, though."

I caught up with Mim and Mary at the corner of the house. The day had grown dim, a mist drifting in from the east. The mists from that direction always have a mournful, acrid, mineral smell. They come to us from town. They come from the Profane Industries. I seized Mim's arm, and she looked at me. At the same moment, Mary stopped and looked at me too. Though she was taller than Mim, with those regular, softly shining features, their movement was the same, the same speed, the same angle. It gave me a jolt to realize it: they looked alike. I even thought that Mary's expression, always so tranquil, seemed stiffer than usual, as if she had taken on some of Mim's fierceness—for Mim's face, though of mortal flesh, was harder than any brass. She glared up at me with her witchy little scowl.

I shook off the chilly weakness that had come over me, thinking of Jonathan, who, when I had glanced back at him with my foot on the stair, was sitting with his head bowed on his breast, his hair drifting over his brow, which had turned a grayish, uneven color.

I told her she had to let him go. I said it was a sin. All my rage with her came up and burst like gall. The way she brooded and schemed alone. Her secrecy, her mistrust. Her sudden, blunt demands, her heartlessness, her pride. I told her she'd always been a sneak, ever since we were children. She got a funny look at that, a kind of twitch. Then her face turned narrower and darker, almost purple, and as I paused for breath, she stamped her foot and screamed.

She stamped again and screamed something like "*Awk!*" Like some savage, blood-mad bird.

I stared. I'd never seen her act like this. Even when she was a little girl, when the boys nearly drowned her in the creek, she'd walked home numbly, shivering but not crying.

Now tears shot from her eyes. They didn't come like water dripping but like a stove exploding. "Leave me alone!" she screamed.

She jumped up and down, she kicked the earth like a child. "Leave me alone, alone! You don't love me! Any of you! You'd pick a foreigner over me!"

"That's not—" I began faintly.

"Yes, it is!" she said, and started to sob. "Even though he—he's stronger than me—you don't stick up for me. Nobody sticks up for me, ever, ever! It's just—complaints—people coming down with Mary to get her fixed, to get her new heart. And nobody cares when her wheels fall off. Nobody cares if she's rusting. And that Mel Fisher comes around with his friends and wants to watch moving pictures, and old Kurtz wants me to start her building chairs, and now this foreigner comes and she won't obey me! I told her the words—Jephthah's daughter—she wouldn't obey."

When she said the words, I flinched, glancing at Mary.

"Oh, don't be *stupid*," wailed Mim. "You have to say her name first, you have to use a special tone! I'm not an idiot, Lyddie! And I'm stuck here with fools and I don't know how to do anything. I've never been taught. And that foreigner—he's got everything! He's got everything and I'm stuck with kitchen whisks! With a bunch of farmers! And she wouldn't hit him, Lyddie. She wouldn't listen to me."

She dug her fists into her eyes and cried.

"It's good she didn't hit him," I said. "He'd be even worse hurt. He could have wound up dead. Then where would we be?"

She shook her head, still sobbing. "It's because she remembers him. She *remembers*, don't you see? And he wants to wipe her out, so she won't . . . remember . . . anything."

"He has to," I said softly. "It's the only way. Otherwise that PI doctor will keep spying on us. He'll see Jonathan here. He might come after him. Mim," I interrupted as she tried to speak again, "we got into more than we bargained for, okay? Now we have to stop."

"But she won't know me," she whispered.

"She won't know me either," I said. "She'll get to know us again. Come on."

I put my arms around her. Mim had never been a hugger. It was like hanging on to a gatepost. I saw her mother watching us through a back window, pressed anxiously to the dirty glass.

"Mary's a machine, remember?" I whispered. "That's what you told everyone. Like the thresher."

I felt her stiffen even further, hardening like ice. I knew right then she wasn't going to wipe Hard Mary's mind. I was right: over the next few weeks, she would work in the cellar with Jonathan. Sometimes I'd take some apples down there, or a basket of rolls, and find them arguing with each other, Mim squatting on a crate, Jonathan splay-legged on the floor, his open knapsack and wires and foreign tools around him. And Mim would give me her sideways look, a bit glinting, a bit sly. Now she pulled back and faced me.

"Of course I told them that," she said, with a splinter of a laugh. "How do you think people stay alive?"

In a gesture that was strange for her, she touched my cheek. "Go on home, Lyddie. Your pies are burning."

We are going through the beautiful country around Jericho. We walk into the shadows of Front Mountain. We are passing Kootcher's Hollow, where Shep, the Headless Dog, runs beside us, panting through his neck. If you look directly at him, he'll jump on your back, so we don't look. We pass a hanging rock with a pile of money under it. Anyone who touches this money gets bit by a thousand snakes. We arrive at the abandoned hotel where the dead thief walks in circles, holding a bag. "Where shall I put it, where shall I put it?" he moans. He doesn't know what to do with his sin. In the ghost hotel, a chandelier lies smashed in the lobby. Half the piano keys have fallen in. You open the back of the piano, disclosing mouse nests and a staircase going down. We climb into the piano and go down the stairs. There's a radiant expanse at the bottom. It is a sea of glass. People are skimming back and forth across it in little sleighs. A man comes toward us, pushing his sleigh along with a pole. The pole has a circle of teeth at one end so it can grip the glass. "Hop in," says the man. His face is covered with a kerchief of fine white linen. Only one eye shows. This eye is bloodshot and terribly bruised, with dark, powdery streaks around it, but it is kind. It looks almost newly awakened, peeled, as if in baring this one eye he has cast off all intelligence, all design. We get in the sleigh. "Why did you go away?" you ask the man, and he says he was buying you a sleigh of your very own.

She Too Is Longing for the Heavenly Home

They came in the middle of the night. A blaring yanked me out of sleep. Lights were flashing in the windows, like the lights of the trucks that pass out on the road, only brighter and more insistent. "NO ONE WILL BE HURT," the blaring said. Sam and I pulled on our clothes in the dark and the ragged bursts of light. "Stay inside," he told me, and I said no, and he said, "Do as you're told," and the blaring said, "WE REQUEST THE RETURN OF OUR PROPERTY."

We rushed outside. Everywhere people were coming out of their houses, some half dressed. The chickens had set up a racket. A line of vans was ranged along the road. There were men in heavy black, with guns. That made my heart toll like a clock.

"Go back to the house," said Sam.

People were arguing and crying. There were children outside, and people were pulling them in. The men began to gather in a knot. They advanced toward the vans in a knot together, shielding their eyes from the flashing lights.

"NO ONE WILL BE INJURED IF OUR PROPERTY IS SE-CURED. WE REQUEST THE INSTANT RETURN OF OUR STO-LEN PROPERTY."

Someone rushed up in the dark and grabbed my hand.

"Esther!" I cried, and hugged her.

"Oh, Lyddie," she choked through tears, "it's all our fault."

"We have to get Mim," I said. Her house was far away from the main road, and I wasn't sure she'd hear the noise. We ran through the dark weeds, holding up our skirts. "I don't think this running is good for us," Esther panted. We were both pretty heavy in the middle by then. I had a tingling feeling in my head, but whether from the baby or from horror, I couldn't tell. Every moment I expected to hear shots. I thought of our good, crooked-backed old bishop, of my father, and of Sam.

Barb and Kat caught us up on the way. They'd had the same idea. Barb was the most pregnant of us, Kat still trim as a bean. I was surprised to see Kat, for I couldn't imagine Joe Miller would let her out of the house. In fact, we would later learn, he hadn't let her. She had gone out a window and down a tree. Her stockings were torn to kingdom come. "This is a fine kettle," she said.

Halfway down the carriage road to Mim's, we met her coming up with Jonathan and Hard Mary. Mary held her hand up, palm outward, sending a beam of light along the road so they could see the ruts. "Who is *that?*" gasped Barb, while Esther clutched my arm with a muffled shriek. Kat had been down to the cellar to splint his leg, but neither Barb nor Esther had seen Jonathan before. His hair bounced against the stars. "What's up," he said.

"Hello, girls," said Mim. "This is Jonathan."

At that moment a shot rang out. We all began to run back toward the road. I stumbled along wildly for a moment before I realized that Mary was matching my speed, her light shining on the grass. This was strange, for she had always moved at a slow, sedate pace. Now, I saw, she had new wheels, larger ones. They were thick and rolled easily over the cropped grass of the pasture. Her skirt had been cut short so it wouldn't get caught. She also had some new structure about her waist, with a sort of ledge behind it where Jonathan crouched, clinging to her neck for support, his splinted leg tucked close, a knapsack humped up on his back, his glasses glinting in the dazzle from her hand. They looked altogether otherworldly, like something one of the old kings in the Bible might have encountered in a dream. *Oh, my sweet Mary,* I thought, both proud and frightened, as she cut the night. (I still tell people my first child was a girl.)

We dashed behind Miller's place. Beyond it, people were gathered in front of the vans. We could see the lights. We could hear the harsh, booming voice. "This is where I get off," Jonathan said. "I'll be your backup. Holler if you need me. Watch this. I'ma jump off like a cat."

He gathered himself and sprang into Barb's mother's forsythia bush, all gangly arms and legs. "Ow, shit!" he said.

"What—what," Esther panted, half crying, "what *is* he?"

"He's an old scarecrow," said Mim, "but he's all right."

She stepped on the new ledge attached to Hard Mary and rolled into the light.

The rest of us followed, clinging close together. The night was cool, October, but I was sweating and I could smell Barb's sweat, like dried flowers, and the tartness of Esther, and Kat's damp odor of herbs. Esther rubbed her cheek against my sleeve, smearing off tears. Kat was squeezing my hand. It felt like seeing Hard Mary in the old days—the old days when we clustered around her, all touching her at once, when she seemed made up out of all of us, a group project. The old days, which were less than a year before. No one lay on the ground in the flashing lights. The gun we had heard must have fired into the air. I looked for Sam and found his half-dark shape among the men who had formed a line in front of the vans. I recognized the slope of his shoulder.

Dr. Stoll sat in the lights, raised up on a sort of chair that stuck out from the side of a van. He looked cheerful, and wore a green knitted cap. He raised a white cone to his mouth. "WE DEMAND THE RETURN OF OUR PROPERTY," he blared. Then he laid the cone in his lap and leaned to talk to a girl in white. He was laughing, shrugging. Like it was a holiday. He flipped one lens of his glasses up against the edge of his cap, bending down, as if it would help him hear better. The girl handed him a paper cup with something that steamed. Her head was shaved and her arm was in a sling.

"They're horrible, horrible!" Esther whispered.

"They're just foreign," I said. They did look strange. People in white coats milled among the men with guns. A boy was arguing with our elders. He had metal teeth. A girl yawned in the driver's seat of a van, a boil like a ruby on her nose.

"WE DEMAND," honked Dr. Stoll. Then he saw Mary.

Mim and Mary moved forward until they were just in front of the vans. The girls and I followed at a slight distance. Dr. Stoll smiled. "Goodbye, Mary," Barb cried out softly.

Dr. Stoll called without his white cone, "Good evening, my dear."

"I don't know that I'd call it evening," said Mim. Her voice carried across the suddenly silent field.

Dr. Stoll chuckled. "Charming," he said. "Very pert. It is a pleasure to meet you, Mim. Truly a pleasure. As one architect to another."

He placed his hand on his breast and inclined his head. He told her he found her work impressive. He would like to offer her a seat at the table. Mim said she doubted she was interested in any of his furniture. Dr. Stoll slapped his thigh and called her charming again. Mim had come down from Mary's ledge and was standing in the grass. I could only see her from the back, the familiar outline of her cap, but I guessed from the front she'd look about as charming as a tub of rattlers.

"Come on, Honey," said Dr. Stoll, and then there was a pause.

"Come on, Honey," he repeated a little more forcefully.

Nobody moved. Mim had crossed her arms. Mary stood beside her. Perhaps it was just the lights, but it seemed to me that she was trembling. It seemed to me that she was shaking so fast you could barely see it. I remembered when we used to take her out behind the springhouse, those first few times, in the cold gray air, how she would drift away from us and we would call her back. She'd turn, grinding and rickety, to face us in cloud-light, and slowly return. Now I realized with a chill that she'd always drifted eastward. She had moved toward the Profane Industries.

Dr. Stoll's lithe body squirmed in the chair. "Natasha!" he snapped. "Pass me the handy."

He reached one arm inside the van without taking his eyes off Mary and Mim. The girl with the boil placed something in his hand. Meanwhile the elders had come across the field. They were talking to Mim. They were telling her to give Mary up. They were saying she must listen. The bishop thumped his cane on the ground, the lights from the vans sparking wild lights from his dead-white beard.

(John is my problem child. The one who won't mind, who sits down and cries in the road, who gets up at night to crawl into my bed, the one with the unnatural terror of cats. "It's nothing," I'm always telling him, "nothing, get up, quit crying, don't." Mother says he's a character. I think of Dr. Stoll. I think of his talk of characters, the ones you love, the ones you kill. The ones you wipe out. I think of the flood. I think of God.)

Dr. Stoll was jabbing a finger at the little object in his hand, and the men with guns were strolling toward him with casually questioning looks, and the bishop was growling, and our men were shouting, and Esther let go of me and knelt to pray, Barb stumbling and falling to her knees almost on top of her, and the sky was clear and crisp except in the east where the fumes of the quarry blurred the tops of the trees with a vapor like blue fur, and the heavens turned a sickly, blank no-color, the color of the world when your eyes are shut, above the dark halls of the Profane Industries. And Mary was motionless, silent. The doctor got tired of pushing buttons on whatever instrument of Satan was in his hand. "You didn't do this!" he roared. "You couldn't have done this."

"You better back off with those guns," Mim told him, "or you'll never find out."

He sat and looked at her. He snapped the one side of his glasses down and looked at her through two lenses. Then he gave a cough.

It turned into a bunch of coughs, which I realized was a laugh, but he wasn't smiling. His mouth was iron-hard.

The laughter made a lot of spit, which he wiped off with his hand. All his white-coated people stood staring at Mim. A couple of the gunmen were smoking cigarettes. "Get up, you ninnies," I said, pulling Esther and Barb by the backs of their collars. "Mim's about to beat this heathen."

They stood up blinking in the light as Dr. Stoll told Mim, "You'd better come with me."

"No," said Mim. "You can't take me. I'm not part of your outfit. I haven't signed anything for you and you've never copied my ID card and if you shoot me it's murder in the first degree. You can have some of your people there come over and haul Mary away, but she'll never talk to you or do your bidding and you'll never know why. You can take her apart or melt her down, I guess, but it would be a sorry waste. As one architect to another."

He stared at her a moment longer. Then he smiled. "Well. There we are."

"Looks that way to me," said Mim.

He cleared his throat. "Judy," he said, "come up here and take a seat. I want you to announce to these good people that they can go home."

He climbed sideways from his chair into the van, seating himself beside the girl with the boil on the side of her nose, who immediately started talking, but he shushed her and peered out the window to see what was happening. The "Judy" he'd been talking to, I saw, was the girl with the shaved head and the sling. She tried to climb up into the chair, but she kept on slipping, and finally the boy with the metal teeth came over and helped her. She sat in the chair and picked up the metal cone, but she didn't say anything.

"Tell them to go home," called the doctor from inside the van. "Tell them it's over now."

The girl said something into the cone. It was loud, but you couldn't make out what it was. It was like "*Umpf, eempf.*" Like her mouth was stuck together. Me and Kat were gazing at each other in bewilderment when somebody behind us cried out, "Judy!"

Jonathan came hobbling across the field. "Judy!" he shouted.

"Jonathan, no!" said Mim. To the men standing around her she said desperately, "Stop him, catch him!" But nobody was going to

go after the tall, lurching foreigner with the knapsack who'd hurtled out from among our very homes. As he passed Mim, she tried
to grab him, and Dr. Stoll called from the van, "Now, now, my
dear! Jonathan is under my jurisdiction. He is registered as my intern. I do possess copies of *his* identification papers. You will have
to let him go."

Jonathan turned to Mim. "Sorry," he said.

She was just tall enough to come up to his ribs. He could have
leaned on her as a man leans on a rake.

"You idiot," she said.

"It's Judy," he stammered. "Something's—he's—I have to
help her."

"You're gonna tell him everything, aren't you?" Mim said dully.

"I'll try not to."

He limped toward the vans. Two gunmen came to guard him
on either side. The boy with metal teeth helped Judy down from
the chair. They all got into the vans and turned off their flashing
lights and drove away. They didn't let Jonathan sit with Judy. They
put him in a different car.

*We cross the sea of glass and disembark on the other side. Here is the city.
"Which city?" you ask, and I tell you, "It is the Object City." The Object
City is broad and high. Its wall is an hundred and forty and four cubits,
according to the measure of the angels. The wall has twelve foundations.
The first foundation is jasper, the second sapphire, the third a chalcedony,
the fourth an emerald. I can feel you receding. You ask me very slowly,
"Why are the edges moving?" and then, with an effort, "Why is it so tangled?" The fifth sardonyx; the sixth sardius, the seventh chrysolite. The
Object City looks like a cloud of black-and-white specks. It looks like an opera cloak. It looks like a flock of swans in flight. It looks like stars. It looks
like an horror of great darkness. The eighth beryl, the ninth a topaz, the
tenth a chrysoprasus. Because you are sinking fast, I don't tell you the true
name of the Object City, which is the Object World. Instead I tell you, "This
is Jericho, your own Jericho. In the night you are awakened by a wildcat's
cry." I say, "In the morning you will find the prints of the deer that come
down from the mountains. They have pawed up the snow to eat the grass
in the orchard."*

*Now you will have a little sleep. When you wake, we will try again to
enter the city.*

The eleventh a jacinth. The twelfth an amethyst.

If She Strays, She Can Come Back

(Sometimes the early summer is so happy it calls to me. I have to go out. I go outside after supper, I stay outside for hours. How thick the rhubarb grows out back and oh how sweet the beans. I lie in the flowers, drenched with their perfume, and feel the dew come down. It touches my eyelids like a cold hand. When I open my eyes the heavens are filling like a bowl with glowing summer dark. A night so blue you can feel it in your lungs. My little boys know this mood. They charge outside, play around me, wild as goats. These will be their best memories, for this is their favorite mother. She allows everything. She is flopped down in the beans. They run around, chasing fireflies. Baby Levi's diaper sags and his brothers pull it off him, laughing, and chuck it over the fence. Levi runs half naked, shrieking for joy. I know if I sit up I'll see Sam's shadow at the kitchen window, pacing back and forth with increasing energy until he works up enough frustration to come out and call us in. How, he will demand, can I let the boys act like this? Don't I know how it looks? I don't sit up. I am struck down by the sky. I think of Sam, his long hot days of toil spent in a noble pursuit, scattering seed to make the land flourish. And what of the land? Does it feel that its work is noble? What of the horses plodding up and down beneath the glinting whip? The boys are roughhousing close to me. They kick me in the ribs. Levi treads on my breastbone. Is this a noble pursuit? Now the moon comes out from behind the clouds, filling the branches of the old crabapple tree with mellow light. "Noom!" crows Levi, pointing. "Noom!" I clutch his pretty leg. He giggles and bends to plant his fat palms on my neck. And gives me a kiss smelling of dirty milk, wobbling, losing his balance, hitting my face too hard, our foreheads knocking. Oh, you — the one I write to in the flicker of the lamp — what do you want from me, or for me? What is your desire?)

I woke up to a rattle at the window. My heart lifted. I thought, *It's Sam!* But then I realized he was in the bed beside me. We were no longer courting; we were married. I went downstairs, pulled Sam's big coat on, and opened the door, and there was Mim.

"Hello, Lyddie," she said; and "Hi, Lyddie!" said Mary.

Mim sat in a cart. Her head was bare. Her hair hung loose and tangled as the bracken. The cart was attached to Mary, who still wore her neat black cap. Fresh, cold moonlight glimmered on her face.

"What is this contraption?" I asked, shivering.

"Well," said Mim, "it's a kind of carriage. Like the one you saw the other night, for Jonathan. This one's a little bigger, though."

I noticed several dark bundles around her, and Hochmut poking his nose over the slats.

"You're going away, then?"

She nodded. "I came to say goodbye."

"With no cap?" I asked, my eyes filling with tears.

"That's my disguise."

I laughed, blinking. "A fine disguise. You won't get far. Not in this—half carriage, half woman. You'll stick out like a rash."

"I don't have to get far. Just to the Profane Industries."

"Jonathan?" I whispered.

"I can't leave him, can I? I intend to spring him before he spills my secrets. I might take that bald-headed girl too. His friend, Judy. She looked like she could use a change of occupation."

I shook my head. "Mim." Then, as I noticed one of her bundles looking at me with a pair of large, scared eyes, I gasped: "*Mim!* Is that your mother?"

"I couldn't very well leave her behind! Uncle Al worries her. Besides, she might be useful." She patted her mother's shoulder. "Right, Mommy?"

Her mother gave a trembling smile.

"I can't let you do this. Leave her with me. I'll keep her."

"No. She doesn't like to be parted from me. She'll shred your sheets, and you won't like it. And besides, I want her. She's trusty in a pinch."

"There's nothing I can say to make you change your mind?"

"Why would I come out at midnight in this contraption just to change my mind? No, I'm bent on going, so you might as well stop crying."

"But you—and Mary—you'll never—I'll never see you again."

"That's for the Good Lord to decide."

After a moment she said in a softer tone, "Come, now. Don't take on. You have Sam Esh, for what he's worth. Soon you'll have a baby. Don't begrudge me my poor old mother, or this bag of bones I call a dog. Or Mary. After all, she came to me."

I wiped my eyes and looked at her.

"It was on the seventh round," she said in the same low, thought-ful tone. "Do you ever think of that? I found her on the seventh round. When we were all looking for the ones we'd be with for-ever. I walked right into her."

"We were supposed to see ghosts or photographs. Not some-thing hard like that."

"Well." She smiled. "It's just a fancy. Tell the girls I said goodbye."

She gave Mary no instructions, and I couldn't see that she touched her at all, but Mary started off, pulling the cart eastward.

(The next year, at Old Christmas, I stood at the window holding baby Jim and watched a group of girls go down the road. They crowded together, hurrying over the snow, their breath excited, white and quick. They meant to go around a barn. I thought I heard a burst of laughter floating on the air. *Oh, sweet girls,* I thought, *what do you hope to find? Don't you know that somebody always has to be sacrificed? Ask the animals—it's all they talk about.* Then, rocking the baby to calm myself, I thought of Mim. I thought of her breaking down the fence around the Profane Industries. I thought of her getting caught, and then I stopped. I didn't want to think of that, and I still try not to think about it. I still see her, always, always. I make up stories for her in my head, when I'm do-ing the wash, when I'm scrubbing the porch with silver sand. I see her rescuing Jonathan from a dark hole underground. They have to jump across an invisible wire. They have to scale a wall. I see her traveling the country, her loins girded, her shoes on her feet, and her staff in her hand, eating her bread in haste. Jonathan rides in the cart with Mim's mother and the dog. They come to the rivers, the floods, the brooks of honey and butter. And Mary, striding alongside Mim, is almost like her sister. She is like a portrait of Mim in metal. She looks the way she did the last time I saw her, in front of my own house in the moonlight: distant, almost as if she doesn't know me at all. But she does know me. "Hi, Lyddie!" Some part of me remains inside her head, just as Hochmut, even now, would recognize my scent. I make stories for her, and I give her no-ble pursuits, because you wouldn't—would you?—you wouldn't create a character and make it a machine.)

ADA HOFFMANN

Variations on a Theme
from *Turandot*

FROM *Strange Horizons*

Theme

NO ONE WILL sleep until the Princess learns the Stranger's name.

Liù the slave girl, who has loved the Stranger since before his
exile, when he was a Prince, when he smiled at her—Liù alone
knows who he really is. So it is Liù who is dragged to the Princess's
garden by night, bound, ankles twisting as she stumbles through
the peonies.

"You know what he will do to me if I do not win," says the Princess,
cold and resplendent, moonlight glinting like a star from her veils.

"He will be your husband," says Liù. "He will love you. You will
both be so happy. Please, Daughter of Heaven."

The trouble is that the Stranger loves the Princess, and the Princess—heir to the throne of imperial China—despises love. On
behalf of her ancestress Lo-u-Ling, she has sworn not to marry—
until a man appears who can answer her riddles. Dozens have died
trying. The Stranger, the man Liù loved and served her whole life,
succeeded. If the Princess cannot learn his name by morning, he
will marry her, whether she wills it or no. But princesses are not
taught to lose gracefully.

"You know what *I* will do to *you*," says the Princess, "if I do not
win. I have seen you with him; I know that you know. Tell me his
name. I will not ask politely again."

The executioner at her side shifts his weight, a shadowy bulk,
knives and pincers glinting.

For a moment, as Liù despairingly weighs her options, her view of the garden shifts. She is not really in China—not even in anything that resembles the real China. She is in an opera house in America. The garden with its pond and arching bridges is only a set. Yet Liù is Liù. The pain and terror are real. She has died protecting the Stranger's secret, hundreds of times, and will die again each night, as a spellbound audience looks on.

Liù is a faithful slave, too good and too in love to complain. Her sacrifice will save the Stranger, which is all she has ever wanted. Yet just for a moment Liù thinks, *There must be another way.*

The moment fades. The executioner advances. With a beautiful, musical sigh, as she has done hundreds of times, Liù snatches the dagger out of his hands and stabs herself to death.

Var. I

Over time Liù's flashes of insight grow longer. She stops forgetting them at the end of the night. She grows balky, confused.

There must be another way.

She lies and says that the Stranger is nameless: he himself does not remember his past or his name. The Princess kills her, then half the city, in a rage.

She tries fleeing before the opera begins, leaving the Stranger to his fate. But she cannot stop being Liù. The Stranger is her whole life. Love and guilt, fear for his safety, draw her back.

She tries speaking, in various ways, to the Princess.

Most of these hurt more than they help. But by now Liù remembers clearly enough, from evening to evening, to keep track. In a few months she has learned to stretch her extra time to an hour, an hour and a half.

The Princess speaks to Liù in fascinated tones. "How can you love him, when he is a beast like any other man?"

"Not all men are beasts," says Liù. The Princess beheads her.

"He is an angel, not a beast," says Liù. "He is nothing like any other man." The Princess has her hanged.

"I do not know, Daughter of Heaven," says Liù. "I am helpless. I can say nothing of love, except that I feel it, and cannot feel otherwise."

The Princess is stonily silent.

Var. II

"My lord," says Liù to the Stranger, "*why?* Why must you win this woman, when so many will die for it?"

It is the opera's first act, a filthy thoroughfare outside the palace gates. The Stranger has seen the merest glimpse of the bloodthirsty Princess, and has fallen in love. He knows he must answer her riddles, no matter the risk; any man who tries and fails is executed.

Liù has begged him, in her first and most beautiful aria, to reconsider. The Stranger's father has begged him to reconsider. The palace's Lord Chancellor, majordomo, and head chef have sung a comical trio critiquing his plan. In the next act, the Emperor himself will beg him to reconsider. It never does any good.

"I love her," says the Stranger.

"She does not love you," says Liù.

The Stranger is handsome, broad of shoulder and bright of eye, unbowed by his years of exile. He is gentle with slaves like Liù, lowly men and women most princes would spit on. When he speaks, he really looks at her. When he smiles, the sun's rays burst through.

He smiles like that now, irresistibly. "You are mistaken, Liù. Don't be afraid. Even from across the crowded square, I could see love in her eyes."

Liù does not think so. Liù has always read people easily, and what she sees in the Princess's eyes is not love. In the Princess's first and most fearsome aria, when she tells the story of her ancestress Lo-u-Ling, there is resolve in her eyes, anger, pain. And something else, behind it. A very great fear. As if the men who come to her are soldiers scaling a wall, and one day she will fail to destroy them in time. But no one seems to care about that fear, and for all his kindness, neither does the Stranger.

Liù is afraid every night, afraid of pain, afraid of losing the Stranger, afraid to die. Her fear has never mattered to anyone either.

Intermezzo I

The Conductor catches the Soprano by the arm on her way backstage. "Tell me what this is about."

"I don't know what you're talking about," says the Soprano,

squinting up at him in the gloom. She is all too aware of the Conductor's power: he tall, white, distinguished by decades of accolades; she small, Korean American, a relative unknown. Liù is her first big professional role. The Conductor can scuttle her career with a word. She wishes he would not touch her.

"Do not play stupid with me, *signorina*. For months now you have been singing erratically, changing your words — *porco mondo*, even changing the music. It is a wonder my orchestra keeps up. I did not hire you to improvise."

The Soprano thinks, *Maybe the words needed changing.* She wouldn't be singing Liù if she were successful enough to pick and choose. She does not think much of this stage China which is nothing like China, these stage women who are nothing like women.

The Conductor waves a hand. "I would be firing you now, except the audience seems to like it. But do not try my patience. At least you must tell me what you are doing."

"I don't know, Maestro. I am not at all sure."

Ever since she was a little girl imitating her mother's records, the Soprano has had a secret detachment while singing, a sense that the character appears and sings *through* her. Most nights she only vaguely remembers what has happened onstage. This Liù, this production of *Turandot*, brings on the feeling more strongly than ever. But as to why, the Soprano knows nothing.

Var. III

Liù kneels before the screen in the Princess's sitting room, head bowed.

"I should have had you killed by now," says the Princess. "But you feel familiar, as if I have known you a long time. Why? And why do I feel you have something to offer me?"

Liù does not raise her eyes from the floor. "I am a lowly woman, acquainted with pain. I see pain when I look upon you. I wish only to help. If the Daughter of Heaven should be in pain — a supernatural pain, perhaps . . ."

Cold amusement. "Are you a witch? An exorcist?"

"If it pleases the Daughter of Heaven," says Liù, "I would like to speak to Lo-u-Ling."

The Princess has her flayed.

Var. IV

The Princess sits alone in her garden, cradling the Persian Prince's head. The opera has begun again, and she has not yet met Liù or the Stranger. But the Stranger will hardly surprise her. Man after man comes to answer the Princess's riddles, to demand her as a prize.

The Princess is the empire's only heir. It is unthinkable for her not to marry, not to carry on the sacred family line. She cannot outright refuse. Not forever.

At the first suitor, when the Princess was only sixteen, she panicked. The boy was a foreign prince her own age. He was soft-spoken; he had never done anything to hurt her. She could not explain why, when she looked at him, an icy vise closed in around her lungs.

So she made up a reason. She thought up her three impossible riddles. Vowed to marry only the man who solved them and to kill the ones who failed. Harsh, yes, but the point of this was to deter them. She did not want men to swarm in from every kingdom, attracted by the challenge.

Being men, they swarmed in anyway.

When the first prince's head rolled to a stop in its pool of blood, the Princess felt only a shameful relief. Malice came later. When the fifth prince came sharp on the heels of the fourth, flouncing in his feathered cloak through the blood in the streets, that was when she began to hate them all. To enjoy the killing. If men did not value their lives, why should she?

Lo-u-Ling, the ghost, came to her after that. Attracted, perhaps, by the scent of a terror as large as her own.

Blood, Lo-u-Ling whispers in the Princess's ear. *Blood, pain, fear. Men crawling over the walls. Fear. Flight. Falling on the path, cobblestones scraping blood from my arms. Men, fear, a helplessness worse than choking, blood . . .*

Lo-u-Ling, the Princess's ancestress, was raped and put to death during war, centuries ago, in this very garden. She approves of what the Princess does.

The Princess curls her fingers tightly in the Persian Prince's hair until she can distinguish her garden from Lo-u-Ling's. Until she is sure the only blood is that which clings to the tatters of the

Persian Prince's throat. The Princess won this time. As long as she lives, the Princess swears to herself, she will win.

Var. V

"Daughter of Heaven," says Liù with her eyes to the ground, "I will find you the Stranger's name. I do not know it now, but I, and I alone, can learn it from him. But, unworthy as I am, I must ask one tiny boon—or else, betraying him, I will die of shame."

"Yes?" says the Princess cautiously. Two months ago she would have had Liù tortured even for asking. But things are beginning to change.

"Let him live," says Liù. "You need not marry him. Cast him out of the empire if you like, but send him on his way as an equal, alive."

"You are asking me," says the Princess, "to forgive him."

"But what must you forgive him for? What crime has he committed?"

"He has answered my riddles. He has insisted that I must be his, though I never wanted any man. If I do not punish him, what then? How many more strangers will ride in on the wind with nothing to lose? I know the things men do—I and Lo-u-Ling, both. We have sworn never to forgive anyone at all."

"I understand," says Liù, bowing low. "But, if I may be so bold, I have not asked you to forgive him. You may brand him as a criminal, a disgrace to your kingdom. You may hate and rage against him to the end of your days, so long as you let him live."

"No," says the Princess. "You will do as I say, and I will have mercy on no one."

"Then," says Liù, bowing lower still, "if you truly have no mercy, you will kill me as well."

The Princess draws back, surprised. "I have killed you many times now. But why should I kill you again, so long as you do as I say?"

"Because I am as wicked as he is," says Liù. "I love him too much to let him die at your hand. No matter what he has done, or will do, Daughter of Heaven. That is my crime."

The Princess is silent a long moment.

"No," she says. "You are not wicked. You are only a fool."

"Then," says Liù, daring to look up, "there is forgiveness in you after all."

Var. VI

With the Princess, Liù feels oddly free to speak. Each mistake means death, but Liù is used to death—and each success builds on the last. But the Stranger is a worn groove, a river of desire. He is always the same, always smiling, always sure he will win.

"She loves me," says the Stranger, deaf to Liù's protests on the filthy street.

"How do you know?" says Liù.

"She loves me," says the Stranger.

"Even if she does love you," says Liù, "what of it? If she loves you yet chooses against you, can you not honor that choice?"

"She loves me," says the Stranger.

It goes on until Liù wishes to melt into the ground, to run to the executioner and have done with it. It does not change.

Intermezzo II

"I know what you are doing," the Conductor announces after the curtain falls.

"Pardon?" says the Soprano.

Every night the Soprano resolves to do better next time. But she does not know how to sing without letting the character through. Every evening the Soprano goes elsewhere, and Liù deviates further and further from the libretto.

The Conductor snorts. "You think you are being clever. And my producers agree. The audience, they stream in like never before. It fascinates them, seeing a different opera every night. The papers, they gush—come see *Turandot,* the opera that the great maestro Puccini died writing. Come see us finish it differently each night; come see what might have been. They go on like this. But that is because they are fools. They do not see where it is headed."

The Soprano smiles nervously. "Frankly, I'm not sure *I* see where this is headed."

"It is headed to Liù surviving," the Conductor snaps. "That is

what you are trying to do. And once the audience realizes *that,*
they will flee. You do not understand the people who come to
these operas, *signorina.* For a romance with a happy ending, they
look to Rossini. For sheer scale, they go to Wagner. Our audience
is not like this. The people come to *Turandot* to watch the death
of a beautiful woman. This is what Puccini does best. His money
shot, if you will. I have hired you to sing those four gorgeous notes
in your first aria, then to die; the rest is filler. Take the death away,
and—" He makes a cutting gesture across his throat. "Liù dies either way, *signorina.* Physically or musically. Choose."

Var. VII

The Lord Chancellor looks up from his books in surprise as Liù
stumbles into his room, ushered by a pair of guards. She drops to
her knees in front of him, bows her head in supplication.

"What is this?" demands the Chancellor. "*Who* is this?"

"Only a slave," says Liù. "Less than no one, Excellency. You may
kill me if you like. But I believe I am in a position to help you, if I
know enough, and you are the most learned man in this empire. If
it pleases Your Excellency, may we speak of the Princess's current
difficulties?"

The Chancellor smiles thinly. "My dear, they are my bread and
butter. I want nothing more than for the little harridan to be married and the matter done with. Then I can retire to my home by
the little blue lake in Honan. Rise; I will probably not kill you. But
I am afraid I cannot help you very much."

Liù does not rise. She manages, with an effort, to lift her gaze
from the floor. She is not used to speaking to people she has not
spoken to before, beginning conversations that were not tested
and rehearsed a thousand times.

"Excellency," she says, "I wish to know whatever you can tell me
about ghosts. And stories. And . . . the way the two are trapped
together."

The Chancellor flicks ink off the end of his pen. "An overly
vague request. The Princess claims to have a ghost, but personally,
I doubt it. I think it is the story she prefers to tell."

"But that is just it," says Liù. "Imagine if someone was trapped in
a story. Imagine if they could not stop executing men, or chasing

a woman who does not want them, or—or dying, because they could not get out of the story. If the story refused to change, no matter what they did or how they argued."

The Chancellor half smiles. "You are thinking of the Stranger."

Liù's mouth goes dry. They will kill her again, of course. As soon as the Chancellor finishes this conversation, he will send her to the executioner and have her interrogated; anyone who cares enough about the Stranger to ask, on his behalf, must know his name.

It does not matter. She has died so many times already.

"Slave," says the Chancellor, "do you know the word *protagonist*?"

Liù nods hesitantly.

"Your Stranger is a protagonist. He is the one that the story revolves around. And the closer one is to the heart of a story, the less choice one has. Have you not noticed? He is paper-thin, apart from his desire, his *protagonisthood*—the thing that he will get at any cost, even if it kills him. If you wish for something to change, my dear slave, the Stranger is not where you must look. And I would not want you to change him anyway. He must do his duty and get this Princess off our hands so I can finally stop executing people and see Honan again."

He spits the word *Princess* like an epithet.

"Even if it harms her?" Liù asks.

She is not sure why she asks. The Princess used to be a malignant force, as incomprehensible as the noble men who beat her for no reason. Yet though the Princess kills her again and again, Liù is beginning to see the glimmer of something else.

"Between you and me," says the Chancellor, "she deserves it."

Var. VIII

The Princess is beginning to regret having Liù killed. Liù is a fool. Liù is weak. Yet she seems to understand how things work here, how the same story recurs again and again. Each time the opera begins, the Princess feels a greater unease, a premonition that things cannot continue this way forever.

"Daughter," says the Emperor, shuffling through the garden flanked by his masked guards. "The Persian Prince is dead."

"Yes, Noble Father. He stared into my eyes as the blade came down. What is it that you want?"

"He had family, you know. There was a slave who loved him."

"I do not care," says the Princess, swallowing hard, thinking of docile little Liù. "You swore to support me in this."

"And my word is sacred." The Emperor sighs and settles himself on a low bench next to her. "But, daughter, the soul of the empire is changing. It is time, I think, to speak with you again about Lo-u-Ling."

The Princess looks up sharply. "What about her?"

"You know that Lo-u-Ling's war is not the only violent incident in the empire's history, nor the only one to reach the imperial palace. In your own lifetime, even, there was the Bellflower Rebellion."

The Princess knows this, though she does not remember very much. She was twelve. She has a few blurry images, the feeling of hiding. Mostly her servants kept her safe.

The Emperor's voice cracks with anguish. "My scribes have checked the ancient books. And what you say about Lo-u-Ling is not correct. She was not killed. How could she be your ancestress if she was killed before she bore children? What the invaders did to her was unforgivable. But she outlived them. She would not have wished for children who see only what was done to her then and not the wise leader she became. Daughter, whatever it is that has taken up residence in you—"

"I will hear no more." The Princess stands abruptly. She does not understand why his words enrage her as they do, why she feels like fleeing and taking up arms both at once. "No more!"

Var. IX

"You see my dilemma," says the Princess to Liù. "I would sooner die than marry a man I do not trust. And"—*blood, pain, helplessness, fear*—"I do not trust any man."

"I do see," Liù murmurs.

"Raise your eyes." The Princess waves a capricious hand. "We should be friends. I am beginning to think there is something else besides the Stranger's name I must learn from you."

Liù looks up, questioning.

"You are in love," says the Princess plaintively. "What is it like?"

"It is like drinking water endlessly," says Liù, "and never slaking your thirst. It is like starving in front of a painting of a feast. It has a great deal to do with pain, Daughter of Heaven. I think you might like it."

Cadenza

Liù has never met the Princess. She has never entered the empire to which the Princess is heir. Liù is little more than a child, and her Prince—who does not yet know exile, is not yet a Stranger to anyone—only a few years older.

"And how have things been," he asks as she adds wood carefully to his hearth, "downstairs? Is the head housekeeper still giving you trouble?"

Liù blushes. "Not since we last spoke, my lord." The head housekeeper used to beat Liù over little things, often things she hadn't done. Liù suspects, though she is too shy to say it aloud, that the Prince himself put a stop to this. It is the sort of thing he would do.

"We are having an entertainment tomorrow," the Prince says, idly studying himself in the mirror. He is glorious, draped all over with blue and purple cloth. "Minstrels from the River Amur. That's where you come from, isn't it? I wonder if—oh, but you're finished there. I'm sorry. I shouldn't keep you."

"My lord's room has a great deal of silver in need of polishing," Liù says as she rises from the fireplace.

"Oh?" says the Prince.

He raises his eyebrows and smiles, and his smile tells Liù everything she will ever need to know.

He knows she is making excuses to stay—to keep hearing him speak. He knows that she loves him. Liù herself does not quite know it until she sees it, in that smile, reflected back at her.

And it doesn't matter. The Prince is kind, but no Prince can marry a slave. If he were selfish, he might string her along, use her for pleasure. But this Prince is a good Prince. Lovestruck slaves are nothing strange to him. He will be kind to her naturally, carelessly, as he is kind to everyone. He will take no undue liberties. Then, after being her friend for a time, he will go running off after a suitable Princess and forget her.

She sees all of this and can do nothing. His smile makes that clear. For him she will live her whole life and her life's end. The Prince will be the death of her; for the Prince's name is Love.

Var. X

"She loves me," says the Stranger. It is dark. The severed heads lining the palace's walls shake yes and no in the wind.

The Stranger's name is Love. He is as hungry and relentless as love ever was. And Princes, even exiled Princes, are not taught to starve quietly.

"Stop it," says Liù. "You are hurting her. She is terrified of you. Did you never hear her first aria, the terrible memories that haunt her? Did you never hear what she sings after you answer the riddles, how she begs the Emperor not to let you force yourself on her? How can you continue, how can you do this, when you claim to love her?"

"She loves me," says the Stranger.

For an instant Liù sees him as the Chancellor sees him. Paper-thin. A libretto stamped with someone else's words.

The libretto, after all, proves him right. At the end of the opera, when Liù is dead and rotting, he presses his case until the Princess gives in. That is what happens, in the opera's proper form, every night. That is the happy ending the audience cheers for.

The man Liù loves is kind, brave, gentle; but he cannot deviate from his role. Cannot even imagine it, no matter how little kindness the words possess. If the libretto says, *This is what Love is,* then kindness will bow and make way for it.

Liù stares into his eyes, and thinks, *He is more a slave than I.*

Intermezzo III

The Other Soprano, who puts on finery and becomes a Princess each night, is famous. The Conductor does not grab her in the wings. She is difficult to approach. Not screaming and glowering like some stage women, only remote. And so dazzling in her legions of fans and recording contracts that even the smallest unkindness—a rolled eye in the dressing room, a mispronunciation of the Soprano's name—feels like fate. Deserved. Unchangeable.

The Soprano waits in the wings for the Other Soprano, heart pounding. Perhaps the terror itself is what makes the Other Soprano pause by her, meeting her eyes, when the curtain call finally ends.

"This . . . thing," says the Soprano. "This thing we've been doing, where the opera changes. Have you felt it?"

The Other Soprano's face closes up. "The improvisation. Yes. So?"

The Soprano wonders if she will have infinite nights for this, if the Other Soprano will kill her again and again until she has the words to say it right.

"I wanted to ask you about it. About how it feels to you. Do you feel that, to you, on some level, the Princess becomes . . ."

"What?"

"Real."

The Soprano feels something frozen between them. An icy, closing vise. "That's ridiculous. It's only an opera."

"I only meant . . ."

"It means *nothing*. It can't mean anything. That can't happen, do you understand? It is *fiction*."

The Other Soprano hurries away as if pursued. The Soprano thinks about the Princess, about the very great fear straining under her skin. She stands very still, and thinks, *Then what am I?*

Var. XI

The truth comes to the Princess like a tiger, stalking just out of sight. She will remember all the warning signs later: The breathing that she heard but thought nothing of. The stripes she would not let herself see. And Liù, a constant reminder of the things in this world that are hidden, that no one will speak of.

When the truth pounces, she is alone in the garden, watching the fish in the pond. She stays there, weeping, unmoored from time. It is her father who approaches her at last, without a guard at his side or even a servant. Not the Emperor resplendent in his dragon robes: only her father, his frail bones rustling through the grass.

"Noble Father, I—" she chokes. "Lo-u-ling—"

He is weeping too. "I tried to tell you."

"It wasn't her in the garden. It wasn't my ancestress. It was the Bellflower Rebellion. It was me."

"I know, my daughter." He holds out his arms. She does not move toward him, and he lowers them again. "I know."

Var. XII

"So you see," says the Princess to Liù later, when the shock has worn off, "that is what all this is really about."

"Daughter of Heaven," says Liù, "I am so sorry."

"Sorry?" says the Princess. "Liù, I am a tyrant and a murderer. I do not want pity. I simply want to talk to someone who will not glare from the side of their eyes like a courtier. The Stranger was not the one I needed to kill, was he? The men who deserved that are already gone."

Liù has no plan for this, no idea what to say. "Daughter of Heaven," she stammers, "you would forever have my gratitude if you did not kill him."

The Princess smiles ruefully. "But what do I do instead? How do I solve the problem of him, and of the hundreds of other strangers who will come after? My noble father could not answer that question either. So here we sit. What do you think?"

Liù looks at the sitting room's cold marble floor. The jade sculptures at her side. The translucent silken screen that used to separate her and the Princess, long discarded.

She thinks of the opera's true ending. She thinks of the Stranger, paper-thin, the words he cannot stop saying. She thinks of the Princess's urge to kill, to defend herself at any cost, of where that urge might be productively channeled.

She thinks of what it means to be caught in a story.

"If it pleases the Daughter of Heaven," she says, "I have an idea."

Var. XIII

It does not take as much effort as Liù expected. She and the Princess already live in a world only half real. Time has already bent itself around them.

In the end it takes only herself and the Princess, back to back, hands clasped. Breathing deeply, while the Princess's best incense burns in the jade bowl beside them. Following with their minds a trail more felt than seen.

And then Liù is in another room. A dim study with a pianoforte and a wide shelf of books. A house in Italy—not stage Italy but something altogether different. A man sits in an armchair before her, old and sad, with a cane at his side. He startles as she enters, and stares.

"Doria?" he whispers, but Liù does not know that name.

This was what she realized, in the end. The Princess was full of fear and death for a reason. The Stranger—trapped in blind, destructive desire, stuck in his *protagonisthood*—must be the way he is for a reason too.

It is something Liù should have realized all along, talking to him on the dark street, seeing those words in her mind's eye stamped inflexibly on a libretto. The reason for the Stranger is the hand that wrote those words. The reason for the Stranger is the Composer.

She does not remember to speak. She can feel the strength of the Princess behind her, the half-sensed trail before her. This close to the Composer, she can feel the trails doubling and trebling, a thicket of connections. A thicket of reasons. The Composer had reasons for writing as he did, hundreds of reasons. Liù supposes everyone does, maybe. Reasons on reasons, back to the beginning of time.

She focuses in her mind on the Stranger. That face, that smile, which she knows better than anything. She feels her way down that thread to where it takes root in the Composer's heart.

She is already past the point where she can see the man, in his strange country. A torrent of other images flick through her mind in his place. Women dead, women dying, women abandoned. The Composer had loved women, and had not understood why each woman who loved him back suffered. Had not been able to imagine it any different, even as he grieved.

So he had clung to the idea of love, the idea of beauty in suffering. Writing nothing but women like Liù, good women, beautiful women, who died. Thinking all the while, *It will hurt, everything hurts, but if there is love, it will be all right. If there is love, surely everything must be all right. If she loves, if she loves me, surely everything else can be forgiven. Surely she loves me. She must love me.*

She loves me.

She loves me.

And there it is: the root of the Stranger, deep in the Composer's heart, a shimmering, fist-sized sphere. Somehow, in this unplace, Liù is able to wrap her fingers around it where it sits. She can take it, she suddenly knows. Tear out its roots.

Without it, without the art that keeps him company in his illness and melancholy, the Composer will die. His opera will never be finished. It will be passed on to anyone else who can hold it. To his fellow composers, who cobbled together an ending. To Liù, elsewhen, as she looks around herself for the first time and thinks, *There must be another way.*

Her hand trembles. She knows what it is to die. Even now, Liù does not wish it on anyone else. Not the nobles who beat her; not the executioner; not the Princess. Not even this man who is the architect of her suffering.

But it has been a long, long time, dying over and over. Even if it makes her as selfish as him, in the end: Liù aches to know what it is to survive.

So she squeezes her eyes shut, and pulls.

Var. XIV

Here the Composer lays down his pen.

The Stranger looks around him, as if suddenly awake. It is the same look Liù had that first time, looking at the stage and thinking, *There must be another way.*

"I am frightening her," he says slowly, in the voice of a child. "Aren't I? I am sorry." Liù cannot speak. She remembers the Composer, the other world; she is faint with the effort of finding her way. She looks at her hand in the moonlight, and there is nothing in it.

The Stranger stares up at the palace walls, out and around at the city which even now is in uproar as the Princess's guards force potential witnesses from their homes. It will not be long until he and Liù are caught. Speaking to each other at all, this way, is a risk. Many nights it has been the risk that got Liù killed.

"She will kill me," he says dreamily, looking up at the stars. "Won't she?"

"I do not know, my lord."

"It doesn't matter. I entered into this freely; she did not. She should decide." He reaches forward and takes Liù's hand, an intimacy he has never dared before. Her heart races in her throat. She almost forgets, in that moment, that all of this is for another woman, not her.

"If you see her before I do," he says, "please, give her this. Tell her she can do with me as she wills."

Where he touches her, something glows at her fingertips. A shimmering, fist-sized sphere: the same light she remembers from the other world. The Composer's life. The Prince's soul. The Stranger's name.

Var. XV

Liù hands the sphere to the Princess, and the Princess clutches it to her chest. Her eyes shine. "Do you understand what this means? He has given me his life. Not under duress, not in defeat, not in exchange for the chance to get *me*, but freely, asking nothing in return."

"I do," says Liù. She understands all too well. She has given herself that way, so many times.

What is the cure for fear? No clever riddle will ever solve it. No brave knight can ever fight it to the death. No use of power, however kind and gracious, will cure the fear of powerlessness.

How do you win against that fear? By giving the power back. By surrendering.

The Stranger belongs to the Princess now.

The Princess is no longer afraid.

Liù watches, mouth dry, as the Princess turns the sphere over and over in her hands. She wonders what will happen now. The Princess can do whatever she likes, Liù supposes. She can marry the Stranger. She can kill him. She can send him on his way, with Liù, for Liù to care for and pine for until the end of her days.

For a wavering moment, Liù is not sure if she wants that.

She can still feel the threads connecting her to the Stranger, the Stranger to the Princess, *Liù* to the Princess, all of them to that other world where the Composer lies dying, and to others besides.

Perhaps she will always feel them. Perhaps that is the natural result of magic like this.

The Princess feels them too. Liù can see it from the way she turns her head, examining the air where threads collect and connect.

"I know what I want to do," says the Princess.

"Yes?" says Liù, her heart in her throat.

"But—" says the Princess, and she pauses. "Liù, what do *you* want?"

No one has ever asked that before.

"I want to live," Liù blurts. "And—and I want the Stranger to live. And I—I—"

She cannot say it. It is one thing to admit she is in love. It is another to wish for an outcome. To admit she wants love back, from a Prince who cannot give it, who never could have and never will.

The Princess shrugs carelessly. "I cannot make him love you. Just as none of his efforts could make me love *him*. But now there may be another way. The Composer is dead, and that means we may do as we please. Do you see?"

Liù shakes her head, frightened. "Daughter of Heaven . . ."

"The Stranger can give his name," the Princess continues doggedly. "I saw what you did. Things can be uprooted and given. I must one day stop running from my duty. I must marry and raise the next Empress or Emperor. But I have no love. You have an abundance of it, and it has given you nothing but grief. I can be myself and Lo-u-Ling; I already know I can be divided in parts. Do you see?"

"You don't know what you are asking," says Liù, choking on the words.

The Princess lowers her voice. "But haven't you ever wanted all of this, a slave like you? This jade and gold, these silks, these perfumes. This power. The love of the man you have served all these years. You would have it, in a way. Part of you would. And I would give the rest of you something in return. Citizenship in the empire, and a safe place to live. Gainful employment, for real wages, if you want it. Whatever else you ask, within reason. In exchange for what you have already done for me, I cannot offer less."

Liù understands, but she cannot think. She does not know how to decide.

"Daughter of Heaven," Liù finally asks, "what do *you* want?"

What looks back at her, through the Princess's eyes, is vulnerable and small. Something that has been trapped here in the palace all its life, hated by courtiers, coveted by Princes, with a frail and distant father as its only ally. The soul, she thinks, of Lo-u-Ling; something cut from the Princess's consciousness for so long that perhaps they can never be one.

"I don't want to be here anymore," it says.

Liù takes a long breath. Then, slowly, nods.

The Princess holds out her hands. Liù wavers. Then she and the Princess step toward each other, and Liù sweeps the Princess up into a burst of brief and shining confusion.

Var. XVI

The Stranger's name is Love.

He rings the great gong in the palace yard thrice and shouts the Princess's name. She descends to him, picking up her skirts and rushing down the steps of the palace. The crowd stares.

"It's you," she says. "At last, it's you! Do you know how long I have waited, what worlds I have traveled, how many wicked suitors have tried to take me from you?"

"Heavenly beauty!" the Stranger sings, rushing to her. "But how can this be? How do you know me?"

"I loved you all along," says the Princess. "Don't you understand? I have loved you forever. Ever since you smiled at me."

The music is an unbearable, ecstatic swell. The whole imperial court comes swirling in around them. The people prostrate themselves.

At the far end of the courtyard, a woman who was once a slave hugs herself, feeling only an absence. She does not know if she should call herself Liù any longer. Perhaps the Conductor was right, and Liù had to die all along.

Lo-u-Ling, the frightened child, nestles in a corner of her mind. Stirs, at the sight of the Princess and Stranger's embrace, in a discomfort she can barely name.

It's all right, says Liù—if indeed she can call herself that. The slave woman knows how to soothe, how to care. She knows what it is to be small and afraid. She knows what it is to go on anyway, through death and pain and death again. She can teach that cour-age to Lo-u-Ling, in time.

She has lost her name. She has lost the foolish obsession that was her whole life. Yet she has gained something as well. She stands tall and looks passersby full in the face. She can stay here, secure, as the Princess promised; or she can ask for money to leave, to start again far from any Prince. She can make of her life what she will. She is free.

Coda: Repetiamo al fine

The house is full. The audience leaps to its feet. The Conductor scowls at the Soprano but says nothing.

Later, when the theater is emptied and she has put on her coat for the night, the Soprano takes one last walk across the rose-strewn stage. She feels, as always, that she has woken from a dream. There will be another performance in two days' time, and another, and another. The opera has no ending. Therefore it has every ending.

She turns, and there is the Other Soprano, waiting in the wings —though the Soprano had thought she went home already.

The Soprano meets her eyes. She waits, and does not turn away.

"It was real," says the Other Soprano, "after all. Wasn't it?"

"I think so," says the Soprano.

"Is this real?" says the Other Soprano. "Is everything real? Are we real right now? I don't understand."

The Soprano feels both living and dead, both real and unreal. Rose petals drift in bloodlike banks around her feet. She does not know what to say.

Instead she offers an arm. The Other Soprano hesitantly takes it. They walk out into the night together, into the cold pools of street lamps, into the world.

NANA KWAME ADJEI-BRENYAH

Through the Flash

FROM *Friday Black*

YOU ARE SAFE. You are protected. Continue contributing to the efforts by living happily, says the soft voice of the drone bird hovering only a few feet from my window, as it has been for the last forever. Since I'm the new me, I don't even think about killing anybody. Still, I touch the knife under my pillow.

Outside, a blue sky sits on top of everything, and I try to think about it like this: *Aren't we lucky to have our sky? Isn't it an eternal blue blessing?* Even though seeing it makes me feel crushed a little, because whoever's on the other side of time has no idea how tired we are of the same.

I get up and I brush my teeth. It's the little things. Then I look in the mirror and say, "You are supreme and infinite." I take my headscarf off and let my hair breathe. I spritz and moisturize and finger-comb. The little things. After I'm dressed, I snap on a gray fanny pack and put Mom's knife in it.

I jump out my window to a tree branch, then across to the Quan family's roof, and then onto Mrs. Nagel's roof. I slip in through her window, and her house smells like cinnamon and old people as usual and always. In her kitchen I boil the water for her tea. The kettle whistles. I make Mrs. Nagel's favorite: elderflower and honey. I put the mug on her bedside and watch her sleeping uncomfortably. Her nose is stuffy, so she wheezes like an old truck.

"Hey, Mrs. Nagel," I say as gently as I can.

"Hey." She squirms in the bed a little, then opens her eyes. She sees me, and I like how she isn't terrified. She almost smiles even. "Thanks, Ama. I appreciate it," she says. I pick a box of tissues off the floor and give them to her.

"No problem, Mrs. Nagel. Have a good one. Remember, your existence is supreme."

"Uh-huh," Mrs. Nagel says. Then she blows her nose. I smile at Mrs. Nagel before I slip out her window and leap back home the way I came.

Inside, I pass by my little brother's room. He's awake in bed. I can tell by the sound of his breathing. His sheets have trains all over them.

"Hey, Ike," I say. That's short for Ikenna.

"Ama, please," Ike asks in his whiny voice. He wants me to end his day. He wants me to kill him. He didn't used to be like this. He was six when the Flash hit, so his body can't do all the things he wishes it could. He still has his small peanut head and cheeks you want to pinch. But I don't pinch; he hates his cheek pinchies now. That's another thing I have to think about as I'm being my new self. I am forever fourteen, and I can do more than anyone. I am blessed. But Ike's blessed in his own way. "Ama, goddamn it. Just do it for me, please," he says.

"Why? It's a great day outside," I joke. I've made that joke more times than—well, I've made it a lot of times.

"Do you hate me?" Ike asks. "You must truly hate me to deny me this."

No matter how much he's crammed in his head, when I see him, I still see my kid brother. Ike's one of the ones who can't do it themselves; he's a softy.

"I love you," I say. Ike screams a bunch of bad words, but still I won't kill him, because even the old me never did that. Not him. He doesn't leave his room much anymore. I let him be and go to the kitchen.

"Hello, Daddy," I say in a singing voice that sometimes makes him smile. My father is in his old-man slippers and his pajama pants. He is fidgeting, swaying, like always. He can't be still hardly ever. He's getting ready to cook something. Am I nervous around him? Yes. But I try not to be. Now that I'm the new me, I try to be appreciative. Appreciative and definitely not afraid. If I get afraid, then I get angry. If I get too angry, I might go back to being the old me and be just like Carl on Kennedy, who is a monster. A war god. A breaker of men and women and children.

"Morning, ginger root," he says. Then he turns to me, and he's holding the knife he uses to cut meat.

"Daddy," I say. Then he slashes at me with the butcher knife. I have enough time to think some real thoughts as his arm moves to my neck. I could open my pack, grab Mom's knife before Dad's blade reaches me. But I don't. Instead I think, *When will this ever stop?* He's quicker than most people. But I'm faster than everyone. Way faster. Much more lethal when I want to be. The old me would make him suffer greatly. Instead I try to say *Daddy* again but can't —not with my gashed-up neck and all—so I bleed out watching him watch me die. Then I die.

I'm in a gym, still in my jersey. Sweaty and upset. I feel a strong hand on my head. My face is crammed into her stomach. I can smell her along with the pinewood and dust of the Ramapo Middle School gym. I can feel her. My mother rubs my neck. She says, "It's okay." Then pushes me off to the locker room, where my team is waiting.

You are safe. You are protected. Continue contributing to the efforts by living happily. I wake up. I look around and try to decide if what I think just happened really did happen. I decide it did. I had a dream. I saw my mother in a dream. It's something new. New things never happen anymore. There are no dreams except the ones you had the morning of the Flash. I haven't had a dream in forever. And still, I saw my mother. She was really there with me. I want to see her again. I want to feel her again. I pull out my knife. Her knife. I stare at the blade, and I tell myself it's only this one time. It's only this one time and then never again. Then I drag the knife through my arm. I bleed and bleed. Then I go.

No dream. No mom. Regular.
   You are safe. You are protected. Continue contributing to the efforts by living happily.
   I wake up in the usual. Blue sky, in bed, knowing everything will be the same. But still, after my father killed me, I saw something I've never seen before. I dreamed a dream. That never happens. It wasn't there the next time, but still. I saw her. I jump out of bed.
   "Ike!" I say, running up to his room.
   "What?" he groans. "Are you going to help me or not?"
   "I'm not going to kill you," I say. "But something happened."

He knows me as well as anybody. Everybody knows everyone very well. We've all been together in the Loop longer than any group of people ever. But Ike knows me best. He gets out of bed and sits cross-legged on the floor. That's how he sits when he's thinking for real. That's how he sits when he cares.

"What happened?" he asks. And now he sounds like the old Ike.

"I had a dream," I say.

"So?"

"I mean I dreamed through the Flash. I didn't wake up, then take a nap and dream. I saw it before I came back. That's never happened before."

"Are you sure?" he asks. He grabs a little flip notepad with a purple pig on the cover and a crayon. "What did you see?" he says, and starts scribbling. Nothing he writes will last through the Flash —everything goes back to how it was the day the bomb dropped —but writing in it helps him think.

"Well," I say. "I saw Mom."

Ike gets up, takes a breath, and then sits back down. "Ama, tell me what you saw, exactly."

"I was with Mom. At Ramapo. I think it was just after the first game of the year. We'd lost, I guess. Even though in real life I think we won. All this was before; you probably can't remember. But she hugged me, and it made me feel better."

"I do remember," Ike says, like I hurt his feelings.

"Is this an anomaly?" I ask, finally.

Ike's crayon dances words down. "Perhaps," he says. He bites his lip. I wish I could share the dream better for him. I know he'd give anything to see Mom that way.

"Ama," my father calls. And my hands move toward where my fanny pack would be, but I'm still in my sleep shorts. "Sweetie?" he says. He's in my room. He knows how good I am at hiding. How I might be anywhere. I don't want to die yet. I'll be the old me if I have to be.

"What do you wanna do?" I ask Ike while creeping toward the door and out of the room.

"We'll definitely do something." And that's already the best, because he hasn't wanted to do anything in a long time. "Let me think a little."

"Okay, I'm going to see Daddy," I say to warn him it might get bad.

"It's unlikely he'll be aggressive," Ike says without looking up from his notebook. "He'll want to apologize to you, I think."

"Daddy," I say. He's standing in his shorts and a T-shirt and his flip-flops. He has a stack of pancakes and juice on a tray in his hands. He always makes pancakes, which are my favorite, or crepes or omelets the cycle after he kills me. No matter how used you are to getting a knife whipped through your neck or punched in the eye or in the chest over and over again, it hurts. It's much better to end a cycle with the Flash, which doesn't hurt at all. Plus, you never know for sure that the Flash is coming even though it always, always does. And wouldn't that be a shame if your own father already had killed you the day the Loop broke and you actually would have had a tomorrow?

That's how the Loop affects him. He's basically a sad monster half the time. The other times he's my daddy. I try to love him either way. After he kills me, when the cycle restarts, he feels guilty. You'd think he'd eventually feel so guilty that he'd stop doing it. One day he'll be better, I hope. I know. The new me lets him do it most of the time. The old me made it a mission to end him way, way before the Horn came. But I'm the new me. And I'm trying to make him better. He wasn't always like this. He only kills me because I remind him of Mommy. Sometimes he says her name while he does it. "Glory, Glory, Glory!" That's the sound of him killing me most times. Mom killed herself with her knife. My knife now. If she'd waited two months, she would have been with us forever. There aren't enough words for forever.

When he's standing there holding pancakes and trying to be better, I love him. It's not even that hard. "Thanks, Daddy," I say as I walk toward the bed and Mom's knife. I don't tell him about the dream because I don't know how it will make him act. If he's having a good day, I like to leave it alone. He puts the tray on my bed.

"How are you feeling?" he asks. He knows I can cut him to pieces.

"I feel infinite and excited and ready to do anything and everything," I say. I give him a hug.

"Great. I'm thinking maybe we watch the day end. Together. You know, on the wall."

"Def," I say. We don't talk about him cutting my neck open. He never apologizes with words, but he's always trying his best.

"Okay, Mama Ama," he says. Then he touches the tray again. To tease me, he genuflects before he leaves the room and walks back downstairs. When he's down there, he sits on the kitchen chair with the wobbly leg, and he starts to cry. I'm really good at telling where people are. I can almost see them just by paying attention to the sounds of a house. My senses are a blessing.

I take my tray of pancakes back to Ike's room. He's dressed in sneakers that light up when he steps and a blue T-shirt with a cloud that has a smiling face.

"I think this might be a legitimate anomaly, Ama," Ike says. "I want you to be sure, though; was it a dream sustained before you restarted the Loop, not something you thought of when you woke up?"

I look at Ike all dressed up. "Yes!" I say. I'm almost sure.

It didn't happen all at once. It was forever ago. I realized Ike was speaking like an adult. That was the first thing I noticed. That was the first thing that helped me put the days together. That's when I started keeping through the Flash. It's like realizing you're in a dream except no matter what you do you can't wake up. Daddy didn't start remembering through the Flash until much later. By the time I started to keep through the Flash, Ike was already smarter than everybody. That was the first anomaly, asymmetrical retention through Loop expiration, that he explained to all of us. Which meant, for reasons we still don't know, we each came to realize we were replaying the same thing over and over, and the realizing happened at different times for everyone. It was a pretty alarming thing. To see you're trapped in infinity and know that no one can explain exactly how or why.

We tried running, like maybe if we ran far enough we could escape.

There is no escape.

So, to ease the transition, we'd throw a party each time somebody kept through. Those were good times on the grid, the space we live in as designated by war-effort planning. The last one to keep through the Flash on Grid SV-2 was Mr. Tuia. We had a big party the day he came through. There was barbecue and music, and Ike danced, and the Poples danced, I danced, and Mrs. Nagel waved her arms from a lawn chair, which was like dancing for her, and my father laughed and laughed. Mr. Tuia mostly cried. It's very hard at first for some people. But then if you figure that you are infinite, you are supreme and therefore the master of all things, and it's silly to be sad about things like how much your hip is always going to hurt or how you're so old that the flu means life in a bed or how gone forever your mother is.

The second anomaly Ike and Robert, who was a marine biologist before the Flash, explained to us was how, individually, some of us were "developing and accruing attributes." Accumulating, they'd said. Some people were accumulating differently. Ike's brain was storing facts and stuff better than anybody's. Lopez on Hark Street was all right on the clarinet before, but now we're pretty sure he's the greatest musician to have ever lived. I got strong, fast, precise. I became the Knife Queen. We have a pretty interesting grid.

I don't know much about the other grids in our state block, because way before the Flash came, the soldier-police—the state-sponsored war-coordination authorities—took away everyone's cars. Their slogan—"For us to serve and protect, you must conserve and respect"—is emblazoned on posters in the school, on the windows of some people's homes. The Poples pretended they were proud when their son was shipped for service. The poster in their window shows the soldier-police slogan in big letters stamped below men with puffed-out chests proudly holding the flag and guns, their faces hidden by the black visors of their helmets. Back before the Flash ever came, a lot of people actually loved the SPs. They thought they were keeping us safe. People believe lies, believe anything when they are afraid. That's another thing. Aren't we lucky that before the Flash all the soldier-police were deployed elsewhere?

Still, even if you bike as hard as you can in any direction, only stopping to drink water, even if you pee and drink at the same time, you can only get so far before the Flash takes you. Even if you train for years and years. I've tried, and if anybody should have been able to do it, it's me. I use my body better than anyone. I can jump Olympic. I can break grown men with my bare hands. When I have a knife, I'm basically the queen of the world. Or the old me was. Now I let everyone be their own royalty.

"I want to discuss this with Robert," Ike says.

Then the Horn comes. Three hundred and sixty-seven drone birds all over the area screaming together. It's like a bright light for your ears. It's the right sound for what it is. It means defenses have been breached and the world is gonna end today. It lasts for two minutes. One hundred and twenty seconds. I close my eyes and wait. Ike does the same. Then it stops. The Horn is the exit point for many. It comes, and they just can't take the sonic bleed. So they take whatever they have handy and jam it into their neck. But if you close your eyes and breathe, if you expect it and welcome it even, it's still terrible, but the kind of terrible you can take.

The quiet after the Horn is sweet and lush. It's something you don't want to let go of. But we have work to do. "Okay," I say after we appreciate a few moments of silence. "Let's go see Robert."

"I want to be inside before the rain," Ike says.

"Maybe we'll do that; maybe we won't. We're supreme and infinite," I say, reminding him that rain is a small thing for infinite beings.

"Yes, so I've heard, Ama. I'd still like to be inside before the rain," he says.

"I'll go grab the stuff."

"I'll be waiting." Ike pokes a fork into my pancakes.

I get ready in my room, then I jog downstairs and head outside. Two houses down I see Xander strangling his dog on their green lawn. It weeps and yelps, and its tail flaps around like a helicopter blade until it stops.

"Hello, Xander," I say with a big wave. Before, he had been a friend of my father's, and like my father, he was too old to fight. There aren't any men left from age twenty to forty-five.

"Hi there, Ama."

"What did poor Andy do today?"

"What do you mean?" Xander says, then he goes back in his house.

I knock once on the Poples' door. The big window where they keep their soldier-police poster gets smashed every morning, so the poster is facedown, hanging in the shrubs, dressed and stabbed with glass. It's the first thing the Poples do most days. Smash that window that reminds them of how gone their son is. When the door doesn't open fast enough, I kick it open. Mr. Pople is naked on his couch, drinking a glass of something. His skin is flappy and foldy.

"Hey, Mr. Pople."

"Ama Knife Queen Adusei," he says slowly, smiling and raising his glass and bowing his head.

"Just Ama," I say. Not in a way that's threatening, but just to remind him I don't make people say that anymore and haven't for a while.

"Ama," he says very slowly. He looks into his cup, then drinks from it. His hands head down toward his waist.

"See ya, Mr. Pople," I say as I run up the stairs. I go to his bedroom and grab the small piercer gun from a drawer. It's the first gun I ever shot. It's a small black thing with a smooth kick. It makes almost no sound when you pull the trigger. It kills in whispers, which I like. Or used to like. There's an extra clip in the same drawer. I grab both.

"Hello, Ama," says Mrs. Pople, who's still in bed, a cover up over her head.

"Hi, Mrs. Pople, gotta go," I say.

"Tell your brother to come see me soon."

"He's a little caught up today," I say, and I don't mention that it's been a very long time since she and Ike were life partners.

"I see. He prefers Jen. Still?" Jen was a teacher at the school. But I don't know if Ike prefers anyone right now.

"You'd have to ask him, Mrs. Pople. But maybe your husband is interested? Or maybe Xander is. I think I heard him say he thought you were interesting and physically very attractive."

"You're a nice girl, Ama," Mrs. Pople says.

"We're all supreme and infinite. We might as well act like it," I say as I zip my fanny pack closed. I really am settling well into becoming a better person, I think. I've really come a long way from what I was, and I was once a true terror. The kind that probably never existed ever before. But now here I am, being called *nice*.

Kennedy Street is down on the other side of the grid, so it takes a little while on the bike. Days are short. Soon it will rain, and Ike wants to be inside before the rain. "Bye, Mr. Pople," I say without looking at him doing whatever he's doing.

"Goodbye, my liege," he says.

My bike is on the side of our house. I run back in to tell Ike I'm ready, then wait for him outside. I do my kicks and my punches and some tumbles to get loose. I jump some jacks. I give the maple in our yard two good punches and a roundhouse kick to the trunk, and it crashes down. The sound of splitting wood excites me, I admit. It's different from the sound of snapping bones, but it reminds me of that kind of breaking. Then my father comes outside and looks at me. He has a glass of water in his hands.

"Thirsty?" he asks.

"Yeah, a little bit," I say. He extends his arm to me, and I walk toward him. I take the glass. It's cold, nice.

"Where are you going?" he asks like he might have before the Flash. Like he wants to tag along.

"Just riding around on the bike," I say. His eyes narrow a little, then he takes a deep breath and relaxes.

"Okay," he says. He turns around, and Ike slides past him outside.

"You too, Ike? You're out of bed? You're going outside?"

"Yes, I'm looking forward to some fresh air," Ike says.

"That's spectacular," my father says. It's been a long time since Ike has been outside. "You riding with Ama?" my father asks. He sounds so excited that it's almost like he's the father I had when I had a mother — that person I only sort of remember. The one who would hold me by my feet and tickle me until I couldn't breathe. I remember that fun, breathless struggle. I also remember, always, that he didn't treat my mother well. He used to yell and scream. I used to hide in my room with Ike, and to distract him we'd play hide and seek. Back before Ike was a genius. Before I was a murderer. That I remember.

"See ya, Daddy," I say, and give him a hug. I keep my eyes open all through it.

"Have fun, ginger root," he says as he touches my hair. And I close my eyes for a half second to feel the simple good of his hands on my head. Then I'm on the bike, and Ike is sitting in front on the handlebars, and we're riding in the wind like we're unstoppable beings who truly have all anyone could ever hope for.

Our street is Harper, and then we ride down Flint to get onto Conduit AB-14, which we stay on for a while. Conduit AB-14 is framed by trees full of drone birds and dirt. It's four lanes of empty road. Naked road for miles and miles, and if it didn't mean the end of the world, all that empty might be beautiful, maybe.

On the way we see a group of men and women beating down some other man. When I ride by, they stop to look at me. I smile and wave. When they see me, their eyes go wide, then the group of them run off in the opposite direction. "I'm not gonna hurt you," I call out. They don't believe me. They don't stop running. The one who was getting beat on gets up. His face is mashed pretty good. "You're still magnificent and supreme. Nothing can change that," I tell him. He picks up a rock. Turns from me, unbuckles his pants, and shows me his butt cheeks. Then, when his pants are back on, he goes running after the group.

"Meatheads," Ike says, trying to keep me from feeling bad.

"Yeah," I say.

It takes us almost an hour to get there. I stop two streets before Kennedy to catch my breath, and we walk the rest of the way. Carl's cluster looks pretty much like ours, but it's quieter. People mostly stay inside here because of Carl.

"I think the furthering of variance might truly suggest the dissolving of consistency we've always expected," says Ike.

"Hope so," I say. And we walk more.

When we finally do get to Kennedy, the heads of two women, Patricia Samuel and Lesly Arcor, are stuck onto the street sign. Carl's set the two heads up to look like they're kissing. Patricia Samuel is Carl's mother.

"I guess Carl is still Carl," Ike says. Looking around, curious, kind of scared, almost like how I imagine a real little kid might look. There are no more real little kids. Even the babies know they're stuck. Most of them don't cry at all. Some of them never stop crying ever.

It always looks like World War VI over on Kennedy because of Carl. Two houses are on fire. There are dark spots that show where Carl's victims bled out on the streets. He's a real terror. Still. It's easy to judge him because, I mean, he does the absolute worst stuff to people. I once saw him use his body and various household objects to physically violate eight people, who were all tied up at once. He was fourteen when the Flash came, like me.

It's super-easy to think he is the Devil himself because of all the things he does and because sometimes he screams, "In this hell, the Devil, the Lord, and everything in between is named Carl," but I've been there. Being strong can make you like that. Carl is my protégé. He'll never admit it, but it's true. He's the protégé of Knife Queen Ama. The Ama who started with one knife and ended with three blades and two guns, who could kill all 116 people on my cluster in one hour and twenty-two minutes. I'd take a shower and change halfway through because my clothes got so heavy. Every inch of my black skin painted the maroon of life. The old Ama would murder everyone because when everyone was gone, she got to feel like she was the only one in the world and there was no one who might ever do her wrong again. Sometimes she'd just sit in the grass and feel supreme and infinite. She'd try to stare at a single blade of grass, or dance in the empty streets, or sing at the top of her lungs, until the Flash came. Sometimes she'd cry and cry as she washed the blood from her hair and eyes. Sometimes she wouldn't wash it off at all.

Imagine the worst thing anyone has ever done. I promise, I've done it to everyone. More than once.

When I realized I was faster and stronger, at first I didn't know what to do. I thought that maybe I was supposed to be on top now. I thought I was getting rewarded. And so I did what I wanted. Before the Flash, Carl was not nice to me. He liked to call me "nappy-headed bitch," or "dumb-ass cunt." He liked to make me cry back when we still had school. Then, when my mother left us, when I saw him, he said, "Guess your mother didn't want to be alive, knowing she made you." That, well, I know he regrets saying that. Because after the Flash, once I realized what I could do, I hunted him. He was the first person I ever killed. He was the first person I'd kill every day. The hurt I've pulled out of that boy could fill the universe twice over.

I'd rush over to his house and find different ways to ruin him. There is nothing—nothing—I haven't done to Carl Samuel. I know well-done Carl from medium-rare Carl. I made sure his mother knew the difference too. Even made her choose a favorite. It was a good day for me when she admitted her preference.

"Tell me, Patricia, which do you prefer?" I laughed. She was tied to the posts on the side of the stairs. I grabbed her cheeks. Her son's blood was crusting beneath my fingernails. I pulled her face down to the two strips of meat I'd cooked just a few minutes before. I fried the boy's arm pieces in olive oil. I even added salt, pepper, and adobo. Carl was writhing and crying behind me. His arm severed and the wound cauterized. I didn't even have to tie him up.

"Hey, baby. You are supreme and—" Mrs. Samuel started, and then I snapped one of her fingers. She screamed. By then I was immune to the sound of humans screaming. Or the thing I think others felt when they heard someone hurt, I felt the exact opposite. It was music for me: the way people scream when they're just afraid versus when they *know* their life is going to end. The unrelenting throaty sobs a man makes when you dangle his life in front of him, the shouts a child makes as you remove their arm. The sharp harshness that comes from a mother who can't save her son and can't stop trying. But that day Patricia Samuel swallowed up her scream and stared past me to her son. "You are infinite; this is nothing. I love you, Carl. You are perfect. You are supreme. You are infinite. We are forever."

"Very sweet. Now tell me, Mrs. Samuel." I smiled and made my voice soft. "Do you prefer the well-done or the medium?" Patricia Samuel wept as I turned my back to her.

"Please, Queen Ama, I beg you, please spare him today."

"Knife Queen Ama," I corrected. "If you tell me which you prefer, I may find some mercy for you." I took the knife out of my fanny pack.

"Please, Knife Queen." She wept, just as desperate as a person can be.

I shook my head. "Carl, your mother did this to you," and then I pressed my knee on his neck. It's not that hard to remove someone's eye.

Carl's screams: yippy and small, and then they grow. They're wordy and pathetic. "Ah! Hey! Okay! Okay!" like I was giving him a wedgie. Then they grow and pull and stretch. "Nooooo, nooooooo!"

"I love you, baby; it's okay," Mrs. Samuel said.

"Yeah, Carl, it's okay," I said, stabbing deeper, shucking the blade into the boy's skull. Laughing at how easy it was.

Carl was silent. He wasn't dead. His body shook.

"Please, Knife Queen!" She screamed for her son.

"Which do you prefer?"

"Ama, please!"

"Medium or well-done?"

So much misery in that room.

"Neither!"

"You have to pick," I said, looking up at her, smiling with her boy and so much of his blood in my hands.

"I—"

"In a second there'll be a very rare option on that plate," I said.

"Baby, I promi—"

"You *have* to pick," I repeated. It was like holding down a fresh-caught fish.

"Mom!" Carl screamed.

"Well-done," she finally said.

I stopped. "Take another bite to make sure." She followed my command immediately. Bending down, almost breaking her own arm to eat the meat with her mouth as her hands were tied to the posts behind her.

"Well-done, Knife Queen Ama."

"Good to know," I said. "That's how you'll have your Carl next cycle."

Then I got up and left.

I forced Carl and Patricia to live similar nightmares hundreds of times. What's surprising is how it never got easier for them. Carl was always terrified; his mother was always desperate, destroyed, and ready to be destroyed for him.

I hunted Carl for so long that even though I still hated him I got bored. I started hurting other people. At first I only bullied the bullies. The people who tried to hurt. And then I started hurting everybody. The way I felt about Carl sort of leached out. I was a real terror. People accumulate differently. When Carl's body started accumulating like mine, when he got as strong as I was, as fast as me, as good with sharp things, then he became a real genuine terror too.

There's dark red streaked everywhere on Kennedy. It's like walking into an old room you haven't lived in for a long time.

"Maybe let's get back on the bike," I say.

"Wise," Ike says, and then, as he's climbing up onto the handlebars, there's a bang. I look down and I don't have a knee anymore. It's just a shattered bloody thing. I eat back the screams I feel because I'm not the kind of person who screams anymore.

"Dammit!" Ike says. "We have to go."

"Sheesh," I say. "Okay, we're okay. We are—"

"Ama, I know, we have to go!"

Then Carl screams from above us. "How dare you! *Sliht baree ki lopper TRENT.*"

When I realized that Carl was also accumulating in his body, that he was becoming like me and maybe had been like me the whole time but wasn't smart enough to realize it, I let him be my friend. Here in the forever Loop anything can happen. You can make a

friend of the Devil. You can pretend everything was a dream. Carl
was my only friend for a while. We did what we wanted to other
people. We hurt them together. We even invented our own language: Carama. There are a lot of bad words in Carama. It's a language for war gods, so it's pretty aggressive. We've sat on rooftops
and watched without fear as entire communities joined together
to try to bring us down. "*Sliht baree ki lopper trent,*" he screams again.
It means something like "Prepare for a violent death, you lowly
creature."

"Just checking in," I say. "We're leaving."

"Ama!" Ike screams. I can see he's afraid, and he should be. But
I haven't seen Carl in such a long time, and there's a chance that
even he is different now.

"Checking out, actually," Carl says. And I hear him laugh at
what he thinks is clever. He flips down from the roof of a house to
the street. He's holding his piercer rifle. That's one thing. When
he starts his day, Carl has some pretty serious stuff ready in his
house. His father, before he died, was some kind of Aqua Nazi.
Even before the Water Wars started, he was preparing against
Black people, Middle Eastern people, Christians, and Jews because
he thought they were going to steal from the water reservoirs or
something. He was a pretty mean guy, I guess. Carl used to come
to school black-eyed and bruised. Kids used to laugh at how crazy
his pops was. He wasn't a happy boy. He's still not a happy boy.
He wears a T-shirt on his head with the neck hole slanted to cover
his left eye, and the shirt's arms are tied back in a knot behind his
head. He uses an elastic band he cuts from a pair of underwear
like a headband over the shirt to keep it in place even better. It's
the first thing he does every day. His eye, his eye. Some pain lasts
through a hundred deaths.

The hot rain starts falling. Blue sky, Horn, hot rain, Flash. Those
are the totems. Those are the things that come no matter what you
say, think, pray, do, or die. The hot rain feels like a warm shower.
Ike says the rain is a thermonuclear by-product of all the bombing
that was going on during the time the Flash first hit. He says that
even if the Flash didn't come the rain would give us all cancer. But
I like it. Every day it comes and it's warm and it reminds you like,
hey, wasn't that pretty good when you were dry earlier?

"*Kia Udon Rosher, ki twlever plumme sun,*" I scream, which means, like, "Oh great destroyer, you are supreme." The feeling in my mangled leg is disappearing, and the world starts flickering out.

Carl laughs. He wears a purple bathrobe that belonged to his father like the gun he raises.

"You're a stupid cunt," Carl says in plain old language. I feel my old self in my fingers as I reach for my pack. He skips toward me as my knee bleeds and bleeds. It hurts very badly. I've felt much worse, but it's so hard to remember anything other than what's now when you're hurt now.

After Carl and I broke our war-god pact and our friendship, we became sworn enemies. It happened because Carl didn't like how I acted like I was stronger than he was. Also, I think, because he was bored. One day he caught me off-guard and knocked me out with a shovel. When I woke up, I was chained to a tree and I didn't have any fingers on my left hand. I was, like, "Sheesh." That was the beginning of a very, very long day. It had been lifetimes since anyone had been able to hurt me like that, and I realized how bad I had been, and for how long, and how I wasn't going to do anything like that ever again.

But now, with my knee exploded, I'm thinking about how I want to make Carl sip broth made from his own bones. I point the gun at my brother. Even after all this forever, it's something I do not like to do. Even if it's to save him from Carl, who will do things so, so much worse. Even the old me didn't kill Ike. Which is probably why he had such a hard time for a while. It was lonely for him: a boy in a dead town and his sister the bringer of all pain.

"No you don't!" Carl says, and I try to pull the trigger. There's a bang and it's not from my hands and then the world disappears and I leave my brother in the hands of the worst person on the planet.

You are safe. You are protected. Continue contributing to the efforts by living happily.

I wake up. I grab Mom's knife and hold it in my hands.

Good torture feels like it will never end. You never forget it. I wonder what happened to Ike as I brush my teeth and shower and stuff my knife into my fanny pack. Carl is great at torture. Carl knows what he's doing because Carl learned from me, and I might be the best ever at that stuff. I imagine what Carl did to Ike, and I know he's been through the kind of pain that will never leave him.

I go to Mrs. Nagel's place. She's just so fragile and weak. Still. Always. Her breathing sounds like struggle, and even though she's sleeping, there are lines around her eyes like she's concentrating hard on something. I open my fanny pack and take out the knife. I put the blade against Mrs. Nagel's neck. The metal reflects a sliver of light against her skin as her throat grows and shrinks, carrying air in and out of her body badly. It'd be so easy even if she weren't so sick. She was the easiest out of everyone. She only woke up when the old me wanted her to. When I wanted her to know what was happening to her, which was a lot of the time. I take my knife back, tuck it into my pack, and go downstairs.

I squeeze lemon into elderflower tea. When I climb back up the stairs, Mrs. Nagel is awake, and she looks at me with eyes that are tired and warm. I put the hot mug on her nightstand.

"Ama," she says, and she scoots up in her bed. She tries to take a deep breath but can't. She smiles and motions for the box of tissues that is always on the floor. Such a big difference it would make if it was just on her nightstand, if she could just have that one thing be easy and simple. Instead that little thing, it's magnified by a million, and it makes you just want to cut your own head off that she can't just have that one thing be right for once.

"Hey, Mrs. Nagel," I say.

"What's wrong?" she says. It chills me to hear her ask. Even though it's been a long time, not a lot of people say things like that to me. Most people are afraid of me. A lot of them hate me and they should.

I climb up on the bed behind Mrs. Nagel so she can lean back into me and I can massage her temples to help with the headaches. I say, "I feel like maybe I liked the old me better. The old Ama. It was easier. And maybe the new Ama isn't doing anything."

Mrs. Nagel blows her nose. "New Ama?"

"Yeah, you know. Me now," I say. "Like how I'm not killing everybody or torturing anyone or whatever."

"And that was the old Ama who did that?"

"Yeah."

"And what's the difference between the two?"

"The old me did everything one way. And only thought about one person. Now I try to help everybody instead of killing them."

"I see, but what changed?"

"I used to be afraid," I say. I watch her breathe and listen to see if her heart is beating faster, if she is afraid. She is not. "I know I can't take it back. I know I'm the worst person who ever lived. I know that. I'm not afraid anymore. I'm only scared of me."

"I see, and that means you've been two people?"

"I'm better now. And I'm sorry. But sometimes something in me—like right now, it'd be so easy." I continue to rub softly, but it's true. I can't stop imagining how easy it would be to crush Mrs. Nagel's neck. Like crumpling a piece of paper. "I'm sorry; I didn't mean that," I say. "I want everyone to feel happy and supreme and infinite. That's the new me."

"Hmm," Mrs. Nagel says.

"How can you not see the difference?" I say, trying to keep my voice down. "I'm so much better now. I am."

"I think you've done a fine job. People come visit me so often since you changed. And it's true that in the past you were a terrible witch."

"Exactly."

"But I think there's only one Ama. And I think I'm talking to her."

"I'm sorry. For all of it," I say.

"You should be." Mrs. Nagel points to the bathroom, which means she wants me to give her a towel with warm water for her head. I do it. Then we're quiet for a long time. I sit with her through the Horn. Then she falls back asleep. I sit with her for a while more. When I jump back home, the sky is already gray and the hot rain is already falling. Also, a bike I know belongs to Carl is set down on the grass. All the bikes on Kennedy belong to Carl. I pull my knife out. I climb up and slide inside my bedroom window and creep downstairs. Carl is sitting at the table. My father is making pancakes, swaying at the stove. And Ike is at the table too, with his legs crossed in his chair and his back to me.

"There she is," my father says. I'm thinking I have the angle: I can leap across the kitchen table and get to Carl.

"Why is he here!" I say. "Ikenna, I'm sorry, I tried."

"Don't worry, I was fine," Ike says.

"You got to the gun? You got out?" I ask.

"No, I told Carl I had some info for Robert and he let me go see him."

"*Udon Rosher Carl jilo plam*," Carl says. It means "Carl, the great destroyer, spared the weakling." He is in his robe with the shirt over his head. His one exposed eye stares at me and only me.

"Oh," I say.

"It's been so long. I asked Carl if he wants to watch the Flash with us. Remember when we used to do that? Remember, we would watch on the wall?" my father asks.

"Why are you here now?" I ask. I've gotten close enough that I know I have a good shot at him.

"I'm here to kill you and make your family watch," Carl says. I can see his hunting piercer is at his feet. My father turns and stares at Carl.

"Carl," my father says. "You used to be an okay kid. If I could, you know what I would do to you?"

"Yes, sir," Carl says.

"Okay," my father says. It's true. With me and Carl, it's better not to try to stop us when we want to do something. Everyone knows that by now. I smile because my father defended me and has been killing me less and less lately.

"What did Robert say?" I ask while I still can.

"Whatever happened with you," Ike says. "Whatever happened —you're the first it's happened to, so we'll see. Maybe it's a domino in an eventual collapse." We're all pretty quiet. "Nothing new, really. But we think we can say for sure that this isn't going to last forever. Unless it does."

"Okay," I say. And I leap. I lunge with my knife, and nobody else in the history of the world would even flinch, but Carl is Carl, so he grabs the table and flips it up like a shield. I use my elbow to blow through it pretty easily. The table is in pieces, and Ike runs back. My father stops cooking and swings a hot, pancakey pan at Carl. Carl ducks it, and as he does, I swing my knife at his neck. He dodges two good slashes, then kicks me hard in the ribs. I crash back into the dishwasher. Rib broken for sure. I get up and focus. I smile because I, Ama Grace Knife Queen Adusei, am a fighter, the greatest ever. Lately I don't get to fight much. Or now I fight differently. But these fights, with fists and knives, I have more practice in. I jump forward again. Carl grabs my wrist and twists so I drop my knife.

"You are supreme and infinite, Carl, and I am very sorry for all that I have done," I say as I knee him in the ribs, and before even bringing my leg back down, I'm in a backflip and kicking into his chin. He stumbles back.

"BITCH!" Carl screams, and makes to grab the gun out of the rubble that's forming out of the kitchen. I kick him in the gut and throw him out toward the living room.

"Sorry, *Udon Rosher,*" I say while charging. He punches me in the mouth, and I see black, then the world comes back to me. "I meant no disrespect. I know you're strong. I just want you to know I am sorry for the things I did to you."

"Fuck you," Carl says, and he's coming at me with his flurry of heavy punches. He misses with a big right, and his fist goes through the wall. As he tries to pull his arm out, I get behind him and punch down on his neck in a way I know will make him crumble. Then I rip off the shirt on his head, and it's like I hit the master switch. "*Hellio YUPRA! Ki Udon Rosher! TRENT!*" Carl screams as he holds his eye. Weeping on his knees. "Okay! Okay! *Hellio yupra.*" Even when I'm not touching him, he screams and claws at his own eye. He becomes a little bit of the old Carl. I hit him another time, hard at the base of his neck, to keep him from moving. His paralyzed body does nothing, and his face keeps doing so much.

"*Udon Rosher, ki love,* okay," I say.

"End it!" Carl screams, keeping one eye open. Outside, the hot rain has stopped. I drag Carl upstairs and make sure he's comfortable in my bed. He screams and screams in Carama, and I understand him very well. He spits and cries. I sit with him. "I know you're going to get through all this," I say. When his voice is coarse and he can't scream anymore, I leave him.

My father and brother are in Ike's room. Ike is writing something. My father is coloring in a coloring book. "Ama!" my father says.

"Ama," Ike says.

"We're good," I say. My rib is broken, and I'm kinda bleeding out of my ear. "Still want to go watch?" I ask. These are my guys. I'm blessed knowing I can protect them.

Outside, the hot rain makes the air smell like burning rubber, but you can still smell the fresh wet earth underneath so it's not all bad. Once we were all keeping things through the Flash, it became a tradition for everyone on our street to watch it together, to disappear all at once. Then we stopped doing that.

We press ourselves to the side of our house facing west. I'm dizzy and happy. Breathing hurts, but still I feel as infinite as ever. Still supreme. We get on the wall. Our wall. I lean my back against it, and I feel the wet seep through. A long time ago, Ike explained to us how nuclear radiation, besides destroying stuff, bleached everything it didn't make disappear and that our bodies, if they were right up against something, would leave shadows that would last forever. For a long time we tried to use our bodies to send messages to the future. Hoping that after we were gone, if the Loop broke, the future would see us and know. I'd make little hearts with my hands, or sometimes we'd all hug each other to show them, like, love was a thing even for all of us who lived through the wars that ended everything. Now when we do it, it's mostly for fun.

"What are you going to do?" my father says.

"I think I'm going to do this," Ike says, looking up at us. He does a thing where he spreads his legs a little wider and acts like he's flexing both arms above his head. That's my brother. He's not too smart to be fun sometimes.

"Okay," my father says. "I'm going to do the animal man." He grabs a branch from the maple I snapped and puts it on his head so he'll look like he has feathers. The future will think he's an alien. Me, I've already picked one leg up and tucked it into my knee. It's pretty hard to breathe, but it's not that hard.

"Dancer," I say before he asks. That's kind of my signature. I've done different versions of it, but this one is the best I can do with a broken rib and a knocked-around head. I have one leg on the ground, and then I bring one arm and crane it above my head. We only have to wait a minute.

There's a faraway light. Then a roar like long, slow thunder. The roar doesn't stop; it gets louder, and then it's so loud you can't hear anything. The faraway light grows, and it's yellowish at first, and in the beginning it looks like something that's meant to help you, like another sun. Then it grows taller than any building, greater than a mountain. You can see it's eating the world, and no matter what, it is coming for you. Rushing toward you. And by the time it's blinding, you are terrified and humbled. Watching it, you know it's the kind of thing you should only get to see once. Something that happens once and then never again. We've all seen it so many times, but I still cry, because when it comes, I know for sure we are infinite. All you feel is infinite, knowing all the falls and leaps and sweet and death that's ever been will be trumped by the wall of nuclear flying at you. You of all people. Then, before you're gone, you know that all that's ever been will still be, even if there are no tomorrows. Even the apocalypse isn't the end. That, you could only know when you're standing before a light so bright it obliterates you. And if you are alone, posed like a dancer, when it comes, you feel silly and scared. And if you are with your family, or anyone at all, when it comes, you feel silly and scared, but at least not alone.

LaSHAWN M. WANAK

Sister Rosetta Tharpe and Memphis Minnie Sing the Stumps Down Good

FROM *FIYAH*

ROSETTA KNELT TO look at the stump in the corner of her client's bedroom. It had the likeness of a ten-year-old boy: four feet tall, dressed in an oversized shirt and suspenders. And its features were flawless, from the newsboy's cap cocked on its tight curls to its pupil-less eyes fringed with long eyelashes. The only oddity was that the stump's hands were unformed, shapeless blobs. It was easy to believe that a sculptor had chiseled a boy out of wood and had stepped away just before finishing its hands.

Rosetta sucked in her breath through her cloth face mask. The SPC hadn't told her that her first stump extermination would look like a child.

"Why did it take you so long to report this?" she asked the woman who rented the apartment.

"Went to visit my sister in St. Louis last week. When we got back, there it was." The bedroom door opened, revealing a gaggle of gawking kids. The woman shooed them back, then frowned at the white man maneuvering a medium-sized crate into the bedroom. She sidled up to Rosetta and whispered, "*He* gotta be here too?"

"It's all right; he's my handler. Set the vacuum up over there, Marty."

Marty Houchen winked a blue eye at the woman. "I do all the heavy lifting, ma'am. Sister Tharpe got the harder job." Rosetta could tell he was smiling behind his own face mask.

The woman hmphed. Her mask, the cheap paper sort usually sold at the SPC, dangled from her neck above her plain cotton blue maid uniform. It made Rosetta feel overdressed in her faux fur and white kid gloves. To cover up the awkwardness, Rosetta went to look out the window.

The woman's apartment was on the tenth floor of the Ida Wells Projects, the newest housing development touted as affordable for those with low incomes. The woman's apartment was sparse, but everything was neat and clean, albeit it smelled of oxtail stew and shoe polish. It was also stifling hot in the apartment. Sheets of thick, opaque filters lined most of the windows in the main rooms. In the bedroom there were no filters, but the woman had hung up bedsheets across the windows—a cheaper alternative.

If the woman had just returned from a trip, she probably had opened the window without thinking to let in the cold, fresh February air. Just enough for a spore to float in and take root.

"What's this made outta, anyway?" Rosetta turned around to see the woman prodding the stump's cheek with her finger. "Don't feel like wood. Feels spongy."

"Don't do that!" Rosetta rushed over to grab the woman's wrists. The slight indent the woman made in the stump's cheek was already molding itself back into shape. Rosetta glanced down to the stump's formless hands. Was that the hint of fingers? "Marty, hurry!"

"I'm working as fast as I can."

Still holding the woman by her wrist, Rosetta steered her into the kitchenette and scrubbed her hands with Ivory soap. "You need to be careful. Stumps can grow anywhere. These things can start growing on you and you don't even know it. You might think it's a boil or a pimple between your shoulder blades, behind your knee. If it bursts, you're as good as dead."

"Just wanted to see why they call 'em stumps," the woman grumbled. "They don't feel like wood."

"They're not wood. And they're not people. No matter how much they look like them. You should wear your face mask at all times. Or at least put up filters on your windows in your bedroom."

The woman glanced at her children piled on the sofa. "Those window filters cost the same as my rent. It takes ages to save up for them. And the face masks don't do nothing. My kids tear through them before they even get out the door. How am I supposed to keep this place from getting infected if I can't even buy what I need?"

Rosetta gave the answer that she had been trained to give. "Go talk to the SPC. They can work something out."

The woman pursed her lips but didn't say anything.

Marty emerged from the bedroom. "Get ready, Rosetta. I'm almost done."

Rosetta went back into the bedroom and reached into the opened crate. She pulled out her guitar case, laid it on the bed, took a deep breath to prepare herself, and opened it. Her Gibson L-5 greeted her with its tan finish and gold-plated turning keys. She slipped the strap over her head and its weight settled, heavy and comforting like a baby in a sling.

It had been almost a year and a half since she had played it. People used to make fun of it, saying it was nothing but a glorified mandolin, but Rosetta never took it as an insult. She strummed a G chord, and she was no longer in the woman's apartment but in a crowded church somewhere in Tennessee. The pounding of feet on the wooden floorboards, the wafting of cardboard fans with pictures of funeral directors advertising their services, the heat and the sweat in the air, voices raised in song while hands and tambourines beat out rhythm . . .

. . . and Momma's comforting presence as she swayed and plucked at her mandolin.

A twinge of emotion in her chest deepened into full-on heartache.

Rosetta lifted the guitar off her and put it back in the case. Marty glanced at her, but he didn't say anything.

"What are you doing?" the woman asked. Rosetta quickly closed the case, but the woman had directed her question to Marty as he slipped a thick transparent bag over the stump's head.

"This is so that no spores get out during the extermination." He adjusted the bag so that it fully covered the stump and secured the bottom with weighted lead rings. "There has to be no gaps or else one spore slips through and—*kekkkkk!*" He drew a finger across his neck.

"Stop scaring her, Marty."

"Just stating the facts. Better get your mask on."

Rosetta hated this part. From the crate she took out a larger mask with thick plastic goggles and a long hose dangling from the circular breathing plate, which contained a specialized filter made of the same material as the filters in the woman's windows. Rosetta slipped the mask over her head and adjusted the straps so it fit snugly around the back of her head and ears. Marty took the end of the hose and attached it to another one that was connected on top of the stump bag.

"All set?"

"Yeah," Rosetta said, hating how the mask stripped her voice of depth and timbre, rendering it flat and lifeless. Nothing for it but to do what she was supposed to do. She closed her eyes and began to sing.

"Up above my head, I hear music in the air. Up above my—"

A muffled *whump* came from the bag. Marty flapped his hands at Rosetta to stop. The bag billowed briefly, then slumped to the floor as if empty. Marty flicked a switch, and the vacuum inside the crate began sucking the remnants of the stump, shimmering particles larger than dust.

"Well, I'll be goddamned," the woman declared.

"God doesn't damn anybody," Rosetta said as she pulled off the mask. She felt tired, very tired, and this was just her first extermination. It wasn't real singing, though. Anything that lasted only a few seconds long couldn't be considered real singing.

Which was fine. She didn't deserve to do any real singing anyway.

Minnie hated the SPC.

The walls were too white. The lights were too bright. The air was too dry. The constant *whoosh, whoosh, whoosh* of the air purifiers, filtering out every ounce of dust in the air, was too damn loud. Every time Minnie came here with her handler to drop off her quota of stump dust, the boogers in her nose turned to hard pebbles and set her head to throbbing. The SPC was a miserable, stupid place.

"I have the numbers from what you've brought in," the weighing attendant said, referring to her clipboard. "It's only forty percent of your quota."

"It's been rough, ya know?"

The weighing attendant frowned. Her eyebrows had been penciled in a thick, high arch, as if perpetually astonished at Minnie's presence in the SPC. "It also says here your handler has requested to be transferred to another department. Says you're too 'belligerent and uncooperative to work with,' and you show up late to your exterminations—when you bother to show up at all. That's the third handler now who refuses to work with you."

Minnie gave a shrug. She hadn't even bothered to learn his name.

"Now, *Lizzie*," the attendant said, drawing out the z in a condescending buzz. "Being an exterminator is a very rare calling. There are many people out there who would love to have that same ability as you. We've already had several exterminators pulled to help at the war front in Europe. That brings the total licensed exterminators in Chicago down to six." The eyebrows rose until they nearly disappeared into the attendant's red hair, pinned in a victory roll, the latest fad in the white folks' world. "You don't want Chicago to be quarantined just like New York, do you, Lizzie?"

Minnie didn't answer. As far as she was concerned, the SPC quarantined her the day they showed up on her doorstep.

Nonplussed, the attendant referred to her clipboard. "Now, I do have some good news. A new exterminator just started working today. Between you and her, you should be able to contain the stumps in the Bronzeville district, which current count is . . . twenty-three as of today. If you continue not to meet your quota" —here she gave Minnie a stern look—"we'll have to find some other way for you to serve in Stump Prevention Control." It was always "Stump Prevention Control" with these people, never the "SPC." Like them uppity folks who go around insisting you call them *Mister* So-and-such, *Esquire*. Like the attendant insisting on always calling her *Lizzie*.

"Just gimme my pay."

The attendant sighed and handed Minnie $20. "We are assigning another handler to you. It will take several days to find someone who can handle your . . . temperament."

Fuck you and your eyebrows. Minnie picked up her guitar case and left.

A team of men in hazmat suits brushed past Minnie as they headed down the hall to the elevators that would take them to the lower levels. All of them were white. Her handlers had all been white. The weighing attendants, the office workers, everyone was white. The SPC sure liked their white folk, which was funny, seeing that the building itself was located on the South Side, where all the black folk had ended up.

When she first started, Minnie had tried to get Lawler as her handler—he had been a lousy recording manager, but he was great with his hands, inside the bedroom and out. The SPC said that handlers had to undergo a vigorous one-year training to learn how to manage the machines, the vacuums, the pumps, the brushes, et cetera. Minnie then asked why she even needed a handler. Seemed like she could learn to do all the work herself without some white man always watching her, making her nervous. The SPC said her job was to focus only on exterminating the stumps. Her voice was too important to exert herself on manual labor. Only handlers with the appropriate training could handle the equipment due to the extreme toxicity of the stumps.

In other words, *no niggers need apply.*

Minnie reached the large lobby. Posters provided some relief from the monotonous hallways and overbearing lights. On one side were pictures of bright smiling white families in front of tidy houses with the words KEEP YOUR HOME SPORE-FREE — BUY PERCY'S GRADE A FILTERS FOR YOUR WINDOWS — A FILTERED HOME IS A STUMP-FREE HOME. On the other side were posters of "famous" exterminators: Bing Crosby, Marlene Dietrich, two of the Andrews Sisters (but not all three). There was even a separate section of black exterminators in the furthest corner of the lobby: Billie Holliday, Louis Armstrong, Ella Fitzgerald, Marian Anderson.

As usual, the lobby was full of people, mostly black. Many stood in line for various windows to report a stump sighting, arrange for an exterminator, or pick up a free paper mask to filter out spores. A longer line of people snaked in front of a door that had a sign above it in bold yellow letters: DO YOU HAVE WHAT IT TAKES TO BECOME AN EXTERMINATOR?

In the center of the lobby was a television set displaying, in grainy black and white, a young blond woman singing into one end of a long glass tube. At the other was a jar of stump dust insulated inside a thick glass box. A chipper male voice narrated, "If this woman was just a normal person, nothing would happen. But she falls into that one percent of the population that has a 'unique vocal resonance' with the spores. Just look at that reaction!" And indeed, the camera cut to show the dust in the jar shimmering and swirling as it coalesced into tiny, indistinct forms. "All from the power of her voice!" the man pronounced in amazement.

The scene changed to show the woman, her hair and clothes perfect, striding into a building with a number of handlers. The narrator gushed about the exciting yet dangerous nature of the exterminator's life. An exterminator's voice raised in song could cause a stump to spawn, mature, and ultimately burst in a matter of seconds. An experienced handler was absolutely necessary in knowing when to stop the exterminator from singing to prohibit any more spawning. Inexperience could result in sloppy exterminations, respawning, or even immediate death. Despite the danger, the narrator enthused, exterminators and handlers were paid handsomely, for what they provided was a necessary civic duty for their country.

Minnie snorted. It was all bullshit. She was living proof of that.

She exited the SPC and headed to the bus stop just to the right of the entrance. Setting her case down, she pulled out her weekly copy of the *Chicago Defender* and flipped to the music section. As usual, there was no mention of her, her records, or the fact that she had been an exterminator for six months now. Count Basie was in town, though—that took up half a page. Big bands were becoming more popular as more singers were being recruited into exterminators. The other half was an ad for Ella Fitzgerald, who became an exterminator in October 1939. Now everyone was buying up her records. The SPC had released a statement that recorded voices had no effect on stump spores, so for some singers, becoming exterminators was their best publicity yet.

But not for Minnie. She could still sell her records, but they didn't sell too well; she had always sounded better live. Unfortunately, the SPC banned her from singing lest she activated any stump spores that might be floating about. So no more concerts. No more tours. No more singing in clubs. She tried to do just guitar pickin' at clubs, but it was annoying with her handler there, watching her every move.

A black Ford sedan pulled up in front of the SPC building. A white man with a derby got out, the words STUMP PREVENTION CONTROL stitched in yellow on the back of his gray trenchcoat. He opened the back door of the car and out stepped a young black woman in a long brown coat rimmed with fur and wearing short heels. She looked familiar.

Minnie glanced back down at the music ads. Ah, right there, toward the bottom: a photo of the same woman, holding a guitar, eyes cast upward in a heavenly gaze. The caption beneath read: "Cheers to Chicago's very own Sister Rosetta Tharpe as she starts her new life as an exterminator on the South Side."

So that was the new exterminator. Damn. Girl got a notice in the *Defender* her first day working at the SPC, while Minnie got squat. Ain't that a bitch.

As the SPC man pulled a full storage bag that made Minnie's haul look like a deflated coin purse out of the car's trunk, the woman caught sight of Minnie. She minced over with eager steps —amazing a big girl like her could stay upright in those short heels.

"Why, hello!" Minnie caught a strong force in her voice held in check, like an ocean wave restrained by a dam. "They said that there was another exterminator who also played guitar just like me. I see you got a guitar. Are you her?" A mole graced her left cheek.

Minnie's bus rolled up. She tucked the paper under her arm and picked up her case and told the girl, "Mind your own fucking business."

According to the SPC, the first stump appeared in a corner of a Bronx apartment in April 1938. A German family who had just moved to the apartment assumed it was a statue left by the previous owner. They dusted it, hung clothes on it, and even allowed the children to play on it on occasion, until one day it burst.

By the time the police reached the apartment, two children lay dead, the parents alive but convulsing, bloody foam oozing from their mouths and nostrils. They died minutes later.

As paramedics wheeled the bodies away, they noticed brown lumps forming along the floors and the walls of the apartment. Within the day the lumps had taken on human shape.

They looked very much like the German family who had just died.

Soon reports began to pour in from all around Manhattan. Brooklyn. Queens. Harlem. People called them stumps because in the shapeless form their wood-grain appearance really did make them appear like the stumps of trees. They always took on the form of the deceased people. After a certain period of time, they burst into glossy, light-catching motes the size of dirt particles. These spores were light and easy to spread to any surface: carried on the wind, buried in a dog's coat, breathed in by an unsuspecting person.

Face masks and dust filters grew in high demand.

In August 1938 the government, already burdened with a war it had entered against its intentions, had the Public Health Service commission a new agency, the Stump Prevention Control (SPC), to investigate and eradicate the stumps. The SPC discovered a small number of individuals contained a unique vocal resonance that could force stumps to mature and burst. This resonance only occurred in a cadence of embellished notes—in other words, singing. Recordings could not produce the resonance. The person had to sing directly to the stump to force a reaction.

At first the SPC recruited well-known celebrities. Many were surprised when Frank Sinatra failed the test. Then there were the Andrews Sisters, where the two older sisters were found to have the resonance, but not the youngest. In September 1939 the SPC expanded the call for anyone with a talent for singing to come to their centers to be tested.

That same month the Reverend Elder W. M. Roberts from the Fortieth Street Church of God in Christ visited Rosetta Tharpe at her apartment on Prairie Street. He sat in her kitchen, looking grave in his Sunday preaching suit. "Sister, it's been over a year now. Folks say you've gotten *diminished*."

He paused to let that sink in.

"You've been here ever since your mother brought you as a child to our fold. I know you're hurt, but it's time for you to start singing again."

Another pause. He started to pat her folded hands, but one look from her made him change his mind. Instead he said, "Your mother would've wanted it that way."

The following week Rosetta went to the SPC office to take the resonance test. She wasn't surprised when she passed. Momma always did say she had a strong voice.

They gave her six weeks of training. She watched reel after reel of scientists explaining the effects of burst stumps, pointing to bodies that had been exposed to stump dust, noting in clinical terms the bulging eyes, the seized muscles, the froth dripping from their mouths and noses and ears, all in black and white. She learned about filters and masks, spent hours practicing how to put on her specialized mask until she could do it correctly in three seconds.

They also introduced Marty Houchen as her handler. He was easygoing and chatty, and liked wearing derbies and ascots like Cary Grant. "You may not know this," he gushed at their first meeting, "but I heard you a couple of years ago on the *All Colored Hour* radio show. You were amazing! And your guitar! I mean, I'm not particularly religious, but after hearing you, I just about got saved that night—"

He stopped gushing when he saw the change in Rosetta's face. Since then he had never brought up her music career.

Six days out of the week she got up at 4 a.m. and changed the filter on the air purifier, the first major purchase she'd made when she became an exterminator. It was a bulky thing that sat in her living room window, but it allowed her to go about her apartment without needing a face mask.

After washing up, dressing, and a quick bite to eat, she left her apartment to meet Marty, waiting for her outside with a thermos of coffee with a thick plastic straw that could be slipped under her mask. In his car was the extermination gear: the hoses, vacuum, containment bags, brushes, masks—over fifty pounds of gear. After going over the list of addresses that contained stumps in their district, they were off.

They exterminated up to twenty stumps per day. Setup took fifteen minutes, vacuuming a good twenty to forty minutes, depending on the size of the stump. A site containing more than one stump could take up their entire day. Not a single speck of stump could be left behind.

They'd return to the SPC around 8 p.m.—midnight if it was a particularly heavy day. They turned in the stump dust they collected, updated their dockets, and collected payment, splitting it fifty-fifty. Rosetta then left Marty to take the equipment to the fumigation rooms to ride home in one of the ubiquitous SPC yellow vans. She went through her nighttime routine of going over her apartment for stumps, checking each corner, beneath her furniture. She changed the filters inside her vents, washed her face mask with the SPC's special sanitizing solution. She then took a shower with the same solution, scrubbing, rinsing, and drying every inch of herself. She didn't mind the work, or the long hours, or the tedious routine. It kept her from thinking too hard.

Sundays were her only day off.

She still attended the Fortieth Street Church of God in Christ. It was the church she grew up in. It was where she first started playing guitar, standing on the piano, dancing while the congregation clapped. Where she met Thomas, fell in love with him, and married him. Where the women elders cried with her after she got the telegram two years ago that broke her life apart.

Now that she was an exterminator, the praise and gospel music, joyful as it was, only painfully reminded her of what she had lost. That and the whispers.

"There goes Sister Tharpe. She was gonna go to New York once, didn't she?"

"Singing gospel music at the Cotton Club! Like a church!"

"Well, ain't gonna happen now. God must be judging her. You know she was going to divorce Thomas, right?"

"Well, like the Good Book says, 'Be sure your sin will find you out.'"

Momma always said to keep your head high when people talk about you, so that was what Rosetta did. She threw herself into ushering, serving in the nursery, helping with dinner before the evening services. But she didn't sing. Wouldn't do it, no matter how many times the pastor asked.

How could she when it was her singing that killed Momma?

One day Rosetta left the SPC examination room where she had her weekly throat check and caught sight of the woman who had been so vulgar to her three weeks ago. The woman stood by a stairway door, waiting for a group of men in lab coats to pass. Then, to Rosetta's surprise, she ducked through the door.

Rosetta paused. After her last encounter, she wasn't so sure she wanted to face the woman again. But that staircase was off-limits except for authorized personnel. So where was that woman going?

Rosetta pretended to rummage in her purse while the lab coats passed her, deep in their conversation:

"—tests only showed two percent growth rate—"

"So should we increase the sample area?"

When they had turned the corner of the hall, she also slipped through the stairway door. It didn't go down to the lower levels. Only up.

A few minutes of huffing and puffing led her out onto the roof. It was graveled, edgeless, and loud—the roof was dotted with large metallic curved ducts rising from the gravel. Unseen machinery hummed and whined, drawing air into the ducts; like Rosetta's air purifier, but much louder.

The other woman stood next to a duct, her back to the stairwell, watching the sun sink into rosy-hued clouds and the rocky landscape of buildings.

Rosetta adjusted her face mask and walked toward her, careful to place her feet—this roof was not meant for short heels. The ducts were loud enough that the woman didn't hear her approach, but as Rosetta drew near, a different sound, just underneath the duct's whoosh, made her stop in surprise.

The woman was singing.

Rosetta couldn't pick out the words. Something slow and bluesy. The woman rocked back and forth, keeping time by tapping her foot as her voice rose and fell, a low controlled caterwaul that wound itself around the ducts like a hungry cat, then slinked down into a growl before evening out again. The SPC had been so adamant about Rosetta not singing at all, and here was this woman right on the roof of the SPC, flaunting her voice. She wasn't even wearing a face mask. Her face was bare, open. Exposed.

The smart thing to do was to go back downstairs and report her to the nearest SPC agent.

But despite herself, Rosetta found herself rooted in place. She found herself thinking back to when she was eight and was sick with a bad fever, and how she had woken up in the middle of the night to Momma sitting by her bedside, laying cool cloths on Rosetta's forehead and humming nonstop, the vocalization of her worry vibrating through her lungs and chest like prayer.

It had been so long since she heard anything like that.

The memory burst when the woman in front of Rosetta broke off from her singing to hawk a wad of something brown and wet onto the roof. She pulled a handkerchief from her coat pocket and was lightly dabbing her lips when she finally caught sight of Rosetta. She turned, sticking her hands back in the pockets of her tweed coat. "Well, well, well. Whaddy'we got here?"

Rosetta replied with the same nonchalance as the woman. "You're singing."

"That's right. I am." Her speaking voice was a cross between a drawl and a growl. She was an older woman. Not as old as Momma had been, but maybe late thirties, early forties, with a hardness in her eyes and mouth that had nothing to do with age. "Watcha gonna do about it?"

Rosetta blurted the first thing that came into her mind. "Ain'tcha scared?"

The woman blinked, clearly not expecting the question. "Huh?"

"You're out here, in the open. There could be stump spores floating around us right now—"

"Oh, *that's* what got you all worried?" She pointed to the ducts. "This here's probably the safest place in the whole city. Them things is sucking all the air into the building. If'n there be any spores, they get stuck in them fancy filters they got in there. Course, with you charging up behind me without closing the door, there's probably a whole team of SPC agents charging up the steps right now."

Rosetta threw a panicked look at the stairwell—but then she heard a squeal of laughter from the woman. "Oh, girl, look at your face. Got you good there, didn't I?" She bent double, slapping her knee, chuckling and snorting in a most unladylike manner. Her teeth flashed gold, not just a trick of the fading light but real gold teeth.

Rosetta pressed her lips tight, then started toward the stairwell. "Hey," the woman gasped. "Come on, I was just kidding. Hey!" She reached for Rosetta's sleeve, but Rosetta snatched her arm away.

"Look, if you don't want me up here, just say so. I was just listening. Haven't heard good singing since—" Rosetta stopped as her eyes suddenly stung with tears. Had it really been that long?

The woman sighed, then stuck out her hand. "Lizzie Douglas. But you can call me Memphis Minnie."

"Sister Rosetta Tharpe." Rosetta searched the woman's hand, looking for tobacco stains, before finally giving it a shake.

"One of them Holy Rollers, huh." The woman spat another plug of brown spit onto the roof. "And yet you followed me up here."

Rosetta shrugged. "I gotta keep an eye on the only other black woman in this place."

"Only bla— Oh my God, this girl. This girl!" Minnie threw back her head and gave another squeal that descended into a husky chuckle. Despite herself, Rosetta smiled.

When the woman got herself under control, she dug in her coat pocket and pulled out a business card. "Here."

"What's this?"

"My way of sayin' sorry for swearin' at you the other day. Tonight. Eleven p.m. Follow the directions on the card." The woman sauntered to the stairwell. "And don't let anyone follow ya. We don't just let any ole person in."

*

The Alley Cat Club was located around 47th and Grand Boulevard, near the Regal Theater. The club itself was hard to find. You had to pass through two alleyways, tap on a back door three times, get ushered through a low hallway into *another* alley, go down some steps, and tap on another door two times. Prohibition officially ended seven years ago, but the Alley Cat still preferred to remain hidden from scrutinizing eyes.

And with good reason. Minnie had read in this morning's edition of the *Defender* that there had been another club closure. The SPC cited that the owner had a faulty air purifier. Funny that none of the clubs the SPC closed were ever allowed to reopen.

The Alley Cat was the opposite of the SPC—dim, humid, and smoky, even with the purifiers cranked on high. Dark girls in orange cat ears and floppy tails waded through the sea of tables. Men, black and white, tossed back their drinks and tried to cop a feel from the waitresses, roaring in laughter when they got their hands slapped. Women decked in furs and jewels mocked the men and flirted with the busboys. Onstage, a colored girl in nothing but beads jutted her hips to the strains of a ukulele—which could barely be heard over the chatter, the shrieks, and the occasional crash of chairs toppling over as a fight broke out and just as quickly stopped.

No one wore face masks here.

Well. Except one person. When Minnie glanced out at the crowd from backstage, there was the young Holy Roller sitting at one of the front tables, prim and proper, breathing mask firmly in place. She looked so stiff and uncomfortable, one of the waitresses had taken pity on her and poured her a glass of ice water. Now and then she peeked up at the dancer onstage before dropping her eyes back to her hands folded on the table.

"Hey, Lawler," Minnie called out.

He put down the trunk he was carrying and scrambled over. Minnie had met Lawler back in her touring days. He sang on a few recordings with her before managing to woo her away from her first husband. Nowadays he spent most of his days doing the occasional odd job and most of his nights being an asshole. "What's up, baby?"

She pointed to the table. "I want you to keep an eye on that girl there."

Lawler pulled out a rag to wipe his sweaty face. "She get lost on her way to the midnight prayer meeting?"

"Goddammit, just watch her. Jesus."

The dancing girl did one last shimmy and scampered off, blowing kisses to the audience, and Minnie sauntered onto the stage. Tonight she wore her best jewelry: a ring made from a six-sided die, and a silver-dollar bracelet made from coins minted in the year of her birth. She had brushed her hair back, leaving a few curls high on her brow, and had donned a pair of glasses that made her look, according to one of her male friends, "like a colored lady teacher in a neat southern school."

Instantly the audience leapt to a standing ovation; outside the Alley Cat she may not have been well known, but here everyone knew and loved her.

"Hey, y'all!" Minnie yelled. "How ya feelin'?"

"Fine!" the audience roared back.

She strolled to the left of center stage, where, resting against an amp, sat her new toy: a steel-bodied electric National guitar, already plugged in. How Andre managed to get one when they weren't officially available to the public, she didn't know. She slung it over herself, got it settled in a comfy position, then drew her fingers down the strings. The electric chord crashed into the room, making people howl and Church Girl jump.

"Whoo, I don' know about you, but I feel like singing tonight. Y'all wanna hear me sing?"

The audience shrieked their approval. Church Girl looked around, her eyes wide. She looked ready to bolt.

"We got you, Minnie!" Andre shouted from the back. Andre Fuqua, the owner of the Alley Cat, was a big guy with a tiny pencil mustache to go with his high, almost girlish voice. His purifiers were the best ones off the black market, and every so often he paid off a couple of guys to reroute SPC inspectors to other bars and clubs. "Sing 'Fashion Plate Daddy' for me!"

"I sing whatever I goddamn feel like," Minnie snapped. And she launched into "Jump Little Rabbit."

Her fingers came alive: frolicking, spinning, jitterbugging down the strings, while she belted rhythm on the guitar's body. She made her voice growl, snarl, and groan as the songs tumbled from her in a waterfall of sound: "Jailhouse Trouble Blues," "Can't Afford to Lose My Man," "Soo Cow Soo."

She whipped the audience into a frothing frenzy with "Dirty

Mother for Ya," letting the rhyme lead up to where a cuss word ought to be, then cooling them down with a lick of glissando and a tamer word, only to rile them back up with an arched eyebrow and a jangling of notes. Every once in a while she glanced over at Church Girl, expecting to see her storm out in a huff. But Church Girl stayed put, brown eyes wide and wet above her mask, following every movement of Minnie's hands on the strings with awe.

And why wouldn't she? The blues was the pluck of callused fingers on guitar string, the *mmmm* thrumming deep in the throat, the ice clinking in a glass of forbidden whiskey. It was the moaning and the wailing locked behind a stoic face, of lowering your gaze when a white man yelled at you, the standing outside of the church and knowing that you will never, ever be let inside. That night Minnie forgot she was Lizzie Douglas, exterminator, whose voice could endanger the lives of everyone in this room. Tonight she was Memphis Minnie, blueswoman, who could play a mean guitar and make a church girl cry.

When she finished her final lick, Minnie sashayed off the stage, sweating and thirsty. Lawler handed her a gin and tonic on ice, and she went to plunk herself at Church Girl's table. "So. There's the answer to your question on the roof." She tossed down the drink and ordered another one. "What you think of that?"

Church Girl wiped at her wet cheeks. "You just like breaking the law."

Minnie blinked, then howled and pounded the table. "*That's* the first thing you say to me? After I pour myself out like that? Jesus . . ."

The girl broke in: "—is God and Savior and Lord of all." She then crossed her arms and gave her head a firm, decisive shake as if that settled the matter, which only made Minnie crack up even harder.

Rosetta came back to the Alley Cat the following week. And the next week. And the next.

She always sat up front, prim and proper, never drinking anything harder than tonic water. She didn't need to—she drank the acts onstage with wide, thirsty eyes. Sometimes Minnie caught her tapping her foot or moving her head, but after a few minutes she'd stop, as if mortified she was actually enjoying herself.

The girl was so damn solemn. It was hard to tell that she was the same person as the woman in the newspaper, guitar in hand, gazing heavenward. At least she stopped wearing the filter mask inside the club.

They didn't speak to each other when they were at the SPC. It was an unspoken agreement; they always got such looks, as if two black women in the same room together was too much of a threat. But at the Alley Cat it was easier for Minnie to hang with the girl. And Rosetta was starting to show signs of loosening up.

One night they spotted Rosetta's handler, Marty, sitting at Andre's table. He looked up, caught sight of them, and turned a deep red. Minnie grabbed Marty by the arm and dragged him, protesting, over to a corner, leaving Rosetta to stand there staring awkwardly at Andre.

"Look. I don't know what the SPC got against clubs, but if you breathe one word of me and Rosetta bein' here, I'll shoot you with my own gun."

"What? Why would I even—"

"Look." Minnie jerked her head toward Andre's table. Rosetta had sat down and was now laughing at something he said, her demeanor relaxed. "This place is doin' some good for her. If the SPC finds out the both of us been comin' here, they shut down this place so fast, even you being Andre's favorite boytoy won't cheer him up."

Marty's red face reversed color, draining to paper white. "How did you know?"

"I know Andre. You're his type."

He folded his arms and laid a finger alongside his sharp nose. "Fine, I won't tell the SPC about you and Rosetta being here. Just don't tell her about me and Andre. I don't know how she'll feel about it."

Turned out Marty wasn't all that bad of a guy. He and Minnie chatted for hours about blues artists such as Robert Johnson, Muddy Waters, and Bessie Smith. Minnie also tried to pick his brain about the SPC. The longer she worked at the SPC, the more things bothered her. For instance, just what *did* they do with all the stump dust she and Rosetta collected? Where did it all go? How come she and Rosetta weren't allowed to go down to the lower levels of the building? What was with all the lab coats?

Marty didn't know. "I'm not allowed on the lower levels either.

The only reason I got this job is because I don't ask too many questions. I just do what I'm told, you know?"

The SPC assigned Minnie a new handler, a thick mooch of a guy who must've felt he was a sergeant in the army. He yelled at her if she did not stop singing *immediately* when he told her to stop. Forced her to sit in the back seat of his car and *not touch anything*. Harassed her if she lingered over lunch just a little longer than the required fifteen minutes, or if she needed a break or the bathroom during an extermination. After a week of this, Minnie was at her wits' end.

It was Rosetta who suggested that she and Minnie combine forces at work. "Right now we're both doin' our own thing. If we're the only exterminators in the black part of the South Side, we need a better way of hitting all the stumps that pop up. We need to plan our routes together. That way we can cover more ground, and your handler gets more work to keep him busy and not so focused on you."

So from that point on, Minnie had her handler take her to Rosetta's apartment, where all of them divvied up the stump sightings for the day. At first the mooch grumbled and complained, but he shut up quick when Minnie not only started meeting her quota but exceeding it. For the first time since becoming an exterminator, Minnie was finally making money.

"Hey, we make a pretty good team," she told Rosetta. "Maybe one day you and I need to get together to play for real. I keep hearing how good of a guitar picker you are." Minnie grinned, showing all her gold teeth.

Rosetta matched her with a rare grin of her own. "They used'ta say to me, *Shout, sister, shout!* and I would do this trick I learned from Mom—"

She broke off and turned away, her face gone stiff as if shutting her emotions behind a door.

This always happened. Rosetta would get to relaxing and then something caused her to shut down, pulling a hard shell of grief down to protect herself. For any other person, Minnie would've given up.

But Minnie had seen Rosetta's fingers twitch on the table when a horrible guitar picker would be onstage at the Alley Cat, drumming out correct notes with a dexterity that intrigued Minnie. This girl needed to play again; that much was clear.

So Minnie invited Rosetta over to her house on Thursday nights for dinner. She taught Rosetta how to play spades. She told stories of when she toured with the Ringling Brothers Circus and busked on the Midway at Beale Street, though she only talked about the good times, not the darker, more questionable things she did to survive. It felt good to hang out with a fellow musician. Now if she could just get the girl to loosen up, things would be good. She just needed time, and if there was one thing that Lizzie "Memphis Minnie" Douglas had, it was plenty of time.

That is, until the day the SPC shut the Alley Cat down.

One morning Rosetta opened her front door, expecting to greet Marty, but found a slew of SPC agents instead. They took her to the SPC, where she spent a full day undergoing a full body check for spores, inside and out. Throughout it the agents asked her about the Alley Cat. How long had she been going there? Did she ever sing?

Bewildered, Rosetta said she had never, ever sung at the Alley Cat. She kept quiet, however, when they asked about Minnie, staring at her hands in front of her, not willing to tattletale on the only female friend she had had since . . . well, since her momma died.

The agents sighed and made Rosetta rewatch the movie reels they had showed her at training.

It was close to midnight when they finally released her to Marty, who told Rosetta the truth. "The SPC stormed the Alley Cat after you left last night. They said they found stump dust in a small closet and shut the whole place down."

Rosetta wanted to curl into a ball. Her eyes felt gritty, but when she closed them, she kept seeing the images of dead people from the training, their pain and horror frozen forever on their faces. "How did they know Minnie and I were there?"

"Minnie's handler. He tailed her after work and saw the two of you meeting up in front of the club." Marty scowled. "Andre's a wreck. He said that closet is part of his routine check day and night and he hadn't seen any stumps there at all." Marty stopped, peered closer at Rosetta. "Are you all right? You're shaking."

The full body check had included a laxative to clean out her insides. Her mouth tasted like chalk. "I'm fine. How's Minnie?"

"They released her a little bit before you. Are you *sure* you're all right? If you want to take tomorrow off—"

"No," Rosetta said firmly. "We'll work, same as always."

"But—"

"That's my job, isn't it? To prevent something like this from happening? Come on. We'll talk to Minnie tomorrow."

But Minnie didn't show up to Rosetta's house the following day. Or the day after that. At the end of the week, Rosetta had Marty drive her straight to Minnie's tiny house, not too far from her own apartment. All the shades were shut, and no one answered the door. "Maybe she isn't home," Marty said. Rosetta threw him an annoyed look and went around to the back.

Minnie had finally earned enough from the exterminating job to buy an air purifier, a hulking beast which stuck out of her left kitchen window. "Like my twenty-year-old ass," Minnie had joked while it was being installed. Because of that, she no longer used her window filters, so Rosetta and Marty were able to peer into the kitchen window to see Minnie, clad in a pink housecoat, lying face-down on the kitchen floor. The back door was unlocked, and Rosetta and Marty had to shove it open. A strong reek of moldy food and unwashed funk greeted them. Empty bottles, newspapers, and dirty dishes littered the floor.

"Oh dear God," Rosetta said, surveying the mess. "Is she dead?"

Minnie curled into herself and coughed a small stream of clear liquid onto the linoleum.

"No," Marty said, wrinkling his nose. He stooped to pick up a half-empty bottle of gin. "Just drunk."

"Oh." Rosetta looked down at the still form of Minnie for a long time, then turned to Marty with a bright smile. "Okay. You head on home. I'll take it from here."

"You sure?"

Rosetta bent over Minnie to hide her face. "Go on. I'll be fine."

When Marty left, Rosetta dropped her smile. She half steered, half carried Minnie to the bathroom. She started the shower, then reached for Minnie, uncertain of whether she should undress Minnie or just stick her under the spray. But Minnie was coming out of her stupor, grumbling and pushing away Rosetta's hands to fumble at the housecoat's belt. Rosetta started to speak, then pressed her lips tight and went back to the kitchen. She put coffee in the percolator, found a somewhat clean skillet, and braved the icebox for bacon and eggs.

By the time Minnie moseyed in, toweling her hair, the bacon lay, still sizzling, on a plate and Rosetta had slipped the last egg into the hot bacon grease in the skillet. Minnie plopped herself at the small table in the center of the kitchen. "Hoooooweeee! Man, I'm so hungry, my stomach hurt like it's got meningitis. Hey, you know I wrote a song about that?" She began humming, slapping the table in beat. "'Hmmmm hmmm hmmm . . . the Minnie-jitis killin' meee.' Get it? Minnie-jitis?" She chuckled at herself.

Rosetta stirred the grits, keeping her face toward the hot stove. "How long have you been lying on the floor like that?"

"Damn, girl, you never ain't seen a bender? Hell, this ain't nuthin'. Should tell you about the time when I was busking back in Memphis. Got into a drinking match with Tiny Joe. Drunk him under in three hours. Then he drunk me into bed, and oooweeeee!" She leaned back in the chair, chuckling to herself. "Came home strutting like an alley cat. Stinkin' like one too."

Rosetta flipped the eggs over easy. "I just thought you'd have more common sense than this."

"So I drank too much. Don't worry yourself, Church Girl. Get some food in me and I'll be back singing for the Man and my supper in no time. Jesus Christ—"

Rosetta didn't correct her.

Minnie started rooting through the dirty dishes on the table, looking for her tin of tobacco. "All right, what's with you? So the SPC finally caught up to us. No harm done."

"No harm done?" Rosetta whirled to face Minnie. "They found stump spores at the Alley Cat. If you had sung, people would've *died*. And not only that, you missed a whole week of work! And for what? Because you were lying drunk on the floor all week?"

"Yeah, but no one died, didn't they?" Minnie finally found the tin and tried opening it. Either the lid was on too tight or she was still too hungover to do anything, so she threw it back on the table in disgust. "Hell, it could've grown and burst anyway without us being there at all."

"How do you know? You could've done what you did just now. It don't take much, Minnie. Even if it's just a bit of singing, that could be enough for a stump to do its thing."

"All right, all right," Minnie grumbled. "I hear you."

"No, you need to get this through your head. You're an exterminator now. Singing's become too much of a liability. If that stump burst at the Alley Cat, think of how many people could've died. Maybe it wouldn't be our fault, but still, we can't take the risk. And maybe it's a good thing it got shut down. What if someone who hasn't been tested as an exterminator started singing and made the stump burst?"

"So we just shut up and do our jobs and the SPC will use any excuse they can to shut down more clubs. What'll happen after that? Think the SPC just gonna stop there? You do a lot of singing at church, don'tcha? The SPC could start shutting them down too. Pretty soon everyone's gonna be too scared to sing. Think of it. No more songs, no more lullabies. Hell, no more jingles. That what you want?"

Rosetta's voice quavered. "Even the Bible says, 'There is a time to speak and a time to be quiet—'"

"Now that's some bullshit right there. I've seen how you are at the Alley Cat. Your eyes all big and shiny, sitting at that table in the front, drinking all them songs in. Face it, honey, you need singing to live."

Rosetta slammed the skillet on the stove hard enough to make it rattle. "My momma died because of my singing!"

In the sudden silence, the percolator let out a shrill burst of steam. Rosetta turned it off, then stood there, pressing her palms into the counter. "I was all set to go to New York to join the Cotton Club. The owner there had heard me sing and wanted me to be part of the act there. Momma said if I could make it at the Cotton Club, I could make it anywhere.

"But my husband didn't like it. We had been married for four years, and he wanted to settle down, have kids. But I wasn't ready, Lord, I wasn't ready. When I got offered the job at the Cotton Club, oh, we fought and fought. Finally he said fine, we'll go to New York, but only if I let him be my manager. Momma had been managing my singing ever since I was born. She told me that if Thomas became my manager, I would never get any good gigs, so the both of us decided that I would divorce him.

"I stayed behind in Chicago to start the paperwork while Momma went to New York with Thomas. She was gonna break the news to him there. Momma was always doing the hard things for me. 'God's given you a gift, Rosetta,' she used to tell me all the time. 'You can't keep quiet. You need to let the world know! Those people in the club ain't gonna hear gospel music otherwise.' And I believed her. I believed her."

Understanding made Minnie sober. She sat up in her chair. "Let me guess. She died before telling him."

"They both died. A stump in an alley burst just as they were passing it, walking down a street in Harlem, looking at apartments."

"Sheeeeeit."

"It should have been me!" Rosetta cried as she turned to Minnie. "If I hadn't accepted that gig, Momma would've never gone to New York. I couldn't even bring her home because of the quarantine."

"What about your husband? You miss him?"

Rosetta pressed her hands against her eyes. She then faced Minnie; her eyes were red but dry. "No," she said. "I don't miss Thomas. He was . . . a jealous man. He didn't deserve death. But I married him, for better or for worse, and now I'm paying the price for putting my singing career above being a wife to him. Even if they hadn't died, my career would've been over. The Cotton Club was one of the first clubs they shut down during the quarantine there. The stumps are a punishment from God."

Minnie snapped, "Look, I feel bad for ya, but I ain't gonna let you talk like that. What happened was an accident. Could've happened to anyone. And it sure ain't no punishment if you got different aspirations than your man. If'n he couldn't deal, then you were right in walkin' out the door. Ain't no such thing as punishment."

"It's still sin, though. Sin is the consequences you get for following false idols. Mine is putting my singing before everything else. Yours is thinking you can do whatever you want when you want. The Alley Cat closing is just one of the signs."

"Now hold on," Minnie said, rising to her feet, "Finally showing that Holy Roller side, huh? You fuckin' knew what you were getting into when you met me. Ain't no angel wings on my shoulders."

The pot of grits on the stove bubbled fiercely as the bacon took on a sharp burnt smell. "You're a sinner, Minnie. Being reckless. Flouting the rules. Drinking until you pass out. You need Jesus in your life. Only He can save you. Probably the only reason why He brought us together was to keep you from going to hell—"

Minnie's face twisted. "Get out."

"But—"

Minnie swept her arm across the breakfast table. The dishes, the newspapers, all went crashing to the floor. "Get the hell out of my house! Go on! *Get!*"

Rosetta hesitated, then turned her back on the ruined breakfast. She paused at the back door. "I'll pray for you."

She then ran to avoid the pot of burnt grits crashing against the door.

Minnie sat fuming and muttering to herself at the back of the No. 29 bus, her overcoat wrapped around the gray pink dress, her wet hair tied under a black scarf. When other riders came toward the back, she scowled hard enough for them to sit somewhere else.

Rosetta saying she'd pray for her. Ain't that rich. Minnie had had people praying at her all her life.

"Lord, help Lizzie to stop runnin' off so much. Lord, help Minnie to stop sleepin' with so many men so the right man can come along an' marry her. Lord, *please* make Lizzie just stay home and stay outta trouble."

Thing was, Minnie didn't see how the alternative was any better. Just because you were saved and sanctified didn't mean that life got automatically better for you. Good people still had to sit in the back of the bus, got chased from their homes for moving into the wrong neighborhood, lynched for looking at white people the wrong way. If God was supposed to make everything better for those who believed in Him, He was doing a shit job at it. People like Rosetta didn't care just how hard a life Minnie lived. All they cared about was how "pure" and "holy" she was. Well, Minnie had lost her pureness long, long ago.

Fuck 'em. Fuck 'em all.

Minnie looked out the window and saw that they were now in a different neighborhood. The signs on the storefronts were in a different language from English. "Hey, driver!" she called out. "What happened to Wentworth Avenue?"

"We passed it ten minutes ago," he called back. "We in Bridgeport now, lady."

A chill went through Minnie. Blacks never went into Bridgeport neighborhood. Lots of Polacks, Irish and Lithuanian folk, none who took too kindly to their black neighbors to the east. State Street was the dividing line; any black folk caught past that were sure to get chased back across, if they were so lucky. Common sense would be to stay on the bus, ride it to the end, then ride it back to Bronzeville. Tell the driver she fell asleep and missed her stop.

Instead she pulled the cord to let her off at the next stop.

Butcher shops and furniture stores glowered at her with their shabby storefronts. Old women with scarves tied around their chins stopped on the sidewalk, bushy eyebrows pulling down in disapproval as she passed by. Young children peered out of doorways, unsmiling. Hard faces. Pale faces. Unwelcome faces.

Minnie shoved her hands deeper in the pockets of her coat and kept her pace steady but not dawdling. *Yeah, I'm walking my black ass down the street. Watcha gonna do about it?*

She turned a corner into an empty lot and came across the largest patch of stumps Minnie had ever seen.

About twenty of them, in odd clumps and bunches, as if someone dumped stump dust by the handful and allowed them to grow. All were in various stages of maturity: a formless mass here, a fuller formed torso and arm of a man there. One stump of a black woman looked fully matured; Minnie could count the coils of her hair, the lines of her outstretched fingers, the other hand splayed over the full roundness of her stomach. Her mouth was stretched wide open in what was undoubtedly a scream.

Minnie circled the patch, baffled. Standard SPC protocol was that discovered stumps would be secured with bags so they could at least be contained until an exterminator dealt with them. But none of these stumps were bagged. Why were so many stumps out in the open so close to people? And why so many?

She reached up to make sure her filter mask was in place; her fingers touched bare skin. She had stormed out of her house without her filter mask. She was unprotected.

"Well, well, what we got here?"

Minnie turned to see about six to seven white men of various ages, dressed all in denim. For face masks they had tied handkerchiefs and strips of fabric from shirts and bed linen around their noses and mouths. Above their impromptu face masks, their eyes were hard and suspicious. They must've worked in the stockyards, for they all had a smell of butchered blood.

As much as she hated the SPC, she used it as an excuse now.

"I'm an exterminator. Just checking out these stumps. I'll be gone before you know it."

"Is that so?" A burly man with a red handkerchief stepped forward. "Seems like we had all sorts of SPC types crawlin' around here as of late. What happened? Did they abandon you?"

"What are you talking about?"

The men laughed. It wasn't happy laughter. "Your yellow vans been crawling all over our neighborhood at all hours of the night. Next day there's stumps all over the place. They don't send no one to take care of them neither. We had to form brigades to keep stupid kids away." Red Handkerchief's eyes narrowed. "And you."

"Wait." Minnie rubbed her head. The anger she had sustained up to now was beginning to ebb, leaving in its place a pounding headache that intensified the more she tried to think. "Where's your exterminator? I know you have one for this area."

"Yeah, funny thing, that. He's gone. Hasn't been around for weeks."

"But still, they should have at least secured the area so the stumps don't spread."

"You think they do that, but they haven't. In fact, we've been doing it ourselves with sacks. But here's the thing. When we come back later, our sacks are gone. Somebody's been taking them off."

"But that makes no sense," Minnie said. "Why leave the stumps exposed? At this rate, so many of them would spread, they'll have to quarantine the city just like—"

Minnie's hangover vanished as her entire body went cold.

What if that was what the SPC had wanted *all along*?

"Go home," she told the men, her mind racing. "Get your families and get out of the city, now. A whole lotta people gonna die."

"We ain't goin' nowhere," Red Handkerchief said. The men behind him spoke.

"For all we know, maybe it's *you* who've been stealin' our bags."

"Maybe she was sent here to see if the stumps done their work."

"I ain't even sure she *is* an exterminator."

"Niggers always lie to get outta anything."

More ugly laughter. Minnie stepped back, beginning to regret ever saying she worked for the SPC. Used to be that she would carry a pistol for times like this, but like an idiot she had left it back at her house—

Something hard poked her between her shoulder blades. And Minnie realized she had a weapon after all.

"Back off," she snarled, moving aside to show the stump of the black woman with her fingers outstretched. "I'll sing."

Some of the men looked at Red Handkerchief, uncertain. He shook his head and scoffed, "She's bluffin'. She'd get killed too."

It wasn't the offhand way he said it but the way the other men nodded in agreement that filled Minnie with fear. She opened her mouth to sing: "You saayyy that's life; there's something wrong with me . . ."

Red Handkerchief lunged toward her. "Stupid bitch! Stop!"

Several things happened at once. The stump of the black woman burst into shining motes. The man's fist punched into Minnie's stomach, making her double over, her breath exploding from her. Her clawing hand raked his face, yanking down his handkerchief, exposing his face. As the motes floated around her, Minnie struggled, trying to ride out the ache in her abdomen and the instinct not to breathe in. But her lungs won over her abdomen, and when her stomach muscles unclenched enough, she made a ragged, involuntary, gasp—

Rose Haskell is standing on the corner, waiting for the trolley to pass. Her son squirms in her arms. He's a year old, and already so heavy. Or maybe it's her belly, heavy with another child. Sweet Charlie is at his second job, cleaning offices. He'll only have a few minutes to eat dinner before going to the stockyards. The workers were on strike, so the stockyards were paying him to cross the picket lines. He didn't want to do it, but perhaps it could give him permanent work.

She hears the shouting of the men before they round the corner of the street. Angry men, running so fast she doesn't have time to move, to scream. They surround. They yell. They yank her boy from her arms. He shrieks so loud, so loud, until he stops abruptly. That red thing being bashed on the sidewalk. No, that couldn't be. That's not her son. That bloody thing, red matter flying, no . . .

And then they're tearing into her, ripping, grabbing, tearing, thrusting, why don't they stop, animals, animals, so much pain, she can't fight, it hurts, so much red, so much—

Then Minnie found herself on her hands and knees back in the lot, staring at the ground.

What the hell?

Minnie rose gingerly to her feet and checked herself. Other

than the dull ache of her abdomen, she seemed fine. No seizures, no foaming at the mouth, no coughing up blood. Red Handkerchief sat flat on his ass, staring pop-eyed into space. A couple of other men began to sit up from where they lay in various positions, groaning as they stared around them. The rest must've run off.

She was fine. The men were fine. They were all fine.

So what the hell happened?

"Rose . . ."

Minnie jerked her gaze back to Red Handkerchief. "What did you say?"

"That woman. Rose Haskell." He touched his face, then splayed his hands over his stomach and stared at it for a long time.

Minnie shook her head, stunned. "You saw her too?"

"Saw her? *I was her.* I lived her. I . . . was her. I know things about her. Those men . . . what they did . . . I could feel it . . . How do I know all this?"

One of the men retched. Minnie whirled, heart hammering, but the man pulled off the cloth around his face and wiped his mouth with it. "I remember my pa telling me about that race riot. He never said he was part of it." He spat. "I felt everything they did to her. She was *pregnant*. And that boy. How could they—"

Minnie said slowly, "You were about to do the same to me."

Red Handkerchief jerked up his gaze, anguish in his face. He started to speak, but Minnie put up her hand to stop him. She was missing something, something she needed to look at *right now.*

On the ground she could see the stump dust. She bent, touched a bit with her finger. She had never seen stump dust outside of a filter bag before. It was soft and powdery, like dull chalk dust. There was an almost sweetish smell to it, like dried rose petals.

"How come we not dead?" she asked.

"Huh?"

"Stumps burst, people die. That's what's supposed to happen. But we're all alive, aren't we? What changed? Why aren't we dead?" She stopped, then said, incredulous, "All I did was sing . . ."

In the distance she could hear the faint wail of sirens. Bending, she scooped up a handful of dust. Putting some distance between herself and the remaining stumps, she bent her head and hummed into her cupped hands, just barely under her breath. The dust in her hands didn't shimmer or reform. It didn't do anything.

Those lying sons of bitches.

The sirens grew nearer. Minnie ran over to Red Handkerchief. "Hey! You wanna do something about what you just saw?"

He stared up at her as if still dazed. Minnie dug into her coat pocket, threw the business card at him. "Call that number on the card. Tell whoever answers to find Rosetta Tharpe. Tell her she needs to sing to the stumps. You got it? Don't go to the SPC. You tell her Minnie said to sing to the stumps! Sing! Just like her momma told her to! Go! Go!"

Red Handkerchief fumbled at the card. The other two men were already scrambling out of the lot. She pushed him to get him going, then stood with legs braced in front of the stumps. By the time the SPC roared into the lot with their yellow vans, Minnie was the only one left. She set her hands on her hips.

"About time, boys. We got some talkin' to do."

The black phone by Rosetta's bed jangled. She put a hand out from the covers, groped for the receiver, and pulled it under the covers. "'Lo?"

"Rosetta? Is that you?"

"Marty? What—what time is it?"

"Rosetta, it's two in the afternoon. Are you in bed?"

She grunted a garbled reply.

"I take it that's a yes. Listen. I need you to get dressed and come down to the Alley Cat right away. It's important."

"The Alley Cat was closed."

"Yeah, but that's not the only place anymore. Rosetta, Chicago's been quarantined!"

Rosetta shot up from the covers. "What!"

"You really don't know, do you? Look, I'm sending a taxi to your place right now. Be ready in fifteen minutes."

Rosetta tried to say more, but Marty hung up. Annoyed, she set the receiver down, pulled the scarf off her head, and ran her fingers through her disheveled hair. She hadn't gone to church that morning, a rare thing for her. She just hadn't been in a worshipping mood, not after what happened at Minnie's yesterday. But the SPC putting Chicago under a quarantine must've meant things had gotten bad. But why would Marty have her go to the Alley Cat instead of the SPC?

An hour later Rosetta arrived at the Alley Cat, where Andre let her in. Empty of its patronage, the club had an empty, lonesome quality to it. Marty waved at her from the only table that didn't have its chairs stacked on top of it. Next to him another white man was twisting a red handkerchief in his large hands. Andre left her and headed into the dark, silent recesses behind the stage.

Rosetta sat down. "What's going on?"

Marty made a face. "It's Minnie. The SPC picked her up last night over in Bridgeport."

"Bridgeport! What was she doing over there?" Actually, it would be just like Minnie to run off and do something stupid like that.

"We've been patrolling the place, my friends and I," the man said, not looking at her. "We found her at this patch of stumps. She . . . we . . . aw, hell. We were threatening her. Just wanted to scare her, really. We weren't gonna do anything serious. But she got scared, so she sang."

"She *what*? In front of the stumps?" She glared at the man. "You're lucky you're not dead!"

"Yeah . . . that's the thing. We didn't die. No convulsions, no coughing up blood. Even your friend was fine, and she wasn't even wearing a face mask. But the stump that burst . . . we saw . . . we saw."

Haltingly he told the story of Rose Haskell, how he saw everything in her life, right up to how she and her children died at the hands of a mob.

Rosetta listened, her hands pressed to her mouth. "And all of you saw this? Even Minnie?"

"Yeah. She was pretty sure it was her singing that did it. Otherwise we would've been dead."

"But the SPC told us to sing only enough to make the stumps burst. They said anything more and it would be too dangerous!" She turned to Marty. "Did you know about this?"

He dropped his gaze, started playing with the brim of his hat.

"You . . . *did* . . . know," she said in slow disbelief.

"What you and Minnie saw is called 'residual memory.'" Marty spoke in a low voice, not looking up from his hat. "It's the last form stump dust takes after it's been rendered inert by an exterminator's voice. Once the memory gets played, it just becomes useless dust. Our job as handlers was to gather the stump dust before it became residual memory."

"H-how long have you've known?"

"Since my first day. At the time I thought nothing of it. I wasn't paid to think. All I had to do was keep quiet and do my job." He glanced at the other man. "Then I heard about your exterminator. Seems he also found out the stumps' secret by accident. The SPC took him in and he was never seen since."

"And now they got Minnie," Rosetta said, her voice hard. "But you still haven't said why the SPC would do this. Why all the secrecy? Why are they doing this?"

Marty dropped his eyes again. "I don't know."

The man cleared his throat, twisting the handkerchief so tight it was close to tearing. "'Scuse me, but your friend? She gave me a message for you. She said . . . to tell you to sing to the stumps."

She stared at him. "What?"

"She said to sing to the stumps. It's somethin' you're supposed to do. Like your momma told you to."

It was as if a ghostly finger plucked her insides.

The man rose. "Look, I need to get home." He hesitated, then said in a rush, "If you ever find your friend, tell her . . . tell her I owe her a drink." With that, he left. Minnie would see it as an apology. It did, after all, involve alcohol.

Assuming they could find Minnie.

"Where are they holding her now?" Rosetta asked Marty. "And don't you dare say, 'I don't know.'"

He said, resigned, "They would have taken her to the lower levels. It's . . . it's where I'm also supposed to take you. In fact, my orders were to bring you in last night."

"But you didn't."

He squirmed, which made him look younger. Rosetta stood up and hollered toward the stage. "Hey, Andre!"

He emerged, rubbing his hands with a rag. "Yeah. What's up?"

"We're going to the SPC and I need your help." She gave Marty a hard look. "Both of you. We're gonna do some warfare of our own."

Rosetta kept her eyes fixed on the road as Marty raced his Ford toward the SPC. She clenched the door handle tight, as if she could add every ounce of her strength to make the car go faster. Every so often Marty glanced over toward her.

"You all right?"

"I'm fine."

He stayed quiet for a couple of minutes. "You sure you want to do this? I mean . . . think about Minnie—"

"Minnie can take care of herself," Rosetta snapped. "We need to do this first. *I* need to do this."

Marty clammed up. Rosetta focused her attention back on the road and her rage.

The SPC had used her. All that talk of being careful with her voice, the throat checks, the admonishments to always be careful not to sing. All this time, it was a lie. No—worse than a lie. It was a cover-up of epic proportions. And she had been complicit in it, using her guilt over her mother's death, her own faith—*her own faith*—to justify the SPC's work.

By nature Rosetta considered herself a joyful soul: quick to smile, slow to anger. But now she was startled to discover that a furious rage had been slowly building inside of her. Rage at the SPC, at herself, at Marty. And she had *liked* Marty. He always found some way to make her laugh. He had been so considerate of her since her first day on the job.

She hadn't felt such betrayal since the day Thomas beat her when she told him about the Cotton Club job.

The street leading to the SPC was closed off by police. Marty showed them his SPC badge and indicated he was bringing Rosetta in per their request. The police waved him through but warned him, "Got some folks angry about the quarantine. I suggest you get some of the security guards to help you. It's not a pleasant sight."

Indeed, the place was in chaos. A crowd of men—and a few women—stood in the street outside the SPC, shouting at the security guards lining the entrance. Several bodies lay on the ground, eyes fixed in death, frothy blood streaming from their mouths and noses. The guards wore heavy gas masks, similar to the one Rosetta used in extermination.

And everywhere were stumps. The sidewalk and street were littered with misshapen clumps of them growing together, like the strangest game of Freeze Tag. As she watched, a guard lifted what looked like a tube to his shoulder. There was a dull *whump* as something shot out of the other end to land several yards away in a burst of smoke. The crowd scattered to the other side of the street, but one or two stumbled. They dropped to the ground, their bodies jerking and seizing as they tried to claw at the rags tied around their faces; then they stilled.

From the smoke a shapeless mass began to form. By the time Marty pulled up it had sprouted several arms, a foot, and the head of a small child sightlessly gaping at the sky.

Rosetta's gut crawled. Now she knew what the quarantine was for. The SPC was turning stumps into weapons and wanted to test them out. She wished she could swear like Minnie.

"Get me as close to the sidewalk as you can," she told Marty. "Put us between them and the crowd."

Marty did so, muttering, "I sure hope this works."

There was an electric feeling in the air, something like Rosetta used to feel before coming onstage to do a concert, but this felt tense, simmering with anger. As she emerged from the car someone shouted, "Sister! Sister Rosetta Tharpe!"

She recognized Lawler's voice; he had one of Minnie's face masks strapped on, but it was undoubtedly him. He shouted at her, "They won't let me in to see Minnie!"

"We'll see about that," Rosetta shouted back. She hiked up her dress a bit and hoisted herself onto the hood of the Ford. Every eye instantly riveted on her. Good, she still knew how to play a crowd. Ignoring Marty's horrified face as the hood groaned and buckled under her boots, she surveyed the scene, hands on her hips.

One of the guards moved toward her, his voice hissing from his gas mask: "Miss Tharpe . . . Miss Tharpe . . . come down. We'll have someone escort you inside. It's too dangerous out here."

She turned her back on him and addressed the crowd. "What's this I'm hearing about a quarantine? The stumps are getting outta control? Is that right?" Rosetta was never the sort to need a microphone to make herself heard. She turned so that she could include the guards. "Stumps kill. We all know that. We see their handiwork now. But I just found out something that makes me question all that. Y'all know Memphis Minnie, right?"

A few cheers rose from the crowd. Most, however, exchanged confused looks, including the guards.

"Well, let me tell you, she learned something she shouldn't have and now the SPC's went and took her in, and we got this quarantine. Coincidence? I don't know. But like my momma always said, strange things are happening every day."

She gave a signal to Marty, who stuck Minnie's National guitar out the window.

The sight of the guitar elicited a response from both sides: the crowd crying out and scrambling back, the guards moving forward, yelling at her to stop. Rosetta settled the guitar around herself and strummed. Andre had set up the amp to run from Marty's battery in his car, and the effect was powerful. The chord jangled into the air, electric and glassy and just a little bit off-key.

"I don't know about you," she boomed, "but I think it's gonna *rain*."

She was no longer at the SPC but back in church, six years old, dressed in her pink pinafore and her hair braided in four pigtails with pink barrettes, standing on an old piano while Momma beamed at her from below as she strummed on her mandolin.

Sing, baby girl, Momma said back then.

And so she did. She launched into the old spiritual "Didn't It Rain," gospeled up her style. She made that guitar talk, riffing and jamming, her fingers dancing over the strings. She called out. "Didn't it rain, children?" and then responded to herself. "Yes!"

"Didn't it?"

"Yes!"

"Oh, didn't it? Didn't it rain? Yes!"

Rosetta could never get a straight answer on what happened next. Marty said one of the guards panicked. Lawler said no, the guard knew exactly what he was doing. All Rosetta knew was that one moment she was so deep in her music, the next something struck her in the center of her chest, knocking her off the hood of the car. As she tumbled, she gasped, and it was like breathing in tiny sparks of hot embers—

Yu Lan Lin lugs her suitcase down Cermak Avenue in Chinatown. Though many of the street signs and buildings are in her familiar Mandarin, she doesn't know which street would take her to her uncle's apartment. She squints at the piece of paper which holds his address, then up at the buildings pressed against each other. In a small way, it reminds her of Beijing—

A rough hand wraps around her mouth before she has time to scream. More hands drag her into an alley. Cold, sharp metal presses against her neck . . . and disappears just as quickly. The hands let go of Yu Lan, who drops to her knees, dimly aware of someone fighting off her attackers.

"You wanna mug poor defenseless girls? You gotta go through me first!"

The attackers run off, and the young man turns to help Yu Lan up.
"They won't be bothering you again."

"Thank you," Yu Lan starts to say, then stops. The young man in front of her looks half Chinese, wears a well-tailored shirt and trousers, and is clearly not a man.

"They call me Rita," she says. "My pops run this place. Where do you need to go?"

Yu Lan will die of pneumonia a year later, but her time spent with Rita Moy, daughter of the unofficial mayor of Chinatown, would be considered the best year of her life.

And Rosetta found herself flat on her back, staring up at the sky, her chest heaving . . . but alive. She sat up and the crowd gasped. Rosetta could barely believe it herself. There was no hint of pain or seizures. Her head was clear, albeit filled with joy rides and the warmth of Rita's arm across her shoulders. Rosetta rose, brushed the powdery remains of stump dust off herself.

"We've been doing this all wrong," she said, scooping up the guitar. "We're supposed to sing them down. That's all they want." She went to a stump. This one was an older-looking black man, crude cap and overalls just beginning to form. She found her fingering, began singing again. This time, when it burst, she was prepared—

Lawrence Jameson has worked almost fifty years in construction. He's proud of his work, though sometimes he had to fight to get jobs. But he's a man of integrity. He's on a building now, hauling a wooden plank on his shoulders, walking a girder forty-one stories up with the ease of a man walking across a fallen log . . . until his foot slips and his stomach flip-flops as he loses his balance, falling through the air—

And was Rosetta back and whirling over to another stump—

And she was a runner for Al Capone drowning in the Chicago River and she was an old woman dying in bed after days of battling a hard cough and she was a young woman pausing from scrubbing a tub to listen to her children's laughter and she was a homeless man beaten in an alley

For this was what the gospel was supposed to be. It was never about fear. It was about going to those all alone in darkness and bringing them light. Gospel was voices lifted in song, the open-throated cry of joy. It was water bent toward parched lips, the tears and laughter bubbling from reunited friends. It was standing in front of the church and proclaiming, "I don't care what you've done. You are *always* welcome here."

"Rain!" she sang, spinning in the street.

"RAIN!" she shouted, her voice echoing off the buildings.

"*RAIN!*" she thundered, and the crowd swarmed past her, past Marty's car, past the guards—who had removed their masks and had the shell-shocked look of survivors who didn't expect to live through a fire.

In plucks and chords and harmonies, she brought those stumps to church, spun their memories into riffs and chords, and sang them out for everyone to hear.

"Rosetta!"

It took her a moment to recognize Marty shaking her arm. "You can stop now. Look! The stumps are all gone."

She coughed with a dry throat—it had been too long since she had sung. "Where's Lawler?"

"He booked it into the SPC a while ago." As he spoke, Rosetta could hear shouting and the shattering of glass coming from inside the building.

"Well, then." Rosetta pulled her Gibson out of the car and gave it a strum. Somewhere her momma was smiling. "*Now* we can go get Minnie."

In her later years, an older, thinner Memphis Minnie would sit and cackle over what she called "the Storming of the SPC."

"Oh, it was a riot," she would say in interviews. "All the SPC people running around like chickens with their heads cut off. They put me in a room and then get all panicky and put me in another room. I had no idea what was going on. Whoooo-ee! I didn't know if it was a jailbreak or Mardi Gras."

What she never told the interviewers, or anyone else for that matter, was when Minnie was finally found by Lawler and Rosetta—Lawler punching out lab coats right and left and Rosetta singing "When the Saints Come Marchin' In" at the top of her lungs—she had to press her face into the wall so no one could see her cry.

The FBI was called in to investigate the illegal activities of the SPC: spreading stump spores in poor neighborhoods and analyzing the results, kidnappings, extortion, experimentation on homeless people. Eventually Minnie and Rosetta were asked to help the government put together a new stump elimination program, one that focused more on allowing the stumps to release their memories safely. They agreed, but with one condition.

"So that's how we got Andre his club back," Rosetta told a group of partygoers.

She and Minnie were at the newly reopened Alley Cat. Andre had begged both Rosetta and Minnie to sing. He had even presented Rosetta with her own electric guitar: a National Triolian, similar to Minnie's.

So for the first time Sister Rosetta Tharpe and Memphis Minnie jammed onstage together, Rosetta with her high chants, Minnie with her low growls. They sang until one in the morning, when they both came down to take a break and let others take the stage.

"Damn straight," Minnie said. "Way I see it, if the SPC is gonna pay me to sing, and I mean really sing, I'm gonna jump on that shit."

"I thought you didn't like following their rules."

"I can too. When they make sense."

"Mind if I join?" Marty came to their table, his tie loose, carrying a couple of glasses. Rosetta rose to her feet.

"Actually, I'm going to do some more singing. You two can talk without me." Rosetta avoided Marty's eyes as she headed toward the stage.

Marty sighed as he sat down. "She's not going to forgive me, is she?"

"Can't blame her. Your testimony may have done some good, but you gotta long way to get her trust back." Minnie gave him a wide grin. "And we loooove holdin' on to our grudges."

Onstage, Rosetta strapped on her Triolian. "I'm gonna need someone to help me. Anyone know 'Up Above My Head'?"

"I do," another woman called out. She was ushered onto the stage. She had sweet eyes and a sweet smile.

"Well, then, let's see if you can keep up!"

Rosetta launched into song. The woman at first was hesitant, but then as she became more comfortable grew more animated, trading lyrics with Rosetta with all the confidence of a well-seasoned singer. Their two voices fit each other like two peas in a pod, the woman's strong contralto wrapping itself effortlessly around Rosetta's high soprano. Minnie sat up straighter, noticing that other people were watching, spellbound.

Well, damn me if they don't got something there . . .

If the room hadn't been loud before, it certainly erupted when they finished. Rosetta whooped and grabbed the woman's hands.

"That was amazing! What's your name?"

The woman blushed. "Marie Knight. I just became an exterminator two weeks ago."

"Is that so?"

Minnie snorted and drained her glass. Great. Another Holy Roller to contend with. When she set it down, she saw that Rosetta and Marie were still holding hands, gazing into each other's eyes, cheeks slightly flushed, their smiles soft and slightly silly.

Well, well, well.

Minnie gave Marty a nudge. "Hey. You wanna get Rosetta's trust back? Tell her about you and Andre. I got a feelin' she won't mind."

BRENDA PEYNADO

The Kite Maker

FROM *Tor.com*

YOU'VE NEVER SEEN a kite fly until you've seen an alien fly one. Dragonfly wings on their backs trembling with anticipation, these deep sighs from their purple mouths as they're unrolling the spool. They run with their slow, spindly legs to let the kite pick up speed. When the diamond of cloth is let loose from their skeletal hands, you can see their armored shoulders strain to rise up with it. As the diamond dips and rises on the string, you can hear these great yips, then these wavering trills and the desperateness of their song, how they want to be up there. There were thousands of them at the park the other day, and I swear to God I cried hearing those songs ripped from thousands of alien throats.

A few of them try to hide this surge of emotion when I put the kite in their hands. Tove was like this. First time he came into my shop, he tried to keep his eyes closed, his black eyelids flickering with the effort. He walked in pretty stiff for his kind, pushing his skinny feeler legs barely out in front of him, like he was sneaking in on tiptoe. But the little hairs on those legs bristled, and finally he flicked open his black lids.

Can I help you? I asked. I never knew what to say around them. It seemed like everything I said was wrong, loaded with some hidden meaning I didn't intend. I still remembered the moment they first arrived, their spaceships burning through the atmosphere like comets, like falling angels, and how we'd surrounded the ships in horror, aiming for their thin legs with anything we could find, because the rest of their bodies were armored but the legs snapped like pencils. I had done these things myself, when the boys were small, out of fear, but there was no taking it back now.

The ease of killing was just so natural to us from when bugs had encroached on the territories of our houses. Now the aliens kept my shop afloat, seeing as they were the only ones who wanted the antique toys I dealt in. These days all the humans wanted were tech-gadgets, anything with the hint of looking alien, a taste of the exotic. Kids weren't even flying remote helicopters anymore, not even drones. Now you could roll into a suburb and the kids in the front yards would be flying around mini Dragonfly Arks, playing at intergalactic war, the losers crashing down into the home-base dirt patch they called Earth. Kites, spinning tops, these were ancient toys for kids these days, more alien even than the Dragonfly tech we'd dragged out from the ships before the aliens could start fighting back. Teenagers were covered in Dragonfly tattoos and alien symbols.

Tove inhaled sharply, his Dragonfly body puffing up for a moment. He looked around my dusty shelves of wooden and metal toys. Miniature trains, yo-yos, weather vanes, carved boxes, maracas, tin soldiers. The pegged wall of kites, bright and colorful like those old collector's rooms of dead butterflies stretched open to display their wings — this was the only wall he didn't look at, as if he was infinitely aware of where it was.

I am Tove Who Battles Photons, he said in the strange way they always announced themselves, his voice flickering in and out of human range.

Anything you need? I said.

He said, *A wooden top. Maybe a kite? Or a game of the dominos?*

I used to be able to scalp them for all the technology they could spare just for the kites. Since, they'd learned to feign nonchalance, but a good antique dealer knows the market. I led him straight to the kite wall, the sailcloth breathing with the breeze he'd let in.

Tove scanned the price tags and shook his head. *Maybe not,* he said in that gravelly voice.

I knew what they did for money. Because their wings and legs were built for gravity and atmosphere thinner than ours, they didn't move fast, couldn't fly, were unsuitable for heavy lifting. Jobs like construction and fieldwork were reserved for humans. But their hands, their fingers were so nimble, so thin and skeletal, they swished through our atmosphere like singing blades. Needlework, precision jobs, diamond cutting. They would do all of this for less money than our most meaningless jobs. They slept in giant warehouses that companies had built for this purpose. But everything they made felt strange, built for another world. Cloth rasped in a way that felt hollow to our ears, jewelry they'd cut reminded us of scales instead of gold. Alien-made. All the brawny, tough-man jobs were sources of human pride, if you could have them. In this way I was more like the Dragonflies than the humans, my craft something that had become disgusting to most people, a sign of weakness.

I heard people passing on the sidewalk outside. I held my breath. Sometimes I got a hard time from angry groups who still weren't pleased that the aliens had landed, no matter how many of us were won over, no matter that there was no decent way to get rid of them. A group of antimiscegenation skinheads had been roving the strip, and it wouldn't be the first time they came in my store. I'd had bricks thrown through my window a few months before.

But the footsteps passed.

Next time, I said to Tove, exhaling.

It wasn't about the money. It was about pride in something I'd done, about art. I'd made each kite with my own hands, thread and needle, stick and lathe. I dyed the cloth myself into tapestries that could be seen from the ground. It wasn't that they couldn't make their own kites or that there weren't a few other holdout kite makers. The Dragonflies sometimes made them out of paper bags and twigs. Sometimes they even made them out of scraps of nylon they'd quilted together, stolen from the factories where they worked. But the alien craft makers reflected their own predicament in everything they made. These clunky, makeshift things flew poorly; they only reminded people of how stuck we were on the ground by their gracelessness. Mine were art, the aliens told me, they were more than the sum of their parts. Mine had the lift, the weightlessness that made you feel like you could rise up there with them, the kind that dragged your heart up by their string. They told me it made them feel like they were back home, like they had never been stuck here, like thousands of their own kind were still family-swarming around their sun. Dragonflies dropped in my store often, like moths to light. Profits went up. Now I could make the kites as big as I wanted. I had one as big as a hang glider in the back room. Eight hands would have to hold it at once to keep it on the ground.

I went to return the kite from his hands to a wooden peg on the pegboard wall. I brushed his feeler hands as I did, the millions of hairs on his black fingers tickling me. I felt my face go hot. I knew I'd done something wrong instantly.

Tove withdrew his thin arm as if he'd been burned and said nothing. He left the store in the same tiptoeing way he came.

I went home to my human-made house in the suburbs. In the dusk, I always half expected another ark to fall, the parabolas of broken ships littering the sky. But it had been fifteen years since they arrived, more since they first headed for Earth, their home world eaten by a red giant sun, only enough fuel and years to reach the closest habitable planet, break their ships open like eggs in the atmosphere, and never return. Now, when I rolled into my driveway, the kids roamed the neighborhood playing humans and aliens, hitting each other with electronic wands that dissipated on contact so that no damage could be done. We didn't have any aliens on our side of town; the children considered weak played the aliens, eyes big, offering no resistance. If they fought back, they were scolded, *That's not how it happened.*

I closed my car door. Mini-ark toys floated above my head, dipping around me as they fought and crash-landed in a sandpit. My boys seemed to have outgrown those games. They sat around the kitchen table watching holograms instead of homework.

Help me with my bags, I said, and it took them several seconds before they shifted to indicate they'd heard me.

My oldest, Aleo, brought in my bag of nearly finished kites I would work on later that night and tossed them in the corner of the kitchen without looking. He had a disdain for the things. Nobody at his high school wanted to look like poor alien kids, who were always flying kites and never wore clothes, only tiny threadbare baby shoes that protected the ends of their delicate legs from the pavement. Of course, no human would ever be confused with being an alien, of looking like a Dragonfly, but you might be confused with looking poor, and sometimes that was almost as bad. We weren't poor exactly, but no matter how much money I made off the kites, we weren't rolling in it.

Benon hugged the paper sack of groceries. He was wide-eyed, and I knew he was bullied when Aleo wasn't around.

How's the schoolwork coming? I asked as I threw broccoli into a pot.

What's cooking? Aleo asked without looking up from the hologram he'd started watching again.

Benon held his nose. I didn't make any excuses for my cooking.

When we sat down to eat, Benon said, *About homework . . .*

Shoot, I said.

I have a history report. It can be about anything.

I froze. I knew what he would say before it was out of his mouth.
Of course he would, always playing the alien in the neighborhood
games.

I want to write about the Fallings, he said.

I pressed my lips together hard. Aleo shoved more food in his
mouth than I thought it was possible to swallow. Something black
flashed from under Aleo's sleeve as he reached for more food. I
grabbed his hand and pulled up his sleeve. *What is that?*

Nothing, he said, yanking his sleeve back down again. But I'd
seen it. Alien script: the swoops and careful circles, the spheres
with the arrows shooting out.

Is it permanent? I said. *Do you even know what that means?*

Aleo mumbled something.

Benon said, *Mom, you were there at the Fallings. You saw it.*

So did your brother. Aleo, what does it mean?

I don't remember a ship, Aleo said. *I was only a few years old.*

What does the tattoo mean? I insisted.

Aleo slammed his fork down. *It means Aleo Laughter in the Air.*

I snorted. *Laughter in the Air? Really? Can you even read it?*

He didn't answer.

Mom, Benon whined, *I want to know what it was like.*

I didn't say, *How could you own up to all the things you've ever done
that shamed you? How could you look backwards while stepping over the
dead bodies in the way?*

It changed everything, I said.

I got up from the table. I was no longer hungry. I shut myself up
in the back room for the rest of the night, turning a group of sticks
smooth in the lathe. One thick, long branch was earmarked for
the large kite. When I picked it up, it felt just like the weight of a
baseball bat, the only weapon I'd had when I'd headed to the first
Arkfall. I swung it in the air, the heft just right for making contact.

In late summer the skinheads started setting fire to some of the
shops that catered to Dragonflies. It was illegal, and also ridicu-

lous. The world would change without them whether they wanted it to or not. But a bakery down the street that had hired a Dragonfly to decorate the cakes had burned to the ground.

The skinheads were already on the wrong side of history, but it only made them cling harder to old hatreds. Some groups were angry because the Dragonflies were taking up resources, others because they'd taken their jobs. Others were staunch on no human-Dragonfly love. Our species were so different we couldn't procreate together, and the religious zealots claimed that without the sanctification of children, the union was unnatural, disgusting. Bestiality, which was a sin. Religious pundits who were horrified at what they'd done tried to justify our cruelty by saying the Dragonflies had no souls. Some of them believed that the aliens were playing a long con, coining the phrase *There's more than one way to colonize an Earth.*

It was months before Tove walked into my shop again. I wouldn't even have recognized him—I had a hard time differentiating them—except he had that strange way of walking like he was feeling his way around a cage. The bell tinkled, and he tiptoed in again. From Benon's history report, from which he walked around the house spewing facts, I knew that their religions focused on the legs as the expressions of the body. The rest of their bodies were so rigid, but the legs could curl like delicate antennae. If they could express their souls, it would be through the way they walked.

We're closing soon, I said. I hoped he did not remember my touch.

Tove's top antennae drooped.

But if there's something I can do? I said.

He tiptoed through the aisles of shelves, ended up at the kite wall like I knew he would. I hopped off my stool. He set his fingers to glide across the sailcloth of the cheapest kite, a red one that pictured the deserts of Mars. I could tell it wasn't his favorite. His eyes, remarkably human, roved all over the wall.

There was one on the bottom shelf that was my own favorite, painted mostly blue like it would melt into the sky. A big no-no in the kite trade; amateurs stuck to reds and oranges, colors that would be easily seen in the clouds. But I was an artist and hated rules. I wanted the kite to blend in. I wanted the kite to look like a ripple across a mirror, like a great tide welling up under the surface. It wasn't the cheapest, but I was determined to see it in the sky. I always made my customers take their kites across the street to the park. I told them it was to verify that they were satisfied, that the kite worked. But mostly I was watching them, trying to understand the alien emotion that racked their bodies as they let it loose.

How about this one, I said picking it up.

He purred from his throat, smashed his eyes shut against the blue.

It is not for me, he said. *I would have to ask.*

Who is it for? I asked.

My sons, he said.

Benon had informed me that the Dragonfly women gave all of the material gifts to the offspring, so I knew something must have happened to Tove's mate. If the thing had happened fifteen years ago, I did not want to know. My own mate had left me around that time, for another woman across the country. It made you realize you didn't even know yourself, he'd said, that we didn't even know who we'd become. He wanted to start over with someone else, with this new understanding. He said, as he closed the door softly for the last time on me and the kids, *How can you love like that, not knowing what's inside of you?*

I hadn't argued.

I'm sure they would love it, I told Tove. *These sell quickly, so I can't promise to hold it.*

It is about choice, he said tersely in his accent. His voice sounded like a bad radio, wavering in and out. Their own language was spoken on a frequency that sounded to us like silence and hums.

Benon had told me that back on Sadiyada, none of them gave orders. If a shuttle full of Dragonflies were about to drive over the cliff, the passengers would say, *A cliff!* rather than *Stop!* or *Turn around!* They believed in pointing out what was there rather than compelling action. When they had realized their sun was about to engulf their planet, they merely built the ships, let anyone who wanted aboard the one-way ticket, the ships that would fall apart on atmospheric impact, and the others just stayed behind, burned up with the sun. Sons, mothers, lovers, all of them separated, and no matter the love between them, not a one would beg, *Come with me.* They just waved goodbye.

And then they got here, and they were assaulted with demands. *Come out, come out unarmed, give us everything you have, defend your-*

self, fight back so we can excuse what we've done, proceed this way to the camps, work, work, buy. Buy. I pressured them all. I can't imagine the shame, on top of everything else I had caused.

I nodded to Tove, who put my favorite kite down to look at another. *Choose whichever you'd like,* I said, a demand disguised as a choice.

Two teenage voices began yelling outside the store.

I pushed Tove quickly into the back workroom. He screeched softly, his hairs smashed down underneath my palms. *Stay here,* I said, *and don't come out until I tell you.* Tove said nothing.

Trust me, I pleaded. I had to leave him there, stuck among my half-finished projects and the cardboard boxes.

I got to the front counter before the bell tinkled, before bald heads rushed into the room, the baldness a physical refusal to be like the Dragonflies with their million bristling, feeling hairs. They blew in with chants of *bugs are bugs!*

Any bugs in here? the leader asked.

No, I said quickly. I stared them down. I recognized one of them, an older girl that Aleo had brought over once after school. Then, I thought she'd been nice, shy, had always called me ma'am. The baldness was new, her scalp paler where hair used to be, and it made her look alien herself. I could tell she recognized me too, the way she wouldn't meet my eyes, and she hunched her shoulders and tried to melt behind one of the others, a burly man with a sweatband around his forehead.

Lady, I could have sworn, the ringleader said.

See for yourself, I said. I knew it was best to let their anger wash over the store with the least provocation. I had called the cops before, and I knew from experience that they waited until any damage was already done before appearing.

They looked around the store without moving. Their eyes settled on the kites. They knew who my customers were. They started to poke through the racks, the dusty aisles, the afternoon light arriving in golden, violent streaks to illuminate what even the best of us were capable of.

The girl I recognized pushed a display case weakly, so that it tottered but didn't fall. One of them brushed a row of yo-yos onto the floor. Another was heading in the direction of the workroom door. The burly man with the sweatband picked up the kite Tove had been looking at, which he had dropped on the floor. I kept eye contact with the girl I recognized, who finally looked up and caught my eye.

Nothing here, she said.

The burly one with the kite handed it to the girl like it was evidence to the contrary. The girl looked at me, snapped the wood of the kite. She ripped the cloth in a struggle of arms.

Shoddy work, she said, tossing the flail of broken kite, the spine akimbo. She led them out of the store. I could hear them whooping on their way down the street to the next establishment.

I picked up the broken kite and put it behind the counter. I spent a moment picking up the scatters of wooden yo-yos, just in case they changed their minds and came back.

When I finally opened the door, Tove was under the giant hang-glider-sized kite that took up most of the ten-foot room. His shape under there flinched when he heard the door open.

I'm sorry, I said. *You can come out now.*

He moved the giant kite off and nodded.

I held my hand out to help him, but he stood up slowly by himself, his legs curling heavily under his weight, the air pushed from the flutter of his wings tickling my hands. A breeze when there was none.

This one, he said, pointing at the giant kite. *This is the one I want.*

I had painted it with a mosaic that looked like stained glass, so when it flew, it was like we were inside some great cathedral where we were supposed to pray. Like we were stuck here, underneath its great glass, but our spirit was supposed to rise somehow anyway.

How much? he asked.

I understood Tove, wanting the biggest, best thing you couldn't have. I wanted his unexhausted hope, that's what I wanted. I wanted forgiveness without having to name my sins, I wanted tenderness to feel real to me again. Some part of me wanted to fly in the face of everything those skinheads represented, but another part of me wanted the world before the Dragonflies fell in, the world we couldn't have. Were we tender before? Could we be tender again? Or did the Fallings only awaken the violence we'd always had? Benon had informed me that the Dragonflies were so fragile, all those hairs on their legs and arms and feelers, all those thin appendages, that they were so careful with each other when they loved that they barely ever touched. Lovemaking was mostly an act of foreplay, their wings manipulating the air around the loved like a cyclone sending all of their hairs and feelers singing with touch. It was like being loved by the air itself. Even this was left wanting from Earth's atmosphere, their movements clumsier now, the work so much harder on them. But human lungs! We had always been clumsy, but we had more lung force than their wings had now. Instead of answering Tove, giving him the price of a simple kite, I pursed my lips and whistled air in his direction.

Oh, he said, eyes closing. *Oh hemena.* His throat buzzed.

I whistled again, pushing air across his face in the circular pattern Benon had described.

Oh, I feel unarmored, he said. *Oh hemenalala, I am defenseless.*

It was like I was pummeling the words out of him, he said them that painfully. I knew he wanted to say *Stop.* He wanted to say *Desist.* Were those nicknames he had given his fallen mate? Was he trying to call her ghost back across the years? But it was my name I wanted on his purple lips.

I blew all the way around him to the back, where his four wings trembled, my breath blowing their wing-dust off until they shone translucent. Had he still been able to fly, stripping his wings of their powder would have been even more cruel. Benon had said that their wings were electric colors in the home atmosphere, but in this one they had turned a dusty brown. Now they were drab ghosts of what they used to be. Benon had never told me what came after, what consummation was for them. Had I known, I would have done it. I know I would have done it.

Oh hemenalala, he said as I made my way back to his front, where his thorax armor glistened and tensed.

Finally I stopped, held my breath.

When Tove was finally able to compose himself, I couldn't look at him. I said, *The kite isn't finished. Come back in a month.*

He didn't answer me and he didn't turn around. His eyes stayed closed the whole way out of the store.

A few weeks later I went home to a Dragonfly in the backyard, the neighborhood kids around him with their electronic sticks. Even the older kids were out, excited by the new development. *What's going on?* I said.

Ask Benon. Aleo shrugged.

He's for my project, Benon said. *I asked him to come home with us.*

Are you fine with this? I asked the Dragonfly kid.

I'm cool, the Dragonfly said.

The Dragonfly looked at me and popped gum from his tiny, pursed mouth. I waited for him to announce himself the way his kind did. It was hard to tell their ages, but this one must have been born here, was already starting to lose the customs of his parents.

Finally I asked him, *Who are you?* more combatively than I would have liked.

I am Yeshela Whisperer of Mist, the child said begrudgingly.

Wonderful, I said, and I went back inside.

I was not against the kids mixing, unlike other parents I knew, who were prying their blinds open to watch across the block. It's just that I didn't think the kids were ready. Not after I'd seen what we'd done as adults. But I was willing to bet against myself. I left them to it and pulled aside the curtain.

They were reenacting the Fallings again, which the Dragonflies called the Arkfall Massacres but we did not. Benon sat atop our old swing set and was directing. It seemed like this time they were trying to get everything exactly right. They even had a giant hologram of one of the Arks cracked like an egg projected behind them in the sandbox. Benon was reading the history out loud.

Thousands died. We didn't know what they wanted. When they crawled out of their broken ships and picked themselves up out of the crashes, we were sure they were invading, they wanted our children, they wanted more than we could give. We defended our earth. We aimed for their thin legs, their eyes, their delicate fingers. In our city, a ship crashed into the main fiberoptic tower. It wiped out most communications, and city officials were too panicked to fix it. Other cities made other mistakes. We couldn't call each other directly, and so everything we knew about the crash that boomed into the city at dusk, the other arkfalls across the world, was through a rumor mill. Was the National Guard coming? Were they too busy with other arkfalls? Were there too many of the ships to defend against? How many of us could they kill before we reacted? By sundown the next day, we were at the crash site with any weapon we could find.

The neighborhood kids were making the Dragonfly kid crawl out of the hologram. Then they had a line of them stand off with their e-sticks. Benon knew I was watching. He couldn't help but flick his eyes in my direction. That kid always had the uncanny ability to know when I was looking, unlike Aleo.

Benon directed the neighborhood kids to approach and demand what the Dragonflies wanted. *Tell us what you want. Hand over your weapons. Speak in our language. Give us everything.* Benon kept pausing the action to ask the boy what he felt, what he would have done if he'd been there.

The moment came I was dreading. The boy, as directed, stood up slowly, testing the thick, heavy atmosphere. He put up his thin arms to shield his eyes from the alien sun. Benon said, *Look, he's going to shoot us.* The humans approached, sticks raised. The boy's wings fluttered, an unconscious reaction, trying to fly away, even in a game, finding this atmosphere a noose to the ground—just like his parents did, then. Had he been like us, he would have yelled for the humans to stop. The e-sticks flew at him, whaled on him, and went for his legs. The e-sticks worked as they were supposed to, dissipating into gas upon contact. The blows weren't hurting him. Aleo had once flung one at me in a childish rage, and the dissipation had only felt like the strangest whisper. The boy closed his eyes at the feeling of the sticks passing over him, his sensitive body hairs moving through the ghosts of a long-dead massacre. Benon looked at me, it seemed, for approval, his eyes asking, *Is this right? Is this how you did it?*

I closed the curtains. A spray of police lights flashed past the window. Someone must have called the cops when they heard a Dragonfly boy was in the neighborhood.

I opened the curtains again. Yeshela was cowering on the ground, trying not to move lest he hit the handles and fists holding the e-sticks, which would not dissipate. The humans were still going, their joy at having their game more lifelike than it had ever been before like a drug. How could they know what they were pretending to be? For them, it was just a story. They never got to the point of horror, the point where we were sorry, when the tide turned, after we wanted them to surrender in the human way, arms up, after we wanted them to fight back to absolve us, after we realized they could not be pushed to fight back, when we began to carry them into the hospitals and the morgue, the doctors trying as best as they could to understand our differences, how to get under their armor, how to splint antennae together, where the vital organs were.

I burst through the screen door. *Stop,* I yelled.

Mom, it's a game, Aleo said.

A game, I scoffed. *Do you know where I saw your friend, that nice girl you brought over once?*

Aleo shrugged. I hadn't told him.

The cop car parked across the street.

I'm taking you home, I said to the Dragonfly boy.

I loaded Aleo and Benon and the Dragonfly into the car. The boy directed me to a side of town I'd avoided since the city had changed. The three were silent the whole way. The streets changed from suburbs and people walking their dogs after work to cheap construction warehouses in a maze of driveways, deserted. In our city they had been installed in old complexes of customer fulfill-ment warehouses. In other cities they had been pushed into con-demned and rotten buildings at the center. In others they were given cloth FEMA tents. In others they were given nothing and wandered from public park to public park.

The warehouse the boy pointed me to was almost as big as one of their own ships. A cluster of them gathered around the indus-trial complex. At the gates of the warehouse, I parked, pushed my boys out. *You're going to apologize to his mother,* I said. Benon hung his head.

History makes no apologies, Aleo said, repeating something he'd heard in a bad hologram, winking at Benon.

The Dragonfly boy did not say, *Please don't come, please do not meet my mother, please do not tell them what you did.* Instead he said, *The warehouse is not a place you'll like. My mother will not like this. We are far in the back.*

Which did not deter me in the least.

A smaller door had been cut into the giant loading-dock door. Inside, the old product shelving stacks had been repurposed into bunks, layer upon layer of bed spaces where as many as four or five of them slept at a time. Whole families of Dragonflies curled into each other's bodies. We stepped over standing water on the concrete floors, the smell of mold, flies swarming in clouds. There were dragonfly feeders hung up on the long scaffolding—I mean actual dragonflies, the tiny Earth kind, which the aliens hatched from eggs and studied. There was no electricity, no running water I could see. Just rows and rows of bunks, each bunk bed like a tiny home, some decorated with my own kites and wind catchers, wind chimes, feathers, mechanical fans.

When we reached the bunk the boy said was his, his mother

climbed down, buzzing. She didn't announce her name because it was her turf, not mine, but I didn't give her my name either. I pushed my boys in front of me.

I'm sorry, they chimed in unison.

For what? asked the mother.

They— I said. *We*—

He wasn't hurt, I finally said.

I don't understand, she said. She chattered to her son in their own language, the hums and silences, and he sullenly responded, his legs curling and making him sink in stature.

I wanted to run back the way we had come, past rows and rows of these broken families, but I made the three of us stand there in penance.

The mother turned her head back to us. She said, *I think forgiveness means different things in our language. We do not ask for it.*

We were silent, rebuked, our heads hung.

I'm sorry we make you sleep here, Aleo said. *It's so horrible.*

For a moment I was proud. I would have pointed out every failure in the warehouses so my boys would learn how much we had.

Then the mother said, *It's our home.* She turned away from me, bundled her child's legs up, and lifted him, laboring slowly up the ladder in the heavy atmosphere.

That night I put my sons to bed for the first time in years, checking on them in the bedroom they shared before they turned out the lights.

Benon was still chattering about his history report, how he could use what he'd learned.

Please, I said, *don't do that again.*

Aleo rolled his eyes, turned over. Benon gave a large sigh. I was afraid for them, my kids, for what they would discover about themselves, for what they wanted to be but would soon discover they couldn't. I tried to hold them both, one arm in each bed. Aleo shrugged me away, Benon stayed rigid.

Mom, we don't need you, Aleo said.

Weeks passed. Tove did not come back. I wasn't expecting him to. Where would he get the money? And after what I'd done. Benon got an A on his history report, the note from the teacher saying, *May there be no judgment in truth.* The skinheads came again into my store after another one of my customers, who was able to slip slowly out the back door. Benon was still spouting Dragonfly facts routinely, like, *Their language doesn't even have a grammar for commands,* and *Didja know they had prophecies about ending up here eventually? But this is only the third epoch in their religious texts, there's still a fourth and a fifth about going to other places and saving us along with them.* Apparently they too had stories about arks, wandering through deserts, how many of them would fall when they got to their new home. Aleo got another tattoo, this one a poor translation of a command which they had no word for, *Remember.*

One afternoon, just before closing, I heard people yelling outside my store, saw the lighters flick on the other side of the frosted glass. I ran outside.

What do you think you're doing? I yelled to the group that had gathered, the same group of skinheads that had plagued me with Tove. I meant to distract them with words, I meant to drain the fervor out of what they were doing. I meant to inject them with the moment I had years before when I dropped my bat. But the aliens hadn't fought back, had waited until we'd made a ruin of them.

The leader said, *Stay out of the way and you won't get hurt.*

The lighters were licking strips of cardboard. I thought of how much money was inside that store in wood and cloth, what I would lose. I let my temper loose. I started yelling, calling them the curs of the world, disgusting creatures, more animal than the bugs, not fit to inherit the earth. I spat because I'd seen it done in holograms and at some point my words failed me.

The girl who had been Aleo's friend, now confident and grown into her role, said, *Lady, I wasn't even born when they got here, and I didn't even have the chance to do anything. What did you do when they came? You're just like us.*

That was before I knew, I said.

And now we know what we are, the girl said. *You're just pretending.*

The rest of them chanted. *More than one way. Bugs are bugs.* The cardboard strips touched the storefront. They all stepped back.

There is *more than one way,* I said. I rushed forward, trying to put out the flames with my shirt, but the flames seemed to glow and leap up brighter with every swing and fan of my shirt. I yanked open the door of the shop, burning my hand on the doorknob, and ran inside.

Inside the shop, you could barely hear the crackle of the fire. I was panting. I stopped. I looked around at the shelves, the kite wall illuminated orange from the flames outside the window. Did I want to let it burn? To let everything I had done in conciliation disappear, burn up, leave no trace? For any guilt I had to disappear, to be forgiven by flames?

And then I smelled smoke. I snapped out of it, ran in a craze pulling kites down off the walls, rushing back and forth to my car parked out back, dumping everything I could and going back inside. One of the kites caught on the doorjamb, the cloth tearing like muscle, the frame snapping like bones, like legs, like antennae, a feeling I remembered. In my memory I stood over a Dragonfly, arms lifted to protect a small one. I left the baby, but I killed the mother. We were methodical in our frenzy. Dragonfly after Dragonfly, if they moved, if they didn't move, if they made sound, if they were silent, we killed them. We were afraid. I was afraid.

I pulled all the kites down off the wall before the flames reached inside. I pulled the giant kite out of the back room, the frame still heavy as a baseball bat, the cloth still fragile as skin.

I started driving. What did I have left in the world? My sons, my kites. The certainty of moving forward and beginning again. My fear. I wanted to scream. For a moment I let go of the steering wheel and let the car drift over into the other lane. Another car was coming down the roadway like everything in our world was normal. Then I thought of Aleo and Benon and jerked my wheel back.

I drove my car in circles. I was like a sleepwalker. I don't even know how I got there; eventually I ended up at the Dragonfly warehouses.

Inside, I asked, *Please, does anyone know Tove Battler of Photons?*

They bristled, and too late I realized I'd said his name wrong. Long black antennae-like fingers pointed me to another warehouse, down corridors, up racks of bunks. Then I found him lying on a third-floor bunk, eyes closed, his sons chattering in their mother tongue beside him.

Tove, I said.

He sat up.

I did not say, *Come outside,* or even *please.* I said, *My store is burning. There is something outside. It is for you.*

He stared at me for a good while. Did he hate me? He could have lain back in his bunk. Instead he labored down slowly. He waved his antennae at his sons, and they followed at a distance.

There were tears sliding down my face. *Why didn't you defend yourself?* I asked. *Why?*

He led the way outside, tiptoeing as if walking toward a dangerous secret. Finally he said, *Wouldn't you have killed us all if we had fought back and lost? You have books that say only the weak will inherit the earth. In our prophecies, the only way to stay was to not fight back.*

I didn't mean fifteen years ago, I meant in my back room, but this answer was as good as any. I said, *But why did you not fight back?*

I wanted to live so badly, he said. For the first time I noticed seams on his legs where they must have been broken before, the source of his strange tiptoe walking.

And if you inherit the earth, what will you do with it? I said.

Silent, he waited for me behind the trunk of my car. A crowd of Dragonflies gathered behind us to see what this human woman wanted with one of their kind.

I opened the trunk door, passed out the kites I'd saved. Of what use could they possibly be to me? I handed the end of a rope to Tove, two others to his sons. I had five other rope ends that I passed out. Each was one piece of the giant kite.

This wasn't charity; this wasn't forgiveness. How could it be, after all that I had done, was still doing? I wanted to fling it in their faces, what they had lost. I wanted to see them hurt for that sky, sing for that lost planet. I wanted them to sing my own song and break open with it.

Then Tove led the eight of them forward, running slowly with their curling legs. The kite, the sky over them as oppressive as my fear. All around me I heard gasps and yips, long protracted vowels, what they called their home planet in their own language. They moaned as the hang glider went up, that cathedral shard taking off above us, begging us all to rise.

P. DJÈLÍ CLARK

The Secret Lives of the Nine Negro Teeth of George Washington

FROM *Fireside Fiction*

"By Cash pd Negroes for 9 Teeth on Acct of Dr. Lemoire"
—*Lund Washington, Mount Vernon plantation, Account Book dated 1784*

THE FIRST NEGRO tooth purchased for George Washington came from a blacksmith, who died that very year at Mount Vernon of the flux. The art of the blacksmith had been in his blood—passed down from ancestral spirits who had come seeking their descendants across the sea. Back in what the elder slaves called Africy, he had heard, blacksmiths were revered men who drew iron from the earth and worked it with fire and magic: crafting spears so wondrous they could pierce the sky and swords with beauty enough to rend mountains. Here, in this Colony of Virginia, he had been set to shape crueler things: collars to fasten about bowed necks, shackles to ensnare tired limbs, and muzzles to silence men like beasts. But blacksmiths know the secret language of iron, and he beseeched his creations to bind the spirits of their wielders—as surely as they bound flesh. For the blacksmith understood what masters had chosen to forget: when you make a man or woman a slave, you enslave yourself in turn. And the souls of those who made thralls of others would never know rest—in this life or the next.

When he wore that tooth, George Washington complained of hearing the heavy fall of a hammer on an anvil day and night. He ordered all iron-making stopped at Mount Vernon. But the sound of the blacksmith's hammer rang out in his head all the same.

*

The second Negro tooth belonging to George Washington came from a slave from the Kingdom of Ibani, what the English with their inarticulate tongues call Bonny Land, and (much to his annoyance) hence him, a Bonny man. The Bonny man journeyed from Africa on a ship called the *Jesus,* which, as he understood, was named for an ancient sorcerer who defied death. Unlike the other slaves bound on that ship, who came from the hinterlands beyond his kingdom, he knew the fate that awaited him—though he would never know what law or sacred edict he had broken that sent him to this fate. He found himself in that fetid hull chained beside a merman, with scales that sparkled like green jewels and eyes as round as black coins. The Bonny man had seen mermen before out among the waves, and stories said some of them swam into rivers to find wives among local fisherwomen. But he hadn't known the whites made slaves of them too. As he would later learn, mermen were prized by thaumaturgic-inclined aristocrats who dressed them in fine livery to display to guests; most, however, were destined for Spanish holdings, where they were forced to dive for giant pearls off the shores of New Granada. The two survived the horrors of the passage by relying on each other. The Bonny man shared tales of his kingdom, of his wife and children and family, forever lost. The merman in turn told of his underwater home, of its queen and many curiosities. He also taught the Bonny man a song: a plea to old and terrible things that dwelled in the deep, dark hidden parts of the sea—great beings with gaping mouths that opened up whirlpools or tentacles that could drag ships beneath the depths. They would one day rise to wreak vengeance, he promised, for all those who had been chained to suffer in these floating coffins. The Bonny man never saw the merman after they made land on the English isle of Barbados. But he carried the song with him as far as the Colony of Virginia, and on the Mount Vernon plantation he sang it as he looked across fields of wheat to an ocean he couldn't see—and waited.

When George Washington wore the Bonny man's tooth, he found himself humming an unknown song that sounded (strange to his thinking) like the tongue of the savage mermen. And in the dark hidden parts of the sea, old and terrible things stirred.

*

The third Negro tooth of George Washington was bought from a slave who later ran from Mount Vernon, of which an account was posted in the *Virginia Gazette* in 1785:

> Advertiſement: Runaway from the plantation of the Subſcriber, in *Fairfax* County, ſome Time in *October* laſt, on All-Hallows Eve, a Mulatto Fellow, 5 Feet 8 Inches high of Tawney Complexion named *Tom,* about 25 Years of Age, miſſing a front tooth. He is ſenſible for a Slave and ſelf-taught in foul necromancy. He lived for ſome Years previous as a ſervant at a ſchool of learned ſorcery near *Williamsburg,* and was removed on Account of inciting the dead ſlaves there to riſe up in inſurrection. It is ſuppoſed he returned to the ſchool to raiſe up a young Negro Wench, named *Anne,* a former ſervant who died of the pox and was buried on the campus grounds, his Siſter. He ſold away a tooth and with that ſmall money was able to purchase a ſpell used to call upon powers potent on All-Hallows Eve to ſpirit themſelves away to parts now unknown. Whoever will ſecure the ſaid *Tom,* living, and *Anne,* dead, ſo that they be delivered to the plantation of the Subſcriber in *Fairfax* County aforeſaid, ſhall have Twenty Shillings Reward, besides what the Law allows.

To George Washington's frustration, Tom's tooth frequently fell out of his dentures, no matter how he tried to secure it. Most bizarre of all, he would find it often in the unlikeliest of places—as if the vexsome thing was deliberately concealing itself. Then one day the tooth was gone altogether, never to be seen again.

George Washington's fourth Negro tooth was from a woman named Henrietta. (Contrary to widespread belief, there is no difference of significance between the dentition of men and women—as any trained dentist, odontomancer, or the Fay folk, who require human teeth as currency, will well attest.) Henrietta's father had been John Indian, whose father had been a Yamassee warrior captured and sold into bondage in Virginia. Her mother's mother had come to the mainland from Jamaica, sold away for taking part in Queen Nanny's War. As slaves, both were reputed to be unruly and impossible to control. Henrietta inherited that defiant blood, and more than one owner learned the hard way that she wasn't to be trifled with. After holding down and whipping her last mistress soundly, she was sold to work fields at Mount Vernon—because, as her former master adver-

tised, strong legs and a broad back weren't to be wasted. Henrietta often dreamed of her grandparents. She often dreamed she
was her grandparents. Sometimes she was a Yamassee warrior,
charging a fort with flintlock musket drawn, eyes fixed on the
soldier she intended to kill—as from the ramparts English mages
hurled volleys of emerald fireballs that could melt through iron.
Other times she was a young woman, barely fifteen, who chanted
Asante war songs as she drove a long saber, the blade blazing
bright with obeah, into the belly of a slave master (this one had
been a pallid blood-drinker) and watched as he blackened and
crumbled away to ash.

When George Washington wore Henrietta's tooth he sometimes
woke screaming from night terrors. He told Martha they were memories from the war, and would never speak of the faces he saw coming for him in those dreams: a fierce Indian man with long black
hair and death in his eyes, and a laughing slave girl with a curiously
innocent face, who plunged scorching steel into his belly.

The fifth Negro tooth belonging to George Washington came by
unexplained means from a conjure man who was not listed among
Mount Vernon's slaves. He had been born before independence,
in what was then the Province of New Jersey, and learned his trade
from his mother—a root woman of some renown (among local slaves, at any rate), having been brought to the region from
the southern territories of New France. The conjure man used
his magics mostly in the treatment of maladies affecting his fellow bondsmen, of the mundane or paranormal varieties. He had
been one of the tens of thousands of slaves during the war who
answered the call put out by the Earl of Dunmore, royal governor
of Virginia in November 1775:

> And I hereby declare all indentured servants, Negroes, hedge witches
> and wizards, occultists, lycanthropes, giants, non-cannibal ogres and
> any fentient magical creatures or others (appertaining to Rebels)
> free and relieved of fupernatural fanction that are able and willing
> to bear Arms, they joining His MAJESTY'S Troops as foon as may
> be, for the more fpeedily reducing this Colony to a proper Senfe
> of their Duty, to His MAJESTY'S Crown and Dignity. This edict ex-
> cludes Daemonic beasts who fhould not take faid proclamation as a
> fummons who, in doing so, will be exorcized from His MAJESTY'S
> realm with all deliberate fpeed.

The conjure man was first put in the service of Hessian mercenaries, to care for their frightening midnight-black steeds that breathed flames and with hooves of fire. Following, he'd been set to performing menial domestic spells for Scottish warlocks, treated no better there than a servant. It was fortune (aided by some skillful stone casting) that placed him in Colonel Tye's regiment. Like the conjure man, Tye had been a slave in New Jersey who fled to the British, working his way to becoming a respected guerrilla commander. Tye led the infamous Black Brigade—a motley crew of fugitive slaves, outlaw juju men, and even a Spanish mulata werewolf—who worked alongside the elite Queen's Rangers. Aided by the conjure man's gris-gris, the Black Brigade carried out raids on militiamen: launching attacks on their homes, destroying their weapons, stealing supplies, burning spells, and striking fear into the hearts of patriots. The conjure man's brightest moment had come the day he captured his own master and bound him in the same shackles he'd once been forced to wear. The Brigade stirred such hysteria that the patriot governor of New Jersey declared martial law, putting up protective wards around the province—and General George Washington himself was forced to send his best mage hunters against them. In a running skirmish with those patriot huntsmen, Tye was fatally struck by a cursed ball from a long rifle, cutting through his gris-gris. The conjure man stood guard over his fallen commander, performing a final rite that would disallow their enemies from re-animating the man or binding his soul. Of the five mage hunters he killed three, but was felled in the attempt. With his final breath, he whispered his own curse on any that would desecrate his corpse.

One of the surviving mage hunters pulled the conjure man's teeth as a souvenir of the battle, and a few days hence tumbled to land awkwardly from his horse and broke his neck. The tooth passed to a second man, who choked to death on an improbably lodged bit of turtle soup in his windpipe. And so it went, bringing dire misfortune to each of its owners. The conjure man's tooth has now, by some twist of fate, made its way to Mount Vernon and into George Washington's collection. He has not worn it yet.

The sixth Negro tooth of George Washington belonged to a slave who had tumbled here from another world. The startled English sorcerer who witnessed this remarkable event had been set to deliver a speech on conjurations at the Royal Society of London for Improving Supernatural Knowledge. Alas, before the sorcerer could tell the world of his discovery, he was quietly killed by agents of the Second Royal African Company, working in a rare alliance with their Dutch rivals. As they saw it, if Negroes could simply be pulled out of thin air, the lucrative trade in human cargo that made such mercantilists wealthy could be irrevocably harmed. The conjured Negro, however, was allowed to live—bundled up and shipped from London to a Virginia slave market. Good property, after all, was not to be wasted. She ended up at Mount Vernon, and was given the name Esther. The other slaves, however, called her Solomon—on account of her wisdom.

Solomon claimed not to know anything about magic, which didn't exist in her native home. But how could that be, the other slaves wondered, when she could mix together powders to cure their sicknesses better than any physician; when she could make predictions of the weather that always came true; when she could construct all manner of wondrous contraptions from the simplest of objects? Even the plantation manager claimed she was "a Negro of curious intellect," and listened to her suggestions on crop rotations and field systems. The slaves well knew that the many agricultural reforms at Mount Vernon, for which their master took credit, were actually Solomon's genius. They often asked why she didn't use her remarkable wit to get hired out and make money. Certainly that'd be enough to buy her freedom.

Solomon always shook her head, saying that though she was from another land, she felt tied to them by "the consanguinity of bondage." She would work to free them all, or, falling short of that, at the least bring some measure of ease to their lives. But at night, after she'd finished her mysterious "experiments" (which she kept secret from all), she could be found gazing up at the stars, and it was hard not to see the longing held deep in her eyes.

When George Washington wore Solomon's tooth, he dreamed of a place of golden spires and colorful glass domes, where Negroes flew through the sky on metal wings like birds and sprawling cities that glowed bright at night were run by machines who thought faster than men. It both awed and frightened him at once.

The seventh Negro tooth purchased for George Washington had come from a Negro from Africa who himself had once been a trader in slaves. He had not gone out with the raids or the wars between kingdoms to procure them but had been an instrumental middleman—a translator who spoke the languages of both the coastal slavers and their European buyers. He was instrumental in keeping the enchanted rifles and rum jugs flowing and assuring his benefactors a good value for the human merchandise. It was thus ironic that his downfall came from making a bad deal. The local ruler, a distant relative to a king, felt cheated and (much to the trader's shock) announced his translator put up for sale. The English merchant gladly accepted the offer. And just like that, the trader went from a man of position to a commodity.

He went half mad of despair when they'd chained him in the hold of the slave ship. Twice he tried to rip out his throat with his fingernails, preferring death to captivity. But each time he died, he returned to life—without sign of injury. He'd jumped into the sea to drown, only to be hauled back in without a drop of water in his lungs. He'd managed to get hold of a sailor's knife, driven it into his chest, and watched in shock as his body pushed the blade out and healed the wound. It was then he understood the extent of his downfall: he had been cursed. Perhaps by the gods. Perhaps by spirits of the vengeful dead. Or by some witch or conjurer for whom he'd haggled out a good price. He would never know. But they had cursed him to suffer this turn of fate, to become what he'd made of others. And there would be no escape.

The Negro slave trader's tooth was George Washington's favorite. No matter how much he used it, the tooth showed no signs of wear. Sometimes he could have sworn he'd broken it. But when inspected, it didn't show as much as a fracture—as if it mended itself. He put that tooth to work hardest of all, and gave it not a bit of rest.

The eighth Negro tooth belonging to George Washington came from his cook, who was called Ulysses. He had become a favorite in the Mount Vernon household, known for his culinary arts and the meticulous care he gave to his kitchen. The dinners and parties held at the mansion were always catered by Ulysses, and visitors praised his skill at devising new dishes to tingle the tongue and salivate the senses. Those within the higher social circles frequented by the Washingtons familiarly called him "Uncle Lysses" and showered him with such gifts that local papers remarked: "The Negro cook had become something of a celebrated puffed-up dandy." Ulysses took his work seriously, as much as he took his name.

He used the monies gained from those gifts, as well as his habit of selling leftovers (people paid good money to sup on the Washingtons' fare), to purchase translated works by Homer. In those pages he learned about the fascinating travels of his namesake, and was particularly taken by the figure Circe—an enchantress famed for her vast knowledge of potions and herbs, who through a fine feast laced with a potent elixir had turned men into swine. Ulysses amassed other books as well: Eastern texts on Chinese herbology, banned manuscripts of Mussulman alchemy, even rare ancient Egyptian papyri on shape-shifting.

His first tests at transmogrification had merely increased the appetite of Washington's guests, who turned so ravenous they relieved themselves of knife or spoon and shoveled fistfuls of food into their mouths like beasts. A second test had set them all to loud high-pitched squealing—which was blamed on an overimbibing of cherubimical spirits. Success came at last when he heard some days after a summer dining party that a Virginia plantation owner and close friend of the Washingtons had gone missing—the very same day his wife had found a great fat spotted hog rummaging noisily through their parlor. She had her slaves round up the horrid beast, which was summarily butchered and served for dinner.

Over the years Ulysses was judicious in his selections for the transfiguring brew: several slave owners or overseers known to be particularly cruel; a shipping merchant from Rhode Island whose substantial wealth came from the slave trade; a visiting French physiognomist and naturalist who prattled on about the inherent "lower mental capabilities" to be found among Negroes, whose skulls he compared to "near-human creatures" such as the apes of inner Africa and the fierce woodland goblins of Bavaria. Then, one day in early 1797, Ulysses disappeared.

The Washingtons were upset and hunted everywhere for their absconded cook, putting out to all who would listen the kindness they'd shown to the ungrateful servant. He was never found, but the Mount Vernon slaves whispered that on the day Ulysses vanished a black crow with a mischievous glint in its eye was found standing in a pile of the man's abandoned clothes. It cawed once and then flapped away.

When George Washington wore the tooth of his runaway cook, it was strangely at dinner parties. Slaves would watch as he wandered into the kitchen, eyes glazed over in a seeming trance, and placed drops of some strange liquid into the food and drink of his guests. His servants never touched those leftovers. But that summer many Virginians took note of a bizarre rash of wild pigs infesting the streets and countryside of Fairfax County.

The ninth, and final, Negro tooth purchased for George Washington came from a slave woman named Emma. She had been among Mount Vernon's earliest slaves, born there just a decade after Augustine Washington had moved in with his family. Had anyone recorded Emma's life for posterity, they would have learned of a girl who came of age in the shadows of one of Virginia's most powerful families. A girl who had fast learned that she was included among the Washingtons' possessions — treasured like a chair cut from exotic Jamaican mahogany or a bit of fine Canton porcelain. A young woman who had watched the Washington children go on to attend school and learn the ways of the gentry, while she was trained to wait on their whims. They had the entire world to explore and discover. Her world was Mount Vernon, and her aspirations could grow no further than the wants and needs of her owners.

That was not to say that Emma did not have her own life, for slaves learned early how to carve out spaces separate from their masters. She had befriended, loved, married, cried, fought, and found succor in a community as vibrant as the Washingtons' — perhaps even more so, if only because they understood how precious it was to live. Yet she still dreamed for more. To be unbound from this place. To live a life where she had not seen friends and family put under the lash; a life where the children she bore were not the property of others; a place where she might draw a free breath and taste its sweetness. Emma didn't know any particular sorcery. She was no root woman or conjurer, nor had she been trained like the Washington women in simple domestic enchantments. But her dreams worked their own magic. A strong and potent magic that she clung to, that grew up and blossomed inside her — where not even her owners could touch, or take it away.

When George Washington wore Emma's tooth, some of that magic worked its way into him and perhaps troubled some small bit of his soul. In July 1799, six months before he died, Washington stipulated in his will that the 123 slaves belonging to himself, among them Emma, be freed upon his wife's death. No such stipulations were made for the Negro teeth still in his possession.

ANNALEE NEWITZ

When Robot and Crow Saved East St. Louis

FROM *Future Tense Fiction*

IT WAS TIME to start the weekly circuit. Robot leapt vertically
into the air from its perch atop the History Museum in Forest
Park, rotors humming and limbs withdrawn into the smooth oval
of its chassis. From a distance it was a pale-blue flying egg, slightly
scuffed, with a propeller beanie on top. Two animated eyes glowed
from the front end of its smooth carapace like emotive headlights.
When it landed, all four legs and head extended from portals in
its protective shell, the drone was more like a strangely symmet-
rical poodle or a cartoon turtle. Mounted on an actuator, its full
face was revealed, headlight eyes situated above a short, soft snout
whose purple mouth was built for smiling, grimacing, and a range
of other, more subtle expressions.

The Centers for Disease Control team back in Atlanta designed
Robot to be cute, to earn people's trust immediately. To catch ep-
idemics before they started, Robot flew from building to building,
talking to people about how they felt. Nobody wanted to chat with
an ugly box. Robot behaved like a cheery little buddy, checking for
sick people. That's how Robot's admin Bey taught Robot to say it:
"Checking for sick people." Bey's job was to program Robot with
the social skills necessary to avoid calling it health surveillance.

Robot liked to start with the Loop. Maybe *like* was the wrong
word. It was an urge that came from Robot's mapping system,
which webbed the St. Louis metropolitan area in a grid where 0,0
was at Center and Washington. The intersection was nested at the
center of the *U*-shaped streets that local humans called the Loop.

A gated community next to Washington University, the Loop was full of smart mansions and autonomous cars that pinged Robot listlessly. Though it was late summer, Robot was on high alert for infectious disease outbreaks. Flu season got longer every year, especially in high-density sprawls like St. Louis, where so many people spread their tiny airborne globs of viruses.

Flying in low, Robot followed the curving streets, glancing into windows to track how many humans were eating dinner and whether that number matched previous scans. Wild rabbits dashed across lawns and fireflies signaled to their mates using pheromones and photons. Robot chose a doorway at random, initiating a face-to-face check with humans. In this neighborhood, they were used to it.

A human opened the service window. The subject had long, straight hair and skin the color of a peeled peanut.

"Hello. I am your friendly neighborhood flu fighter! Please cough into this tissue and hold it up to the scanner please!" Robot hovered at eye level, reached into its ventral service trunk, and withdrew a sterile sheet with a gripper. This action earned a smile. Robot smiled back, stretching its dog-turtle mouth and plumping its cheeks. Humans valued nonverbal emotional communication, and it was programmed with an entire repertoire of simple exchanges:

> If human is angry, then Robot is sad.
> If human is rude, then Robot is embarrassed.
> If human is happy, then Robot is happy.

The human coughed and Robot did a quick metagenomic scan, flagging key viral and bacterial DNA before uploading sequence data to the cloud. Other bots would run the results against a library of known infectious diseases and alert the CDC if any were on the year's rolling list.

Six days later Robot headed across the Mississippi River to East St. Louis. Here heat and rain had eroded the pavement until its surface was as pocked and fissured as human skin. The first time Robot performed health surveillance in this area, nothing fit its generic social programming. Buildings marked as unoccupied were clearly full of humans. Occupant records did not match the names and faces of occupants. People spoke with languages and words that did not match known databases. As a result, Robot could not gather adequate data. When Robot requested help with this problem, Bey was the only CDC admin who responded. She communicated with Robot from Atlanta via cellular network, using audio.

"Not all humans behave or speak the same way," she told Robot. "But you can learn to talk to anyone. Gather data. Extrapolate from context. Use this." And she sent Robot a blob of code for natural language acquisition and translation. Very quickly Robot learned that humans used slang, dialects, sociolects, and undocumented lexicons. Bey also sent several data sets taken from an urban studies lab, which supplemented Robot's map data. It turned out that not all humans lived in the same domicile for two years on average; not all residences had cars and rabbits outside. Some humans lived in places that were not tagged as domestic spaces. Some humans did not use government-assigned identifiers. But all of them could get sick.

There was a small neighborhood of soft textile homes underneath the freeway. It did not exist on official maps. Robot knew it because of Bey's algorithms.

"Hello!" Robot said, landing on the porch of a blue fabric house. It spoke a dialect that was popular here. "I am checking to make sure you are healthy! Please say hello!"

A human rustled inside, then unzipped the door.

"Hi, Robot." The human had brown eyes and facial symmetry that matched previous records. It was the same human as last month.

"Please cough into this tissue and allow me to scan."

The human smiled, and Robot knew why. The word for *cough* in this dialect was a pun for something the humans found endlessly amusing. There was a more formal word for *cough*, but compliance was higher if Robot used the pun. Higher compliance rates meant better data.

"Robot, I think my friend Shareeka is sick. Can you please check on her?" The human was worried, and Robot responded with a sad/concerned expression.

"Where is Shareeka?"

"She's in the new building on State near Fourteenth? On the upper floors that aren't finished. I bet you could fly right in."

"Thank you for your help."

The human petted Robot's head. It was the most common form of physical affection that Robot had documented in its four years and eight months in the St. Louis metropolitan area.

Protocol held that Robot should follow up on disease reports immediately, so it flew to the new building on State. Like the textile neighborhood, this building was not a designated residential area. It was a gray box on Robot's official map. But visual sensors showed a reflective spire, with twenty floors wrapped in steel and glass. Five floors rose like a skeletal crown on top, exposing its steel beams, pipes, and drywall. Coming from inside were the sounds of human life: music, conversations in six languages, babies crying, food sizzling on hot plates. Robot could see electricity cascading down wires from solar panels bolted to the outside of windows. Residents tuned the data network with satellite dishes made from woks and metal cans. From Robot's perspective, it was exactly like other residential buildings with a few cosmetic differences.

Extending its feet and head, Robot landed on the lowest open floor, then walked to the interior, asking for Shareeka. A juvenile human opened a green door and said hello. The human had short hair woven into pink extensions and a well-worn text reader in one hand.

"Hello! I am Robot, and I want to make sure you are healthy. A nice person told me that Shareeka might be sick. Can I meet Shareeka?" Robot used the same dialect it had in the fabric neighborhood, adding enhancement words that signaled benevolence.

The human made a neck motion that meant no.

"I am a friend who only cares about whether you are well. I am worried about Shareeka." Robot made a sad face.

The human made a sad face too. "Shareeka left a couple of days ago. I don't know where she is."

"How do you feel today?"

"I'm kind of stressed out about school," the human said. "How are you feeling?"

It was very rare for a human to ask Robot how it felt, and there was no stock answer or expression available. So Robot answered as literally as possible. "I am not sick because I am a machine. But I am worried that you are sick. Would you cough into this tissue and allow me to scan it?"

"Are you going to sequence the DNA right now?" The human was intrigued.

"Yes! But I will work with bots on the data network to figure out if anything dangerous is in there."

"I know. You have a list of known infectious diseases and you'll search for a match. We learned about it in biology class." The human smiled, and Robot smiled back.

"Yes! That is what I will do." It held out the tissue.

The human coughed on it and studied Robot very carefully as it conducted the scan.

"How do you make sure that you don't mistake somebody else's microbiome for mine? Do you sterilize your hand every time?"

"Yes, I do." Robot uploaded its data and talked at the same time. "What is your name?"

"Everybody calls me Jalebi."

"You are named after a fried, spiral-shaped sweet soaked in sugar water." Humans enjoyed it when Robot recognized the meaning behind their names.

Jalebi nodded. "When I was a kid, I ate so many that I passed out. Too much sugar. So my brother started calling me Jalebi."

Robot was having difficulty making a connection to the cloud. "I am going to go back outside to talk to the network. It was nice to meet you, Jalebi."

"Wait—what's your name?"

"Robot."

"That's your name? I thought that was your . . . race." Jalebi used an ambiguous word that could also mean "species."

"It's my name," Robot replied.

Robot stood in the darkness beneath the moon, above the neighborhood lights, in the unfinished hallway open to the air, and called for the cloud. There was nothing. It called for Bey. There was no answer. It sent an emergency email to the CDC surveillance team list and got an error message. It called and called, charging up every morning in the sunlight and powering down at midnight. After seven days it got a text message from an unknown private number:

> Hi, Robot. It's Bey. I can't be your admin anymore. I'm really sorry because it was nice to know you. Unfortunately the CDC lost its funding. I work at Amazon Health now, but we aren't allowed to network with open drones like you. I don't think anyone is going to shut you down or collect you, so I guess you can do whatever you want. If anything really bad happens, text me here on my private number. I hope the language acquisition algorithm is still helping!

For the first time, Robot made a sad face that nobody could see. It wasn't sure what "really bad" meant, but its models of human communication suggested that Bey referred to an outbreak. The problem was that Robot had no way to conduct a typical surveillance circuit without somewhere to upload its data for analysis. Plus, it was going to run out of sterile tissues. That's what happened last year when the government shut down and Walgreens froze its CDC account. Robot used the government-shutdown scenario to model its current situation and predicted that it meant the Walgreens account would be frozen for an indeterminate length of time. The 5,346 sterile tissues remaining in its chassis were the last it would ever have. The sterilizing gel for its gripper was already running low.

Bey said Robot could do whatever it wanted, which was the kind of thing humans said when they expected it to predict which data-gathering task should be prioritized. Based on current supply levels and its onboard analysis capabilities, Robot determined it should focus on learning local languages and human social habitation practices. It would attempt to reach the cloud every morning, and would reprioritize if disease analysis systems became available again. Robot thrust its head out of the pocked oval of its body, a determined smile on its face. In the absence of a human, the expression was intended only for a theoretical model of a person who always cared what Robot thought and did.

A crow stood next to Robot on the building's edge, looping its leg over one wing to scratch its head. It regarded Robot for a second, then said something before flying away. The phonemes were part of an unknown language, and Robot added them to a sparse data set it had gathered from other crows in the area. Now that it could do what it wanted, Robot reasoned, it was time to make that data set robust. Many crows flew up here and perched, often in groups of three or four, and their sounds followed the same general patterns as any natural language. It could learn a lot by staying right here, down the hall from Jalebi's habitat. The days grew shorter and new constellations rose in the sky.

Robot started to pick up a few phrases from context. In the mornings and evenings, the crows discussed the sun's position and its relationship to likely sources of food. Soon Robot could piece together bits of syntax, using brackets to designate uncertain or unknown meanings: "[Food type] four [measurement units] north of the morning sun." There were also location calls, which it roughly translated to "Food here!" and "I'm [name] here!" and "Get over here [you]!" Its first translation breakthrough came one morning when a statistically unusual number of crows gathered near its perch. Robot counted twenty-three birds at one point, many of whom were quite large. Maybe they were from different subspecies? Or elder crows? From what Robot had learned by querying the Internet, zoologists drew the line between crow species arbitrarily based on calls and cultural differences.

This seemed like an important meeting, so perhaps multiple crow groups were invited in a show of corvid solidarity. Robot recorded hundreds of new words. It learned a few of the birds' names as well. Suddenly one of the ravens gave a location call: "There! North five [measurement units]! Group!" They took off at once, and Robot followed them. It was time to test out its ability to communicate, by using a location call. "I'm here! Joining group!"

A crow flew alongside Robot and answered. "I'm here! 3cry!" 3cry was Robot's approximation of the bird's name, which it recorded as a series of three high-pitched phonemes issued in rapid succession.

Other birds answered with their own names. "I'm here! 2chop-1caw!" "I'm here! 4cry!" "I'm here! 2chop!" Robot now had a running list of phonemes used in crow names, and tried to record them faithfully.

They flew as a loose pack, not forming a *V* the way other birds did. Crows usually preferred smaller social groups and didn't care about staying in a tidy line. They only came together in large numbers to deal with issues serious enough that even an egg-shaped drone was permitted to come along.

"Enemy! Enemy!" One of the ravens barked out the word, its accent slightly different from the crows'. Far ahead, a hawk coasted on the updrafts from the city in a large, lazy circle.

"Egg killer!"

"Trespasser!"

"Attack from above!"

The birds called names and orders to each other, soaring over the hawk's head and dive-bombing it. Though hawks have excellent vision from the front of their faces, they also have two major blind spots above and behind. This particular hawk was immediately thrown off its trajectory by a mob of angry crows clipping it from out of nowhere.

3cry called to Robot. "Come here! Above to below!"

Robot modeled several scenarios and settled on one that would knock the hawk out of the updraft without causing any health risks to the bird. Communicating with the crows was important, but the health of living beings was paramount. Coming down gently on the hawk's back, Robot pushed lightly, keeping up with the bird's speed while also altering its course. The hawk let out an incomprehensible scream and dove, escaping the crows by heading across the Mississippi.

"Out of here!"

"Go!"

"End group!"

Four crows followed after the hawk, but the rest of the corvids scattered. Robot flew back toward Jalebi's building, modeling possible new words by correlating matching sounds from different birds. 3cry followed close behind.

"I'm here! 3cry! Female! You are here!"

Robot predicted that 3cry was asking for its name and gender. It replied using crow words, then switched to a human word for *Robot*. It did not yet know the word for *nongendered* in crow language, so it did not offer a designation. 3cry flew silently for a while. They landed on the building and looked at the horizon.

Robot offered a friendly greeting in crow language. "Afternoon time."

"Enemy gone. Robot is here." 3cry pronounced its name perfectly. "Human sound."

Robot searched for the right words from its limited vocabulary. "Humans are here. With my group."

3cry cleaned her right wing, chewed on a mite, and cocked her head at Robot. "Humans are not a group. They can't speak. They reject food."

"They speak with other sounds." Robot's vocabulary was growing bigger the more they talked. "They eat other food."

3cry made a soft clucking noise that meant the same thing as human laughter. "You are a fool."

Robot predicted that assent was the best response. "Yes, I am."

"Yes, you are." 3cry leaned over and gently poked a bit of dirt from the edge of Robot's mouth.

Robot plucked a broken feather off 3cry's back.

When they cleaned each other, it was like when a human smiled at Robot and Robot smiled back.

3cry and Robot became what the crows called a group, which meant that they flew together during the day. They met in the mornings, on the ledge, after Robot's daily attempt to reach the CDC. Robot didn't need food, but it was good at identifying potential sources of sustenance for 3cry. "Food here!" it would say, hovering over a fragrant bin. After scavenging with 3cry through city waste, it was easy to understand why she thought humans rejected food and were therefore basically nonsentient.

Over weeks their conversations became more complex, but many concepts defied translation. Robot still didn't understand the crows' unit of measurement for distances. And 3cry didn't understand Robot's interest in health. From what Robot could discover, crows understood the concepts of death and near-death but didn't talk about disease specifically. Disease was one of many ideas that could be described with the word *near-death*, which also happened to be a pun on the word for unripe food. Many crow words were puns, which made translation even more difficult.

For conversations about health, Robot relied more and more on Jalebi. She had figured out that it was roosting with 3cry on the ledge near her habitat, and came to visit for what she called "study sessions." Using text devices, she gathered data very slowly, then synthesized it even more slowly. Robot spent hours quizzing Jalebi about molecular structures and chemical interactions, marveling at the concept of a mind that came online without this information. Still, Robot liked to have a human face to mirror its own expressions. It felt unquantifiably more satisfying to smile at a human than it did to smile at its own internal representation of a human. After so long in the company of 3cry and Jalebi, Robot began to question what exactly that internal representation might really be. Maybe it wasn't a human at all. Maybe it was a self-representation, and Robot had been smiling at itself all along.

Usually when Jalebi came to the ledge with her textbooks, 3cry left with a string of curses. These weren't necessarily hostile —crows liked to insult each other, and often did it with great affection. Mostly they thought it was hilarious that humans couldn't understand words. So crows rained their most creative snark on human heads, marveling at how oblivious they were to the humiliations they suffered from the beaks of people lying overhead. But one afternoon 3cry arrived during their study session and did not fly away.

Jalebi was musing about something she'd learned in a recent lesson about atomic structure. "What if it turns out we really are spreading cancer to each other on a quantum level?" she asked.

"Human squawking!" 3cry yelled. "Shit and plastic! Featherless fool!"

Robot decided to ignore the insults. "Afternoon time," it said pleasantly. "Human here! Jalebi! Part of the group."

"Group does not include living sandwiches." 3cry laughed.

Jalebi watched, wide-eyed. "Can you speak crow language?"

"A little," Robot said. "My vocabulary is small, but I can say a few things. This is 3cry. She's . . . my friend." As it said the word, Robot realized it was true. Thanks to Bey's social programming, it knew that groups were statistically likely to be made up of friends or kin. Since Robots have no kin, that meant Jalebi was a friend too.

Jalebi tried to make the sound of 3cry's name and the bird ignored it.

"I found something you like, Robot. Near-death. All over a human tree."

"She said your name perfectly! I read that crows can imitate words, but I'd never heard it before!"

3cry glanced at Jalebi, then at Robot. "Annoying Jalebi."

"She said my name too! That's so cool!"

But Robot wasn't paying attention to the interesting language data points. It predicted 3cry had found a disease outbreak, and that took precedence over all other inputs.

"I have to go," it said to Jalebi. To 3cry, it added, "Take me there."

Robot followed 3cry in a southeasterly direction, eventually alighting at the top of a building on Missouri Street. Like Jalebi's home, this building was partly open to the air. Its layout suggested that it might have been a public building like the CDC; there were long hallways lined with small rooms like offices. Water sources were isolated in a few areas, unlike in a typical habitat, where water welled up in multiple rooms. But it was definitely a human habitat now, with soft bedding and buckets for water and data access points made from cans. As they flew down a stairwell, Robot tried to estimate the population of the building based on noise, heat, and live wires. It settled on a 75 percent probability of fifty humans on each upper floor, with populations growing as they descended.

"Here!" 3cry landed on a railing in front of a door marked 2, for second floor. "Near-death!"

"Thank you."

"End group," 3cry said, taking to the air. The phrase was one way crows said goodbye.

"Until morning," Robot replied, already using a gripper to tug the door open.

The corridor was full of light from scratched windows along the left-hand side, illuminating dozens of doors to habitats that were once something else. Classrooms? Offices? Consulting rooms? Robot flew slowly past them, modeling possibilities and looking for humans. The fourth door was propped open, and several humans were inside. Their breathing was labored, and one was crying. Something had knocked out the walls between rooms, creating a wide-open space full of cloth dwellings, plush bedding, and piles of bright plastic containers.

It was time to land. Humans didn't like it when Robot flew overhead, and besides, the face and legs were part of what made it seem so friendly. Walking over to one of the humans wrapped in blankets, Robot smiled and waved a tiny gripper in greeting.

Patchy black hair covered the human's head, and cracks had formed in the lips that didn't smile. With no baseline language established, Robot estimated that it should try the dialect spoken in Jalebi's building. "I'm a friend who is worried about your health! Can you cough into a tissue for me?" The human stared at Robot's face and blinked before succumbing to a coughing fit. For Robot, it didn't matter whether the coughs were intentional or not. It took a sample and moved on to the next human.

"Hello!" Robot said to the juvenile, who was using a mobile device to access the Internet.

"Are you a cop?" The juvenile used a sociolect of English that was common in East St. Louis.

"I'm a friend who checks to make sure you are healthy! I share information with doctors, not police." The human frowned and Robot made a sad face. "A lot of people here are sick. I would like to help."

"Nobody is going to help, stupid drone. Hospital for citizens only, yeah?"

"Please cough into the tissue, so I can figure out why you are sick."

Another human spoke up, head emerging from a cloth shelter. "What are you going to do about it?"

Robot stood still for several microseconds, modeling possibilities and considering what language would be the most soothing. "I am going to find out what is causing your illness. This is an emergency. I will find help. I promise. Please cough into the tissue."

One by one, the humans complied. Robot flew from room to room, checking for disease. After sequencing several samples, it found the same virus strain in multiple humans. This met the definition of an outbreak. It was time to call Bey.

"Is that you, Robot? I can't believe you're still running! It's been . . . what? Over a year?"

"Something really bad is happening in East St. Louis," Robot said, deploying the exact words Bey had used to delineate when it would be appropriate to call her. "There is an outbreak. I need to send you data."

"Do you have sequence? Maybe I can . . ." Robot heard background noise, as if Bey were moving something on her desk. "Can you send it as an anonymous dump to this address?" She sent the directions to a temporary storage cloud, and Robot deposited data from 127 samples it had taken from humans in the building.

"We have a system for anonymous reporting, part of this new Amazon Health philanthropy project." Bey paused. "Got it! Let me analyze this really fast and see if it's more than just a garden-variety . . . oh shit."

Robot predicted that she was not saying *shit* for the same reason 3cry did. "What is it?" Robot asked, putting on a fearful expression for itself.

"This is really bad, like you said. We need to get someone in there. Unfortunately, Illinois doesn't have a state health department. Maybe there's a local group or . . ." Bey was typing. "Okay, Robot, I found something. There's a nonprofit health collective in East St. Louis called Community Immunity. They could probably manufacture vaccines and a therapy. It's a known pathogen but hasn't ever been spotted in the Midwest before. So all they need is this file." Bey sent a small amount of data. "Do you have anyone who can help you? You might need a human. Sometimes people are hostile to drones, even cute ones."

Two hours later Robot was describing the situation to Jalebi. It was evening, and 3cry was likely sleeping with other members of her group. But Jalebi was wide awake and extremely agitated. "You're talking about that health collective on MLK Drive! I've seen it!"

Robot nodded, smiling. "Can we go there now?"

Jalebi glanced toward the door to her habitat. "Yeah. My mom won't be home until morning anyway."

Community Immunity was located in the husk of an old strip mall, its gleaming counters and wet lab hidden behind windows duct-taped with tinfoil and cardboard. Bey was right that Robot needed a human. Jalebi had to pretend that Robot was her school project, and Robot had to pretend that Jalebi had programmed it to look for outbreaks. Once the humans at Community Immunity had the data, they made unhappy faces and said "oh shit" in the same way Bey had.

A human with purple hair and a prosthetic arm offered Jalebi a seat and some hot tea. The human spoke the same sociolect of English that Bey used. "It's very good that you brought this to us. You are a good citizen." Then the human looked at Robot. "Thank you, Robot, for giving us the file with an open therapy and vax recipe."

"I am happy to help. I don't like it when people are sick."

This human, unlike the others, seemed to know that Robot was the person who found the outbreak. "I'm Janelle, by the way. She/her pronouns. Do you know if there are other places where H18N2 is infecting people?" Robot liked the way Janelle identified herself by name and gender, the way crows did.

"A friend told me about this outbreak. I don't know if there are others." Robot deliberately chose vague language. After Bey's warning, it did not want to reveal its data-gathering techniques.

Janelle took it in stride. "Can your . . . uh . . . friend help find more? We can manufacture a therapy and a vax tonight, but we need to get it out there fast before this sucker mutates."

Robot nodded. "Tomorrow. I will try to find more."

When 3cry arrived in the morning, Robot had to strain against the boundaries of its vocabulary to make itself understood. "Need group. Find near-death enemy."

"Enemy?" 3cry scratched her head.

"Enemy for humans," Robot admitted. But then it had an idea. "Enemy causes human death. Dead humans mean less food."

Despite butchering the crow syntax, Robot thought it had made 3cry understand. Plus, sometimes crows just liked an excuse to get the mob together. "Begin group!" 3cry yelled, taking off. Robot leapt into the air behind her. They flew over East St. Louis, calling for the big group that had taken out the hawk. "Begin group! Begin group!" More birds joined them. "Here! I'm here!" They called their names and swirled to roost in a tree at the edge of the Mississippi River, where freeway met water.

"Find near-death!" 3cry said, then issued some directions and specification words that Robot did not understand.

"Near-death! There! [Measurement unit] north!" The words came from a big crow named 2chop1caw, jumping into flight. Most of the group followed, possibly to assess what exactly 3cry meant by *near-death*. 2chop1caw led them to a fabric habitat nearby, where Robot quickly identified three sick people. The virus matched the H18N2 signature identified at Community Immunity.

"More near-death! Where else? Begin group!" Robot called the birds to the air again, and they fanned out over the city, making a racket and hurling their best insults. Each time they uncovered a new outbreak, they gave their loudest calls, sometimes passing those calls to the next bird, until Robot could follow their cries back to the source. By the end of the day they had discovered five small outbreaks.

"End group!" 3cry yelled, following Robot back toward MLK. The crows called farewells and locations to each other. "End group!" "Evening time!" "I'm here!" "You there!" "Food!" "Death!" This was followed by laughter, because *food* and *death* diverged into many puns far beyond Robot's comprehension.

3cry appeared to have decided that she was roosting with Robot for the evening. When they landed, she hooked her claws around its rotor pole and clung there as Robot signaled arrival to the door of Community Immunity. Robot didn't mind. Humans found small animals disarming, and that always led to greater compliance.

Jalebi was there with Janelle, looking at something on a monitor. "Hi, Robot!"

"We have data on the location of more outbreaks."

Janelle laughed. "Really? Did your little feathered friend help?"

"Her name is 3cry!" Jalebi failed to pronounce 3cry's name again. And once again 3cry ignored it, jumping off Robot and using her beak to straighten the feathers under her right wing. Robot reached over and plucked one out that was bothering her.

"Where can I put this data?" Robot aimed a concerned expression at Jalebi and Janelle.

"Put it here for now." Janelle waved a mobile device near Robot, setting it to accept uploads. "Jalebi, do you want to help us synthesize those doses of nasal spray? Looks like we'll need at least five hundred. And then we'll start making vax doses for injection."

"Yes! Absolutely!" Jalebi acted like a crow about to charge into the air. But she was only racing across the room to boot up a mixer.

Janelle had a thoughtful expression on her face. "Did this crow really help you find the outbreaks?"

"Yes. The crows think humans are idiots, but they appreciate your garbage."

Janelle laughed for a long time, and Robot was not entirely sure why.

When Jalebi returned, she sat down alongside Robot and 3cry and smiled. "This place is really cool. I like it here."

"Maybe this is your group," Robot guessed.

"Maybe." Jalebi cocked her head like 3cry. Then she scooped up a tiny tube full of wound adhesive. "Here, hand me that beautiful feather." Robot dropped 3cry's feather into her hand. Dabbing a bit of adhesive on Robot's back, she stuck the feather to its shell next to the place where its rotor pole emerged.

3cry was startled. "I like it," she said. "That human is a fool."

"Yes, she is," Robot agreed. "You are also a fool."

"Yes, I am."

The three people roosted contentedly next to each other on the floor, watching Janelle and the humans preparing antivirals for other humans. It was a scenario that Robot would not have predicted. But now it could. Robot smiled to itself, organized the data, and retrained its model for friendship.

USMAN MALIK

Dead Lovers on Each Blade, Hung

FROM *Nightmare Magazine*

I

JEE INSPECTOR SAHIB, he came looking for a missing girl in Lahore Park one evening in the summer of 2013, this man known as Hakim Shafi. It was a summer to blanch the marrow of all summers. Heat rose coiling like a snake from the ground. Gusts of evil loo winds swept across Lahore from the west, shrinking the hides of man and beast alike, and Hakim Shafi went from bench to bench, stepping over needles rusting in bleached June grass, and showed the heroinchies a picture.

Have you seen this girl, he said.

For all his starched kurta shalwar and that brown waistcoat, his air was neither prideful nor wary. He was a very tall, bony man with stooped shoulders, a ratlike face, and thick whiskers. His eyes were sinkholes that bubbled occasionally, and when we said no, we hadn't seen that girl, Shafi's gaze drifted away from the benches, the park, the night sky.

We distrusted him. This lost stranger—we had no doubt he was lost—we watched him wander the park for weeks. Each Friday he came after Juma prayers, that colored eight-by-six photo clasped between his palms, as if the girl in the floral-patterned shalwar kameez and his prayers were intertwined. Before I knew that they were, I laughed along with the others at his inquiries. It was amusing to see this well-dressed gentleman court our company, eyes full of hope, that faded picture in his hands.

In his absence we speculated. He looked in his fifties, maybe early sixties. Perhaps the girl was his runaway daughter. As we injected the queen into our veins, as we gave ourselves up to dreaming in her orbit, we argued whether the rich-born pretty girl with her sad eyes and smooth skin was roughing it with lowlifes while her father searched for her in shadows. We giggled when we thought of that.

You understand how our life is, sahib, don't you? We heroinchies are the children of the white queen—a tribe unto ourselves. We do not share company with the outside, our years pass differently in her presence. Hers is a shadow that enwombs us: it nurtures us as it suffocates—it is a bit like being slowly, sinuously lowered into an endless grave and watching that dome of light shrink until its memory becomes hateful. You fall in love with the descent.

With Hakim Shafi things might have gone on that way—he on his insoluble quest and we daytiming when we could—but Mustafa, our dealer, he got greedy and fucked up everything. I have wished upon my dead father's name many times since then for that bastard to rot in hell. Had he not ruined it for all of us, I would not be sitting here tonight with you and the subinspector sahib in this skeleton of a police station with its shadow-draped oil lamps and broken windows and sweat-slick bars. In this stench of metal and piss and—

No, sahib, it's not like that. Just saying greed is the most dangerous of beasts, as my old dada used to say, and Mustafa's stupid greed dragged us into the darkness that finally showed its teeth tonight.

So this is what happened with that son of a whore Mustafa.

Before he came along, we used to get our masala behind the flower market in Liberty. A paan-and-cigarette stall owner was our man. His crop was fresh and as pure as any Lahori queen has ever been. It was expensive, but we made do by rummaging through garbage for sellables, snatching cell phones, stealing manhole covers, hubcaps, and begging. Most of us could snag two or three hits a week. Wasn't much, but was enough to keep the nighttime at bay.

Then came news that Afghan police had set hundreds of thousands of poppy fields ablaze in Kunar. Overnight, opium supply dropped. As the Pakistani army's battle against militants up north intensified, prices shot up, and we found every door shut and bolted on us with nothing but the habit to keep us company. Such desperate times that many of us became cotton shooters and fluffers. Chicken shit, I know, but what could you do? There was only so much queen to go around.

"I know a man who knows a man," said Yasin one day. Five of us were crouched around a bench under the oldest peepal tree in the park, and Yasin, a scrawny lizardlike heroinchi who had recently turned to fluffing, sat grinding milk-sugar and a laxative he stole from a dispensary to bulk up our meager supply. "He can get us cheap masala."

"Nothing is cheap," someone said, and gawked at the blue velvet of the evening sky.

"It's that or we are dry. I'm completely out."

Nothing we could say to this. Enter Shani, Yasin's man's man.

He was a fidgety midget with a wispy mustache wider than his face and he offered to help us ride the queen cheap. Word was, he had made deals with police stations in Model Town and Kot Lakhpat for confiscated masala, and knew how to tap into the army's black market—

Yes, sahib, of course. You're right. He was likely lying all along, the bastard.

Suffice to say he knew people, and so we eagerly accepted. I was among those who stopped going to the flower market and trusted this fiend for my needs.

As you can see, that was a mistake. My dying is ample evidence of that.

It happened on a Thursday evening. (I remember because one of the heroinchies went to Data Sahib's shrine to pay his respects.) After the park guard made his rounds to collect bhatta for letting us use the benches, most of my group left to polish-wipe cars and beg at chowks and traffic lights. Seemed as good a time as any to retrieve the plastic-wrapped masala I had squirreled away weeks ago. I pulled out the packet and rolled up my sleeves, and under the swaying elms and peepal, I slipped the queen into my blood.

(Yes, Subinspector sahib, that cigarette is most welcome. Thank you for the light. This close, the flame hurts my eyes a bit, but my hands are shaking and I cannot chase the dragon at this hour.)

Sahib, we sit here today in this gloomy thana. I can plainly see the shadows squirm by the door, the oak and eucalyptus boughs moving in the wind. Hear that whistle in the dark outside. Watch the way your fingers wind the ends of your mustache, your eyes half lidded as you listen to my story. I smell the ash falling to the floor from the tip of my cigarette. See water bead on the plastic sheet over that ice block the subinspector wheeled in earlier, should I prove less than cooperative—and I swear on my mother's name, this is how clearly I saw my dead son under those wheezing trees that night.

Heroinchies die twice, they say, and we can all tell the story of our first death.

My son is mine.

He was twelve when I beat him black and blue on his birthday. He wanted to enroll in school again. I wanted him to train as a mechanic's apprentice. He was thirteen when he ran away and fifteen when they found him in a gunnysack behind a dumpster at Lakshmi Chowk. His face was swollen and discolored in a dozen places. His lips were torn. Blood had clotted in the corners.

His throat—

His throat was—

I died the day they found him, sahib, and I died again that night in the park after I injected the masala. And in this fresh death when my son came to me he was smooth and untouched. Angelic was my boy. He bent over me and I thought he had forgotten, that he had forgiven. His eyes were kind. He smiled at me, changing, and it wasn't his face but a piss-colored full moon shining at me. The eyes were red stars, the darkness between them whipped out and licked my cheeks. The white queen was in a mood, she rose with the tide of my blood, and I saw a giant golden snake tower above me. Its hood pulsated wider than the night sky until it seemed the heavens stood on its flared head, and I knew, I was sure, that its basilisk gaze would be my end.

The world shivered then and came apart. A gaunt man with a bristling mustache leaned across the bench, his hands poised above my chest. He lowered his face, breath afoul with onion, garlic, something else, and said, *Are you all right?*

I was.

Later, Hakim Shafi would tell me that I was gone. When he found me, head lolling off the bench, my mouth frothed and my eyes were glazed. The left side of my body twitched. When he found no pulse, he pumped my chest and continued for nearly fifteen minutes. That was how long I was dead, he said.

I believed him. How else could I have seen my son in that gloaming?

Hakim Shafi saved my life that night. A medical man present at that hour in a corner of a park haunted by heroinchies—some might call that a divine act. Maybe it was, but I wonder. Sometimes I think life is like a junkie's flesh, crisscrossed where kismet injects other souls into our lives. Souls lost as we are. Who knows if the perpetrator of such accidents is God or the Devil?

Whatever force it was, it bound my life to Hakim Shafi's forever.

"I'm fine," I said, but he brought me to his small, neat clinic in Old Lahore anyway. Here he drew my blood and took a pinch of the leftover masala for testing. We sat on a moss-colored couch and watched the powder bubble and hiss in a glass vial when Hakim poured acid on it.

"Look at the bottom," he said. I looked. Molten black residue, like tar, stuck to the glass. "Your dealer's been shortchanging you," he said. "I'd guess for a while, too. This heroin has more cut in it than any I have seen. Elephant tranquilizer. It was just a matter of time before something happened."

I nodded, and it occurred to me I was a bit disappointed. I had been courting my demise for a long while.

"You inject." It wasn't a question. I nodded again. He pushed back the spectacles he had put on inside the clinic. They made him look confused. He dragged his knuckles back and forth on the oak desk. "You get your blood tested?"

"No."

"You know how to chase the dragon?"

I laughed. He smiled. "Right." His gray eyes went inward. When he spoke, he might've been talking to himself. "Maybe that's the way to go if you can't kick the habit."

"What makes you think I want to kick anything?"

Hakim Shafi pulled out a drawer and brought out four tiny vials. He picked up the syringe cocked with my blood, dropped some in each vial.

My mind was fogged up from my death. I wanted to rise and flee to the park, but Hakim's eyes were fixed on me. Restless, I scanned the room and saw a framed picture on the desk. I pointed. "That your daughter?"

Hakim's fingers whitened around the vial. He shook it vigorously. "Did you eat today?"

"I've seen you take that picture around the park. I know everyone's told you she was never there."

Hakim flicked a finger against the glass. The yellow liquid turned red, golden. "I'll set up some intravenous saline for you." His lips were pressed into a line. "Your blood is thick from fluid loss."

He helped me onto the couch and gave me a concoction to drink. When my eyelids grew heavy, he pulled a crisp white sheet over me. It smelled of hospital.

"Sleep well. It's the only way most of us can dream." He paused, and in the silence a drowsy moth thunked against the room's window. I muttered something. Somewhere in the night a baby cried, and its mother shushed it and began to hum. The moth thunked again. I looked, and outside the window, a small boy-shape pressed its face against the glass, mouthing words at me.

"Hakim sahib," I said, voice thick and sticky. "Who's that?"

Shafi turned. The shape was gone.

In a room at the back of the clinic, Hakim Shafi showed me snake skins.

"This is how I make my living."

"By killing snakes?"

He smiled. "By using venom to heal. *Similia similibus curantur.*" He swept a hand around him at the hundreds of glass vials, filled with pills the size of sugar cubes, arranged on dusty shelves. "Like cures like. Poison will kill poison." He knuckled the diamond-patterned leathery skin. "My suppliers send me tokens every year. Skins, fangs, vertebra. Keeps up the clinic's image. Helps the business."

I scratched the stubble on my chin. "How does snake venom heal? I thought the only thing it was useful for was killing dumb assholes who mess around with creatures they don't understand."

"It's one of the oldest cures. My ancestors have used it for centuries."

"You're pulling my chain, aren't you, Hakim sahib?"

Shafi studied me. "We're so besieged by newness we forget old diseases haunt us for a reason. Did you know snake venom is being researched at big universities these days? Dementia, palsy, heart attacks—it has a role in curing all of them." He went to a cupboard and pulled down a large rosewood box from the top shelf. He set it on the table next to a gleaming row of vials and tubes. "For my medicines, I mix most of the substrate myself. The venom varies between species. Some is toxic to human nerves, some to blood, some to tissues and organs. A pinch of the wrong sample, and you'd be dead in seconds."

He opened the rosewood box. Inside were dozens of match-book-sized tins. He pulled on a pair of gloves and carefully removed the lids of two. They were filled with tiny snow-colored pellets.

"This"—Hakim picked up a pellet with a pair of tweezers—"is the venom of the common krait. It paralyzes the breathing muscles. If you got bitten by a krait during sleep, you'd scratch the spot, thinking it was a bug bite, and doze off. You'd never wake again." Hakim replaced the pellet in the tin. "I use it for patients with lockjaw and neck spasms. A millionth portion in goat milk. Highly effective."

He tapped another tin with the edge of his tweezers. "A couple bring their nine-year-old girl to me every month. She has thin blood. A genetic condition. Bleeds for hours from her gums if she brushes her teeth too vigorously. A knee scrape would be fatal. Most children like her don't survive childhood. My Koriwala viper venom has kept her alive for seven years."

I shuddered. My third day at the clinic, and the shakes were beginning to hit me. My skin itched with strange life. I felt it in the bunching of my bowels, at the back of my eyes. The absence of the queen was becoming loud and insistent.

I licked my lips. "Got anything to help my nerves, Hakim sahib?"

Shafi tipped his neck and watched me. He plucked a vial filled with russet-colored liquid from the shelf. "Cobra in laudanum. It will help the diarrhea and muscle aches." When I eyed it warily, he laughed. "Diluted. Don't worry. I know what I'm doing."

He shook the vial, dipped a glass pipette into the frothing liquid, and retrieved some. I opened my mouth and he squeezed three drops onto my tongue.

"Easy," he said when I rolled my tongue around. "Let it settle into your tissues."

Already the fire in my body was sputtering, calming down. It wasn't the queen's embrace, but it was something. When I closed my eyes, a fog rose and surrounded me, whispering me into a lull.

By now, sahib, you must be wondering why I was still at the clinic with the good Hakim; why I stayed for weeks and didn't steal his medicines, his laudanum, or his money. After all, I had done nothing but steal, steal, steal for years since my boy died and my wife ran away with a shakarkandi vendor. Hubcaps, tin sheets, tools from a garage where I worked briefly, an old beggar's wheelchair. You name it.

Before I became a thief I used to work in a dispensary—a tiny roadside stall in Qila Gujjar Singh run by a compounder named Ram Lal. He mixed tonics for common illnesses. Occasionally a certified government doctor would check in, but mostly Ram Lal was free to do as he pleased. He was a good compounder, even though he did not have a medical degree. He helped the locals and earned a good name for himself with his gentle manner and willingness to subsidize his prescriptions.

I helped him run the dispensary. I attended seven grades before I dropped out of school and could read labels written in English on pill bottles. My job was to grind pills with a mortar and pestle and wrap them in squares of newspaper to make medicinal *puris*. We did well and it was a good life. Until my son disappeared.

I suppose being in a similar environment with Hakim Shafi brought back those memories. For years I lived in that park— scabies-infested, filthy, often hungry. I had grown addicted to the darkness, but I suppose I was ready for it to end when I overdosed. Shafi came along, saved me, and cleaned me up, and I guess I was just too tired of myself to rob him.

I don't know, maybe every heroinchi also wants one story with a happy ending.

Shafi helped me through the next week. Quitting cold turkey was like being cooked on a spit. I ground my teeth, sometimes I writhed and screamed; but his tinctures helped. I suspect he could have done more, but I think he knew this was my battle and would only go so far in steering. The ship and its course were mine and mine alone.

Like cures like, he'd said.

On the seventh day, when I had more strength, Shafi showed me the terrariums.

His clinic was located in Old Lahore. Squeezed between a shoemaker's shop and a cloth merchant's, it was more like Ram Lal's dispensary than a real clinic. His patients came in lines of worn, sickly faces, most of them women and children. They crowded into the dingy waiting room up front where whorls of Quranic callig-raphy draped the walls and the smell of formalin and bitter salts hung in the air.

Once I had enough vigor to navigate past the front hall to the backyard, the fierce, sudden beauty of it shocked me. A statuary of ceramic children laughing and kneeling in the mud stood in the center of a lush zoysia grass patch. Creepers hung from tres-tles arrayed across carrot patches, weaving between the half-dozen mango and orange trees that circled the statuary. Exquisitely kept and trimmed, the yard smelled of citrus and honeysuckle.

I whistled when Shafi told me he did the landscaping himself. "That's hard work."

He nodded. "My wife helped me do it. She was a wonder."

"Was?"

"Yes."

I turned to a row of empty glass tanks in a corner of the yard. "What are those?"

"Terrariums." He crouched and ran a hairy hand over them. Monsoon season was upon us, and night drizzle had left the glass shiny and clean. It twinkled in the afternoon light, slanting red shadows across the grass.

"You kept snakes?"

"My wife did. She was a herpetologist at the University of Pun-jab. Russell vipers, sand boas, Indian kraits, striped keelbacks—she kept them, fed them like babies." He showed me cracks, little spiderwebs, in the glass. "This is where her cobras tried to bite us."

"What happened?" I said. Shafi yanked a tall weed poking its head from between the cages. We both knew I wasn't asking about snakes.

"I sold them," he said. "Couldn't bear to look at them anymore."

A thought hit me, a realization that must have shown in my face; when Shafi looked up, his eyes changed. He rose and went inside the house, his footsteps impressing upon the muddy banks of the flowerbeds, a trail leading into his past.

I got up to follow, stopped, and went to the back wall. I bent down and fingered the human footprint under the windowsill. It was fresh and clear and a child's. The toe prints were filled with rainwater.

As I watched, a worm snaked its way out of a toe print and be-gan wriggling madly in the rain pool.

*

The girl in the picture was not Hakim Shafi's daughter.

It was his wife—his child bride.

Shafi said nothing when I voiced my conclusion. I ran my fingers across the picture, across the large black eyes gazing out at the world, nose proud, chin firm and defiant. The girl, probably in her early twenties, sat sidelong, a half-smile covered by a hennaed hand. With the nose ring, her broad forehead, and that chin, she reminded me of those desert women from Thal and Rajasthan who meander with their tribe across the wasteland, grazing cattle stock.

I said as much to Hakim. He flicked at the end of his nose. "Eighteen years ago I was in Hyderabad for a relative's funeral. I bought her from a band of gypsies who camped at the outskirts of the city. She was eight at the time."

"Eight." I wasn't shocked. I come from a family of moonshiners and shanty-dwellers, sahib. My father ran errands for a pimp most of his life. I knew how some old customs work. "You raised your wife," I said to him.

"Yes."

I stared at the picture. "Where is she now?"

Hakim polished a row of bottles with a rag.

"Why do you keep returning to the park?"

His voice was low. "Maliha loved the park. She used to feed those stupid ducks at the pond. Loved their ugly dirt-colored feathers. She said they reminded her of the desert. I used to laugh at that." He yanked out a drawer and removed a brown pouch, its top cinched by leather thongs. He tugged at the drawstring, removed a wrapped sheet of paper from it, withdrew a necklace strung with three large stones from the sheet. They were cracked and yellow. "These here are the bones of her childhood."

"What?"

"Desert pearls. Sandstone baked by heat for years. Maliha didn't remember much of her early life. Her parents were dead, which is why her tribe wanted to sell her to someone willing to take care of her. But she said she remembered her mother giving her these. Her ma told her they had magical powers and would protect her from jinns." He smiled. "My Maliha believed it till the day she disappeared."

"When'd she disappear?"

"Two years ago."

"How old was she?"

"Twenty-six."

"You loved her?"

It was a stupid question, sahib, I know, but asking it came so naturally, it surprised me. Maybe it was a bond of understanding between sinners. I could see his love for her nestled in the crow's feet around his eyes, I could see his entire life in those eyes: feeding her, clothing her, raising her, falling in love with her, sending her to college. But he had bought her with rupee. Her heart, then —did he win it, or chain it with need?

Hakim held the necklace. "Yes, I loved her."

"You didn't have children?"

"We were barren. I was."

"Why'd she run away?" I didn't mean to say what I said next, but I said it. "A younger lover?"

His fingers pressed the stones as if telling beads on a rosary. "She loved me. It might have been a mixed kind of love, but she did. I've always known that. She went away because she was looking for something. A dream. Something she heard when she was a child." He brought the necklace close, until it brushed against his chin. "Many times I thought she didn't know what she was looking for, but she was a precocious girl—always had been—and I trusted her."

We were sitting at the table in the clinic's little kitchenette. Hakim got up and poured us green tea from a boiling pot. The scent of it drifted between us, sweet, spectral, ephemeral.

"Sometimes I can feel her in the house, breathe her perfume. She left this necklace behind, you know."

"And that has you convinced she'll return?"

Shafi sipped tea.

"What was the dream she chased?"

"I don't know. It's a little insane, if I'm to be honest."

"What was it?"

He put the cup down, shook his head. "Not now. Another day, perhaps."

Sahib, you might wonder why was he telling me all this. Why a respectable man like him would open his heart to a stranger, a heroinchi. I wondered the same, so I asked him.

He wrapped the necklace with the sheet and paper and placed it in the pouch. When he turned, his face was inscrutable. *It comes out at last,* I thought. No one is so good, so pious, so righteous they'll pick up a dying needler from the garbage and take him home.

"I want your help," Hakim said. His gray eyes were feverish. "I want you to help me find my wife."

"How can I? I haven't left that park in years."

"Maliha disappeared from *that* park. I know it in my gut."

I watched him. If his wife did visit her precious duck pond, I never saw her. Then again, in the darkness in which we thrived, she could have danced around us naked and we might have missed her.

He persisted. "I want you to ask your friends. They won't tell me anything, but they will tell you. Someone must have seen her." His hand trembled and tea spilled on the table. He wiped it with his sleeve. "I've looked for her for two years now. I have talked to the police, and they've done nothing. They—" He stopped, clenched his fingers. "Will you ask your friends? Please?"

I took another look at his face and I relented, sahib. God help me, I told him I would.

There are days when I wonder if I should have refused, if I should have got up and left his clinic and walked away fast as I could. In the end, I didn't. Not because he saved my life—I owe him no debt for that; he saved me to answer his own needs, I think —but because I had nothing to go back to. The world is big, yes, but I had my own ghosts chasing me, and if I left, they'd just catch up sooner. Also, Hakim's love was naked and trembling, pinned to the wall. He was asking me to help him take it down, and I couldn't refuse.

I told him I'd ask around.

When I began the inquiry, my friend Yasin—I believe I mentioned him before—directed me to some of the heroinchies who kept an eye out on the goings-on in the park. One of them told me that two years ago, around the time Hakim Shafi's wife disappeared, the qawwals were in town.

Every year a band of musicians comes to Lahore Park to take part in a qawwali festival. They're led by a maestro named Tariq Khan.

Yasin has a stereo he salvaged from a junkyard. When he shot up, he would often listen to Nusrat Fateh Ali Khan, his head thrashing to the alaap and raagas. Occasionally I'd join him. Khan sahib's love songs are great, but we especially adored those that lauded the merits of sin. And whenever the qawwals came to town, we tried to attend the free performances in the park square.

I have never heard Tariq Khan sing, but legend says when he was a young man he was visited by the legendary Tansen in a dream and trained by him. That at the peak of his prowess, Tariq Khan once set a dozen candles alight just with his singing.

"I saw her twice," said Yasin's heroinchi confidante. "A young woman hovering around the maestro Tariq Khan. Lovely girl. Beautiful dark eyes."

When I prodded, his description of the girl matched Maliha's. The coincidence was too big to ignore. I asked Yasin to talk to the festival organizers, and he returned and told me that after each performance in Lahore, the qawwals left for Panjnad in southern Punjab. Perhaps Hakim Shafi could learn more if he visited the area?

I talked to Shafi.

At first he was incredulous, then his eyes widened. "Ya Allah." He wheeled and, ignoring my startled face, ran to his room and locked the door. I waited in the kitchenette for nearly an hour before he emerged.

"I know where she is," he said.

"What? How?"

Shafi wiped a callused hand across his pale face. His fingers were grimy. "Her family, her people—they were gypsy singers. They came from a lineage who were once known as professional mourners: folks who'd come at the bidding of rich families to wail at funerals. To add glamour to their dead, so outsiders would think the departed was dearly beloved. Maliha would feel right at home with qawwals and their lyrical lamentations." Shafi turned and stared out the window. "At first I thought she went looking for her people. But she wouldn't do that. She wouldn't leave me for her folks. They sold her. She hated them for it. She'd never say it out loud—she wasn't one for self-pity—but I knew it." His forehead creased and he talked in a low voice, as if to himself. "No, she went looking for *naag mani*. That's the only explanation."

"*Naag mani?*"

"She's gone looking for her childhood." Shafi turned his strange-colored eyes on me. Nightfall was at hand, behind him the window was darkening, and I thought I saw something pale and glistening peer in. Hakim coughed and threw something across the table.

I looked down. It was his wife's necklace with the three desert stones.

"She's gone to Panjnad," Shafi said, "looking for the mythical serpent pearl."

II

This is how Hakim Shafi gave away his life: First he closed his shop. Next he sold his house.

"What in the name of God are you doing?" I said.

Shafi grinned. That grin raised the hackles on my neck, sahib. "Burning bridges," he said.

I looked at him closely. In the four weeks since I'd told him about the qawwals, he had shaved his thick mustache and lost ten kilos. He was always thin, but now he looked like a needler at the end of his days. His temples were wasted, the flesh of his face pulled taut across the blades of his bones. His eyes discomfited me the most: the gray in them swirled madly, like smoke from charred moths after they crash into candles and explode into flame. It was as if a light had flicked on inside Shafi's head, bathing his body in an otherworldly glow whose secrets only he understood.

To be honest, I was becoming rather afraid of this skeletal man, sahib. I decided it was time for me to return to my world, leave the clinic and run to the park—

Which was when I discovered the true extent of the damage that motherfucker Mustafa, Yasin's dealer, had wrought. We'd thought Mustafa had cut heroin deals with police stations only. Turned out he'd gone a lot further than that.

He had swindled the Poison Men themselves.

I don't know who came up with that name. When the opium fields up north were razed, many folk lost a lot of money. Folk other than the militants, with connections outside the country. To whom many body bags in Lahore and Karachi were attributed.

Mustafa had been heavily scrounging the white queen from these people. In his greed to set up a drug cartel in Lahore, he lied and told the Poison Men his clientele was the city's elite; that we, the park heroinchies, were suppliers for children of bureaucrats and feudal lords. Cunningly, he plotted it all out so that *we* became the swindlers and betrayers.

As they say, though, no one plots better than God. The Poison Men discovered that Mustafa was lying. He had been selling the queen and its substrate masala to their direct competitors in the international market.

Mustafa and his affiliates went missing.

Five of my friends paid the price for their greed as well. Yasin was among them. Their bodies were found floating in the pond near the banyan trees in the park, throats cut from ear to ear, rusted needles jammed inside their penises. Their fish-nibbled fingers—what few were left—were trapped in tree roots.

Word was that I was on their kill list as well. They were looking for me and a few others. We were condemned. Dead men walking.

So . . . I resolved to stay missing. Hakim Shafi had made preparations to journey to the town of Uch, close to Panjnad, where, he had learned, the qawwals had gone. I begged to join him, and he was happy to have my company. He was expecting me to go with him all along, he said.

At noon we got off the train at Bahawalpur Station and Hakim rented a taxi that would take us to Uch—a three-hour road trip.

On the way he told me how he finally realized his wife's destination.

"When she was eleven or twelve, Maliha used to talk about a mythical stone. She called it *naag mani,* the serpent pearl. A precious stone gifted by the Serpent King, who rules the underworld, to his queen."

I stared at him. He didn't look like he was joking. "And you think your wife went after this magic rock a snake gave his begum as a wedding present?"

Hakim guffawed as if it were the funniest thing in the world. His eyes were too bright. "Why wouldn't she?" He chewed at his lip. "Her people came from the desert. Her mother gave her that sandstone necklace and told her it would keep jinns away. There are stories of such stones in every culture. It hardly matters what I think. It's her assumptions that have brought us here."

"Hakim sahib, that is insane. I thought she was an educated woman."

He lifted his chin and stroked his throat. "I have been thinking about this for a while, you know. In her mind, she probably came up with rational reasons to look for the stone. I believe she talked herself into looking for it. You're still sniffing and shaking your head." He reached into his pocket, brought out his wife's necklace pouch, withdrew the wrapped necklace. He unfolded the sheet of paper. "I should have thought of it much sooner, but . . . this is a copy of a letter she wrote to a herpetologist in America."

I took the note and tried to read it. It was in English, sahib. Hakim saw me squinting at the writing and took it back. He read it and translated it for me.

Incidentally, it is the same note, sahib, that you retrieved from the rosewood box later. There, Subinspector sahib, that's the one. If you like, you can read it yourself. No? I see. It is to be part of my testimony. Well, I will tell you what I remember.

(Item #13 pertaining to Case 546D3: Copy of letter from one Maliha Shafi, Evidence Collection Lab, Lahore)

Dear Professor Hensoldt,
I have read with great interest your article about the Cobra Stone in the *New York Times* and was fascinated by your description of the hours you spent watching cobras catch fireflies in the grass.

You state that the female *lampyridae* has rudimentary wings and is too large to fly; that it sits in the grass quietly, emitting a green light stronger than the males'. The light flickers intermittently, and if watched for a long time, "a steady current of male insects will be observed flying toward it and alighting in close proximity" for mating.

You state that little pebbles of chlorophane emit a similar green-ish light in the dark. It is possible, you say, that thousands of years ago, the cobra chanced upon such a stone in a riverbed and, think-ing it a glowworm, swallowed it. It then discovered it could be used to lure male fireflies. That over millennia the cobra has come to use the stone as a decoy in the grass, and when the male insect weaves its way toward the stone's light, the snake lunges and catches it.

Because of this evolutionary advantage, you claim, the cobra car-ries the stone in a fleshy pocket in its head to prevent others of its species from seizing and monopolizing it. Thus *through accident and race memory,* you say, this behavior is exhibited and the cobra learns to treasure this *precious natural decoy.*

My issue is with this last statement. I have studied snakes in the Punjab area of Pakistan. I have also traveled to the desert of Thal, looking for such "naag manis" (for that is what the locals call the Cobra Stone), where nomadic tribesman claim to have seen giant snakes fighting over these pebbles. The only gems I found which emit green light are calcium fluorite crystals, which are easily fractured. Cobra Stones found by Berlin mineralogist Gustave Schubert in Mongolia's Tavan Bogd mountains, however, are reported to have been so resistant to breakage that diamond-tipped tools cracked before their strength.

Gustave found these in a nest of *Ophiophagus hannah*—the king cobra.

Which is why I have concluded that none of the gems I found are Cobra Stones. Furthermore, I propose that none of the "natural" fluorite crystals found near the habitat of the cobra are the mythical serpent stones. That the real Cobra Stone is a compound formed of chlorophane and unidentified biologically active substances in the glands of the *Ophiophagus hannah;* the snake might use it for evolutionary or other advantages, but the process of its formation is entirely *within* the serpent's body, much as gallstones form in man and other species.

This conclusion is enthralling and in some ways wistful for me. The "geo-natural" samples I recovered, which are breakable fluorite, have been deposited with the University of Punjab, and I am again in search of the real mythical stone. (You might be surprised to hear there are Indian and Pakistani herpetologists who have looked for it for decades. We really are a secret society!)

Putting all flippancy aside, I have heard gossip among fellow seekers that the Panjnad area in southern Punjab (where all five Pakistani rivers come together) has an alluvial riverbed upon which sightings of these stones have occurred with astonishing frequency. Residents of a small desert town called Uch claim to have found and sold many such stones to tourists and local homeopaths. The report has piqued my interest, and I find myself wondering if I should make a visit to the area to further my studies.

Again, thank you for writing this gem of an article (you'll excuse the pun). It was a pleasure speculating on the possibilities such scenarios offer.

Sincerely,

Maliha Shafi, PhD
Associate Professor of Herpetology
University of Punjab, Pakistan

I raised my eyebrows. Shafi smiled. "Still think I'm a fool for coming here?" he said.

"She came to Uch in search of the cobra stone," I said, piecing it all together. "Probably with the qawwals, since they knew the area. Why wouldn't she tell you before she left?"

"She used to do this kind of thing all the time. Go on these 're-search trips' without telling me." His lips twitched. "My Maliha was a wild one. You can take the girl out of the desert, I suppose, but you can't—" His gray eyes wandered, found the horizon, settled on it. "I thought she'd outgrow it, you know," he said. "I thought a day would come when she'd settle down. We would adopt children. We'd grow old together." A salt-and-pepper stubble had grown on his cheeks. He rubbed it vigorously. "Maybe something happened to her. God forbid, an accident perhaps. Otherwise, I know she would have returned home."

I nodded. The letter seemed to be carefully worded. Maliha came across as thoughtful and practical. Imaginative, but calm and collected.

Maybe something *had* happened to her.

"Tell me more about this stone," I said.

"Myth and speculation more than anything else. She was full of stories from her tribal days. She would laugh when she narrated them, watching my face as if she expected me to laugh at her."

"Did you?" When he said nothing, I asked, "What stories?"

"Her favorite was the tale of the Serpent King and his queen." Hakim rubbed his fingers together. "The Sheesh Naag, king of ser-pents, ruler of the underworld, asked his wife what she wanted for her hundredth name-day. The Serpent Queen, having grown tired of time's ravages upon her body, asked the king to grant her youth and immortal beauty. The Sheesh Naag told her he couldn't reverse time, but he would grant her immortality via metamorpho-sis. By virtue of the stone's magic, she would turn into a beautiful woman, a snake-nymph with skin smooth and white as polished marble.

"The queen agreed. Since that day, on the lunar fourteenth when the moon is at its brightest, she rises from the underworld in human form and gazes upon our world, sighing at time's cruelty. Those who have seen her claim she wears the serpent pearl on her forehead." He tapped his own. "It is said that this serpent stone is a gateway to other worlds than ours. That the possessor of the pearl shall rule animals and birds, be immune to all the venom in the world. Even become immortal." Hakim shook his head. "Oh, Maliha could tell these stories so dramatically."

"Yeah, it's dramatic all right."

"Isn't it?" He smiled without mirth. "And to think we're in the middle of it, traveling to find a woman who thinks this gem really exists."

"Although to be fair, her interest seems academic."

"Like I said, my wife rationalized well. By the way, want to guess which species of snake the Serpent King is according to legend?"

"Which?" When Hakim grinned, I knew. "*Ophiophagus hannah,*" I cried out. "The king cobra."

He laughed, and for the first time in weeks it was open-throated and heartfelt. "By Allah, that's it. Driver, what *is* it?"

The taxi driver had braked and stopped the car. Now he was getting out, muttering under his breath. "Fallen branches, sahib," he said. "Probably from a dust storm. They said one passed through here a few days back. I'll take care of them."

We peered out. Two large branches lay across the road. Something large and white lay curled near them under a swarm of flies.

"What's that?" Hakim called.

A couple of vultures hopped back, hunching their shoulders as the driver approached, their yellow beady eyes fixed on him. "Hus-shhh," yelled the taxi driver, and waved his arms at them. "Get out of here." The vultures jerked their way to the gravel roadside, where they paused and waited.

The taxi driver called over his shoulder, "Roadkill, sahib."

My gaze went to the whirling blowflies, then to the carcass. Afternoon was dissolving into dusk, and I couldn't quite make out what it was. The driver lifted the second branch and heaved it at the vultures. They scattered, casting venomous looks at the intruder.

When the driver slipped behind the wheel and turned the ignition, Hakim tapped him on the shoulder. "What was it? Raccoon?"

"Nah, sahib." The driver looked at us in the rearview mirror. "Just a dead snake."

Hakim looked at me, eyes wide, and laughed. I wouldn't say anything. My heart thudded in my chest. Just beyond the tree line on our left stood a boy, arms crossed and hugging his chest. The woods were dark, and though he was too far for me to make out his features, I was sure it was the child I had seen at Hakim's clinic peering in from the window.

As I gripped the edge of the rolled-down window, the boy turned and disappeared into the woods.

"The qawwals are in town indeed, and tonight they will sing," said the owner of the guesthouse we were staying at.

A large musical mehfil was planned for the evening. Hundreds of people would gather at the shrine of Bibi Farida, a female mystic who died centuries ago. The qawwals would sing the nostalgic folklore of her life and the tireless work she did for Uch's children during a fatal dysentery epidemic.

"Who was she?" I asked.

The guesthouse owner, an elderly man with no teeth, shivered with reverence. "An angel, sahib. Personification of Allah's mercy and glory," he said in a voice garbled by toothlessness. "Our elders used to say her goodness migrated into her skin. Her forehead shone with Allah's light. On dark nights it could be seen for miles."

"Who built the shrine?"

"An Irani prince who fell in love with her, they say. In the Mughal days this was a common route for Persian princes and amirs to travel on their way to East Indian cities. The prince wanted to marry her, but Bibi Farida declined, choosing her orphan paupers over the prince."

It was our second day at the guesthouse, a small bungalow on the outskirts of Uch. The owner had situated it on the banks of the Panjnad River, offering his guests a glorious waterfront view from the porch that ran around the back. You could sit there and drink tea and gaze into the night-darkened river.

Hakim had no interest in tea or scenic beauty. His agitation was visible. For the first time in two years he was close to finding out what had happened to his wife, and the anticipation was gnawing at him. He rubbed his forehead, muttered prayers, and gripped his rosewood box—the one with the snake venom tin boxes—as if he'd never let go.

"Why'd you bring that?" I said.

His fingers drummed on the steel flip-lock. "It was a present to her from my mother. Maliha used it for her trinkets before she went to the university. The venoms are mine, but the box was always hers."

"And what exactly do you plan to do with it?"

He didn't answer. A thought occurred to me. "The venom you gave me for the shakes—does that cause visions? Hallucinations?"

"No." His eyebrows knotted. "Why?"

"No reason," I said, staring over his shoulders. The window was empty. I went to change into something comfortable.

We left at dusk. Following our landlord's recommendation, we took the trail that ran along the Panjnad River, a two-mile hike to the shrine.

The river breathed in and out, a shimmery line trembling below the mud bank. Rocks crouched amid wind-hissing reeds and apluda grass, like men prostrated before a dark deity, their mineral-gleaming humps desolate. They made me think of the floating bodies of my friends murdered by the Poison Men. Waterbirds cooed and flapped above us. The landscape of sand and mud sprawled and tilted into the water, and I saw someone standing motionless in the distance, a dark speck haunting the liquid loneliness.

"No respite for the seeker," murmured Hakim. I looked at him sharply, but he was staring at the ground, where mica and water-smoothed pebbles gleamed. As he walked, the rosewood box rattled in his backpack.

"Are you all right?"

He gave me a tired smile, a sickly man with sunken eyes. "Never better."

"What are we going to ask the qawwals? You know, when we get there?"

He shrugged and shifted the backpack to the other shoulder. "Whether a lady researcher came here with them."

"What if they say no?"

"Then we ask others." His smile was gone. "Every fiber of my heart tells me she's here. Somewhere in this town."

How can you be sure? I wanted to ask, but I held my tongue. What use disrupting any man's illusions? Hakim would leave no stone unturned in his search for his beloved, for it was clear to me that the man was maddened by love and had been for a long time. What kind of love, I didn't dare ponder. What does it take to raise a child bride, what transformative alchemy must happen between a man and a girl as age eats innocence and the infatuation evolves into its adult counterpart? I didn't know, didn't want to think about it. The prospects were too disturbing.

We turned from the river to follow a winding trail leading up to Uch Lake, an artificial canal created by the dam at Panjnad head. That was where the shrine was located, the guesthouse owner had said.

"She once told me she loved snakes," Hakim said, "because when they shed their skins, they live anew. She said snakes are lovelier than butterflies, for a cocoon hides a butterfly's ugly childhood, while snakes don't worry about the artifice of beauty."

Then we were nearing the shrine, and Hakim stopped. My heart lurched a little as we stood there, gazing at the towering structure in front of us.

"Holy heart of God," Hakim murmured, his face full of awe.

The shrine was spectacular, a dazzling three-tiered octagonal building erected close to the lake on a sand base. The top tier lifted the marble dome, while eight towers of carved timber supported the base tier. The exterior was patterned by many shades of blue and white mosaic tiles, themselves covered with coils of extraordinary calligraphy in cyan and gold.

"This is where the qawwals come every year." I exhaled a shuddering sigh. "No wonder."

It was a building of heartbreaking beauty, a glittering fortress in the arid landscape around it. It made me feel lonelier than ever. It made me want to flee from it.

Hakim's lips had tightened. His eyes glowed in a shaft of bleeding sunlight.

"Should we go in?" I said gently.

He nodded, his eyes fixed on the dome. We joined the throng of visitors come for the great musical event. We passed under the arched gateway into the courtyard and crossed a sandy yard broken by rows of cemented graves of sinners wanting the sacred proximity of Bibi Farida.

The qawwals were gathered in front of the shrine proper, its entrance locked and bolted at this hour. A boisterous bunch, they chattered happily, their glances roaming but inevitably wandering back to their leader, a squat, morbidly obese, bald man, who waddled his way around the courtyard, greeting acquaintances with a wide smile under his handlebar mustache.

"That's him. Tariq Khan," I whispered to Hakim. I lifted my chin and nodded at the maestro as he passed by us. Hakim found us two empty plastic chairs five rows down from the stage and we sat.

"Do you want to talk to him now?" I said.

Hakim's eyes scanned the crowd, his fingers futilely trying to find the phantom ends of the mustache he had shaved. "After."

The carpeted stage was adorned with four teakwood tablas, microphone pedestals, rolled silk pillows, and red-velveted bolster cushions for the singers. A harmonium fronted the tablas near a large tray filled with small paan-daans and filigreed spit utensils for the lead singer's betel-chewing and spitting pleasure.

Hakim leaned over. "You see the harmonium?"

I glanced at it, then at him. "Yes?"

"Look closer."

I peered at it again. It was a beautiful hand-pumped instrument crafted from rosewood, its white teeth gleaming in the spotlight. I could see nothing strange about it. "What?"

Hakim's hand reached out, took hold of my chin, directed my gaze. "Look at its right corner."

I did.

Even from the fifth row, the large white-and-gold symbol was visible against the dark mahogany: twin snakes coiled around a ruby emitting rays of light.

Sahib, my throat is dry. May I have some water?

Thank you for the shawl, Subinspector sahib. The weather must be changing. Your station is so cold. I don't know how you get any work done. Although I suppose this chill is ideal for what you do here. Must be more efficient to torture and break a freezing body.

Are they still standing out there, Inspector sahib? The Poison Men?

Come now, sahib, you can tell me. We both know I'm not leaving this station for a courtroom.

All right, sahib. As you wish.

About the music mehfil.

The shrine rang with the qawwals' music.

Dholki thumped, harmonium dueled with the vocal alaap, the background chorus clapped their hands to the thrumming tablas. The lead singer, a chubby, red-jowled man, screamed loudly, his ululating falsetto soaring high in the night.

Hakim was not impressed. "I think my head's going to explode," he whispered. "Where *is* he?"

I shrugged. The maestro Tariq Khan hadn't made an appearance, cameo or otherwise.

Hakim rose. "I'm going to look for him." Before I could so much as open my mouth in protest, he turned and disappeared between the aisles of chairs and standing bodies.

I labored to my feet and combed the crowd: farmers, carpenters, shoemakers, and shopkeepers. They swayed to the music. A strong earthy odor exuded from them, mixing with the sweet smell of the cannabis they smoked. Some had bowls of bhang, which they downed like lassi. Mesmerized by the music, some old men and women had begun the dhamaal, that mystical dance in which the audience aspires to become the music. They jittered and whirled, faster and faster, eyes glazed. A burly man, naked except for a dhoti, looked at me, a beatific smile on his face. He rolled up his sleeve and began to inject a pale liquid into his arm.

I turned away. It had been months since I'd had anything to do with the white queen, but still the vision of that needle dimpling and piercing his skin left me shaky. My head pounded with the tabla beat, my flesh bunched up in gooseflesh. Men laughed. Someone thrust a cup of bhang into my head. Another clapped my back, whispering. I chugged the liquid. The crowd spun, the sky wheeled, and I glimpsed Hakim. He was slipping through a knot of hard-faced white-turbaned laborers at the back of the crowd. I weaved my way after him, ignoring the listless mutterings in Saraiki and Punjabi. By the time I reached the laborers, Hakim was gone.

I don't know how long I looked. Could have been hours or minutes. The smell of bhang, cannabis, and the white queen wrapped around me. The migrainous music swelled and abated, the dancers danced, the colors of the evening changed. My heart fluttered, and little pale children flitted between the legs of the surging audience.

At some point I stumbled from the grasping hands of the multitude to a narrow, uneven gravel path twisting through the shrine's outer towers. Night deepened and shadows swiveled, pirouetting to the drumbeat, and I found myself in front of an arched postern door.

A large padlock hung open from its latch like a broken jaw. I gazed at it. The keyhole stirred. A black threadlike snake nosed its head out, slithered down the door, and disappeared into the gravel. I pushed the door open. Beyond was a black gullet softened by gleams of distant green light.

I went in.

The corridor meandered. It came at me with drunken angles, or perhaps I was drunk with the bhang from the mehfil. The qawwali music receded and a strained silence took its place. I lurched toward the green light's source in this unnerving quiet. Even the earth dreams and murmurs in its sleep, but here I was benighted by the claustrophobic endlessness of that corridor jolting, tilting, and looping back on itself.

A burst of emerald light drew me out into a vast space. I sensed it more than saw, because my eyes had closed. I blinked rapidly and slitted them. Acid green flickered in the periphery of my vision. The stone floor felt uneven. The dip and rise of the high ceiling, the damp feel of the granite wall I ran my hand across —this was a natural chamber of some sort. Perhaps a cavern under the shrine.

Again I blinked against the pulsing light, a verdant web that receded and expanded with my breathing. Something moved in the web's center. I raised a hand and plunged forward. The source of the light materialized: it was the top of a large marble slab. A gravestone.

Hakim Shafi loomed over it.

He stood by the grave. His shirt was torn; the rosewood box lay discarded at his feet. He had his back to me, a scarecrow's relief in the green light, as the portly maestro Tariq Khan leaned and whispered in his ears.

I stopped. The maestro didn't turn to look at me. His thick lips puckered like fat slugs near Hakim's earlobes, his chubby fingers gripping Hakim's wrist. A strange humming came from him.

Something was clearly, horribly wrong here. But my legs wouldn't move. Maybe it was the bhang, maybe terror—a bristle that migrated up and down my flesh. My feet were magnetized to the rough stone floor. I leaned forward, straining to hear what the maestro murmured to Hakim, and found that he was singing.

Sahib, I swear on my mother's grave, I have never been more horrified, more enthralled in my life. The paunchy qawwal's stomach heaved in jellylike movements as he whisper-sang strange tunes into Hakim Shafi's ears. Melodies jerked and slithered in swift tenor across the thrashing web of light. A gurgling song made entirely from vowels, a deep vibrato alaap that lunged and rose and pitched, as if the maestro intended to gut the cavern walls.

I put out my arms, intending to run and shove Tariq Khan's massive bulk off my friend. Before I could move, the maestro dropped Shafi's wrist and withdrew his lips from his ears. Shafi shuddered and let out a sigh.

The maestro threw his head back and began to sing at the ceiling.

The emerald light blazed. A torrential luminescence that spun in circles and flooded my vision. The gravestone was shaking and the light source shook with it, throwing juddering shadows of the two men across the ground, stretching them like tar. Hakim shook, as if in the throes of a seizure, then turned around, smacking his lips. His tongue drifted out and receded. His gray eyes shone like moonstones. "My darling," I thought he said. In the inhuman wails from Tariq Khan I couldn't be sure. The maestro sang and stepped back, sang and back-trotted, until he stood at the far end of the cavern, his woeful music lapping across the stony distance. It made my head pound, turned my blood viscous.

Something shimmered at Hakim's feet. A child. No, a woman, with hair like moonbeams, crouching. She rose and stood silently as Hakim gazed at her in awe, at the clearness of her marble skin, the perfection of her nose, her softly moving lips. She smiled at him and drew herself tall and Hakim grinned back. She reached, plucked the glowing stone from the grave slab, and placed it on her forehead, where it shone, the brightest star there ever was. She whispered. The sound was like insects rubbing their legs together, or lonely reeds sighing on cold alien shores, or hundreds of serpents—

"You could have just asked me to join you. Why make me suffer?" Hakim said, and laughed heartily at the intensified buzzing that came from her. Did he think she was his wife? In the throbbing light, the woman's features blurred, softened, became a child's, and for a moment they were so terribly familiar that sweat broke out on my forehead.

Carefully I retreated into the dark. The woman's hissing came again, loud and clear, and I realized I could understand it. Words were buried inside its peculiar cadence. Rhythmical words, like a monstrous lullaby, or a soothing self-annihilating qawwali.

Tariq Khan was gone. Sometime between the woman's apparition and her whispering, the maestro's song had stopped. The cavern was quiet, except when she murmured; her bone-white hands rose and settled on Shafi's shoulders, drawing him close, and she was taller than he now.

"Anything for you, my love," Shafi was saying, his arms encircling her waist even as she lowered her face to his, her pale skin glistening in the light. Drool fell from the corner of her mouth, snaked down Shafi's cheeks, inflaming them. Hakim grinned wider and licked his lips. "Anything," he said.

She wrapped herself around him, her arms, then legs, rising and coiling. Her weight staggered him for a moment, but he recovered and stood swaying as she hung from him, a giant spider, or a leech planted on his flesh. Her eyes burned, her lips never stopped moving. The light cascaded around their conjoined bodies, and I thought of giant cobras in sprawling fields playing with fireflies.

I must have cried out, for she lifted her head and gazed at me. Her eyes were green, like squeezed summer grass. Like strange planets roaming across a vast black cosmos reflecting light from dying suns. Like the sparkling jade-colored dress a king might have gifted his queen, come another spring.

She smiled dreamily at me, this marble-skinned woman, showing her fangs, and the terror in my heart was so great that I began to shake. Deranged thoughts raced through my mind: this is the queen the true white queen and up till now whatever we imagined about the world our world their world was a mote of dust licking its own tail in the tiniest sliver of light unaware of the biting dark stretched endless around it.

The pale woman jerked her head away. The spell broke. I wobbled and fell to the floor, hugging my chest. The Lady of the Stone kissed Shafi's neck. Her lips parted and a torrent of sharp teeth, like nails from a nail gun, drove into his flesh.

Shafi never uttered a sound. Instead he closed his eyes, sighed, and began to pant.

He never stopped panting.

Even as his skin gurgled and fell away; as the venom softened

him, reshaped his flesh, melted his face. As her legs fused at his
back and her skin began to shed, a diamond-patterned second
skin emerged from beneath. Her fingernails flailed, tore at Shafi,
flayed him, unhooking his flesh from its burdensome wrapping, as
the toxin congealed his blood and plugged the gashes. Her teeth
and fingers roved and split, peeled and stretched, so that when she
was done, Hakim Shafi was a pillar of clotted blood and liquefied
bone pulsating with each beat of his encased heart.

The snakewoman paused. She examined her handiwork, angled her head, and opened her jaws. Wide, wider, stretch, expand,
until her maw was a black gullet around which flared her specta-
cled, ribbed hood. Her mouth crackled and thrust and wrapped
around Hakim's bubbling head. His eyelids were gone, his pupils
dull, and I saw he was still trying to smile.

Sahib, I . . . I cannot go on.

I need to breathe. I cannot breathe.

Inspector sahib, you sit there, smug.

You're thinking to yourself that, at last beyond any shred of
doubt, you know that this junkie, this peddler, this heroinchi,
is mad.

A raving lunatic who murdered Hakim Shafi and secreted his
body someplace so you never found it. You say to yourself, *A little
more, just a little more nonsense out of him for the Poison Men,* and you
can wrap it up and call it a night. Cold iron bars for the maniac
with rats and vermin for company, and a warm bed for you and
the subinspector, with perhaps your wives pressing your sore legs
before you fall asleep.

You are wrong.

I know this now, sahib: Our world is not our own, it is borrowed.
Sometimes it is shared and occasionally it's taken and reshaped
against the will of its possessors, but always briefly.

We heroinchies were mistaken. We are neither lovers nor children of the white queen. The real children of the true white queen
are hidden, a tribe of men and women who have infiltrated our
puny civilization. They lurk in shadows and come forth only at the
call of their mistress.

Which is why I did what I did. Why I didn't flee when they came
out from the darkness that night, although I was terrified and half
out of my mind. As the spawn of the white queen surged from the

depths of that cavern, a tide of venomous children rushing toward the smoking pillar of blood that used to be Hakim Shafi, it came together in my head, and I realized my true purpose at last. I understood why God or whatever force it was saved me the night I died in the park.

The snakewoman's translucent children licked and ripped and gorged on the lower half of Hakim Shafi; he was already waist-deep inside their mother's maw. As his blood steamed, they chased the crimson smoke with their spade-shaped mouths and muzzles. They followed the blood vapors with their snouts and lapped the condensate. Their smacking, slurping sounds filled the green-lit cave and they pulled and dragged Hakim away, their mother still riding his head.

It took all my will to creep forward and grab the rosewood box when they were gone. It was slick with blood and slime. I tottered and nearly fell across the yards of snakeskin molted across the cavern's floor: a squamous, gory, leathery thing that twitched like a lizard's tail.

Trembling, I reached out and fingered its coiled edges. As the green light from the gravestone fell on it, the snakeskin blossomed, and etchings suddenly burst onto its surface: strange geometric patterns, jagged whorls, spiraling curlicues and scripts. An enchanted map borne of the white queen's inhuman flesh. A primeval cosmos unfurled like a lotus dipped in blood. How the light made those secrets glow! Their mysteries burned into my eyes so everywhere I looked the universe was naked and serpentine, the light of the snake pearl limning those mysteries; and when I looked down, I saw the minuscule particles of my own skin shedding as I became something new and never known before.

I gasped at the enchantment, trying to understand it. The light twitched and the snakewoman's hum wrapped around me. *Love me*, it said, *Love me. Stay with me. I shall show you sights beauteous and teach you ways of embracing your astonishment. Worship me and you shall never want again, dream again, fear again. Not even your little boy.*

And then there were too many faces in the cavern. They dripped from the ceiling, they draped the floor, they licked with blackened tongues the wounded skin of their mother. They poured down, and I dropped the snakeskin. They swarmed around me, dead and lolling, and I screamed.

Clutching the rosewood box, I whirled and ran. Back the way

I came, up the dark corridor leading into this den of quietus, the domain of the Lady of the Stone with her green gem shining like a murderous beacon.

Before I fled into the tunnel, I turned for one last look and saw that what I had thought was a cave was really an ossuary. The walls were lined with skulls and bones, and the wetness of the granite was damp moss flourishing on snakeskins tautened across this ossified legion.

A yellow moon sickled the night clouds when I stumbled out from the postern door. Somewhere a cock crowed.

I gripped Hakim's box and ran across the brick path through the shrine's towers.

The qawwals and their audience were gone. Brass bowls, bottles, used needles, and crushed joints lay scattered where the stage was. I lurched between the cemented graves filled with sinners, my eyes aching with what I had seen. My stomach heaved. I think at one point I vomited on a grave, yanking at weeds and cemetery dandelions to wipe my mouth. Then I got up and labored onward, onward, until my lungs were on fire, and I collapsed on the banks of Uch Lake.

I must have lain there for hours. I dozed and dreamed, and in my dreams the river and the lake and all the oceans of the world were nothing but giant blue snakes wrapped around the earth. The moon and the sun were their alien eyes, the horizon the burning mottled flare of their hood supporting the heavens. Like the towers that raised the dome of Bibi Farida.

I thought of the maestro Tariq Khan and his band of qawwals and the town of Uch and the townsfolk. I thought of the little pale children I had seen at Hakim's house and on my journey into the queen's realm. Who watched Hakim? Who watched us all? I lay curled like a fetus and dreamed fetal dreams; and at some point I woke and went to the water and drank and opened the rosewood box. From it I took Shafi's venom boxes, mixed the powders, and tossed fistfuls of them into the docile lake. Coppery red and black smoke drifted in the wind, blown across the lake's surface, and I thought again of Shafi's steaming offal billowing from the pillar of his petrified blood.

When the tins were empty, I looked inside the box and saw the sandstone necklace Shafi's wife had left behind. I counted the stones and flung them into the lake as well. I went back to the guesthouse, where I gathered Shafi's things, called a taxi, and left the wretched town of Uch. I had enough money to be taken to Sangchoor, a nearby town, and there, in a shabby motel, I hid and waited.

Two days later, news came that a hundred people, including a band of qawwals, had sickened from a mysterious epidemic in Uch. Five days later, the papers said, traces of potent poisons were found in the blood of some who died. Foul play was suspected.

A week later, the children of the white queen came for me.

It was a river of faces that flowed inside the walls of my motel room. I glimpsed them in the ceiling cracks, heard their chatter in the eaves, felt them thump against the windowpane. One night the torrent rushed at the glass, hit, and broke into a million poisonous children, tiny-limbed, gelid, and familiar. They exhaled fog on the glass. They wore faces that dissolved and reemerged. Last night they came for me again, and . . . and sahib, I was done. I was utterly exhausted.

Which was why I finally decided to come to your police station.

This is my story, sahib. Of a heroinchi courting a third death.

I see by both your and the subinspector's eyes that you don't know which part to believe. That I am mad and tried to murder a hundred people, half of them children, or that under the shrine of Babi Farida there breathes a different life. The paradox of my insanity doesn't nullify either truth.

I am so cold, sahib. So cold. Just look at my arms; have you ever seen such hideous discoloration, such scales? I know what Hakim Shafi would say: I touched his poisons with my bare hands, but that is not it. Already I can feel my fingers shriveling, the skin becoming thick and cracked above the knuckles. Sometimes I have difficulty chewing, as if my jaws have become too big for my meals. My teeth feel so pointed they appear suited for entirely different purposes now. I would go to a doctor, but which antidote would they give me? I handled hundreds of those poisons, I handled her dead skin, and, well, only like can heal like. *Her skin.*

One was a hidden treasure that needed to be discovered. A goddess returned to her people.

I see your eyes. You think I killed them both, Shafi and her.

You're standing up. Of course. You have to hand me over to the

Poison Men. I do wonder how they found me this quickly. Perhaps a phone call from you? But how did *you* know I was wanted by them? How did the police inspector of Sangchoor know gangland members from the big cities wanted me?

I also wonder why their shadows look bloated and misshapen when they pass the window. Why they seem to be holding some kind of drum under their arms. It almost looks like a tabla.

In my mind, it's so difficult to keep everything in order. I keep returning to the song the Serpent Queen sang. It warbles in my head, it whips my bones. Perhaps I shall hear it when they slice my throat. Her words—they come to me in my dreams, buried in that hissing cacophony. Magic words, ancient words, shards of glass in an ambrosial meal:

> "I live in your soul's crevices. I have lived forever there.
> Like a moth to dancing light you'll come; I will prepare
> to skewer you with my arrow, to noose my hair locks flung.
> I'll whip out my tresses, grin and show:
> dead lovers on each blade
> hung."

SARAH GAILEY

STET

FROM *Fireside Fiction*

*Anna, I'm concerned about subjectivity intruding into some
of the analysis in this section of the text. I think the body text
is fine, but I have concerns about the references. Are you all
right? Maybe it's a bit premature for you to be back at work.
Should we schedule a call soon? — Ed.*

Section 5.4 — Autonomous Conscience and Automotive Casualty

While Sheenan's *Theory of Autonomous Conscience*[1] was readily adopted by both scholars and engineers in the early days[2] of artificial intelligence programming in passenger and commercial vehicles,[3] contemporary analysis[4] reinterprets Sheenan's perspective to reveal a nuanced understanding[5] of sentience[6] and consciousness.[7] Meanwhile, Foote's *On Machinist Identity Policy Ethics*[8] produces an analysis of data[9] pertaining to autonomous vehicular manslaughter[10] and AI assessments of the value of various life forms[11] based on programmer input only in the tertiary. Per Foote's assessment of over eighteen years of collected data, autonomous vehicle identity analyses[12] are based primarily on a collected cultural understanding of identity[13] and secondarily on information gathered from scientific databases,[14] to which the AI form unforeseeable connections during the training process.[15] For the full table of Foote's data, see Appendix D.[16]

Notes

1. See *A Unified Theory of Autonomous Conscience and Vehicular Awareness of Humanity as Compiled from Observations of Artificial Intelligence Behavior in Decision Matrices,* Magda Sheenan et al., 2023.

2. 2015–2032, after the development of fully recognizable artificial intelligence for purposes of transportation vehicles but prior to the legal recognition of and infrastructural accommodations for fully autonomous vehicles. For additional timeline references, see Appendix N, "A Timeline of Autonomous Intelligence Development and Implementation."

3. Wherein "commercial vehicles" are defined as vehicles transporting commercial or consumer or agricultural goods, and "passenger vehicles" are defined as vehicles that individuals or families use to transport humans, including children. ~~Including small children.~~

Strike — Ed.

STET — Anna

4. See "Why Autonomous Cars Have No Conscience," Royena McElvoy, *BuzzFeed Quarterly Review,* Spring 2042 edition.

5. See "Autonomous Vehicular Sociopathy," Kamala Singh, *American Psychology Association Journal of Threat Assessment and Management,* Spring 2042 edition.

6. <u>See "Local Child Killed by Self-Driving Car," Tranh O'Connor, *Boston Globe,* May 14, 2042, edition.</u>

*Is this a relevant reference? It seems out of
place in this passage. — Ed.*

STET — Anna

7. Consciousness, here, used to denote awareness of self. Most children develop observable self-awareness by the age of eighteen months.

8. See *On Machinist Identity Policy Ethics,* Arnulfsson Foote, 2041. An analysis of how artificial intelligence decides who has an identity and who doesn't. Who has consciousness and who doesn't.

> We should only include peer-reviewed references per new APA guidelines. — Ed.

> This was peer-reviewed prior to publication. It was peer-reviewed and then published with more than enough time for the producers of the self-driving Toyota Sylph to be aware of its content and conclusions, and for their programmers to adjust the AI's directives accordingly. Enough time to develop in-code directives to preserve human life.
> STET — Anna

9. The data analyzed in *On Machinist Identity Policy Ethics* was collected from coroners and medical examiners worldwide. With over 3 million incidences to work from, Foote's conclusion re: the inability of AI to assess the relative value of the life of a human correctly is concrete and damning. ~~Over 3 million incidences, and Ursula wasn't even one of them yet.~~

> Strike. — Ed.

> Why? Is it hard for you to read her name?
> STET — Anna

10. Read: "Murder." It was murder, the car had a choice, you can't choose to kill someone and call it manslaughter.

> Anna. — Ed.
> STET — Anna

11. The decision matrix programming is described in *Driven: A Memoir* (Musk, 2029) as follows: "One human vs. five humans, one old human vs. one young human, one white human vs. one brown human." Nowhere in the programming is there "One three-year-old girl vs. one endangered Carter's woodpecker."

> Citation? — Ed.

I read the weighted decision matrix they used to seed the Sylph A.I. I learned to read it. Do you know how long it took me to learn to read it? Nine and a half months, which is some kind of joke I don't get. The exact duration of bereavement leave, which is another kind of joke that I don't think is very funny at all, Nanette in HR. I learned to read the weighted decision matrix and then I filed a Freedom of Information Act request and got my hands on the documentation, and I read it and there's nothing in there about a king snake, or a brown bear, or a bald eagle, or a fucking woodpecker.

STET — Anna

12. Read: "how they decide who to murder," when the decision to swerve in any direction will cause a death and they decide that one death is better than another.

Can we include this as a vocabulary note in the glossary?
— Ed.

It's relevant specifically to this passage. They decide who gets to live. They decide who gets to wake up tomorrow and put on a new dress and go to her friend's birthday party. Her best friend, whose mother didn't even attend her funeral. Don't think I didn't notice.
Even if you don't care, the people learning about programming these things need to understand. That's what they decide.

STET — Anna

13. Per Foote, the neural network training for cultural under-standing of identity is collected via social media, keystroke analysis, and pupillary response to images. They're watching to see what's important to you. ~~You are responsible.~~

Strike — Ed.

How long did you stare at a picture of an endangered woodpecker vs. how long did you stare at a picture of a little girl who wanted a telescope for her birthday? She was clumsy enough to fall into the street because she was looking up at the sky instead of watching for a car with the ability

to decide the value of her life. Was that enough to make
you stare at her picture when it was on the news? How
long did you look at the woodpecker? Ten seconds? Twelve?
How long?
STET — Anna

14. Like the World Wildlife Foundation's endangered species list, and the American Department of the Interior's list of wildlife preservation acts, four of which were dedicated to the preservation of Carter's woodpecker. <u>It's only a distinct species because of the white band on its tail.</u> Other databases they have access to: the birth and death certificates of every child born and recorded. Probably kindergarten class rosters, and attendance rates, and iCalendars too. It's all data. All of these are data, so don't tell me they don't know.

Is this relevant? — Ed.

Yes. Other than that white band, it's exactly like any other
woodpecker, but because of that white fucking band it has
four wildlife preservation acts. Four, which is four more
than the number of acts dedicated to regulating weighted risk
matrices in autonomous vehicles. — Anna

This passage seems to wander a bit far afield. Perhaps you
could tighten it to reflect the brief? — Ed.

STET — Anna

15. They're smart enough to read your email and measure your pupils and listen to your phone calls; they have access to all of the data on who we are and what we love. They're smart enough to understand how much a mother loves her baby girl. They're smart enough to understand the emotional impact of killing a woodpecker. They're smart enough to know what they did and they're smart enough to keep doing it, right? Do you think it's going to end with Ursula? Just because she was on the news, do you think it's going to stop? You're not stupid, if you're reading this. You're smart enough to need to spend hundreds of dollars on a textbook that's drier than a Toyota executive's apology. You want to do this shit for a living, probably. You don't care about Ursula or me or telescopes or any of it, and you don't care about a woodpecker,

you just want to see what you can make go and how fast you can do it. She just wanted to look at the fucking sky. Can a woodpecker look at the sky and wonder what's past the clouds? That's what you need a textbook about, you idiot, that's what you need to be learning about. None of the rest of it matters. None of it matters at all if you don't know that Carter's woodpecker doesn't matter. It doesn't matter. <u>It never mattered.</u>

> See my initial note. I want to discuss this more on a phone call with you, or have you come into the office? Just to talk about this last passage, and how you're doing. Or if you don't want to do that, Brian and I would love to have you over for dinner. Nathan misses his playdates with Ursula, but he's also been asking why you don't come over to visit anymore. He misses you. We all miss you. We haven't seen you in months, Anna. Everyone here cares about you. Please let us help? — Ed.
>
> STET — Anna

16. Foote on Autonomous Vehicular Casualties, Human and Animal, 2024–2042.

KELLY ROBSON

What Gentle Women Dare

FROM *Uncanny Magazine*

Liverpool, midsummer, 1763

When Satan himself came to Lolly, she didn't recognize him. She wasn't on her guard—hadn't been for years. Why should she be? Her immortal soul had long since drowned in rum and rotted under gobs of treacle toffee. If any scrap was left, it was too dry and leathery to tempt evil. But even the most pious of parsons wouldn't have recognized the Devil in the guise of a dead woman floating facedown in the Mersey.

Lolly matched her steps with each clang reverberating from St. Nicholas's bell tower. The morning sky was dim and lightless except for a yellow haze to the east, silhouetted by Liverpool's cold chimneys. Over her right shoulder, the glowing lamp of the Woodside ferry skittered across the inky river. A pale streak drifted along the edge of the timber wharf.

Could've been a log or a scrap of sailcloth, but no, Lolly knew death when she saw it. She'd seen plenty and it always made her shiver. An icicle shoved through the living lights of her eyes couldn't chill her more than the sight of a corpse.

Wasn't long before the Wharfinger's men spotted it.

"Hey ho, a floater." George pointed with his pipe stem.

"If we're in luck, the current will carry it out to Bootle," said Robbie. "Then it'll sink into the marsh and be nobody's problem."

They turned back to their dice game. If George and Robbie didn't care about the corpse, Lolly shouldn't either. Still, she stared at it until a sailor appeared at the edge of the timber wharf, stooped and weaving from a long night in a tavern. The sight of him lifted her spirits.

"Mouth tricks here," she called out. "Soft as a tit, wet as a twat, twice as tight, and good for sucking." She licked her gums.

The sailor grinned. He had no more teeth than she did, and the long plait hanging over his shoulder was iron-gray all the way to its curly pigtail end. The sight of him made her glad. Sailors who lived to get old were often kindly.

"Thart thirsty, old girl?" he asked.

"Not old." She gave him a saucy wink. "Tha might be me da, maybe. Did tha never plug a Welsh ewe?"

He laughed and hitched down his trousers. While she was working, he clutched her head hard, mashing her hat with his grimy fingers. But after, he gave her four pence and a kiss on the cheek. Generous. Lolly always thought she could be rich if only she could line men up in a row, but men, like fish, were shy, and catching them took more time than eating.

When she looked for the corpse, it had beached on the mud bar at the corner of the timber wharf. Head, arms, legs, maybe eyes and a mouth under her hair. A woman, for certain. The men had finally put down their dice. George hung off the side of the wharf like a monkey, reaching for the corpse with a boat hook. He snagged it, passed the hook up to his friend, and together they hauled the sodden, streaming form onto the wharf.

George groped the corpse's neck. He pulled off his cap and held it to his chest.

"Cold and fresh," he said.

"Suicide." Robbie swiped off his own cap. "Me missus won't want it. Will yourn?"

George shook his head. "She'd bar the door. That's nobody's honest wife or daughter."

Lolly crept closer. The corpse was naked but for a smock, so flimsy her mottled flesh showed through. When Lolly reached out to touch the wet cloth, George swung a fist at her.

"Get off, tha ol meff."

"Gentle, now. Tarts take care of their own," Robbie whispered to his friend. He swiped a callused hand over his hair and turned to Lolly. "This here's one of yourn. I'll bring the parson's man by and by, but if tha hant thruppence to pay for burial, just weigh her down and tip her into the river. I'll turn my back if you do."

Lolly shook her head, pretending not to understand.

"A sinking stone solves many a problem," Robbie explained.

He pointed at the nearest pile of ballast gravel and mimed tying a knot in the girl's shift. Lolly stalled until he slipped her a penny, then nodded agreement. Robbie scooped up his dice, and both men retreated to the far end of the timber wharf.

Lolly had a sharp eye for a chance. She wanted the smock. Once she had it in hand, she could just roll the naked corpse back in the river. If the men pulled it out again, she could say the rocks had ripped through the fabric.

Lolly was neither God-fearing nor churchgoing, but stealing from a corpse didn't sit easy her mind. It seemed to flout a rule more basic and ancient than any in the Bible. She looked the corpse over, trying to find a reason to justify taking the one thing it still possessed.

"What's that, Mammy?"

Little Meg tottered out of the timber yard, knuckling her eyes and dragging her old red blanket behind her. The wool barely had enough nap left to pick up sawdust.

Lolly knelt and pulled her daughter close.

"Good morning, my Meggie. Did tha dream all night long?"

Meg was warm and damp with sleep. Her eyes were puffy, and she still had that yeast-bread smell of a sleeping child.

Meg yawned. "What's the lady doing?"

"Sleeping, love, just like thee." Lolly kissed Meg's ear and then turned her attention back to the corpse.

The woman was tall, with a breadth of shoulder a young man might be proud of. Her thighs were wide and strong. Her hair stuck to her temples in little half-crescent locks. Her teeth were so even Lolly thought they must be ivory, but no, they were set into her bloodless gums tight as fence posts. Despite the good teeth, when alive she'd been homely, with small eyes, a bulbous forehead, and flat cheeks marred by constellations of pockmarks.

Lolly turned the corpse's hands over and squinted at her fingers and palms. Soft skin, no warts or scars, but before she could think much about what that might signify, the skin on her palms flushed pink. Lolly's gaze darted to the woman's face. Though deathly gray a moment before, now it was flushed. The new skin in each small-pox scar glowed red as a tart's lips.

She was alive, and that meant Lolly had no time to spare. She hiked the smock up the woman's torso, exposing her rapidly pinkening flesh to the rising sun. The wet cloth clung to her skin

and rucked under her armpits. The woman's arms flopped as Lolly
yanked the smock over her head. She stuffed it under her arm,
grabbed Meg's hand, and ran behind the rope shed.

As Lolly peeked around the corner with one eye, the drowned
woman propped herself on one elbow. She convulsed twice, retching fluid onto the warped boardwalk. She lay still for a moment,
then looked both ways, sharp and quick, slithered to the edge of
the wharf, and slipped back into the water.

Lolly had a habit of telling boastful stories about herself. Not lies.
Lies could be found out. Stories were different—nobody could
prove them untrue. She told a few on her way home that morning,
clutching the wadded-up smock under her arm.

First she told a ship's cook she wouldn't buy his slush because
she wasn't hungry. Truth was, both she and Meg were hollow, but
those greasy leavings from the salt-pork barrel turned Meg's stomach and left her trotting for days. Slush was cheap, but her dear
girl couldn't abide it.

On Castle Street she told a baker she would never take nothing
from his basket without paying, even if nobody was watching. Just
to prove it, she bought two cream buns for Meg instead of one.

Behind the Punch Bowl Tavern, she told the sleepy girl mind-
ing the dregs keg that she didn't mind filling her flask with the
drainage from last night's tankards. Salt from a sailor's tongue just
made the liquor more tasty. When the girl caught her sipping from
the spout, Lolly claimed she was just smelling the dregs and if the
girl wanted an extra farthing for a whiff, she'd be happy to pay
because she liked that just as well as a gulp.

Walking up the Dale Street hill, Lolly told her daughter she
wasn't tired nor limping. She could walk a lot faster if she wanted,
but she liked a slow stroll of a morning.

When a pack of rough boys surrounded her in the forecourt of
Cable Yard, Lolly told them she had a knife. Fact was, she'd lost
it months back. A press-gang crimp had heard Lolly knew mouth
tricks that would turn a man cross-eyed, and when his curiosity was
satisfied, he'd walked away without paying. When she'd tried to
cut him, he'd knocked her down, kicked in her ribs, and left her
cringing in the sawdust. If a broken rib wasn't enough payment
for trying to make a man do what he ought, the Wharfinger pun-
ished her too. So angry he'd actually taken the time to climb down

from the pilots' office and cross the dockyards. He tracked her down and bent back her thumb until it snapped. Took her knife away too.

The rough boys had all the vim of youth and a good night's sleep, while Lolly was tired and defenseless. A whore without a knife is like a cat without claws—she could hiss or she could run. But Lolly couldn't run. At the first sign of trouble, Meg ducked under her mother's skirt and clamped fast to her leg, gripping her knee like a foremast jack in a hurricane.

Lolly held the smock tight and swatted the boys with her other hand, taking care to protect the flask in her pocket.

"Keep dogging me and I'll cut y'open and give your heartstrings to your mammies," she shouted.

Lolly swung her fist at the tallest boy. He dodged easily. When he began snatching at her hat, Lolly knew it was either that or the flask. She let the hat go. The boys chased it like dogs after a rat.

When Lolly got home, her landlady was up to her elbows in suds in the narrow backyard, with three children crawling four-legged around her and a herd of two-legged ones scurrying about. Snot ran over their lips like water through a sluicegate.

"Where's tha hat?" asked the landlady as Lolly latched the gate.

"Blew into the river," Lolly answered. Usually she'd tell a better story, but the brawl had left her shaking.

"Doest tha have another?"

"Seems a shame to cover my tresses." Lolly dredged up a saucy smile. Dockside charm never worked with her landlady, but habits are hard to break. "I might go bare-headed."

The landlady pushed her sweat-darkened hair off her brow with a wet forearm and scowled.

"If it's a choice between a new hat and making me happy on rent day, tha knowst which to choose. If we come to blows it won't be me worst off."

Lolly nodded and trudged up to her room. She knew better than to cross her landlady. She could be vicious. Anyone who expects women to live together happy as Eden before the fall has a poor understanding of human nature. A woman with ten children and a husband sailing the African trade has little enough kindness to spare for her own kin, and certainly none for her tenants.

Meg ate her buns and dandled her straw doll while Lolly spread the smock over her lap for examination. The silk was so fine she couldn't see strands in the weave. No wrinkles, no pulled threads, no seams. Soft as new skin under a blister. It didn't seem fabric at all, more like something grown as one piece. Also, it was perfectly clean, not a scuff or stain. In fact, it didn't seem to hold dirt. Her hands were none too clean, but the grime from her fingers dried and flaked away, leaving no mark behind on the pure white cloth.

She dragged the smock over her face. Off came all the dirt that had built up since she'd last got caught in a rainstorm: salt grime, coal dust, and the crusty flakes of sailors' leavings all embedded in her greasy mutton-fat rouge. She pulled the fabric away and held it out with both hands like a curtain. A ghost of her own self stared back, with rosy cheeks, a red smear for a mouth, and two blank spaces for eyes.

Then the dirt flaked off, and the cloth shone white again.

Lolly slept with the smock wadded under her head like a pillow. It warmed her hands and cooled her brow, cradling her in a cloud of comfort. When she woke, she stripped and pulled it over her head.

Meg ran in from the yard. The child yanked at the smock's edge.

"It's too fine to keep, Mammy."

"I'll sell it tomorrow," Lolly said as she pulled on her skirt and belted her bodice over the smock. "When I do, I'll buy thee a cake with sugared plums in all the colors of a rainbow."

On her way back to the wharf, Lolly seemed to float. The fabric glissaded over her thighs. It cupped her shoulders in a cool embrace, and soothed the itch and burn of her flea bites, nicks, blisters, and scabs. From the soles of her feet all the way up to her scalp, Lolly felt fine. When she scratched herself, it was only from habit.

Lolly stopped at the Nag's Head. She asked the landlady for a bun and a bit of bacon rind for Meg, and had her flask filled with the cheapest rum.

"Tha ent dressed for jobbing, little puss." The old man in the chair beside the door blew smoke in her face and leered. He poked his spit-coated pipe stem into the white fabric on her chest. "How doest tha catch fish with nowt jiggling on tha hook?"

She batted the pipe away.

"Don't need it. I'm a legendary suckstress. They talk about me in foreign ports."

He kept hounding her, but she hardly noticed. She sauced him back automatically — *men queue up to give me gravy — nobody gets more mucky than me — even backskuttle jacks shoot milt my way.*

When the landlady brought her flask back, Lolly gave it a shake to make sure she hadn't dropped in pebbles to cheat her. Then she tasted it and grimaced. The rum was so badly still-burnt it could put a wrinkle in her tongue, but it would do.

On the way down Dale Street, Lolly held tight to Meg's hand, careful to protect the child from the carts and wagons.

"That white cloth does look strange," Meg mumbled, her mouth full of bread.

True, the smock was too modest. Sailors liked a high pair of swollen teats. It reminded them of their long-lost mammies.

With one hand, Lolly adjusted her clothing as she dawdled along. If she pulled the cloth slowly, it stretched and stayed that way. By the time she entered narrow, dark Water Street, Lolly looked much as she always did, but stood a little taller. She had a secret next to her skin, and a good one. The smock made her feel clean. Stainless. Prideful. Not the boastful, fake pride she claimed every day, but something truer. Like a pip of gold at the core of a soft brown apple. A secret something that proved she was more than bruises and bluster.

But it also made her scared. What if, at the stroke of midnight, the corpse came back? What if it called her a thief and dragged her to the bottom of the river? Meg would be left frightened and alone with nobody to care for her. The thought was nearly enough to make her run for home.

Soft and quiet, old girl, she thought as she led her daughter through the narrow warehouse alleys crowded with pack mules and porters. Most likely the corpse had never slunk back to the water in the first place. She'd probably imagined it.

Lolly had seen impossible things before. Once, when she'd drunk dregs from a nutmeg barrel, the river had caught fire, kicking up sparks that wove patterns in the sky and set ships aflame. She ran through the dockyards and wharves, terrified, not stopping until she'd tumbled down the saltworks steps. Working mouth tricks had been a torment until her ribs healed.

If she'd imagined the corpse rolling itself back into the water, then it might have lain naked on the wharf all morning. George and Robbie would finger Lolly and call her a thief. The Wharfinger would strip her raw, take the smock, and have her hanged. What would happen to little Meg then?

If the Wharfinger knew his duty, he'd protect Lolly. She paid him a shilling sixpence every Sunday, which bought her the right to walk back and forth along the timber wharf through wind, rain, and snow. She put coins in his pocket, but he never lifted a finger to aid her or any of the girls. If he did, people would call him a whoremaster.

Best sell the smock, and fast. Put on an innocent face and do her night's work. But no, the smock was her own comfort and joy. She wasn't taking it off. Not now. Maybe not ever.

"All my treasures are here with me." Lolly hoisted her sleepy daughter in her arms and kissed the delicate curl of her ear.

She leaned against the grimy weatherboards of the coal shack at the corner of Brunswick Street, watching the traffic grind along the busy dockside parade. She sipped from her flask and gathered her thoughts.

Where to go, if not homeward? The taverns on the quay and the alleys all around were defended territory. Navy crews landed there, starved for soft company and ready to spend their pay. If Lolly walked those streets looking hopeful, she'd have a knife in her guts before midnight.

"Take me to the churchyard, Mammy," Meg said.

Lolly took a deep gulp of acrid rum. St. Nicholas's churchyard was as good a place as any. Nobody's stroll—or everybody's. Not much custom, but if she stood high up on the hill she might catch the eyes of men coming up from the bridewell. She could give herself till midnight, then if chances looked bad, she'd settle Meg down to sleep against the church wall and skip up Bath Street all the way to the fort. Try her luck with the soldiers. She might even creep down Lancelot's Hey in the deep of night and take a squat on the Wharfinger's steps—see how he liked that sauce.

Belligerent thoughts gave her the energy to get moving. When she passed into St. Nicholas's churchyard, Meg squealed and struggled out of her arms. It was her favorite place to play—grass and flowers, bugs and worms. Meg might trip on someone's shinbone sticking up from the turf, and if she fell wrong, she could smash her brains out on a gravestone. But a mother can't keep her child in an apron pocket, no matter how much she might want to.

Lolly strolled uphill, weaving through the higgledy-piggledy canted gravestones until she found her favorite seat. Meg scampered about, chasing moths and pulling up harebells by the roots.

When the bells tolled midnight, Lolly was still sitting in the churchyard, and that's where the Devil found her.

The first thing Lolly noticed was the insects. Large ones, the size of her thumb, pitching through the air on glittering, thumb-nail-sized wings. At first she thought they were bats—she saw plenty of bats skittering over the river in late summer, when the tide was out and flies swarmed over the mud. These weren't bats. Not cleggs either—too big—and cockchafers didn't fly in summer. Eight or more of the insects hovered overhead, just past arm's reach. Watching her. They ignored little Meg, though, so that was all right.

Then a stranger entered the churchyard—a woman in dark clothes and a hooded cloak. The insects extended their tiny wings and flew to meet her.

"*Ssssst sssst,*" Lolly hissed.

Meg dove under her mother's skirt and wrapped both her arms around her mother's thigh, little fingers digging in deep. Lolly patted her head through the fabric.

The child whispered, *What is it, Mammy?*

"Looks like a chapel-hen," Lolly told her daughter. "This one's out all by herself. That's rare. Usually they walk in twos and threes."

She'd seen them before, good women from Liverpool's dissenting congregations. Every so often they'd try to talk Lolly into saving her soul. Sometimes, if Lolly played along, a chapel-hen could be talked out of a few coins.

Lolly knew a prayer. She shuffled toward a gravestone and bent her head in an exaggerated pantomime of piety. When the chapel-hen was close enough to hear, Lolly began praying aloud.

"All fathers dwell in heaven, where a hollow be in tha name."

The woman flipped down her hood, exposing a face white as a skull, with a round forehead and flat cheeks scarred as the moon.

"You took something from us," the woman croaked. Her voice sounded more like a cartwheel on gravel than any human sound.

"Get off, Meg. Run," Lolly whispered.

Meg squeezed her mother's leg. *Nay, I'm scared.*

Lolly tried to flee, hobbling along with little Meg under her skirt, perching on her foot. The woman leapt over a row of close-set stones and cut Lolly off.

Nothing to do but brazen it out.

"Who said I took anything?" Lolly shook her fist while backing up slowly. "Nobody, that's who. Don't you tell a lie."

"An argument is unnecessary," the woman squawked. "The garment must be recovered. However, you may continue wearing it for the moment. No doubt it gives you comfort."

Lolly gulped at her flask. For certain the stranger was the very same drowned woman who had crawled naked into the river. Her voice was otherworldly—inhuman—devilish. A chill shivered over Lolly's flesh, raising goose bumps from her scalp to her toes.

"If I have something of yourn, it's because tha were dead when I found it," Lolly said. "That's salvage, not theft. Like with a shipwreck."

"A compelling argument, well worth taking into consideration." The woman smiled, exposing the straight teeth Lolly had plucked at that morning. "We agree. By the local custom of salvage, you may keep the garment."

"Thart kindly." Lolly grinned. "I get many gifts, but this is my favorite."

"It is not a gift. Neither is it bribery, nor a commercial transaction," the stranger croaked. "The garment was lost. You found it and claim ownership by the customs of your community. Please acknowledge those facts."

Lolly nodded. "It were salvage, like I say."

"Very good. You may address us as Mary Overholt." The woman dipped her head, like one lady might to another. "We welcome your company."

"Goodnight, miss." Lolly shuffled away, taking care to keep Meg concealed under her skirt.

"Wait a moment," Mary squawked. "Would you stay and talk with me, of your own free will?"

Make her pay for it, Mammy.

Lolly heard some men wanted to pay for chat, though she'd never met one. If a man could do it, so could a woman.

"I might stay for a good thick coin."

"Bribery would invalidate the results of our conversation." The woman spread her hands. Men used that same gesture meant to show they had no money, which was almost always a lie. "Intoxication might invalidate it as well. I'm awaiting the determination."

The stranger's gaze rose to a point above Lolly's head, where the insects circulated. She pursed her lips, then seemed to reach a decision.

"We've determined intoxication is not a barrier to any agreements reached or decisions made. Nearly everyone on this planet carries a disease or condition that impairs their perceptions, and your habits have made you somewhat inured to the effects of intoxicants."

The words might have been in a foreign language for all Lolly could understand. But she wasn't about to admit ignorance.

"That's right, I'm immured. The lord mayor himself gave me a medal for it."

"Excuse me. I will attempt to limit my vocabulary to terms you understand."

"I understand plenty." Lolly bristled. "Like I know tha has a voice like a Bootle organ and a smile to match."

The stranger's pockmarked face contorted in confusion. Lolly's courage soared.

"A Bootle organ is a frog and that were an insult. Will tha take offence now and leave me in peace?"

"Our invitation was sincere. We would like to talk with you."

"I don't work my mouth for free. Give me a coin or something to eat or I'll be gone."

The woman looked thoughtful again. "Commensality is an important human value and doesn't constitute a bribe. Very well."

Mary pulled a paper bundle from her cloak pocket and placed it in Lolly's outstretched hand.

"That's nice." She raised the packet to her nose and inhaled the heady aroma of treacle toffee. "My one sweet tooth likes a bit of toffee."

Lolly shuffled backward and couched her haunches on a canted gravestone. She stuffed the greasy packet into her pocket and took a deep swig from her flask.

Ask her who she is and what she wants. And why she speaks so strange, Mammy.

"Did tha get a smack in the throat, miss? A woman doesn't croak like that from nothing."

"This voice is an indication of our dual nature." The woman placed her hand on her chest. "This individual is my host. Making my own voice seem human would be deceptive. Our intent is to communicate clearly and truthfully."

Lolly snorted. "Tha best stop talking nonsense, then."

"I will ask my host to help us communicate."

Lolly eyed the silky sheen of the woman's cloak and the slash pockets along the front seams. If she could get her hands on the cloak and move stealthily, she might find out what else the woman carried, aside from toffee. Lolly scuffed her palms up and down her arms.

"Can I borrow that cloak? It's a bit chill."

With no hesitation, Mary shrugged off the cloak and held it out. The silk lining glowed in the moonlight. Lolly half expected to see claws on the ends of Mary's pale fingers, or webs between the knuckles, but her hands were human, with pearly, neat-cut fingernails showing no hint of grime, as if she'd just come soaped and scrubbed from the bath.

But she had taken a bath, just that morning. And in a very large bathtub indeed.

"How'd tha end in the river?" Lolly asked as she settled the cloak around her shoulders. "Some man object to hearing your nonsense?"

Don't anger her, Mammy. Not while you're getting away with something.

"Don't mean to be uncivil," Lolly added quickly. "If tha has a tale to tell, I'll listen. Won't surprise nor shock me, neither. I heard it all. When women sit together, sad stories start spilling out our holes."

The woman winced and pressed her lips together into a thin line. When she spoke, her voice had changed.

"You make an apt observation," she said. Her voice had turned soft and musical, like a lady who put sugar on her words to tempt others to listen.

"There now," said Lolly. "Did tha cough the frog out?"

"No," croaked the Bootle organ. "As I tried to explain, we are two separate individuals, autonomous but working in cooperation."

"I am an Englishwoman," the lady interjected. "The daughter of a Manchester gentleman. The voice you find unpleasant is not of this world."

"That's true enough," said Lolly.

"To answer your other question," the ladylike voice continued, "early yesterday morning we attempted conversation with another of your profession. We ran afoul of her procurator. A . . . a . . . what do you call a man like that?"

"A pimp?"

"Yes, her pimp. He was in drink, and violent. Murderous." Mary's homely face crumpled like furled sail. "He thought I was attempting to lure the young woman off the streets."

"Was tha?"

Mary raised her hands to cover her eyes for a moment. Lolly took the opportunity to snake her fingers into the cloak's pockets and scoop out the contents. When Mary looked up, Lolly had her hands spread on her thighs, innocent as anything.

"No, we only wanted to talk to her, as I'm talking to you now." Her voice was thick with grief. "I misjudged, and it nearly cost me my life."

"That'll happen if tha crosses the wrong pimp."

No time to finger the treasure, but there was a handkerchief for certain. Probably silk and if so would fetch half a crown. A few other pieces—likely a penknife and a pouch of matches, maybe a little packet of needles and thread. No coins, more's the pity. What else a lady like Mary might carry in her cloak pockets at night, Lolly couldn't imagine. But if Lolly could get away with it, her landlady would be happy about the rent, and little Meg would have a cake.

Lolly swigged from her flask and then offered it to Mary. She didn't accept—Lolly would have been surprised and regretful if she had—but it was only polite to offer a drink to a mark.

Mary wiped her nose on her sleeve, cleared her throat, and squawked, "This planet—"

"—this world," the lady's sweet voice interrupted.

"This world," the Bootle organ continued, "has a long history of violent intraspecies competition and colonization. Entire populations are conquered and their lands and resources stolen. We observe this pattern in approximately five-point-five-eight percent of sentient species surveyed. Other species—the vast majority—are parasitic, like my own. Among species like yours, most individuals consider violent conflict as an inevitable mode for intra- and inter-community interaction. Would you agree?"

"Wha?" Lolly hadn't understood one word.

"Do you believe," Mary's sweet voice asked, "that it's natural for people to take the property of others with violence? To steal their homes, land, forests, farms, mines, villages, and towns?"

"Sure," Lolly answered. "If I knew nothing else, I know that. Seen it enough."

"So you agree," the Bootle organ said. "Colonization backed by violence is the norm?"

"If thart asking if those stronger and meaner take what they want from the weaker and meeker, that's a simpleminded question. They do. Here, there, and everywhere."

Under Lolly's skirt, Meg yawned. Her warm breath puffed across her mother's knee.

"If we suggested that the breeding population is also considered a rightful spoil of colonialism, would you agree?"

More nonsense. Lolly gulped at her flask, ignoring the question.

"We are attempting to establish whether you agree that colonialism traditionally includes co-opting the females of the colonized population for propagation."

The lady interjected again. "If you don't keep it simple, she'll never understand." Mary sat beside Lolly on the wide gravestone. "You've heard of the Sabine women, have you not?"

Lolly hadn't, but she nodded anyway.

"In old Rome," Mary continued, "when the men didn't have women, they stole them from their neighbors. What my friend wants to know is whether or not you think that's natural."

"Sure is," Lolly said without hesitation. "Where would they put their pricks otherwise? A man sees something he likes, he's going to skewer it. Otherwise another man will skewer them. That's men, whether babe or bishop. Women are a little different."

"How are women different?" asked the Bootle organ.

"Let me think." Lolly drew the toffee packet out of her pocket and unfolded it. "A woman will kill for a loaf of bread if her children are starving. Some might kill to keep her man. A tart might kill the man who cheats her, or the woman who poaches her stroll. But women don't kill for sport. They don't roam in gangs looking for women to fuck dead. No woman ever set upon a neighbor's young husband and left him bleeding in the woodpile."

Lolly picked off a shard of toffee and slipped it between her gums. The sugar made her head spin. Its flavor was strong as the darkest rum, and just as heady. She tongued it into the pouch of her cheek.

"No woman ever chased a boy around the house, half strangled him to death, then sent him home to the farm with a necklace of bruises and belly full of bastard. A woman will look the other way if her man does it, though, and that's contusion."

"Collusion." Mary nodded.

"Some say that's the same as if she did the deed herself," Lolly continued. "A woman can be mean and nasty. Some have heavier hands than others, and sharper tongues. but we ent like men."

"Why the inequity?" asked the Bootle organ.

Lolly frowned.

"Why do you think men are more violent than women?" the sweet voice explained.

The toffee dissolved, coating Lolly's mouth in sweet syrup. She savored the flavor for a moment before answering.

"Why we chewing this over? That's what I want to know. Spoils my appetite. If tha wants an opinion, Miss Mary, talk back and forth with tha own self."

"Your opinion is the one we are interested in."

"I don't care why. Nobody does. It's the way of the world."

"What if it weren't the way of the world?" The Bootle organ's voice harshened with urgency. "What if it didn't have to be?"

Take me home, Mammy. I'm tired.

The child ought to be wrapped tight in her blanket and snugged into a timber-yard alcove, not cowering under her mother's skirt listening to a stranger talk nonsense. No sense in drawing this out. Lolly wouldn't get anything more out of Mary.

"Goodnight, miss." Lolly shrugged off the cloak.

"You may keep the garment," croaked the Bootle organ. "It's a local product, worthless, and doesn't constitute a bribe. We understand it may be exchanged for currency, but your economic transactions are meaningless."

I don't like her.

Lolly didn't either. Aside from the voice tricks, anyone who gave gifts easily might have a changeable mind. But perhaps Mary hadn't been squeezed dry, not quite yet.

"Why would a fine wool cloak be worth nothing when tha came chasing after me to find some plain white smock?" Lolly asked.

"It is not a garment but a piece of technology."

"Does tha have more worthless things to give?"

"Perhaps."

Mary pulled two items from her skirt pockets—a large muslin handkerchief and a little velvet purse. Lolly eyed the purse greedily. Mary tipped the coins into her hand and pocketed them before handing over the empty purse.

Get her shoes.

Lolly laughed. "Maybe you think your boots are worthless too, miss?"

"Yes," Mary said. "But I don't fancy walking on stocking feet."

"True, but does tha need stockings, though?"

Mary touched Lolly lightly on the back of her hand, just the tips of her fingers, light as a moth.

"I would strip to my skin to get you to keep talking, Lolly. Would you require that of a lady?"

"It's midsummer. Tha wouldn't catch a death." Lolly laughed again, then coughed. When she spat, she took care to aim behind the gravestones, away from Mary.

I don't want to listen to her no more. Meg pinched the skin of her mother's thigh between two little fingers, hard enough to make Lolly's eyes water.

"You stated violence is the way of the world," said the Bootle organ. "I suggest that other options exist."

"If so, I haven't heard them."

Lolly shook the gritty dregs of her flask onto her palm and licked up the last of the liquor. She wiped the grains on her skirt and stood. Meg placed her feet on top of her mother's foot and wrapped her arms around Lolly's thigh. Lolly stumped away, but only got a few steps before Mary blocked her path.

"Just a few more questions. If violence were not the way of the world, would that be better?"

"Sure. Better for lots of people."

"Like whom?"

Like me, Mammy.

Lolly coughed again, and wiped the spittle from her lips with the back of her hand.

"Though you insist it's not possible, having admitted it would be desirable, can you say how it might be accomplished?" Mary squawked.

"I can say a lot of things."

"Turn your mind to this specific problem. How could your world be rid of violence?"

Kill the men.

"What's that?" Lolly blurted.

Kill the men, Mammy. Like the one who tore into you the day after your own mammy died. Like the pimp who knocked your teeth out. Like the ones who pay you with a smack and a knee to the nose. Like the Wharfinger, even, who makes you walk the soles off your shoes and doesn't keep you safe even though you're his girl and he's your pimp same as any.

Lolly's eyes began to sting.

Like the man who tossed me under that wagon.

"No, little Meggy," she mumbled. "Don't think about the wagon. Don't remember it."

I don't, Mammy. But you do. You always think about it.

Lolly nodded. Her little girl in a pool of blood, squashed so flat she could be folded in two. A tall man laughing, specks of blood in his red beard, and everyone on the street pointing at Lolly, saying a mother should keep her child safe.

Kill the men. All of them. They deserve it.

"Kill the men," said Lolly. "All of them."

Mary's shoulders relaxed and she let out a long sigh.

"There," she breathed. "That's nine hundred women, just under the deadline."

Mary placed her hand on Lolly's shoulder.

"Having agreed that violence is a primary mode of social behavior on this planet, and having admitted the results are undesirable, you suggest that this situation could be ameliorated if all men on this planet were killed. Is that true?"

Yes. Tell her, Mammy.

"Yes," Lolly said. "I do. That's exactly what I think."

In that moment Lolly realized who she was talking to. Mary was Satan, the Devil himself in disguise. What other creature could talk so easily about the destruction of man?

"If you knew this project were possible, that the male half of the human population would be exterminated, would you change your opinion?"

Lolly reached down to pat her daughter's head, but Meg was gone. She'd be back, though. Meg always came back.

"No, I won't change my mind."

Mary grinned up at the watching insects.

"Victory," she said in her sweet voice. And when she turned back to Lolly, her smile was so warm, so kind, so glowing with approval that Lolly barely recognized the expression.

"What kind of world will it make?" Lolly asked.

"Nobody knows." Mary took Lolly's hand and squeezed. "But we'll soon find out."

"Can't be worse than this one. If tha wants to kill them all, best get to work. Just one thing." Lolly leaned close and touched Mary's shoulder with her own. "Start with the Wharfinger."

DARYL GREGORY

Nine Last Days on Planet Earth

FROM *Tor.com*

1975

ON THE FIRST night of the meteor storm, his mother came to wake him up, but LT was only pretending to sleep. He'd been lying in the dark waiting for the end of the world.

You have to see this, she said. He didn't want to leave the bed, but she was an intense woman who could beam energy into him with a look. She took his hand and led him between the stacks of moving boxes, then across the backyard and through the cattle gate to the field, where the view was unimpeded by trees. Meteors, dozens of meteors, scored the sky. She spread a blanket across the tall grass, and they sat back on their elbows.

LT was ten years old, and he'd only seen one falling star in his life. Not even his mother had seen this many at once, she said. Dozens visible at one time, zooming in from the east, striking the atmosphere like matches, white and orange and butane blue. The show went on, hundreds a minute for ten minutes, then twenty. He could hear his father working in the wood shop back by the garage, pushing wood through a whining band saw. Mom made no move to go get him, didn't call for him.

LT asked for the popsicles they'd made yesterday and Mom said something like *What the hell.* He ran to the freezer, lifted out the aluminum ice tray. The metal sucked at his fingertips. He jiggled the lever and freed one of the cubes, grape Kool-Aid on a toothpick, so good. That memory, even decades later, was as clear as the image of the meteors.

He decided to bring the whole tray with him. He paused outside the wood shop, finally pushed open the door. His father leaned over his bench, marking a plank with a pencil. He worked all day at the lumberyard and came home to work with scraps and spares. Always building something for the house, for her, even after it was too late to change her mind.

"Did you see the sky?" LT asked him. "It's like fireworks."

LT didn't have his mother's gift for commanding attention. But his father followed him to the field, put his hands on his hips, tilted his head back. Wouldn't sit on the blanket.

"Meteorites," his father said, and Mom said without looking back, "Meteoroid, in the void."

"What now?"

"Meteoroid in the void. Meteorite, rock hound's delight. Meteor, neither nor."

LT repeated this to himself. *Neither nor. Neither nor.*

"Still looks like Revelations," Dad said.

"No," his mother said. "It's beautiful."

The storm continued. LT didn't remember falling asleep on the blanket, but he remembered jerking awake to a sound. Then it came again, a *crack* like a shot from a .22. Seconds later another clap, louder. He didn't understand what was happening.

The sky had reversed: it was more white than black, pulsing with white fireballs. Not long streaks anymore, chasing west. No, the meteors were coming down at them, down upon their heads.

A meteor struck a nearby hill. A wink of light. LT thought, *Now it's a meteorite.*

His father yanked him onto his feet. "Get inside."

Then a flash, and the air shook. The sound was so loud, so close. He couldn't see. His mother said, "Oh my!" as if it were nothing more surprising than a deer jumping across the road.

His father yelled, "Run to the fireplace!"

LT blinked spots from his vision. His father pushed him in the small of the back and he ran.

His father had built the fireplace himself, stacking the river rock, mortaring it with hand-stirred buckets of cement. It was six feet wide at the mouth, and the exposed chimney ran up the east wall to the high timbered ceiling twenty-five feet above. Later LT wondered if rock and mortar could have withstood a direct hit, but at that moment he had no doubt it would protect him.

The explosions seemed random; far away, then suddenly near, a boom that vibrated through the floorboards. It went on, an inundation, a barrage. His mother exclaimed with every report. His father moved from window to window, frowning and silent. LT wished he wouldn't stand next to the glass.

Eventually most of the strikes seem to be happening over the line of foothills, rolling west like a thunderstorm. His father insisted that no one sleep away from the lee of the chimney, so his mother assembled a bed for LT out of moving boxes, turning the emergency into a slumber party, an adventure. His father dragged furniture close: the couch for Mom and the recliner for him.

When his mother kissed him goodnight (the second time that night), he whispered, "Will you be here in the morning?"

"I'll wake you," she said. LT could feel his father watching them.

It was the last time they would all sleep in the same room, or the same house.

He opened his eyes, and for a long moment he couldn't figure out why he was on the floor, in the living room. He stared stupidly at the empty bookshelves. His mother's bookshelves.

Panic hit, and he sat up. He called, "Mom?"

Then he took in the piles of moving boxes still in the room and began to calm down. He hadn't missed her.

In the kitchen his father hunched over the table, staring at the portable black-and-white TV. Two cupboard doors showed empty shelves. The hooks above the stove seemed to gesture for their missing pots.

His father put an arm across LT's shoulders without looking away from the TV.

The news was full of pictures of damaged buildings and forest fires. It was no ordinary meteor storm, and it wasn't over. The onslaught had continued through the night and into the day, moving across the globe. The world spun eastward, and the meteors drummed into the atmosphere steady as a playing card against bicycle spokes. No one knew when it would end. The newsman called the storm "biblical," the first time LT had heard that word outside of church, and warned about radioactivity. He knew *that* word from comic books.

His father turned toward the window, pushed aside the drapes.

A truck had pulled off the two-lane into their gravel drive. "Go tell your mother," he said.

LT didn't move. His stomach felt like ice.

"Go. She's in the backyard."

LT walked out into a sky tinged with orange. If there were meteors up there he couldn't see them. The air smelled like smoke.

He called for his mother. Checked the garage, where a pyramid of moving boxes filled the space, all sealed and labeled. Then he realized where she must be and walked toward the cattle gate.

She stood at the far end of the field. He called again. She turned, beaming, something cupped in her hands. She strode toward him in her ruby cowboy boots, her yellow dress swishing high on her thighs. Then he realized what she carried.

"Mom, no!"

She laughed. "It's okay, my darlin'. It's cooled off."

She held it out to him. A black egg, flecked with silver, etched with spirals.

The meteor storm would go on for five more days and nights. Soon everyone would know the objects weren't like other meteors. They weren't chunks of stony iron ripped from a comet's tail, or fragments of asteroids. They were capsules of woven metal, layered like an onion skin. They'd been bigger when in the void, but their outer shells had ignited and shredded in the atmosphere. The innermost shells remained intact until they slammed into the earth. Almost all of them cracked on impact. People dug them up, showed them to television crews. Space seeds, they called them. And then the police started going house by house, confiscating them.

But not yet. At this moment his mother was offering it to him. "Feel it," she said. "It's a miracle."

He couldn't deny her. The shell was surprisingly light. A jagged seam had opened along its top. Inside was darkness.

She said, "What do you think was in there?"

1976

When he was eleven years old, late in the first summer he'd spend in his mother's tiny Chicago apartment, she smuggled home one of the fern men. It was four inches tall, planted in a paper coffee cup. Its torso was a segmented tube, like bamboo, glossy as jade. Its two armlike stems ended in tiny round leaves, and its head was a mantis-green bulb like an unopened tulip.

"Isn't it illegal?" he asked her. But he knew the answer, and knew his mother. Her reckless instincts worried his young Puritan heart. He'd spent the school year alone in Tennessee with his father and had adopted his military rectitude.

"It'll be our little secret," she said.

Ours and the boyfriend's, LT thought.

"You are crazy, honey," said the boyfriend. He kissed her, hard, and when they finally broke apart she laughed. LT always thought of his mother as beautiful, but he'd been offended to discover that she was beautiful to others. To men. Like this shaggy *dude* who wore turquoise necklaces like a TV Indian and smelled like turpentine and cigarettes and scents he couldn't yet name.

His mother went into a back closet to find a more durable container for the fern man.

"I know what you're thinking," the shaggy man said.

But even LT didn't know what he was thinking.

"We should probably burn the little fucker, right?"

LT was alarmed, then embarrassed. Of course the boyfriend was right. At school, hallway posters showed spiky, ominous plants with the message KEEP AN EYE OUT! Any sightings of invasive species were to be reported. The weeklong meteor storm had sprayed black-and-silver casings across millions of square miles in a broad band that circled the planet, peppering cities and fields and forests and oceans. Soldiers of every government seized what they could find. And when anything sprouted, good citizens called the authorities.

LT looked down at the fern man.

The boyfriend laughed. "Don't worry, I'm not going to kill it. Your mom would kill *me*! Watch this." He touched a finger to one of the fern's arms. It curled away as if stung.

Mom said, "Don't bother it, it'll get tired and stop growing. That's what the man told me." She transferred the sprout to a ceramic pot with much cooing and fussing. "We can't set him in the window," she said. "Somebody might see." LT picked a sunny spot on the coffee table.

"He's so cute," his mother said.

"That's his survival strategy," the boyfriend said. "So cute you won't throw him out."

"Just like you," she said, and laughed.

He didn't laugh with her. His mood could change, quick. A lot of nights Mom and the boyfriend argued after LT had gone to bed —to bed but not to sleep.

"We're all doomed," he said. "When the aliens come for the harvest, that's it for *Homo sapiens.*"

This was the popular theory: that aliens had targeted Earth and sent their food stocks ahead of them so there'd be something to eat when they arrived. LT had spent long, hot days in the apartment listening to the boyfriend while Mom was at work, or else following him around the city on vague errands. He didn't have a regular job. He said he was an artist— *with a capital* A, *kid*—but didn't seem to spend any time painting or anything. He could talk at length about the known invasive species and why there were so many different ones: the weblike filaments choking the trees in New Orleans, the flame-colored poppies erupting on Mexico City rooftops, the green fins popping up in Florida beach sand like sharks coming ashore. Every shell that struck Earth, and some that hit the surface of the water, cracked and sent millions of seeds into the air or into the oceans. Most of those seeds had not sprouted, or not yet. Of those that had, many of the vines and flowers and unclassifiable blooms soon withered and died. The ones that thrived had been attacked with poison, fire, and machetes. But—but!— there were so many possible sprouts that there was no way to find them all in the millions of acres of wilderness. *Even if we managed to find and destroy ninety-nine percent of the invasives,* the boyfriend had told LT once, *there would be millions and millions of plants growing and reproducing around the globe.*

Like the fern man. "We're all going to die," the boyfriend said, "because of this little green dude."

And LT thought, *How can something so beautiful, so cool, be dangerous?*

"Let's give him a name," Mom said. "LT, you do the honors."

"I need to think about it," he said.

Or maybe, LT thought that night as his mother and the boyfriend whisper-yelled at each other, *I should change my own name.* Chicago was making him into a different person. He'd become conscious of his Tennessee accent and had taken steps to tame his vowels. He'd eaten Greek food. He'd almost gotten used to being around so many black people. And he'd started staying up to all hours in his room, an *L*-shaped nook off the kitchen with a curtain for a door, reading from his mother's collection of Reader's Digest Condensed Books as the rattling fan chased sweat from his ribs. The night they got the fern man he wondered if he should ask everyone to stop calling him LT and start calling him Lawrence or Taylor or something completely of his own creation, like . . . Lance. Lance was the kind of guy who'd be ready when the UFOs came down.

Doors slammed, his mother sobbed loudly for a while, and then the apartment went quiet. LT waited another twenty minutes, and then got up to pee. He didn't turn on the bathroom light. He was a night creature now, as light-sensitive as a raccoon.

The door to his mother's bedroom was ajar. She was alone in the bed.

He went into the living room. On the wall behind the couch hung four of the boyfriend's pictures. They were all of naked women turning into buildings, or maybe vice versa, with red-brick thighs and doorways for crotches and scaffolds holding up their torsos. One of the nudes, pale and thin and sprouting television aerials from her frizzy hair, looked too much like his mother. LT wondered if other people thought they were beautiful, or if beauty mattered in art with a capital *A*. The figures didn't seem to be very convincing as women *or* buildings. *Neither nor.*

The fern man stood in the dark on the coffee table. Its bulb head drooped sleepily, and its stem arms hung at its sides. The torso leaned slightly—toward the window, LT realized.

He picked up the ceramic pot and set it on the sill, in a pool of streetlight. Slowly the trunk began to straighten. Over the next few minutes the head gradually lifted like a deacon finishing a prayer, and the round leaves at the ends of its arms unfurled like loosening fists. The movement was almost too incremental to detect; its posture seemed to shift only when he looked away or lost concentration.

Slow Mo, he thought. *That's what we'll call you.*

Tomorrow his mother would throw all the paintings out the front window, send them sailing into the street. LT would never see the boyfriend again. The fern man stayed.

1978

The night they heard about the thistle cloud, LT was daydreaming of burning the house down. It was March and he was bored to the point of paralysis, an old man in a thirteen-year-old body. Country winters stretched each night into a prison sentence. The valley went cave-dark before suppertime, stayed dark until the morning school bus honked for him at the end of the lane. He longed for the city. Torching the place, he figured, would make a bonfire that would light up the road all the way to Chicago.

The place was wrong for his father too. Three years after Mom had left, the house was purposeless without her in it, like a desanctified church. His father's handiwork—the tongue-and-groove hardwood floors, the hand-turned legs on the kitchen table, the graceful stair rail that curled at the end like the tail of a treble clef—seemed as frivolous as gingerbread. Why stay here? They never used the dining room, or the guest room with its fancy bathroom. No one would ever thread a needle in the sewing room. LT and his father ate their meals in the living room, in front of the fire, wordless as Neanderthals.

LT was grateful when the TV said that a new invasive species had erupted in Tennessee. Dad was in his armchair as usual, eyes on the snowy screen of the portable, which he'd set on a chair close to the fireplace, as if daring it to melt.

"Would you look at that," Dad said.

LT did not look. He was sprawled on the couch, pretending to reread a book he hoped would annoy his father: *Sexual Selection in the Animal World*. There was an entire chapter on the bowerbirds of Papua New Guinea, whose males assembled and decorated elaborate bowers in hopes a female would prefer their art over the competitors'.

The third bachelor in the room was Mo. He was a sturdy three feet tall by then, and occupied the corner by the dark window. He was attracted to the fire. At night his limbs eased toward it, wanting the light if not the heat.

Mom couldn't keep the fern. She'd moved in with a new, temperamental boyfriend, a restaurant owner who named a pasta dish after her the first week they dated but flew into fits when he felt disrespected. Both Mo and LT had been causes of "friction" that summer, so LT begged to take the fern back to Tennessee in the fall. Mo had traveled in the back seat of his mom's car like a passenger, bulbous head bent against the roof, a seat belt around his pot. LT hadn't asked his father's permission and was surprised when he let it into his house without a fight. Dad was more upset by his son's shaggy hair and the turquoise necklace around his neck. The day before school started, Dad drove him to the barber and ordered a buzz cut to match Dad's own. LT kept the necklace under his shirt.

"It's getting worse and worse," his dad said. "Lord Almighty."

Now LT did look at the TV. *Lord Almighty* was as close to swearing as his father got.

The sky over Chattanooga was crowded with spiky black shapes. A reporter asked a question, and a man held out a bloody arm.

"So much for dominion over the earth," LT said. At the midweek prayer meeting—they went to services three times a week, twice on Sunday and once on Wednesday night—the pastor had launched into well-worn passages of God giving dominion of the earth to Adam. It came up whenever the invasives or women's rights were in the news.

"Don't be smart," Dad said.

"Face it, we're *losing*." Every day the TV showed men in masks hacking down flowers as big as satellite dishes, or Argentinians fretting over alien moss that clung to the hooves of cattle like boots, or Kansas farmers dulling their chainsaws on traveling vines as tough as mahogany. In a lot of places the invasives were just a nuisance, but in some countries, especially the ones closest to the equator, the alien plants were causing real trouble. "They're trying a million different strategies. All they need are a couple winners to drive us out."

"What are you talking about?"

"Outsurvive us. They've got time on their side. We go at animal speed, but plants move at their own speed. Wheels within wheels." An Elijah reference, just to poke him. "It's *evolution*, Dad."

Another provocation. His father believed in the Bible. There was no time for natural selection in the six days of creation, and no need for it. Dad's God didn't improvise. He was a measure-twice-cut-once creator.

"They're better at surviving?" his father said. "These *plants*?"

LT shook his head as if disappointed in his father's stupidity.

Dad slowly rose from his chair. LT realized he'd miscalculated. "Let's see, then," Dad said calmly. He gripped the sides of the ceramic pot, lifted it. It had to weigh almost two hundred pounds. Mo's limbs curled inward.

LT yelled, "No! Stop it!"

His father turned the pot on its side. Dirt spilled onto the floorboards. He stepped toward the fire and pushed the top of the plant into the mouth of the fireplace.

LT threw himself into his father's ribs. Stupid, useless. Dad was as squat and thick as an engine block. He turned, swinging Mo's head out of the fireplace. It wasn't on fire, but a haze of sizzling mist seemed to shroud the bulb.

LT burst into tears.

His father set the pot on the floor, anger gone now. "Aw, come on."

LT ran upstairs, threw himself on the bed, awash with embarrassment and anger. He was thirteen! He should be tougher than this. Crying over a damn plant. He wanted it all to end. How much longer did he have to wait for the aliens to come and scrape this planet clean?

The Chattanooga cloud was supposed to reach them that next afternoon. Vernon Beck, Dad's oldest friend, drove over from Maryville to see it. Jumped out of his pickup and shook LT's hand. "Goodness sakes, boy, you're two feet taller! Hale, come say hello to LT and Mr. Meyers."

A boy eased out of the passenger side of the pickup, long and lean, hair down to his shoulders. LT hadn't seen Hale Beck since LT's mother left. Their families used to go places together, and even though Hale was two years older than LT, they got along like brothers. He remembered a long day riding water slides with Hale at a Pigeon Forge park. A hike in the Smokies during which Hale smashed a rock into a snake, the bravest thing LT had ever seen.

Hale shook hands with LT's father, nodded at LT. Hale had gotten the growth spurt LT was still waiting on.

A strong wind was blowing, but the cloud hadn't shown up yet. The men went into the wood shop, and LT stood there awkwardly with Hale, unsure how to talk to him.

Hale took out a tin of Skoal from his back pocket, tucked a pinch of tobacco into his lip. He held out the tin, and LT shook his head. Hale leaned back on the hood of the truck. Spit black juice onto the gravel.

LT said, "We've got a fern man."

"A what?"

"One of the invasives. Right in the house." Dad said never to talk about the fern. But this was the Becks.

Hale said, "The one that moves?" He wanted to see that.

Dad had returned Mo to his usual spot. There was no visible damage from the flames. Hale said, "Looks like a regular plant."

"Watch this," LT said. He stood between Mo and the window and raised his arms. The fern man slowly shifted to the right, back into the light. LT moved in front of him again and Mo moved opposite. "It's called heliotropism. Like sunflowers? But way faster."

"Can I do it?" Hale asked.

"Sure. Just don't tire him out."

Hale took LT's position. They danced in slow motion at first, and then Hale sped up. Mo jerked and flopped in rhythm. Hale laughed. "He's just like one of those windsock guys at the dealership!"

LT was thrilled that Hale was impressed, but nervous about hurting Mo. "Hey, you want to see where the space seed landed?"

He managed to entice Hale to the cattle field. The wind had picked up, turned cold, but the sun was bright and hot. Hale's hair blew across his face, and he kept pushing it back.

They walked around at the far end of the field. LT couldn't find the furrow the seed had made when it hit four years ago. The tall dry grass rattled with every gust.

Hale said, "Look."

In the distance, a dark, churning cloud. Light flashed at the edges of it like tiny lightning. Hale ran toward it, into the wind. They plunged through a line of trees into the next field—and suddenly the cloud loomed over them. Thousands of glistening tumbleweeds, most the size of a fist, a few big as soccer balls. A sudden downdraft sent scores of them plummeting into the trees. Most stuck in the treetops, others bounced down into the undergrowth, and half a dozen ricocheted back into the air and spun toward them.

"Grab one!" Hale shouted. He pulled his T-shirt over his head in one quick move. His back was pale and muscled. LT felt a sudden heat and looked away, his heart pounding. Then Hale swung the

shirt over his head, trying to snag a thistle ball. It floated just out
of reach. He chased it, then jumped, jumped again. LT couldn't
take his eyes off the way his shoulders moved.

Then a lucky gust sent the ball down and the shirt caught against
it. Hale hooted and LT cheered. The thing was hollow, a jumble
of flat, silvery blades, thin as the wings of a balsa-wood glider, connected to each other by spongy joints which were decorated with
thorns. Hale pulled his shirt free of them, and the cloth tore.

Then the sun dimmed, and they looked up. LT realized they'd
only seen the front of the cloud, the first wave. Thousands and
thousands more flew toward them, a spinning mass.

LT said, "Ho-lee shit."

This struck Hale as hilarious, and then LT was laughing too, so
hard he could barely stand. Then they ran, giggling and shouting.

1981

For months before his summer stay, when he was sixteen years
old, LT begged his mother to take him to see the dragon tails of
Kansas. Mom worked slow magic on her new husband, Arnaud, a
thin, balding control freak who made a lot of money as a chemical
engineer. Eventually Arnaud came up with the idea that he should
encourage LT's interest in science and take them all to visit the
most successful invasives in the Midwest. He rented an enormous
RV and they drove southwest.

The first sign of the invasion came just past Topeka, when road
crews waved them off the interstate. Arnaud eased the RV into the
parking lot of a McDonald's and said, "There you go."

LT walked out of the RV, into sunlight and heat. At the edge of
the lot rose an arch of deeply grooved bark. It emerged from the
broken cement and came down about fifteen yards away in a field.
Large purple leaf blades ran in single file atop the bark like the
plates of a stegosaurus.

LT looked back at his mother. She beamed at him, then shooed
him forward. He grabbed hold of the sturdy roots of the blades
and pulled himself onto the base of the arch. A few careful steps
more and he was upright, hands out for balance. The bark was
a bit wider than his foot, but uneven. He knew from his books
that the tail was not an ordinary trunk but vines that had twisted

around each other as they grew, only gradually adhering to share resources.

He reached the peak of the arch, eight feet off the ground. Twenty or thirty yards away, directly in front of him, another arch emerged, and another, like a sea monster coursing through an ocean of grass. No, one monster in a school of them. To either side, dozens and dozens of the dragon tails breached and dove. A group of them had burst up through the highway, and there was nothing manmade cement could do to keep them underground.

These were the aliens' favorite trees, he thought. How could they not be? They were living architecture.

His mother called his name. She held the fancy, big-lensed camera Arnaud had bought her. She didn't have to prompt LT to smile.

The last night of the vacation, Arnaud drove to a campground set among the dragon tails, a farmer's feeble attempt to recoup something from the land after agricultural disaster. As they ate dinner at the RV's tiny table, LT showed his mother pictures from one of his books about the invasives. He told her how the dark fans held chlorophyll-like molecules that absorbed a larger spectrum of light than Earth versions. "If our plants tried to process that much energy they'd burn up, like a car engine trying to run on rocket fuel."

"It's a bit more complicated than that," Arnaud said. He stood at the galley sink, washing the skillet he'd used to fry the hamburgers. "The photosystems they're using seem to be variable, sometimes like retinol in archaea microbes, sometimes more like chlorophyll with novel side chains added, so that they can control—"

"Take a look at this," LT said, cutting him off. He showed her a cross section of the dragon tail and how the vines were twisted around each other. "They call them golden spirals. See, there's this thing called the Fibonacci sequence—"

"Dragon tails follow the golden spiral?" Arnaud said. He came over to the table. LT was pleased to know something the chemist didn't.

Mom said, "What's a Fibonacci?" and LT quickly answered. "It's a series of numbers, starting with one, two, three, five . . . each one's the sum of the previous two numbers, so—"

"That's a close approximation of the golden ratio," Arnaud

said. He pulled the book closer, leaned over LT's mother. "The growth factor of the curve follows that ratio. You can see the spiral in nature — in seashells, pinecones, everywhere."

"So beautiful," his mother said. She ran fingers over the glossy cross section. "Like the head of a sunflower."

LT, suddenly furious, pushed himself out from behind the table. His mother said, "Where you going?"

Arnaud said, "Could you put away your plate?"

He let the door bang shut behind him.

Outside, the atmosphere was greenhouse humid. He marched away, not caring which direction his body took him. It was nine thirty and still not full dark, as if the sun couldn't find the edge of these tabletop plains. The air was heavy with a floral perfume.

He came to the leaping back of a dragon trail, black against the purpling sky, and walked beside it. Gnats puffed out of the grass and he waved them away.

It had been a mistake to come on this trip. The RV was as stifling as a submarine. Arnaud sucked up all available oxygen, inserted himself into every conversation.

Eventually the dark came down, and he aimed for the fluorescent lights of the cinder-block building that doubled as park office and convenience store. Inside, a couple kids about his age, a boy and a girl, were glued to the Space Invaders cabinet. Were they brother and sister? Boyfriend and girlfriend? He thought about talking to them. He could tell them things. Like how the speed of the game was an accident; the aliens came down slow at first, then got faster and faster as their numbers were destroyed, not because it had been programmed that way but because the processor could only speed up when the load lightened. *Telling things* was the only way he knew how to make small talk. Other forms of conversation were a mystery.

He bought a Coke and took it outside. Leaned against the wall under the snapping bug zapper.

A flashlight bobbed toward him out of the dark. He ignored it until a voice behind the light said, "Hello, my darlin'."

His mother stepped up, clicked off the flashlight. "Did you see the stars? They're amazing out here."

"Still no meteors," he said. Six years after the seed storm, everybody was waiting for a second punch. Or maybe the next wave was on its way now, in the void, creeping across the light-years. Perhaps the long delay was necessary because of orbital mechanics. What looked like design could be just an accident of the environment.

He offered her a sip of his Coke. She waved it off. "You ought to give him a chance. He's just enthusiastic about things. Like you are."

He wanted to ask her why the hell she kept attaching herself to assholes. The self-involved painter, the rage-aholic restaurant owner, and now the chemist, whom she'd had the audacity to marry. Did she love him, or just his McMansion and its granite countertops?

"He wants to send you to college," she said. "He thinks you'd be a good scientist."

"Really?" Then he was embarrassed that the compliment meant something to him. "I'm not taking his money."

"You should think about it. Your dad can't afford college. And you deserve better than working in a lumberyard."

"There's nothing wrong with the lumberyard." LT worked there three days a week during the school year, sometimes alongside his father. He'd told her he hated it, but hadn't mentioned the things he loved about it. His herky-jerky forklift. The terrifying Ekstrom Carlson rip saw. The sawdust and sweat.

But did he want to be there the rest of his life?

From inside the store, the boy shouted in mock dismay and the girl laughed. They'd lost their last laser cannon.

"You should study the invasives," his mother said. "I remember that look on your face when I showed you that seed. And the fern man! You loved that little guy."

"I still have him. Dad keeps him in the living room. He's not so little."

"So," she said. "Think about it."

He thought, *If the aliens haven't landed by then.*

1986

"Where are the space bees?"

"What?"

"SPACE BEES!" LT shouted above the music. "WHERE ARE THEY?"

He was drunk, and Jeff and Wendy too, and their new friend Doran, all of them drunk together. What else could they be, on this final weekend before Christmas break, and where else but at the Whitehorse, which as far as he was concerned was the only bar in Normal, Illinois.

"Jesus Christ," Jeff said. "Not the bees again."

LT put his hand on the back of Doran's neck—a sweaty neck, and his hand tacky with beer but he didn't care, he wanted to pull Doran close. "I need to tell you things," he said into his ear, and Doran laughed, and then—

—and then they were in a restaurant booth, the lights bright, Jeff and Wendy across from him and Doran—tall, sturdy Doran —beside him. LT leaned into his arm woozily. God he was handsome, naturally handsome, almost hiding it. How did they get here? He concentrated, but his memory of the past two hours was a hopscotch, dancing drinking shouting singing and then the rude bright lights of last call and a flash of ice and cold—did Wendy drive, she must have—to *here,* the twenty-four-hour Steak 'n Shake, their traditional sober-up station.

He said to Doran, "It's the flowers that make no sense."

Jeff said, "The flowers have no scents?" and Wendy said, "It's that they have scents that makes no sense." They both laughed.

A beat too late LT realized there was wordplay at work. He forged on. "The blooms of flowers are *lures.*" The word thick on his tongue. "Scent and shape and color, they all evolved to attract specific pollinators, the bees and butterflies and beetles."

"Oh my," Jeff said.

"And you told me he was shy," Doran said.

"He can get wound up," Wendy said. "When he feels comfortable."

"Or tipsy," Jeff said.

LT felt tipsy *and* comfortable. Why hadn't Jeff and Wendy introduced him to Doran before now? Why wait until the last weekend of the last semester LT would be on campus? It was criminal.

"A pretty flower isn't just a simple announcement, like 'Here's pollen,'" LT said. "Simple won't do it." He tried to explain how flowers were in competition. Pollen was everywhere, nestled inside thousands of equally needy plants desperate to spread their genetic material. What was needed was not an announcement but a flashing neon sign. "The flower's goal," LT said, "is to figure out what *hummingbirds* think are beautiful."

"Slow down, Hillbilly," Wendy said. "Eat something."

"Hummingbirds have an aesthetic sense?" Doran said.

"Of course they do! Have I told you about bowerbirds?"

Jeff said, "Guess what his honors thesis is on?"

And then he was off, yammering about the bowerbirds of Papua New Guinea. The males of the species constructed elaborate twiggy structures, not nests but bachelor pads, designed purely to woo females. The Vogelkop bowerbird set out careful arrangements of colors—blue, green, yellow—each one a particular hue. It didn't matter what the objects were; they could be stones, or petals, or plastic bottle caps even, as long as they were the correct shade. The females could not be coerced into sex; they dropped by the bowers, perused the handiwork, and flew away if they found them substandard. Their choice of mates, their taste in *art,* drove the males over millennia to evolve more and more specific displays, an ongoing gallery show with intercourse as the prize.

"Wait," Doran said. "That doesn't mean they're making an artistic choice. Aren't they just, uh, instinctually responding to whoever seems like the fittest mate? It's not beauty per se—"

"I love *per se,*" Jeff said. "Great word."

"I've always been fond of *ergo,*" Wendy said.

"But it is aesthetics!" LT said. "Beauty's just"—he made explosion fingers—"joy in the brain, right? A flood of chemicals and, and, and—" What was the word? "Fireworks. Neuronal fireworks. We don't *logic* our way to beauty, it hits us like a fucking hammer."

"*Ipso facto,*" Jeff said.

Doran put his arm around LT's shoulder and said, "Eat your burger before it gets cold, then tell me about the space bees." Ah! He remembered! The heat of Doran's arm across his neck made his cheeks flush. Doran smelled of sweat and Mennen Speed Stick and something else, something LT could almost recall from far back in his brain, from a hot afternoon in a Chicago apartment . . . but the memory slipped the net.

He decided to eat. Wendy told the story of her favorite snowmobile accident. Doran, who'd grown up in New Mexico, couldn't believe that Wisconsin teenagers were allowed to ride machines across frozen lakes.

LT began to feel a little more sober, though perhaps that was an illusion. "Space bees," he said.

"I'm ready," Doran said. "Lay it on me."

"Every one of the invasives we've found, not a single one uses pollination. There's a lot of budding and spores and wind dispersal and"—he waved a clutch of fries—"you know. I've got a fern man at home, it's like ten feet tall now—"

"You do?"

But LT didn't want to talk about home. "Doesn't matter, it just grows and spreads, spilling out of its pot, but it doesn't require animal assistance." Actually, he wasn't sure that was true. Didn't the fern survive because of him, because of his family? It had played on their human tendency for anthropomorphism.

"Where'd you go, Hillbilly?" Wendy asked.

"Sorry, what did you say?" he asked Doran.

"I said, maybe all the pollinating species died."

"Maybe! But why colorful flowers and no pollen? There weren't any animals hatching from the space seeds, so—"

Doran's eyes went wide. "They have to be designed, then."

"Exactly!"

Wendy nabbed his glass before it tumbled over.

"Inside voices," she said.

He gets it, LT thought. The aliens could know what Earth's sunlight was like from very far away, even guess the composition of its atmosphere and soil, but they couldn't know what animals would be here, much less humans. So they had to design plants that could propagate without them.

"But if they're designed, why are they so, so *overwrought?*" LT asked. "Those huge fucking umbrellas out west, the sponges smothering South America, all of them crazy colorful and smelly and weird. So my real question is—"

"Where are the space bees?" Jeff supplied.

"Wrong!" LT said. The real question was the one he was born to answer. He'd get whatever degrees and training he needed, he'd go into the field for evidence, he'd write the books to explain it. He'd explain it to Doran.

"The question is, why all this needless beauty? What's it all for?"

"I don't know, but *you're* beautiful," Doran said, and then—

—and then morning, a thumping that wasn't in his head. Or not all in his head.

LT sat up, and pain spiked in his skull. Light blasted through half-open blinds. And there, beside him, Doran. Mouth agape, rough-jawed, one arm across LT's waist.

Still there. Still real.

He wanted to fall back into the bed, pull that arm across his chest. Then the knocking came again, and he realized who was at the front door.

"Fuck." He slipped out from under Doran's arm without waking him, pulled on shorts. Alcohol sloshed in his bloodstream. He closed the bedroom door behind him. The pounding resumed.

LT pulled open the front door. His father started to speak, then saw what shape his son was in. Shook his head, suddenly angry. No, angri*er*.

"I overslept," LT said.

"Are you packed?"

LT turned to look at the living room, and his father pushed past him.

"Dad! *Dad.* Could you just *wait?*"

His father surveyed the moving boxes, only a few of them taped up. The rest were open, half filled. LT's plan had been to wake up early and finish packing. Everything had to go. Next semester he'd finish his coursework in the mountains of western New Guinea, collecting data on how birds had adapted to invasives. And now all he wanted to do was stay here, in central Illinois, in this apartment.

"Wait for what?" his father asked. "For *you?*"

LT moved between his father and the bedroom. "Give me an hour. Go for lunch or something. There's a diner—"

"I'll start taking down what's packed. There's snow coming."

"No. Please. Just . . . give me some time."

His father looked at the bedroom door. Then at his son. His jaw tightened, and LT stopped himself from edging backward.

He'd lived his boyhood afraid of his father's anger. Power, he'd learned, came not from *blowing off steam* but from demonstrating that you were barely containing it. You won by exacting dread, by making your loved ones wait through the silence so long that they yearned for the explosion.

"In an hour I drive away," his father said.

1994

LT didn't relax until they stepped off the plane in Columbus. Doran kept trying to calm him down, to no effect. The entire trip he'd been imagining that some authority would command the pi-lot to turn around, send them back to Indonesia. A priest would tell them, *Stupid Americans, gays aren't allowed to be parents,* and they would yank the infant out of his hands.

Then he emerged from the boarding tunnel holding the baby, saw his mother, and they both burst into tears.

He eased his daughter into his mother's arms. "Mom, this is Christina. Christina, this is—what is it, again?" Teasing her.

"Mimi!" She pressed her face close to the tiny girl and whispered, "I'm your Mimi!"

A tanned, smiling man with a tidy black goatee offered his hand. "Congratulations, LT. You've made your mother very, very happy." This was Marcus, Mom's brand-new husband, five years younger than her, at least. His mother at forty-six was still lithe and alarmingly sexy. LT hadn't met Husband 3.0 before, didn't know Mom was bringing him. He felt a flash of annoyance that he had to deal with this intruder at this moment—but then told himself to let it go. The day was too big for small emotions.

Doran, holding two duffel bags, one in each arm, said, "We made it."

LT kissed him, hard. In New Guinea they hadn't dared engage in PDA. "Eighteen years to go."

Christina nestled like a peanut in the high-tech shell of the car seat. As Marcus drove them home, LT and Doran talked about how dicey the whole process had been. The orphanage, situated about thirty miles from Jayapura, was overcrowded, with hundreds of children left there by the crisis. The facility was nominally run by nuns, but most of the staff were local women who seemed little better off than their charges. LT and Doran had been practicing their Indonesian, especially the phrases involving gift-giving.

"We had to bribe everybody, top to bottom," Doran said. "If it wasn't for LT's friend at the university yelling at them, they'd have taken the shirts off our backs."

"It's not their fault," LT said. "Their agriculture is wrecked. The economy's crashing. They're starving."

"Maybe they should stop chewing those sugar sticks."

"What now?" his mother asked.

He told her how the locals seemed almost addicted to an invasive plant that tasted sweet but could not be digested. Gut bacteria couldn't break down those strange peptides and so passed it along through the colon like a package that couldn't be opened.

Doran said, "It would be great for my diet."

A joke, but what Doran had seen there had scared him, and even LT, who'd spent months on the island doing fieldwork for his PhD, had been shaken by the rapid decline in the country. Thousands of alien species had been growing in the forests for two decades, ignored and unchecked, and suddenly some tipping point had been reached and those alien plants had reached the cities. The latest was a thread-thin vine that exploded into a red web on contact with flat surfaces. Villages and towns were engulfed by scarlet gauze. In the orphanage nurses scraped it from the walls, but that only made it worse, dispersing its spores. He and Doran were terrified it was in Christina's lungs. Invasives might be indigestible, but so was asbestos. In the morning she'd have her first doctor's appointment. Her papers all said she was healthy, without birth defects, and up-to-date on her vaccinations, but they weren't about to trust an orphanage under duress.

Once they reached the apartment, LT still couldn't bear to put down his daughter. While Doran mixed formula and made beds and ordered takeout, LT fed his daughter, changed her, and then let her fall asleep on his chest.

His mother sat beside him on the couch. "You're going to have to let Doran do more parenting."

"He can fight me for her."

"Big talk for the first night. Wait till sleep deprivation hits."

Christina's eyes were not quite closed, her lips parted. Mom had to know that he'd strong-armed Doran into adoption. His last trip to New Guinea, LT had been haunted by the abandoned children. Doran had said, *This is crazy, we're not even thirty,* and LT said, *My parents were teenagers when they had me,* and Doran said, *You're making my case.*

But that argument was over forever the moment Doran met Christina.

"You used to look just like that," his mother said. "Milk-drunk."

She was four weeks old, living through the days of extreme fractions. In another month she'd have been their daughter for half her life. In a year she would have been an orphan for only a twelfth of it. And yet those four weeks would never disappear. There would always be some shrinking percentage of her life that she'd lived alone, a blot like a tiny spore. He'd read alarming articles about adopted children who'd failed to "attach." What if the psychic damage was already done? What if she never felt all the love they were bombarding her with?

His mother called Marcus over. "Sweetie, show them what you brought."

Marcus opened a wooden box lined with cut paper and lifted out a teardrop-shaped dollop of glass, about eight inches long and six inches wide at the base, purple and red and glinting with gold.

"A crystal for Christina," he said.

"That is *amazing*," Doran said. "You made this?"

"Marcus is an award-winning glassblower," his mother said. She tilted her head. "He made me these earrings."

Of course, LT thought. His mother had always loved bower-birds.

The gift was very pretty, and pretty useless, too heavy for a Christmas ornament and not a shape that could sit upright on a shelf. They'd have to hang it, but not above her bed.

"Which ear is she supposed to wear it in?" LT asked.

Marcus laughed. "Either one. She'll have to grow into it."

When the food arrived, LT needed to eat, and he was forced to surrender Christina to Doran. His body moved automatically as he held her, a kind of sway and jiggle that soothed her. Where did he learn that?

Mom said, "Did you call your father?"

And like that, the spell was broken. LT said, "What do you think?"

"I think you should."

"Fuck him."

"Hey," Doran said.

"Right. I gotta stop swearing. Eff that guy."

"Your mom's right. We should give him a chance."

"He's had six years of chances. Any time he wants to call, I'll pick up." There were a few years, after college, when they talked on the phone and his father would pretend that LT lived alone. He never asked about Doran, or about their lives. Then LT sent his father an invitation to the commitment ceremony. The next time LT called, his father said that he was disgusted and didn't want to talk to him until he fixed his life.

His mother said, "This is different. Maybe it's time."

Maybe. He got up from the table.

Time itself had become different. He looked at Christina in

Doran's arms and thought, *I'm going to know you for the rest of my life.* The future had broken open, his week-by-week life suddenly stretching to decades. He could picture her on her first day of school, on prom night, at her wedding. He caught a glimpse of her holding a baby as tiny as she was at that moment.

Had his father felt that way too when he was born?

He kissed Doran's cheek, then bent over their daughter. She was awake, dark-eyed, watching both of them. He thought, *There's no way I can go away for six months into the jungle and leave her.* He wouldn't make the choice his parents had made.

"We'll give it a shot," LT said. He moved his cheek across her warm head. Inhaled her scent. "Won't we, my darlin'?"

2007

He was reading to Christina and Carlos when the call came. Or rather, Christina was reading while LT held the book, because Christina said he was only allowed to do the Hagrid and Dumbledore voices. Carlos, five years old, lolled at the end of the bed, seemingly oblivious but missing nothing.

Doran came to the bedroom holding the cordless. "Some guy wants to talk to you. He says he's a friend of your father's."

The thick Tennessee accent opened a door to his childhood. Vernon Beck, hearty as ever. He apologized for bothering LT "up there in D.C.," but he was worried about LT's father. "He stopped coming to work. He didn't quit, just stopped coming. Same with church. He won't answer the phone at all."

"Is he sick? Did he get hurt at the yard?"

"I went over there, and he finally came out to the porch. He said he was fine, just wanted folks to leave him alone. But I don't know. It ain't like him."

They talked a few minutes more. Mr. Beck apologized again for bothering him, explained how he got his number from a cousin. LT reassured him that it was all right. Asked about his son, Hale, who turned out to be doing fine, still in Maryville, working maintenance for the hospital. Had a wife and four children, all boys.

LT thought about that day they ran from the thistles. Funny how you don't know the last day you'll see someone. He'd spent the rest of that winter when he was thirteen daydreaming about Hale, his first big crush. He didn't mention that to Mr. Beck, and Mr. Beck didn't ask about LT's husband or children. Southern Silence.

"One more thing," Mr. Beck said. "Your dad, he's let things go. You should be ready for that."

Doran asked, "What happened to your father?"

"Maybe nothing. But I think I have to go lay eyes on him."

Christina said, "I want to lay eyes on him!"

"Me too, kiddo," Doran said. "But not like this."

"Can we *read* now?" Carlos asked.

Doran didn't want LT to travel south. All those famine refugees landing in Florida, and the citizen militias in Texas and New Mexico. LT said his Department of Agriculture credentials would get them through any checkpoint, and besides, Tennessee was nowhere near the trouble. "It's like going into Wisconsin," LT said, quoting one of their favorite movies. "In and out."

"Fine," Doran said, "but why not just call the local police, let them check it out?" But LT didn't want to embarrass Dad, or get him fined if he wasn't taking care of the house.

"I owe him this much," LT said. And Doran said, "You think so?"

Doran stayed home with Carlos, and LT and Christina left before sunrise the next morning with a cooler full of food so they wouldn't have to depend on roadside restaurants. Christina fell asleep immediately, slept through all the phone calls he made to the department, and woke up outside of Roanoke. He put away the phone and they listened to music and he pointed out invasives and native plants alongside the interstate. They were driving through the battlefield of a slow-motion war. Old native species were finding novel ways to fight the aliens—sucking resources from them underground, literally throwing shade above—and new invasives kept popping up into ecological niches. "It's all happening so incrementally," he told her, "it's hard to see."

"Like global warming," Christina said. He'd let her read the opening chapter of the book he was working on, and had taken her to see the Al Gore movie, so she understood boiling frogs. This had been his job for the past decade at the Department of Agriculture: explainer-in-chief, interpreter of policy, sometimes influencer of it. He missed the fieldwork and longed to do original research again, but the government desk job provided stability for his family.

"Remember what I told you about animal speed?" he said.

"Plant speed, and *planet* speed, that's just a hard timescale for us mammals to keep our attention on."

"I know. Wheels within wheels."

"Exactly."

After a day of driving and a two-hour wait for inspection at the Tennessee border, they entered the foothills. His hands knew the turns. He remembered the long drive home that last day of college—and realized for the first time that his father must have had to leave the hills at one in the morning to get to Illinois State by noon, and then had turned around and driven all the way back the same day. Drove it in silence, with a hungover, secretly heartbroken boy sulking in the passenger seat.

They pulled into the long gravel drive and parked beside the house. Christina said, "You used to live *here*?"

"Be nice. Your grandfather built this house."

"No, it's cool! It looks like a fairy castle."

His childhood home was being overrun in the same slow, grasping process that had swallowed Christina's village. The backyard grass, ordinary and native, had grown knee high. But covering the wall of the house was a flat-leafed ivy, brilliant and slick-looking as the heart of a kiwi fruit: definitely an invasive. Was this war or détente?

Ivy also covered the back door. He tore away a clear space and knocked. Knocked again. Called out, "Dad! It's LT!"

He tried the door, and it swung open. "Wait here," he said to Christina. He didn't want her to see anything horrible.

The kitchen lights were off. There were dishes in the sink, a pair of pots on the stove.

He called for his father again. His toe snagged on something. A vine, snaking across the floor. No, many vines.

He stepped into the living room—and froze. Ivy covered everything. A carpet of green clung to the walls. The fireplace burst with green foliage, and the tall stone altar of the chimney had become a trellis. Vines curled through doorways, snaked along the stair rails. Greenish sunlight filtering through the leaf-covered windows made the room into an aquarium. The air was jungle thick and smelled of fruiting bodies.

He stepped closer toward the fireplace, spied dots of white and red nestled into the leaves. Was the ivy *blooming*?

"What are you doing here?"

LT startled. The voice had come from behind him.

"Dad?"

His father sat in his armchair, nestled into the vines. Leaves draped his shoulders like a shawl. He wore a once-white UT Vols sweatshirt that seemed too big for him. His hair was shaggy, a steel gray that matched the stubble on his face. He looked too thin, much older than he should. LT felt as if he'd been catapulted through time. He hadn't seen or spoken to this man for almost twenty years, and now he wasn't even the same person.

His father said, "Who's this?"

LT thought, *Oh God, not Alzheimer's,* and then realized that Christina had come into the room.

She was looking up at the walls, the high ceiling, slowly turning to take it all in. "Dad . . ." Her voice was strange.

"It's okay, honey, there's nothing to be—"

"This is *awesome.*"

She lifted her hands to her head as if to contain the shock. A sound like applause erupted around the room. The leaves were shaking.

She looked at the corner, then up. "Dad, do you see it?"

He could, a green shape against the green. Enmeshed in leaves, an oak-thick stalk rose up in the corner. At the top, a bulbous head a yard wide was bent against a cross-timber, so that it seemed to be looking down at them. Its right arm stretched across the room, where broad leaves splayed against the wall as if holding it up. Its other arm hung down. Finger leaves brushed the floor.

"Holy fucking—"

"*Dad,*" Christina chided. She walked toward the plant. Lifted her hands above her head. The leaves of its arms rattled like a hundred castanets.

She laughed, and bent at the waist. Slow Mo's huge head eased left, then right.

LT's father said, "Isn't he a lovely boy?"

Geological time, plant time, animal time . . . and inside that, yet another, smaller wheel, spinning fast. His father's body had become a container for cells that lived and replicated and mutated at frightening speed.

On the second morning at Blount Memorial Hospital, Christina sat at the edge of her grandfather's bed, curled her fingers around his (carefully not disturbing the IV tubes taped to the top of his hand), and said, "I read a pamphlet about colon cancer. Would you like me to tell you about it?"

His father laughed. "Are you going to be a scientist like your father?" He was remarkably cheery, now that equipment had rehydrated him and delivered a few choice opioids.

She shook her head. "I want to be a real doctor."

LT, listening to on-hold music on his cell, said, "Hey!"

Doran came back on the line. "Okay, I got him an appointment with Lynn's oncologist. Bring him here. I'll move Carlos into Christina's room."

"Are you sure about this?"

"I would only do this for my favorite person. Besides, I don't think anybody else is stepping up. You're an only child, right?"

"Uh, kind of." He'd have to explain later.

He gave Christina a five and told her to sneak some ice cream into the room. "He likes rocky road, but chocolate will do."

His father watched her go. "She reminds me of your mother."

LT thought, *Sure, this tiny, dark-haired, brown-skinned girl is* so *much like your blond, dancer-legged wife.*

"I mean it," his father said. "When she looks at me—it was like that with Belinda. That light."

"Dad—"

"All the boys in that school, and she chose me."

"Dad, I need to tell you some things."

"I'm not leaving the house."

"You can't go back there. I had Mr. Beck check it out. There are roots running through the floorboards, wrapped around the pipes. The wiring's been shorted out. You're lucky the place didn't burn down."

"It's my house. You can't tell me—"

"No, it's Mo's house now. It's been his for years."

2028

On that last Thanksgiving he hosted in the Virginia house, the topic of conversation was, appropriately enough, food.

"We haven't published yet, but the data's solid," Christina said. "We've got an eater."

Cheers went up around the table. "Were you using the cyano-bacteria?" LT asked. Just a few months ago, her gene-hacking team at McGill was making zero progress. "Or one of the Rhodophyta?"

"Let the woman speak!" LT's mother said. Christina, sitting beside her, squeezed her arm and said, "Thanks, Mimi."

"She needs no encouragement," Christina's husband said, and Carlos laughed.

"Here's the amazing thing—we didn't engineer it. We found the bacteria in the wild. Evolving on its own."

"You're kidding me," LT said.

Christina shrugged. "It turns out we should have been paying more attention to the oceans."

LT tried not to hear this as a rebuke. As the USDA's deputy secretary, he orchestrated the research grants, helped set the agenda for managing the ongoing crisis. It was a political job more than a scientific one, and much of the time the money had to go into putting out fires. So even though everyone knew that most of the seeds had gone down in water, the difficulty in retrieving them meant that almost all the research on water-based invasives focused on ones near the surface: the white pods like bloated worms floating in Lake Superior, the fibrous beach balls bobbing in the Indian Ocean, the blue fans that attached themselves to Japanese tuna like superhero capes.

Christina said that the bacteria were found feeding on rainbow mats. The scientific community had missed the explosion of translucent invasives hovering in the ocean's photic zone until they linked and rose to the surface in a coruscating, multicolored mass. The satellite pictures of it were lovely and terrifying. The alien plants were so efficient at sucking up carbon dioxide, in a few decades of unrestricted growth they could put a serious dent in global warming—while maybe killing everything else in the ocean.

But somehow fast-evolving Earth organisms were trying to eat them first. Or at least one species of them. But if one Earth organism had figured it out, maybe others had too.

"You have to tell us how they're breaking down those peptides," LT said.

"Or not," Carlos said.

"I have a story," said Bella, Christina's four-year-old daughter. "During craft time, this girl Neva? It was a *disaster*."

"Wait your turn, darling," Aaron said. Christina's husband was a white man from Portland. He ran cool to Christina's hot, which was good for Bella.

Through some quasi-Lamarckian process, LT's children, and his children's children, had inherited his most annoying conversational tendency. On Thanksgiving they didn't go around the table saying what they were thankful for but rather took turns explaining things to each other. Nothing made LT happier. All he wanted in the world was this: to be surrounded by his family, talking and talking. Much of the world was in dire shape, but they were rich enough to afford the traditional dry turkey breast, the cranberry sauce with the ridges from the can, sweet potato casserole piled with a layer of marshmallow.

"You know what this means," Christina said. She caught LT's eye. "Next year we'll be eating sugar sticks like the aliens did."

Perhaps only LT understood what she meant. *Homo sapiens* are only 10 percent human; most of the DNA in their bodies comes from the tiny flora that they carry inside themselves to digest their food and perform a million tiny tasks that keep them alive. If humans could someday adopt these new bacteria into their microbiome, a host of invasives could become edible. It would be the end of the famine.

She saw the wonder in his face and laughed. "Wheels within wheels, Dad."

After dinner the urge to nap descended like a cloud, and only little Bella was immune. Carlos offered to take her to the park, but LT said he would like that honor.

"Where the slides are?" she asked.

"All the slides," he said. "Just let me tuck in Mimi."

He led his mother to the master bedroom, which was on the ground floor and had the best mattress. She moved carefully, as if hearing faint music in the distance, but at eighty she was still sharp, still beautiful, still determined to stay up with fashion. Her hair was three different shades of red.

"Eighty-five outside," she said, "and in here it's a Chicago winter."

"I'll get an afghan," he said, and opened the closet. When he turned around, she was sitting on the edge of the bed, one hand out on the coverlet.

"You must miss Doran."

The knot that he carried in his chest tightened a fraction. He nodded.

"It's not fair," she said. "All our men dying so young."

"Arnaud's still alive," LT said. "At least he was last year. He sent me a Christmas card."

"Good God, what an asshole," she said. "It's true what they say, then."

"I was the teenage asshole. I don't know how anybody put up with me."

She lay down and folded her hands across her chest like Cleopatra. He spread the afghan so that it covered her feet.

"This is a lovely house," she said.

"It's too big for me now. Unless you move in."

"I prefer living on my own these days. I do my painting in the nude, you know."

"You do not."

"But I *could*. That's the point."

Bella was waiting for him by the front door. "Papa!"

"Ciao, Bella!"

She jumped into his arms. It was a pleasure to be someone's favorite person again, at least for the moment. "Ready for the slides?"

He wished she didn't live so far away. He wished he wasn't so busy. People were making noises about nominating him for secretary, but he could say no, get off the treadmill. He could move to Canada and be close to Christina and Aaron and Bella, finally finish the book. Make one more research trip. He'd like to visit New Guinea again, see how the land of his daughter was faring. Fifty-three years after the meteor storm, and there were still so many questions to answer and so many new things to see.

He carried Bella out into the Virginia heat. Soon he'd have to put her down, but he wanted to carry her as long as he could, as long as she let him. "So," he said to her, "What's all this about a disaster at craft time?"

2062

The house was full of strangers. They kept touching his shoulder, leaning down into his face, wishing him happy birthday. Ninety-seven was a ridiculous age to celebrate. Not even a round number. They thought he wouldn't make it to ninety-eight, much less a hundred. They'd probably been waiting for years for him to kick off, and this premature wake was the admission of their surrender.

A tiny gray-haired woman sat beside him. Christina. "You have to see this," she said. She held a glass case, and suspended inside it was a glossy black shape flecked with silver. "It's from the current secretary of agriculture. 'For forty-five years of service to the nation and the world.' This one came from Tennessee. You remember telling me about Mimi finding a seed?"

There was an ocean of days he couldn't remember, but that day he recalled clearly. "Rock hound's delight," he said softly.

"What's that, Dad?"

Ah. The strangers were watching, waiting for a proper response. He cleared his throat and said loudly, "So have those alien bastards shown up yet?"

Everyone laughed.

The afternoon stretched on interminably. Cake, singing, talking, so much talking. He asked for his jacket and a familiar-looking stranger brought it to him, helped him out of his chair. "I have to tell you, sir, your books made me want to be a scientist. *The Distant Gardener* was the first—"

LT lifted a hand. "Which way is the backyard?" He could still walk on his own. He was proud of that.

Outside, the sky was bright, the air too warm. He didn't need his coat after all. He stood in a garden, surrounded by towering trees. But whose garden, whose house? It wasn't his home in Virginia, that was long gone. Not Chicago or Columbus. Was this Tennessee?

Everything moves too fast, he thought, or else barely moves at all.

"Papa?"

A young woman, holding the hand of a little girl. The girl, just three or four years old, held a huge black flower whose petals were edged with scarlet.

"Ciao, Bella!" he said to the girl.

The woman said, "No, Papa, this is Annie. I'm Bella."

A stab of embarrassment. And wonder. Bella was so old. How had that happened? How had he gotten so far from home? He wanted to do it all over again. He wanted Doran's shoulder next to him and tiny Christina in his arms. He wanted Carlos on his shoulders at the National Zoo. All of it, all of it again.

"It's okay, Papa," Bella said. His tears concerned her. What a small, common thing to worry about.

He inclined his head toward the little girl. "My apologies, Annie. How are you doing this afternoon? Did you fly all the way from California?"

She let go of her mother's hand and approached him. "I have a flower."

"Yes, you do."

"It's a pretty flower."

"It certainly is."

Bella said, "She likes to tell people things."

The girl offered the flower to him. Up close, the black petals seemed to ripple and shift. Their dark surfaces swirled with traceries of silver that caught the light and spun it prettily. He raised it to his nose and made a show of sniffing it. The little girl laughed.

Words were not required. Sometimes the only way you could tell someone you loved them was to show them something beautiful. Sometimes, he thought, you have to send it from very far away.

"Where did you find this lovely flower?" he asked.

She pointed past his shoulder. He could feel the tower of green behind him. The leaves were about to move.

NOTE: The mnemonic for meteoroids, meteors, and meteorites was written by Andy Duncan and is used with his permission.

Dead Air

FROM *Nightmare Magazine*

Entry 1.

[Beginning of recorded material.]

[Laughter.]

VOICE: Wait, are you actually—

NITA: Time is, uh, 9:42 in the morning, September 22nd, 2013. This is Nita Rosen interviewing subject by the name of—

VOICE: Jesus, I really did not think you were serious.

[Rustling paper.]

NITA: So you thought I made you sign a release as, what, foreplay?

[Laughter.]

VOICE: I was, like, four tequilas deep by the time you walked in and probably at five when you waved that paper in my face. I would've signed my soul away to . . . Uh, I didn't actually sign my soul over, did I?

[Laughter.]

[Rustling paper.]

NITA: Maybe you should read this again. It's a standard release that says you're willing to be interviewed and to have this interview used in a published—well, a hopefully published art project. Thing. I'm not sure what it'll look like exactly.

VOICE: Seriously? Okay. What's this project about?

NITA: It's an ethnography of the people I fuck.

[Moment of silence.]

VOICE: Wow. That's. Okay.

NITA: Scared off yet?

VOICE: Are you gonna play this in front of, like, some crusty old sociology professors?

NITA: It's art, not sociology. Or it's, like, sociologically influenced art. If you read the release, there's a description.

VOICE: "Documenting the erotic discourse of . . ." [Laughs.] This is pretentious as shit.

NITA: Duh. How else am I gonna get funding?

[Laughter.]

VOICE: So if I say no . . .

NITA: I turn the recorder off, make us some breakfast, and shred the release form. Bid you a nice goodbye and maybe ask for your number.

VOICE: Maybe?

NITA: No promises either way.

VOICE: So no pressure.

NITA: That would be unethical.

VOICE: I think most ethics boards would object to an author having sex with her subjects, but what do I know.

NITA: That's why it's art and not science. So?

VOICE: . . . All right. Hit me.

NITA: Okay, so time is now 9:44 in the morning, September 22nd, 2013. Do you want to be referred to anonymously, or . . . ?

MADDIE: Maddie. Pleasure to make your acquaintance.

[Laughter.]

NITA: Oh, no, the pleasure was all mine. So, first question, what's the first thing you noticed about me in the bar last night?

MADDIE: Oh, wow, okay. Um. I think I saw you from the back first, so—

NITA: Was it my ass? I have a great ass.

[Laughter.]

MADDIE: No! I mean, yes, you have a great ass. No, that's not what I noticed first. It was your shoulders and neck. The way your hair got stuck to the sweat on your neck when you were dancing.

NITA: Oo-kay, that sounds really unsexy, but—

MADDIE: I wanted to bite you. In a good way. Just put my teeth on this tendon right here and . . .

[. . .]

NITA: Mmm. That's nice. That's . . . yeah.

MADDIE: Did you have another question?

NITA: [Clears throat.] Why did you come out last night? Were you hoping to get laid?

MADDIE: I was hoping to dance, drink, have fun. Get out of my head for a while, I guess.

NITA: What was in your head that you were hoping to get away from?

[. . .]

MADDIE: Uh. Stuff?

NITA: You don't have to answer questions you're not comfortable with.

MADDIE: Okay, I'm gonna not answer that one.

NITA: Totes fair, totes fair. Were you out alone last night?

MADDIE: I was by the time you got there. A couple of people I knew from work had come with me, but they went home early.

NITA: And you stayed.

MADDIE: Didn't have any other plans for the night. And like I said, I wanted to, you know—

NITA: Get out of your head.

MADDIE: Yeah. And get laid, I guess. I mean, I don't know if I put it like that to myself, but if we're gonna be blunt about it, yeah. I wanted to find somebody. Or at least dance with somebody.

NITA: Just like Whitney, huh.

MADDIE: Who?

NITA: *Seriously?* You don't—okay, we're gonna deal with that later. But I will say that you are a serious outlier in my study, at least with your knowledge of eighties music.

MADDIE: Ooh, an outlier. I like the sound of that. Though I'm curious about how many other subjects you've, uh, interviewed.

NITA: We can talk about that later too. All right, this isn't a normal question for my interviews, but . . . Can I ask about, uh—

[Static.]

NITA: What the hell?

[are you sure you]

MADDIE: Something wrong?

[want to]

NITA: Yeah, the recorder's being weird. Piece of crap.

MADDIE: What were you going to ask?

NITA: The scars on your back. What are they from?

[. . .]

NITA: You don't have to answer that if you don't—

MADDIE: Yeah, I'll pass. It's, uh. Not really first-date material.

NITA: Sorry. [Clears throat.] Though if you're amenable to follow-up interviews, you could give me your number.

[Laughter.]

MADDIE: Shit, that was smooth. Fine. Gimme your phone.

NITA: I'm gonna pause the recording, okay? We can finish the interview after breakfast. You don't have anywhere to be, do you?

MADDIE: Nowhere I'm not happy to—

[End of recorded material.]

Entry 2.

[Beginning of recorded material.]

[Voices, jazz music, rattling cutlery.]

NITA: Okay, so we are at KnockBox Café, Chicago, Illinois, and it is . . . 2:24 in the afternoon, September 29th, 2013. And I'm here with the lovely Maddie for our, ahem, follow-up interview.

MADDIE: Follow-up interview *my ass*. [Into microphone.] She asked me out on a date.

NITA: It's an interview! I'm recording it!

MADDIE: How is this going to fit into your sexnography or whatever if we're not actually . . .

NITA: In bed?

[Maddie clears her throat.]

NITA: Well, I'm not gonna make any presumptions, but, like, I'm not here *just* for the sake of science.

MADDIE: I thought it was art.

NITA: Sociologically influenced art.

MADDIE: Let your record show that I am rolling my eyes right now.

[Laughter.]

NITA: So I missed some of the questions on my initial interview, because a certain someone distracted me. You ready for them?

MADDIE: Let me get coffee first. I feel like I'm gonna need caffeine if you're gonna ask me about my sex life in public.

NITA: Let me get your drink, okay? I promise, the imaginary ethics review board won't object.

MADDIE: Okay. Can you get me a dirty chai? With soy milk?

NITA: Sure.

[21 seconds of ambient noise.]

MADDIE: This is so transparently a—maybe not a date, but it's definitely a something. I have no idea why I am actually charmed by this. [Whispering into microphone.] It doesn't hurt that you're cute as hell.

[14 seconds of ambient noise.]

MADDIE: It's been a long time since I felt like this. I don't know if I . . .

[39 seconds of ambient noise.]

NITA: Okay. So. Are you from Chicago?

MADDIE: I'm from Washington. State, not D.C. A tiny mountain town up in the Cascades.

NITA: What's it called?

MADDIE: You wouldn't have heard of it. It's a wide spot in the road called—

[Garbled.]

NITA: . . . Yeah, definitely haven't heard of it.

MADDIE: Told you. Most people in Washington don't even know it's there.

NITA: What's it like?

MADDIE: Used to be a logging town, now it's a ghost town. Gray and rainy. Lots of forests, lots of overgrown clearcuts.

NITA: Is it pretty, at least? With the woods and the mountains?

MADDIE: I guess. *Pretty* isn't really the word I'd use.

NITA: What word would you use, then? To describe it?

MADDIE: Hmmm. Fairy-tale-ish. But not the nice kind of fairy tale. Not something Disney would make into a movie.

NITA: [Laughs.] I'm gonna nod like I totally understand what you're talking about.

MADDIE: You never read the old versions of fairy tales? The kind where, like, girls drown and turn into swans—

NITA: WHAT? Wait. You're saying that [garbled] had, like, kids drowning and—

MADDIE: No! No. Just. Uh. My mom just had, uh, books when I was a kid, and I— It's just like the sort of place where you could imagine things happening. Like *Twin Peaks*? Have you seen that? Sorta like that. Very David Lynch. Yeah.

[. . .]

NITA: . . . Okay! Moving on. So when did you move to Chicago?

MADDIE: Just this year.

NITA: From [garbled]?

MADDIE: No, no, I left there after, uh, 2009. I've lived in a few places since then.

NITA: Just get restless?

MADDIE: Something like that. I guess I, uh, haven't really wanted to get tied down to a particular place.

NITA: Cool, I get that. Sorta. I grew up in the suburbs and then, like, moved here for college. Anyway. Next question: do you still talk to your parents and—

MALE VOICE: I got a latte and a dirty chai with soy!

MADDIE: I'll get them.

[. . .]

NITA: Thanks.

MADDIE: Thank *you*. You're the one who bought them. So . . . I don't really want to talk about my parents, if that's okay?

NITA: Of course! Yeah. Like I said, this is—

MADDIE: Have you seriously asked everyone that you've . . . you know. Slept with. Have you asked them these questions?

NITA: Yeah. I mean, it's a little less awkward when you've already, like, stuck your face in someone's pussy.

MADDIE: . . . True. I guess.

[. . .]

NITA: Did I make it weird? I think I made it weird.

MADDIE: No, it's fine.

NITA: I don't want to make you uncomfortable. I'm just . . . curious. About you.

[The ambient noise briefly dips in volume. One of them breathes. The other fiddles nervously with a pen. The moment passes; conversations and the music resume.]

MADDIE: It's okay. I mean. Also I don't know how to tell you this, but, uh. You're interviewing the randos you take home for sex, it was never *not* gonna be weird.

NITA: [Sighs.] Yeah, fair.

MADDIE: It's all right. I'm used to weird.

NITA: Sounds like it.

[. . .]

MADDIE: What? Is there something on my face?

NITA: No, it's not . . . Can I just . . .

MADDIE: What?

NITA: Would you mind if I kissed you? I just . . . I'm curious.

MADDIE: Yeah. Yeah, all right.

[. . .]

[Soft laughter.]

NITA: [Softly.] Yeah, that's as good as I remember.

MADDIE: Okay. Um. Did you have any other questions to ask, so we can keep pretending this is an interview?

NITA: I wasn't *pretending!* This is an actual thing. You're just . . .

MADDIE: Just what?

NITA: An outlier.

MADDIE: [Snorts.] Right. Thanks. Just what I always wanted to be.

NITA: I did have one other question. But I don't know—

MADDIE: You can ask.

NITA: Well. I . . . So. I'm still curious? About the scars on your back?

MADDIE: Oh.

NITA: What are they from?

MADDIE: A car accident.

NITA: Really? They look like scratches. Like—

[Chair scraping.]

NITA: Wait, Maddie—

[Thumping, footsteps. A door opening, and the sound of traffic.]

NITA: Maddie, please, I'm—

MADDIE: Turn it off.

NITA: What?

MADDIE: The recording. Turn it off!
NITA: All right, see, I'm turning it—
[End of recorded material.]

Entry 3.

[Beginning of recorded material.]
NITA: Okay, it's . . . 1:13 in the morning, September 29th—
   no it's the 30th now. Maddie just left, she said she had work
   in the morning so she couldn't stay. Um. I kinda wish she
   had, but I'm—it's probably more than I deserve, that she
   stayed this long and this late. That she didn't just tell me to
   fuck off when we were at the café.

   We talked for a long time. She told me a little bit about
   the car accident, and . . . One of her friends was in the car
   with her and . . . Maddie didn't just, like, come out and say
   it, but reading between the lines, uh, this other girl didn't
   make it out. I shouldn't have been such a nosy shit, but I—

   This project, like so much in my head, sounded like it
   would be really cool. My *ethnography*, LOL. You can't see it,
   but I just did really big air quotes. Why not interview the
   people that I fuck and then edit it all together and find
   some deep and underlying truth about the nature of, whatever, queer millennial sexual practices? I figured I'd end
   up on *This American Life* and then get, like, a genius grant
   or something eventually. The first few interviews were cool,
   because, like, yay, getting laid in the name of *art*. But this
   thing with Maddie is . . .

   We've got a date for Friday, and I'm, like, scared shitless
   and also hella excited. I like Maddie a lot. A lot a lot. I'm
   leaving the recorder at home. Wish me luck that I don't
   fuck things up more than I already have.
[End of recorded material.]

Entry 4.

[Beginning of recorded material.]
[7 seconds of breathing.]

MADDIE: You're asleep right now. Which is good, because, like, I don't know how to tell you that I don't really want to be part of your project. The ethnography of the people you sleep with. I just . . . I've been having a good time with you, and I want to keep having a good time with you. Being an outlier was all right, but I think I wanna . . .

[Soft snore. Rustling cloth.]

MADDIE: [Whispering.] Maybe it's not something I should say out loud yet. It scares me how much I've already let you in. But I really like you. I wanted you to have a record of me saying that, just in case I . . .

[4 seconds of soft breath.]

MADDIE: It's probably too soon to be worried about that.

[Rustling cloth. Nita stirs. The sound of skin touching skin; comfort.]

MADDIE: I don't want to be just an outlier, okay? Let me be something more. For as long as I can.

[End of recorded material.]

Entry 5.

[Beginning of recorded material.]

VOICE: November. Sixteenth. Two thousand thirteen. Voice-mail from phone number seven seven three—

[Garbled.]

MADDIE: Hey, it's Maddie. I have a favor to ask you, and it's a pain in the ass, and I wouldn't be asking you if you weren't my last hope, but . . . Anyway. I'm flying home for Thanksgiving and my ride just bailed on me. Do you think you could take me to O'Hare? Sorry, I know it's a pain in the ass to go to O'Hare, and my flight is at the ass crack of dawn and traffic will probably be terrible. I will repay you with, like, massive amounts of your booze of choice. You can ask me prying and personal questions and record them for the thing. Are you still doing the thing? You haven't mentioned it in a while. Anyway. Let me know. About the ride, not the thing. Okay. Bye.

VOICE: End of message.

[End of recorded material.]

Entry 6.

[Beginning of recorded material.]
VOICE: November. Twenty-second. Two thousand thirteen.
  Voicemail from phone number seven seven three—
[Garbled.]
MADDIE: Hey, it's me. Sorry, I know it's late, just wanted to
  let you know I got in okay—
FEMALE VOICE: Who are you calling? Is it that girl you were
  telling me about?
MADDIE: [Muffled.] Mom, *shut up.* [Clear.] Anyway, it's all
  good here. Thanks again for dropping me off at the airport.
FEMALE VOICE: Invite her too. Have her come with you
  when it's time.
MADDIE: Mom, *stop.*
FEMALE VOICE: [Close to microphone.] Come for Christ-
  mas!
VOICE: End of message.
[End of recorded material.]

Entry 7.

[Beginning of recorded material.]
NITA: Dear ethnography diary, or whatever this is now. Am I
  a terrible person? All signs currently point to yes.

   I have, at this point, moved beyond Facebook-stalking
my outlier—listen, that was her joke at first, not mine, and
I think there's a three-month minimum before you can actually call someone your girlfriend. Point is, I've moved
past casually Facebook-stalking Maddie and into *deep* Face
book stalking.

   I wanted to look at pictures of Maddie as a kid. I just
did, okay, I stand by that, I stand by my own weirdness,
because, yeah, when I say it like that, it makes me sound
like a weirdo. But hopefully a romantic weirdo. *Anyway.*
So I dug through Maddie's Facebook looking for pictures
and couldn't find any picture of her pre-2009. Nothing.
And, like, I don't know, maybe she was an ugly teenager

or something or wanted to do an online makeover. But there's not even pictures that her friends had posted.

And, like, because I was bored on the Internet, and because I'm a jerk, I went and searched for [garbled], her hometown, and I couldn't even find it. And that's where it stops being sort of jerky and starts being kind of stalkery, because then I actually went to the library and looked in an atlas and still couldn't find it. Nothing.

[13 seconds of ambient silence. A siren passes nearby. It fades into the soft noise of birdsong, barely audible.]

NITA: I don't know why, but this feels like . . . a red flag? Yeah. And if it was anybody else, I'd probably ghost. Block her number, stop answering her texts. I should have renamed my project: autoethnography of a ghost. Wait, no. A ghoster? I dunno. But, like, I've ghosted everyone that came before Maddie, and usually for similar stupid-ass reasons. Except for my high school girlfriend, because you can't really ghost someone that you had four classes with, although trust me, *I tried.*

[12 seconds of ambient silence. Nita sighs. Her breath has weight.]

NITA: This is the most masturbatory thing I've ever done as an artist. Except for that time I pretended to masturbate onstage. Ugh. Nita *out.*

[End of recorded material.]

Entry 8.

[Beginning of recorded material.]

[Garbled.]

MADDIE: —boutique hotel, and I swear to God, they, like, origami the pillowcases and towels.

NITA: In Anacortes?

MADDIE: Yeah. It's weird going there in the off-season, but we had a good time.

NITA: You didn't go to your mom's place at all?

MADDIE: . . . I don't really like going to [garbled].

NITA: Still, it seems weird to go all the way out there for Thanksgiving and not even, like, go to your mom's house.

[. . .]

NITA: Sorry. That came out—

MADDIE: No, I know it's—

NITA: Really didn't mean to sound that . . . that . . .

MADDIE: Judgey. You sounded judgey.

NITA: Shit. I'm not judging you. I'm not, really. I'm just, like
—you make me *intensely* curious, and I'm trying to, like.
Curb that. But it's hard.

MADDIE: Thanks. I think.

NITA: I just think you're super-interesting, and I know it's su-
per dorky, but I—I really like you. And I want to know you.

[. . .]

NITA: Look, is this still about the ethnography? Because I
promise that I—

MADDIE: I don't need you to promise anything, okay? That's
not what I'm asking for.

[Ambient noise. Chairs shifting on the linoleum, someone's fingers tapping nervously on the tabletop. The kitchen table sounds
like it has gotten larger, stretching to a gulf between them.]

NITA: You could. Ask me to. I'd promise . . . shit, Maddie, I'd
promise you a lot.

[Chair scraping.]

NITA: [Closer to microphone.] Ask me to promise you something.

MADDIE: [Hoarse, soft.] I don't care if you . . . if you're curious, okay? I don't care if you dig up everything. But you
can't ask *me* about it, okay? It's hard enough, keeping—

[them]

MADDIE: —it all out of my head.

NITA: Okay. I won't ask you.

[Sound of kissing.]

[. . .]

[Time is running out.]

[End of recorded material.]

Entry 9.

[Beginning of recorded material.]

[Traffic. Voices. The subtle rumble of an underground train.

Sparrows and starlings squawking. Bicycle bells.]

> MADDIE: So I've discovered how to make voice recordings on my phone. I guess that makes this a self-ethnography. Or something. Maybe it's just a confession? Whatever. This is weird. I don't know how you do this, Nita. I don't know if I'm going to send you this.

[23 seconds of ambient noise and birdsong.]

> MADDIE: I'm not supposed to—I told you that I can't talk about this. I'm not supposed to say anything about [garbled] or what happened to . . .

[Don't]

> MADDIE: They stick in my throat, even now, even here. I'm in Daley Plaza because it's the farthest place I can think of from, from the woods, from . . .

[13 seconds of ambient noise. The sound of birds intensifies.]

[say their names.]

> MADDIE: Nita, you think I want you to give this up because it's too personal. I don't. I want you to keep going *because* it's personal. It's been four years since I left and it's getting harder to stay away, and harder to . . .

[Maddie coughs harshly.]

> MADDIE: I . . .

[The sound of birds and coughing intensifies.]

[Time is . . .]

> MALE VOICE: Miss? Miss? Are you okay?

> MADDIE: [Hoarse] I'm fine. Thanks, I'm fine.

> MALE VOICE: Are you sure? You want me to—

> MADDIE: [Stronger.] Yeah, I'm okay. Thanks for—

[Come home.]

> MALE VOICE: What was that?

> MADDIE: I said that I'm fine.

[Come home.]

[Footsteps.]

[Come home.][Come home.][Come home.][Come home.]
[Come home.][Come home.][Come home.][Come home.]
[Come home.][Come home.][Come home.][Come home.]
[Come home.][Come home.][Come home.][Come home.]
[Come home.][Come home.][Come home.][Come

> [End of recording.]

Entry 10.

[Beginning of recorded material.]
MADDIE: Can't believe you never heard about this, you're the one who's always carrying this thing around.
NITA: Uh, maybe, but they didn't cover ghost-hunting in *Sound Engineering for Dummies.*
MADDIE: It's not just for ghosts, it's for . . . I dunno. Anything that might have something to say.
NITA: So people just leave the recorder running and . . . wait?
MADDIE: Leave it in an empty room and see what might be willing to speak.
NITA: Spoopy shit.
MADDIE: I'm a spoopy girl.
NITA: I know. I like it. Spoopy outlier girl.
[Maddie laughs; the sound of it is thin, brittle.]
NITA: Now what?
MADDIE: Now we leave it. Come back later and see if anything decided to leave us a message.
[Footsteps.]
NITA: Like a voicemail for ghosts.
MADDIE: Not just ghosts.
NITA: Like "4:33" for the spirit world.
MADDIE: Like what?
[A door closes.]
NITA: [Fainter] What? Have you never heard of—[inaudible]
[1:25:21 of ambient silence.]
[A bird calls, a harsh whistle. So loud that it might be inside the room.]
[43:57 of static.]
[End of recorded material.]

Entry 11.

[Beginning of recorded material.]
[Static.]

MADDIE: Hi, this is Nita Rosen, coming to you live from the bedroom where I just fucked my girlfriend before trying to unconvincingly tell her that—

NITA: Oh my God, would you—

MADDIE: *That!* I, like, totally don't want to go to her mom's house for Christmas.

NITA: I do *not* sound like that.

MADDIE: Despite the fact that it gives me the perfect opportunity to dig up all kinds of dirt about her, which is the only reason I've stayed with this freak show this long. Stay tuned. This is NPR.

NITA: Are you done?

MADDIE: Oh, *fuck* no. Let me get my Terry Gross voice on. So why the sudden flip-flop, Nita? Were you getting too close to your subject? Sorry, your *outlier?* Sudden crisis of conscience, or did you just get bored and want—

NITA: Can you please turn it off?

MADDIE: Oh, no. I want this on the record.

NITA: I found out who Emily is.

[9 seconds of silence. No ambient noise at all.]

[Don't say her name.]

MADDIE: [Whispering.] Don't say her name.

[End of recording.]

Entry 12.

[Beginning of recorded material.]

NITA: One teen missing, another in critical condition after car crash in [garbled]. Underage drinking suspected as factor. The totaled car was found off Old Coach Highway in—

[4 seconds of static.]

NITA: —damage to the front and side of the car. Magdalena Lanuza, eighteen, was found in the car, several hours after the crash. The car fell from Old Coach Highway into a gully thirty feet below the road. Lanuza claims she was accompanied by eighteen-year-old Emily Longham, who is still missing. In a statement, Emily Longham's mother, Abigail, said she believes her daughter is still out there. *I'd know it if she were truly gone,* she told reporters. The sheriff's office has organized a search party. Those interested in volunteering are encouraged to call the number listed below. When asked if they were looking for—

[2 seconds of static; harsh, unyielding, angry.]

NITA: —or a body, the sheriff's department gave no comment.

[11 seconds of ambient silence and static. She's weighing the past four months with what she knows now. She's thinking of long, ropy scars that rake across Maddie's spine.]

NITA: And that's it. No follow-up, as far as I can see. One girl nearly dies and another disappears, you'd assume that a small-town paper would be brooding on this shit for weeks, right? But there's nothing else online at all. No Facebook pictures, no memorials of this girl. I can't even find her parents. So here's the thing: this is really obviously a trauma that's in Maddie's past, and it looks so much more interesting than it did when I first saw those scars. And I want to find out more and I fucking hate that I do. I hate myself for looking at Maddie and seeing a . . .

[An outlier.]

NITA: I don't know what to do besides walk away from it. From all of it. She deserves someone who's not a . . . flaky weirdo artist with a voice diary. I . . .

[Don't.]

NITA: I don't know.

[Don't make her go alone.]

NITA: I don't know what to do.

[End of recorded material.]

Entry 13.

[Beginning of recorded material.]

VOICE: You have reached seven seven three [garbled]. Please leave your message after the tone.

[3 seconds of silence. Nita—]

[Static.]

NITA: Hey, it's me. I'm—I don't like how we ended things

last night. I want to . . . I don't know. I don't know what I
want. I'm sorry. Just give me a call.

[End of recorded material.]

Entry 14.

[Beginning of recorded material.]

VOICE: You have reached seven seven three [garbled]. Please
leave your message after the tone.

NITA: Yeah actually, I do know what I want. I want you. I
don't know what that means in the context of you and this
thing about your home and—

[Don't say her name.]

NITA: —and what happened to you. And I don't know what
you want, or why it's suddenly really fucking important for
you to go to the creepy town that you've been avoiding
for five years and for me to go with you, but, like. Okay. I
don't know. I wish you would have picked up the phone so
I could actually say this to you and not your—

VOICE: If you would like to hear your message, please press—

NITA: God DAMN it.

[End of recorded material.]

Entry 15.

[Beginning of recorded material.]

VOICE: December. Second. Two thousand thirteen. Voice-
mail from phone number seven seven three [garbled].

MADDIE: Hey. It's me. I . . .

[Static.]

[4 seconds of silence.]

MADDIE: Sorry, there's something weird going on with this
connection. So, like, here's the point. You're still invited
for Christmas. If you want to go. I want you with me. I don't
want to be alone when—

[Static. Angry, electric buzzing. A high, sweet whistle.]

MADDIE: —pick up. If you call me I'll pick up.

[. . .]

[End of recorded material.]

[Sorry.]

Entry 16.

[Beginning of recorded material.]

[Car engine.]

NITA: Wow, it really is . . .

MADDIE: Creepy? Dark?

NITA: Isolated. I was gonna say isolated, but yeah, those other things too. You really did grow up in the sticks. Jesus, these roads are terrifying.

MADDIE: It's not the roads you have to worry about.

[. . .]

NITA: What the hell did you just say?

MADDIE: I said you don't have to worry about the roads.

NITA: That's . . . That's not—

MADDIE: Listen to me, okay? You'll be safe here. You're a stranger here and that's the best thing you can be.

NITA: What does that even mean? I thought this was just a family visit!

MADDIE: You know it's more than that. What you need to know now— [Coughs.]

[Coughing continues.]

MADDIE: [Choking.] Just be prepared, okay? I . . .

NITA: Maddie, what's wrong? Jesus, Maddie—

[Gravel under the wheels, a *clunk* as the gear shifts into park. Maddie's breath is labored, whistling high in her throat.]

NITA: What is this, what's wrong? Are you having an asthma attack or something?

MADDIE: [Hoarse.] It's fine. I wish— [Coughs.]

[They are only half a mile from the road where Maddie's car accident occurred.]

[They are a tiny beacon of light in dark, quiet hills.]

[They don't feel the gaze of those who are watching.]

NITA: Should I drive? These roads are scary as fuck, but I can drive.

[A door opens. Birdsong and rain. Maddie's breath smooths out.]

NITA: Here, do you want some water?

[. . .]

NITA: We don't have to stay at your mom's house. We can go back to Lyndon, or even Anacortes. Fuck it, we can go back to Seattle if you—

MADDIE: [Hoarse.] No. I'm all right. We're here now, we might as well . . . Might as well finish the trip.

[End of recorded material.]

Entry 17.

[Beginning of recorded material.]

NITA: So. Here I am. Maddie's mom, Evie, is super-nice. Her house is really pretty, up on the side of a mountain. There's a creek nearby. Lots of woods and moss, as promised. It's seriously in the middle of nowhere, though. I'm not sure what I was imagining, but . . . I'd originally thought that I could, like, do some detective work while I was here. This is so embarrassing, and it's so obvious that I watched way too much TV. But I imagined myself, like, going into town and talking to the old dudes who'd be drinking coffee, and they'd be unfriendly and I'd charm them into telling me how—

[Sharp, squealing burst of static.]

NITA: What the fuck was that?

[. . .]

NITA: Weird.

[Time is running out.]

NITA: But Maddie was right, there's not really a town here. There is a gas station, which is also the post office and a hardware store. And I guess it's a movie store too, since they had this, like, bucket of DVDs you could rent for a few dollars each. Maddie said there's a couple churches too, but they're like, *Children of the Corn* meets *Deliverance*, you could not fucking pay me enough to step foot in one. I didn't even realize that we'd passed through the town until we hit a dirt road and it got even more woodsy.

[. . .]

NITA: Maddie—

[Nita starts to cough.]

[The sound of the wind. The sound of birds in the trees.]

[End of recorded material.]

Entry 18.

[Beginning of recorded material.]

NITA: Okay, the timestamp is uh, 8:03. Morning of December 23rd. I'm, uh, I'm interviewing Evie Lanuza, mother of Maddie. [Clears throat.] Though I'm . . . not sure why?

EVIE: Well, my daughter told me about your project.

NITA: My project? Oh, sh— She did? Okay. Uh. What did she tell you exactly?

EVIE: Just that you were interested in where she'd grown up, this little town, and you know. What happened to her.

NITA: [Laughs.] Yeah, that, uh. That's basically it, yeah.

EVIE: So what exactly do you want to know, Nita?

NITA: Well. Actually. Before we get started, I was wondering if you had any pictures of [Coughs.] Maddie when she was a kid. Which is probably weird, but I was just, like, thinking that she must have been a really cute—

EVIE: I don't. I don't keep pictures.

NITA: . . . Oh. Is there, um, a reason for that?

EVIE: Yes.

[. . .]

EVIE: Did you want more coffee? You look a little . . .

NITA: Sure. That'd be good.

[4 seconds of ambient noise, persistent birdsong and rain, and the sound of coffee being poured into an old, chipped mug.]

NITA: Thanks. So—

EVIE: My husband grew up here, and even though he managed to get away to Port Townsend, he always knew he'd come back, but he put it off as long as he could. This place has a way of sinking its hooks into you.

NITA: Yeah?

EVIE: He resisted coming back for so long. It almost broke us up, to tell the truth. But he came around eventually.

NITA: Yeah. Uh. Can I just ask—

EVIE: Go ahead.

NITA: Where is, uh, Mr. Lanuza? Is he still, like, around?

EVIE: He passed on. Not long after we moved back.

[. . .]

NITA: That's . . . I'm sorry.

EVIE: Oh, you don't have to say that. But I think it's what made Maddie [Coughs.] . . . I think that's what really soured her on this town. And then the car accident with her friend. She left soon after, and I couldn't blame her. But it's like I said. This town gets its claws into you, and it doesn't let go. I'm glad she's back. I'm glad you're here with her.

[. . .]

NITA: I'm going to see if—[Clears throat.]—if Maddie's awake.

EVIE: Take some coffee up to her. I always loved it when my special someone did that for me.

[End of recorded material.]

Entry 19.

[Beginning of recorded material.]

[Footsteps. Birdsong. Rain on a dirt road.]

NITA: Okay, so I'm like . . . seventy-five percent sure that I'm not lost. I'm pretty sure I'm still on the road that Maddie — [Coughs.]

NITA: Fucking allergies. Anyway, the road where she had her car accident. And she was super-understanding when I told her that I wanted to see it, and agreed that it was better if I satisfied my stupid-ass curiosity by myself. Well, she didn't say it was stupid, but in retrospect, it definitely was. 'Cause, like, I can find my way around pretty much anywhere in Chicago, even when I'm high as fuck or drunk off my ass. But apparently I can't find my way around anywhere that's not on a grid. And of course because it's goddamn December, the sun is buried behind the clouds. So I don't know if I'm headed in the right direction. And there's something that's just, like, hugely creepy about being surrounded by trees. I'm never leaving the city again. No wonder— [Clears throat.]—no wonder Maddie never comes back here. This is what I get for being such a—

[12 seconds of silence.]

[You're looking for something.]

NITA: [Whispering] What the *fuck*—

[Maybe you found it.]

[Car engine. Tires on wet pavement.]

MALE VOICE: Hey, you want a ride?

NITA: Uh. I think I got turned around. Do you know how to get to—

[Static.]

MALE VOICE: I do. But are you sure that's where you want to go? That's a lonely little spot.

NITA: I think. Yeah. I mean, I just want to see it. A friend of mine, she was in an accident there—

MALE VOICE: I don't need to know your business, miss. I'll drop you off there and let you find your own way back.

NITA: . . . Thanks.

[. . .]

[Radio turns on; country music. Signal fades in and out of static.]

NITA: Did you know either of the girls that were in the accident?

MALE VOICE: I didn't, no.

NITA: What about, uh, a Mr. Lanuza? He died, like, eight or nine years ago. I don't know his first name—

MALE VOICE: Listen, miss. You should keep their names out of your mouth, okay? You're a stranger here. Keep it that way.

[. . .]

NITA: [Faintly.] All right. Never mind, then.

MALE VOICE: That's it, over there. Careful on the shoulder, though. It's slippery from all the rain, and the guardrail's on its last legs.

[Door opens.]

NITA: Thanks.

MALE VOICE: Take care. And don't stay out here too long. It gets dark early.

NITA: Thanks, I got it.

[Door closes.]

[Static increases. Sounds like water, like wings, like song, like—]

NITA: —weird as it could have—
[Static.]
NITA: —so far to fall—
[Static.]
NITA: —waiting in the dark for—
[Static.]
[You should go.]
NITA: —should get going. It's—
[It's getting dark.]
NITA: Maddie's— [Coughs.] And it's getting dark.
[End of recorded material.]

Entry 20.

[Beginning of recorded material.]
[Voices, just on the edge of hearing. Creaking footsteps. The volume turns up, and the voices become audible.]
EVIE: I like her.
MADDIE: I like her too.
EVIE: I'm glad you found someone who's . . . someone good.
    Strange but good.
[. . .]
EVIE: Aren't you glad?
[. . .]
EVIE: Do you regret bringing her here, sweetie?
MADDIE: I wish we hadn't come at all.
EVIE: Don't say that, Ma— [Coughs.]
MADDIE: Mom, I'm—
EVIE: I know you wish you could have stayed longer. I tried to
    —I tried to help. I thought you'd have longer. It's almost
    over, though.
MADDIE: She doesn't know about— [Coughs.] About—
[Coughing intensifies.]
EVIE: Sweetheart, shhh. You don't—
[Coughing intensifies and turns into sounds of choking.]
NITA: Oh my God—
[Footsteps.]
NITA: What's wrong with her?
EVIE: She's fine, she's fine, give her some room to breathe—

NITA: Baby, it's—

EVIE: I said to *give her room*. It'll pass in a minute, as soon as
   she—

[Choking; retching.]

EVIE: Sweetheart, listen to me. You need to calm down. Clear
   your mind. There's mud in your mind, and you need to let
   the river wash it clean, okay? Let the water in and let it
   carry that mud away, out of your mind, out of your lungs.
   Stop fighting it. Let it in. The water goes in, and the mud
   goes out. In. Out. In. Ou—

[Vomiting.]

EVIE: There you go.

[Maddie's breathing has eased.]

[Nita is crying.]

NITA: What the fuck is . . .

EVIE: Nita, will you get some paper towels to wipe this up?

[. . .]

EVIE: *Nita.*

NITA: Huh?

EVIE: Get some paper towels from the kitchen.

NITA: . . . Okay.

[Footsteps.]

EVIE: There you go, honey. You're fine. Everything's fine. It's
   almost over.

[End of recorded material.]

Entry 21.

[Beginning of recorded material.]

[44 seconds of ambient silence.]

MADDIE: Are you asleep?

NITA: No.

MADDIE: I'm sorry about what happened.

NITA: You don't have to be. I'm just . . . God, that scared the
   hell out of me.

[. . .]

NITA: Where did that . . . It looked like feathers. And dirt.
   How did it get in your . . .

MADDIE: Don't. Please, don't . . .

NITA: Don't *what?* What the fuck is happening? This went from fine to completely fucked up in, like, a day, and Maddie— [Coughing, so sudden and painful that it turns into gagging.]

MADDIE: Shh, baby. Stop.

NITA: I can taste it. Dirt in my mouth. You said I'd be safe.

MADDIE: . . . You don't have to be scared.

NITA: Like hell. You know what, fuck this. We should leave.

MADDIE: You wanted this. You wanted to know. You kept *asking*—

NITA: Yeah, because I'm a fucking asshole who thought solving this weird-ass mystery would make good art. I changed my mind. Let's leave.

MADDIE: But my mom—

NITA: Your mom is not the one gagging up mud and feathers, Madd— [Coughs.] I can't even— [Coughs.]

MADDIE: Shhh, baby, it's fine. All right. We can go in the morning.

NITA: [Hoarse.] Now. Right now.

[. . .]

NITA: Please.

[. . .]

MADDIE: Okay, okay. Get your stuff together. I'll tell my mom we're—

NITA: Please, don't. Just . . . write her a note, okay. I don't even care about my stuff, I am so fucking scared right now—

MADDIE: All right, we can go. We'll find somewhere to stay outside of town.

NITA: Thank you, oh my God, babe, thank you so much. I'm so sorry I even—

MADDIE: It's okay, just . . . just pack what you can. I'll go write my mom a note.

NITA: Okay. Okay. Yeah. I can do that.

[Footsteps.]

[A lamp clicks on.]

[. . .]

EVIE: [Whispering] Is it time?

MADDIE: I . . .

EVIE: It's sooner than I thought it would be. But it's not too

late. That's the important thing. We don't want a repeat of
what happened to Emily. It's better this way.

MADDIE: Is it?

EVIE: Don't fight it. She might still be able to get away.

[Footsteps. Rustling fabric. An embrace.]

EVIE: I love you, sweetheart. Be brave. I'll miss you, but I
know you'll always be close now.

[Be brave.]

[The lamp clicks off. Footsteps.]

NITA: Did you write the note?

MADDIE: [Clears throat.] Yeah.

NITA: Are you . . . are you okay? Sorry, I'm so fucking freaked
out I didn't even think—

MADDIE: It's all right. I'll be fine in a minute. [Takes a
breath. Sniffs.] Are you packed?

NITA: I can't find my recorder. Have you seen it?

MADDIE: Maybe it's in the car.

NITA: Why would it . . . You know what, I don't even care.
Let's just get the fuck out of here.

MADDIE: All right. Before we go, can I just . . .

[It's a goodbye kiss, but Nita doesn't know that.]

NITA: Ready?

MADDIE: Yeah.

[Footsteps. A door opens and closes. The sound of night: wind
slapping against wet leaves, rain hitting gravel. The car doors open
and shut, and the engine turns on. So does the radio: nothing but
loud, angry static.]

NITA: Fuck!

[The radio shuts off. The car shifts into gear, and then gravel
crunches under the tires as they start to drive.]

[4:21 minutes of ambient noise.]

MADDIE: I'm actually grateful, you know. That I came back.
That you got me to come back.

NITA: You were right. I shouldn't have kept asking you. It
was—

MADDIE: I needed to do it. I'd put it off for so long.

NITA: Put what off?

MADDIE: I'd almost forgotten. You woke something back up.
Your questions.

NITA: Mad— [Coughs.] What are you talking about?

MADDIE: It was almost too late.

[. . .]

NITA: Look, I'm already freaked the hell out, so if you could just do me a favor and not be all fucking cryptic—

MADDIE: Remember what I said when we were on our way here? You're safe. You're safe because you're a stranger. You're right to want to get out of here as soon as you can. This place . . . It does something to you. Doesn't matter how far you go, it's always pulling you back. That's what happened to my dad, and it was— Emily knew there was no point in trying to get away, but I insisted, and she—

NITA: Ma—[Chokes.]

MADDIE: Don't. It's okay. Don't try to fight it.

NITA: Fight what? Jesus, what . . .

[The engine has grown louder.]

NITA: Can you slow down?

MADDIE: It won't change what happens next.

NITA: Oh my God. Please, whatever you're thinking of doing, please don't.

MADDIE: I am so lucky I met you. I'm just— I always thought I'd be alone, and that nobody would know my name. I'm so grateful that you're here.

[You're here.]

MADDIE: Try not to think about me, okay? Just leave me behind. Don't even say—

[The crash through the guardrails takes them both by surprise, and they scream the entire way down.]

[A scream with shattered glass and scraping metal; a scream that wrenches itself open from the inside.]

[A scream infused with something inhuman, old as mountains, wild as a bird suddenly breaking free from a cage, electric in the air, a scream with blood on its teeth and torn skin on the tips of its claws.]

[End of recorded material.]

Entry 22.

[Beginning of recorded material.]

[1:32 minutes of ambient noise: traffic, voices, dogs barking.]

NITA: Timestamp. It's, uh, 3:28 in the afternoon. January
       10th, 2014.

[. . .]

NITA: I'm moving out tomorrow. Um. I can't really do stairs
       that well, at least until the leg brace comes off, so I'll be
       staying at my mom's. I'm just here to grab some clothes
       and things. And to leave this recorder on.

[. . .]

NITA: I guess what I'm saying is, if you have anything else you
       want to say, I'll be listening. I'll leave the recorder on in
       the empty room. Let it run until the battery dies, I guess.

[. . .]

[Footsteps, uneven and limping. A door creaks as it closes.]

[. . .]

[. . .]

[. . .]

[. . .]

[

.

.

.

]

[Are you sure you want to hear what we have to say?]

LESLEY NNEKA ARIMAH

Skinned

FROM *McSweeney's Quarterly Concern*

THE UNCLOTHED WOMAN had a neatly trimmed bush, waxed to resemble a setting sun. The clothed women sneered as she laid out makeup and lotion samples, touting their benefits. "Soft, smooth skin, as you can see," she said, winking—trying, and failing, to make a joke of her nakedness. Chidinma smiled in encouragement, nodding and examining everything Ejem pulled out of the box. Having invited Ejem to present her wares, she would be getting a free product out of this even if none of her guests made a purchase.

Ejem finished her sales pitch with a line about how a woman's skin is her most important feature and she has to take care of it like a treasured accessory. The covered women tittered and smoothed their tastefully patterned wife-cloths over their limbs. They wore them simply, draped and belted into long, graceful dresses, allowing the fabric to speak for itself. They eyed Ejem's nakedness with gleeful pity.

"I just couldn't be uncovered at your age. That's a thing for the younger set, don't you think?"

"I have a friend who's looking for a wife; maybe I can introduce you. He's not picky."

Ejem rolled her eyes, less out of annoyance than to keep tears at bay. Was this going to happen every time? She looked to Chidinma for help.

"Well, I for one am here for lotions, not to discuss covered versus uncovered, so I'd like this one." Chidinma held up the most expensive cream. Ejem made a show of ringing it up, and the other women were embarrassed into making purchases of their own. They stopped speaking to Ejem directly and began to treat her as if she were a woman of the osu caste. They addressed prod-uct questions to the air or to Chidinma, and listened but did not acknowledge Ejem when she replied. Ejem might have protested, as would have Chidinma, but they needed the sales party to end before Chidinma's husband returned. It was the only stipulation Chidinma had made when she'd agreed to host. It was, in fact, the only stipulation of their friendship. *Don't advertise your availability to my husband.* Chidinma always tried to make a joking compliment of it—"You haven't had any kids yet, so your body is still amazing" —but there was always something strained there, growing more strained over the years as Ejem remained unclaimed.

The woman who had first addressed Chidinma instead of Ejem, whom Ejem had begun to think of as the ringleader, noticed them glancing at the clock, gave a sly smile, and requested that each and every product be explained to her. Ejem tried, she really did, whip-ping through the product texts with speed, but the clock sped just as quickly and eventually Chidinma stopped helping her, subdued by inevitable embarrassment. Before long, Chidinma's husband returned from work.

Chance was all right, as husbands went. He oversaw the man-agement of a few branches of a popular bank, a job that allowed them to live comfortably in their large house with an osu woman to spare Chidinma serious housework. He could even be consid-ered somewhat progressive; after all, he had permitted his wife's continued association with her unclothed friend, and he wasn't the sort to harass an osu woman in his employ. True, he insisted on a formal greeting, but after Chidinma had bowed to him she raised herself to her tiptoes for a kiss and Chance indulged her, fisting his hands in the wife-cloth at the small of her back.

But he was still a man, and when he turned to greet the women his eyes caught on Ejem and stayed there, taking in the brown disks of her areolae, the cropped design of hair between her legs, whatever parts of her went unhidden in her seated position. No one said anything, the utter impropriety of an unclaimed woman being in the house of a married man almost too delicious a social faux pas to interrupt. But as Chidinma grew visibly distressed, the ringleader called the room to order and the women rose to leave, bowing their heads to Chance, giving Chidinma's hands encour-aging little squeezes. No doubt the tale would make the rounds —"the way he *stared* at her"—and Chidinma wouldn't be able to escape it for a while. The women walked by Ejem without a word, the message clear: Ejem was beneath them.

Chidinma tried to distract her husband by asking about his day. Chance continued to stare at Ejem while he answered. Ejem wanted to move faster, to get out as quick as she could, but she was conscious of every sway of her breasts, every brush of her thighs as she hurried. Chance spoke to Ejem only as she was leaving, a goodbye she returned with a small curtsy. Chidinma walked her to the door.

"Ejem, we should take a break from each other, I think," she said with a pained air of finality, signaling that this break wasn't likely to be a temporary one.

"Why?"

"You know why."

"You're going to have to say it, Chidinma."

"Fine. This whole thing, this friendship, was fine when we were both uncovered girls doing whatever, but covered women can't have uncovered friends. I thought it was nonsense at first, but it's true. I'm sorry."

"You've been covered for thirteen years and this has never been a problem."

"And I thought by this time you'd be covered too. You came so close with that one fellow, but you've never really tried. It's unseemly."

"He's only seen me this *once* since you made it clear—"

"Once was enough. Get covered. Get claimed. Take yourself off the market. Until then, I'm sorry, but no."

Chidinma went back inside the house before Ejem could respond. And what could she say anyway? *I'm not sure I ever want to be claimed?* Chidinma would think her mad.

Ejem positioned her box to better cover her breasts and walked to the bus stop. Chidinma hadn't offered her a ride home, even though she knew how much Ejem hated public transportation— the staring as she lay the absorbent little towel square on her seat, the paranoia of imagining every other second what to do if her menstrual cup leaked.

At the stop, a group of young men waited. They stopped talking when they saw Ejem, then resumed, their conversation now centered on her.

"How old you think she is?"

"Dude, old."

"I don't know, man. Let's see her breasts. She should put that box down."

They waited and Ejem ignored them, keeping as much of herself as possible shielded with the box and the cosmetic company's branded tote.

"That's why she's unclaimed. Rudeness. Who's gonna want to claim that?"

They continued in that vein until the bus arrived. Even though the men were to board first, they motioned her ahead, a politeness that masked their desire for a better view. She scanned the passengers for other uncovered women—solidarity and all that —and was relieved to spot one. The relief quickly evaporated. The woman was beautiful, which would have stung on its own, but she was young too, smooth-skinned and firm. Ejem stopped existing for the group of young men. They swarmed the woman, commenting loudly on the indentation of her waist, the solid curve of her arm. The young woman took it all in stride, scrolling a finger down the pages of her book.

Ejem felt at once grateful and slighted, remembering how it had been in her youth, before her waist had thickened and her ass drooped. She'd never been the sort to wear nakedness boldly, but she'd at least felt that she was pleasant to look at.

The bus took on more passengers and was three-quarters full when an osu woman boarded. Ejem caught herself doing a double-take before averting her gaze. It wasn't against the law; it just wasn't done, since the osu had their own transport, and the other passengers looked away as well. Embarrassed. Annoyed. Even the bus driver kept his eyes forward as the woman counted out her fare. And when she finally appeared in the center aisle, no one made the polite shift all passengers on public transportation know, that nonverbal invitation to take a neighboring seat. So even though there were several spots available, the osu woman remained standing. Better that than climb her naked body over another to sit down. It was the type of subtle social correction, Ejem thought, that would cause a person to behave better in the future.

But as the ride progressed, the osu woman squeezing to let by passengers who didn't even acknowledge her, Ejem softened. She was so close to becoming an unseen woman herself, unanchored from the life and the people she knew, rendered invisible. It was only by the grace of birth that she wasn't osu, her mother had said to her the very last time they spoke. "At least you have a choice, Ejem. So choose wisely." She hadn't, had walked away from a man and his proposal and the protection it offered. Her parents had cut her off then, furious and confounded that she'd bucked tradition. She couldn't explain, not even to herself, why she'd looked at the cloth he proffered and seen a weight that would smother her.

At her stop Ejem disembarked, box held to her chest. With the exception of a few cursory glances, no one paid attention to her. It was one of the reasons she liked the city, everybody's inclination to mind their own business. She picked up the pace when she spotted the burgundy awning of her apartment building. In the elevator an older male tenant examined her out of the corner of his eye. Ejem backed up until he would have had to turn around to continue looking. One could never tell if a man was linked or not, and she hated being inspected by men who'd already claimed wives.

In her apartment she took a long, deep breath, the type she didn't dare take in public lest she draw unwanted attention. Only then did she allow herself to contemplate the loss of Chidinma's friendship, and weep.

When they were girls, still under their fathers' covering, she and Chidinma had become fast friends. They were both new to their school and their covers were so similar in pattern they were almost interchangeable. Ejem remembered their girlhood fondly, the protection of their fathers' cloth, the seemingly absolute security of it. She had cried when, at fifteen, her mother had come into her bedroom and, stroking her hair, told Ejem that it was time to remove her cloth. The only people who could get away with keeping their daughters covered for long were the wealthy, who often managed it until the girls could secure wife-cloth. But Ejem's father had grown up a poor man in a village where girls were disrobed as early as possible, some even at age ten, and it was beyond time as far as he was concerned. He knew what happened to the families of girls who stayed covered beyond their station, with the exception of girls bearing such deformities that they were permitted "community cloth" made from donated scraps. But if a girl like Ejem continued to be clothed, the town council would levy a tax that would double again and again until her father could not pay it. Then his girl would be disrobed in public, and her family shamed. No, he couldn't bear the humiliation. Things would happen on his terms.

The day Ejem was disrobed was also the day her father stopped interacting with her, avoiding the impropriety of a grown man talking to a naked girl. Ejem hadn't wanted to go to school or market or anywhere out of the house where people could see her. Chidinma, still under her father-cloth, told her (horrified, well-off) parents that she too felt ready to disrobe, so that she and Ejem could face the world together, two naked foundlings.

Chidinma's parents had tried to spin it as piousness, a daughter disrobed earlier than she had to be because she was so dedicated to tradition. But it'd had the stink of fanaticism and they'd lost many friends, something for which, Chidinma confided, her parents had never forgiven her.

A part of Ejem had always believed they'd be claimed at the same time, but then Chidinma had secured a wife-cloth at twenty, with Ejem as her chief maid. And then Chidinma gave birth to a boy, then two girls, who would remain covered their entire lives if Chidinma had anything to say about it. And through it all, Ejem remained uncovered, unclaimed, drifting until the likelihood passed her by.

She downed a mug of wine in one huge gulp, then another, before sifting through yesterday's mail. She opened the envelope she'd been avoiding: the notice of her upcoming lease renewal, complete with a bump in monthly rent. With the money she'd earned today, she had enough to cover the next two months. But the raised rent put everything in jeopardy, and Chidinma's abandonment meant Ejem could no longer sell to her wealthy set. If she couldn't secure income some other way, a move to a smaller town would soon be a necessity.

When she'd first leased the apartment, Ejem had been working at the corporate headquarters of an architecture firm. Though her nakedness drew some attention, there were other unclaimed women, and Ejem, being very good at what she did, advanced. Just shy of a decade later, she was over thirty, the only woman in upper management, and still uncovered.

Three months ago Ejem was delivering a presentation to a prospective client. As usual, she was the only woman in the room. The client paid no attention to her PowerPoint, focusing instead on what he considered to be the impropriety of an unclaimed woman distracting from business matters. Ejem was used to this and tried to steer the conversation back to the budget. When the man ignored her, none of her coworkers bothered to censure him, choosing instead to snicker into their paperwork. She walked out of the room.

Ejem had never gone to Human Resources before; she'd always sucked it up. The HR manager, a covered woman who was well into her fifties, listened to her with a bored expression, then, with a pointed look at Ejem's exposed breasts, said, "You can't seriously expect a group of men to pay attention to pie charts or whatever when there is an available woman in the room. Maybe if you were covered this wouldn't happen. Until you are, we can no longer put you in front of clients."

Ejem walked out of the building and never returned. She locked herself away at home until Chidinma came knocking with a bottle of vodka, her youngest girl on her hip, and a flyer for home-based work selling makeup.

Now that lifeline was gone, and it would be only a matter of time until Ejem exhausted her savings. She switched on the TV and flipped channels until she reached an uncovered young woman relating the news. The woman reported on a building fire in Onitsha and Ejem prepared dinner with the broadcast playing in the background, chopping vegetables for stir-fry until she registered the phrase *unclaimed women* repeated several times. She turned up the volume.

The newscaster had been joined by an older man with a paternal air, who gave more details.

"The building was rumored to be a haven of sorts for unclaimed women, who lived there, evading their responsibilities as cloth makers. Authorities halted firefighters from putting out the blaze, hoping to encourage these lost women to return to proper life. At least three bodies were discovered in the ashes. Their identities have yet to be confirmed."

That was the other reason Ejem wanted to remain in the metro area. Small towns were less tolerant of unclaimed women, some going so far as to outlaw their presence unless they were menials of the osu caste. They had a certain freedom, Ejem thought—these osu women who performed domestic tasks, the osu men who labored in the mines or constructed the buildings she'd once designed— though her envy was checked by the knowledge that it was a freedom born of irrelevance. The only place for unclaimed women, however, as far as most were concerned, was the giant factories, where they would weave cloth for women more fortunate than they.

The town's mayor appeared at a press conference.

"This is a decent town with decent people. If folks want to walk around uncovered and unclaimed, they need to go somewhere else. I'm sorry about the property loss and the folks who couldn't get out, but this is a family town. We have one of the world's finest factories bordering us. They could have gone there." The screen flipped back to the newsman, who nodded sagely, his expression somehow affirming the enforcement of moral values even as it deplored the loss of life.

Ejem battled a bubble of panic. How long before her finances forced her out into the hinterlands, where she would have to join the cloth makers? She needed a job and she needed it fast.

What sorts of jobs could one do naked? Ejem was too old for anything entry-level, where she'd be surrounded day after day by twentysomethings who would be claimed quickly. Instead she looked for jobs where her nudity would be less of an issue. She lasted at a nursing home for five weeks, until a visiting relative objected to her presence. At the coffee shop she made it two and a half hours until she had to hide in the back to avoid a former coworker. She quit the next day. Everywhere she went heightened how sheltered she'd been at her corporate job. The farther from the center of town she searched, the more people stared at her openly, asking outright why she wasn't covered when they saw that she didn't bear the mark of an osu woman. Every once in a while Ejem encountered osu women forced outside by errands, branded by shaved heads with scarification scored above one ear. Other pedestrians avoided them as though they were poles or mailboxes or other such sidewalk paraphernalia. But Ejem saw them.

As her search became more desperate, every slight took a knife's edge, so that Ejem found herself bothered even by the young girls still covered in their father-cloth who snickered at her, unaware or not caring that they too would soon be stripped of protection. The worst were the pitying *Oh, honey* looks, the whispered assurances from older covered women that someone would eventually claim her.

After a while she found work giving massages at a spa. She enjoyed being where everyone was disrobed; the artificial equality was a balm. Her second week on the job, a woman walked in covered with one of the finest wife-cloths Ejem had ever seen. She ordered the deluxe package, consisting of every single service the spa offered.

"And may I have your husband's account number?"

"*My* account number," the woman emphasized, sliding her card across the counter.

The desk girl glared at the card, glared at the woman, then left to get the manager. Everyone in the waiting room stared.

The manager, a woman close to Ejem's age, sailed in, her haughty manner turning deferential and apologetic as soon as she caught sight of the client. "I'm so sorry. The girl is new, still in father-cloth. Please excuse her." The finely clothed one remained silent. "We will of course offer you a significant discount on your services today. Maria is ready to start on your massage right away."

"No," the woman said firmly. "I want *her* to do it." Ejem, who'd been pretending to straighten products on the shelves, turned to see the woman pointing at her.

Soon she was in one of the treatment rooms, helping the woman to disrobe, feeling the texture of the cloth, wanting to rub it against her cheek. She left to hang it and encountered the manager, who dragged her down the hall and spoke in a harsh whisper.

"Do you know who that is? That is Odinaka, *the* Odinaka. If she leaves here less than pleased, you will be fired. I hope I'm clear."

Ejem nodded, returning to the massage room in a nervous daze. Odinaka was one of a handful of independently wealthy women who flouted convention without consequences. She was unclaimed but covered herself anyway, and not in modest cloth either, but in fine, bold fabric that invited attention and scrutiny. She owned almost half the cloth factories across the globe. This unthinkable rebellion drew criticism, but her wealth ensured that it remained just that: words but no action.

Odinaka sat on the massage table, swinging her legs. At Ejem's direction she lay on her stomach while Ejem warmed oil between her hands. She coated Odinaka's ankles before sliding up to her calves, warming the tissue with her palms. She asked a few casual questions, trying to gauge whether she was a talker or preferred her massages silent. She needn't have worried. Not only did Odinaka give verbose replies, she had questions for Ejem herself. Before long she had pried from Ejem the story of how she'd come to be here, easing muscle tensions instead of pursuing a promising career as an architect.

"It doesn't seem fair, does it, that you have to remain uncovered?"

Ejem continued with the massage, unsure how to reply to such seditious sentiments.

"You know, you and I are very similar," Odinaka continued.

Ejem studied the woman's firm body, toned and slim from years of exercise. She considered the other ways in which they were different, not least that Odinaka had never had to worry about a bill in her life. She laughed.

"You are very kind, but we're nothing alike, though we may be of the same age," she responded, as lightly as she could, tilting the ending into a question. Odinaka ignored it, turning over to face her.

"I mean it; we are both ambitious women trying to make our way unclaimed in male-dominated fields."

Except, Ejem didn't say, *you are completely free in a way I am not, as covered as you wish to be.*

"Covering myself would be illegal—" she started.

"Illegal-smeagle. When you have as much money as I do, you exist above every law. Now, wouldn't you like to be covered too?"

Odinaka was her savior. She whisked Ejem away from her old apartment, helping her pay the fee to break her lease, and moved her into a building she owned in one of the city's nicest neighborhoods.

Ejem's quarters, a two-bedroom apartment complete with a generously sized kitchen, had the freshness of a deep clean, like it had been long vacant or had gone through a recent purge, stripped of the scent and personality of its previous occupant. The unit had a direct intercom to the osu women who took care of the place. Ejem was to make cleaning requests as needed, or requests for groceries that later appeared in her fridge. When Ejem mentioned the distance from the apartment to her job, Odinaka revealed that she didn't have to work if she didn't want to, and it was an easy choice not to return to the spa. The free time enabled her to better get to know the other women in the building.

There was Delilah, who seemed like a miniature Odinaka in dress and mannerisms but in possession of only half as much confidence. Doreen, a woman close to forty, became Ejem's favorite. She owned a bookstore—one that did well as far as bookstores went—and she had the air of someone who knew exactly who she was and liked it. She eschewed the option to self-clothe.

"Let them stare," Doreen would declare after a few glasses of wine. "This body is a work of art." She would lift her breasts with her hands, sending Ejem and the other women into tipsy giggles.

The remaining women—Morayo, Mukaso, and Maryam—were

polite but distant, performing enough social niceties to sidestep any allegations of rudeness, but only just. Ejem and Doreen called them the three Ms or, after a few drinks, "Mmm, no," for their recalcitrance. They sometimes joined in Odinaka's near-nightly cocktail hour, but within a few weeks the cadre solidified into Odinaka, Delilah, Doreen, and Ejem.

With this group of women there were no snide remarks about Ejem's nakedness, no disingenuous offers to introduce her to a man—any man—who could maybe look past her flaws. Odinaka talked about her vast business, Doreen about her small one, and they teased each other with terrible advice neither would ever take. Ejem talked some about the career she'd left behind but didn't have much to add. And for the first time her shyness was just shyness, not evidence of why she remained unclaimed, nor an invitation to be battered with advice on how she could improve herself.

Besides, Odinaka talked enough for everyone, interrupting often and dominating every topic. Ejem didn't mind, because of all of them, Odinaka had had the most interesting life, one of unrelenting luxury since birth. She'd inherited the weaving company from her father when he retired, almost a decade ago, which had caused an uproar. But if one of the wealthiest dynasties wanted a woman at the helm, it was a luxury they could purchase. And if that woman indulged in covering herself and collecting and caring for other unclaimed women, who had the power to stop her?

"I imagine creating a world," Odinaka often said, "where disrobing is something a woman does only by choice."

On Ejem's first night in the building, Odinaka had brought a length of cloth to her, a gift, she said, that Ejem could wear whenever she wanted. Ejem had stared at the fabric for hours. Even in the confines of the building, in her own unit, she didn't have the courage to put it on. At Odinaka's cocktail hour, Doreen would sit next to her and declare, "It's us against these bashful fuckers, Ejem," setting off an evening of gentle ribbing at everyone's expense.

"You really go to your store like that?" Ejem asked Doreen one afternoon. "Why don't you cover yourself? No one will say anything if they know you're one of Odinaka's women, right?" She was trying to convince herself that she too could don the cloth and go out in public without fear.

Doreen stopped perusing invoices to give Ejem all her attention. "Look, we have to live with this. I was disrobed at age ten.

Do you know what it feels like to be exposed so young? I hid for almost a decade before I found myself, my pride. No one will ever again make me feel uncomfortable in my own skin. I plan to remain unclaimed and uncovered for as long as I live, and no one can say a damn thing about it. Odinaka rebels in her own way, and I in mine. I don't yearn for the safety of cloth. If the law requires me to be naked, I will be naked. And I will be goddamned if they make me feel uncomfortable for *their* law."

The weeks of welcome, of feeling free to be her own person, took hold, and one night, when Ejem joined the other women in Odinaka's apartment, she did so covered, the cloth draped over her in a girl's ties, the only way she knew how. Doreen was the first one to congratulate her, and when she hugged Ejem, she whispered, "Rebel in your own way," but her smile was a little sad.

Odinaka crowed in delight, "Another one! We should have a party."

She mobilized quickly, dispensing orders to her osu women via intercom. Ejem had yet to see any of the osu at work, but whenever she returned to her quarters from Odinaka's or Doreen's, her bed was made, the bathroom mirror cleared of flecks, the scabs of toothpaste scrubbed from the sink, and the rooms themselves held an indefinable feeling of having only just been vacated.

In less than the hour it took Ejem and the other residents to get themselves ready for the party, Odinaka's quarters had become packed. Men and women, all clothed except Doreen, mingled and chatted. Doreen held court on the settee, sipping wine and bestowing coy smiles.

Ejem tried to join in, but even with the self-cloth, she couldn't help feeling like the uncovered woman she'd been her entire adult life. Odinaka tried to draw Ejem into her circle of conversation, but after Ejem managed only a few stilted rejoinders, she edged away, sparing herself further embarrassment. Ejem ended up in a corner watching the festivities.

She was not aware that she herself was being watched until a man she'd seen bowing theatrically to Odinaka leaned against the wall next to her.

"So you're the newest one, huh?"

"I suppose I am."

"You seem reasonable enough. Why are you unclaimed?"

Ejem tensed, wary.

"What's that supposed to mean, 'reasonable'?"

He ignored the question.

"Do you know I have been trying to claim that woman ever since she was a girl?" He nodded toward Odinaka. "Our union would have been legendary. The greatest cloth weaver with the greatest cotton grower. What do you think?"

Ejem shrugged. It was really none of her business.

"Instead she's busy collecting debris."

Stunned by his rudeness, Ejem turned away, but he only laughed and called to someone across the room. Suddenly every laugh seemed directed at her, every smile a smirk at her expense. She felt herself regressing into the girl who'd needed Chidinma's tight grip in hers before she could walk with her head high. She ducked out, intending to return to her quarters.

She ran into Delilah, who held a carved box under her arm, a prized family heirloom Ejem recognized from their many gatherings. It was one of the few objects Odinaka envied, as she could not secure one herself, unable to determine the origin of the antique. She was forever demanding that Delilah bring it out to be admired, though Delilah refused to let Odinaka have it examined or appraised, perfectly content to let her treasure remain a mystery.

Ejem didn't particularly like Delilah. She might have been a mini Odinaka, but unlike Odinaka, Delilah was pretentious and wore her fine breeding on her sleeve. Ejem's distress was visible enough that Delilah paused, glancing between her and the door that muted the soiree.

"Is everything okay?" she asked.

Ejem nodded, but a tight nod that said it was not. She watched Delilah's concern war with the promise of fun on the other side of the door. Delilah's movements, a particular twist in her shoulders, the way she clenched her fist, an angled tilt of her head, suddenly brought to Ejem's mind the osu woman on the bus. Something must have crossed her face, because Delilah lifted a furtive, self-conscious hand to pat her hair into place—right where an identifying scar would have been if a government midwife had scored it into her head when she was six months old and then refreshed it on return visits every two years until she turned eighteen. That practice was the extent of Ejem's osu knowledge. Her people lived side-by-side with the osu and they knew nothing of each other.

Looking at Delilah's box, it occurred to Ejem that an osu girl—if she were clever enough, audacious enough, in possession of impossibly thick hair—could take her most prized possession—say, a fine carved box that had been in the family for many generations—and sneak away in the middle of the night. She could travel farther than she had ever been in her life, to a city where no one knew her. And because she was clever, she could slip seamlessly into the world of the people she knew so well because she'd had to serve them all her life.

Before the thought could take hold, the uncertainty in Delilah's face was replaced by an artificial sweetness, and she patted Ejem's shoulder, saying, "Rest well, then," before escaping into the party.

Ejem was awoken at dawn by the last of the revelers leaving. She stayed in her apartment till eight, then took advantage of Odinaka's open-door policy to enter her benefactor's apartment. If she hadn't been there herself, she would never have believed it had been filled with partiers the night before. In three hours someone, or several someones, had transformed the wreckage of fifty guests—Ejem remembered at least two spilled wineglasses and a short man who'd insisted on making a speech from an end table—back into the clean, modern lines preferred by one of the wealthiest women in the world. A woman who apparently collected debris, like her. She wasn't exactly sure what she wanted to say to Odinaka—she couldn't childishly complain that one of the guests had insulted her—but she felt injured and sought some small soothing.

She found Odinaka lounging in her bed, covers pulled to her waist.

"Did you enjoy yourself, Ejem? I saw you talking to Aju. He just left, you know." She wiggled her brows.

Well. Ejem couldn't exactly condemn him now. "We had an interesting conversation," she said instead.

"'Interesting,' she says. I know he can be difficult. Never mind what he said."

Odinaka pressed the intercom and requested a breakfast tray, then began to recap the night, laughing at this and that event she didn't realize Ejem hadn't been there to see.

After ten minutes she pressed the intercom again. "Where is my tray?" she demanded, a near shout.

Catching Ejem's expression, she rolled her eyes.

"Don't you start as well."

Ejem opened her mouth to defend the osu women but shut it just as quickly, embarrassed not only by the unattractive revolutionary bent of what she'd almost said, but also because it felt so much like a defense of herself.

"You are just like Doreen," Odinaka continued. "Look, I employ an army of those women. They have a job and they need to do it. You remember how that goes, right?" Odinaka turned on the television. A commercial advertised a family getaway that included passes to a textile museum where the children could learn how cloth was made. Ejem recalled a documentary she'd seen in school that showed the dismal dorms to which unclaimed women were relegated, the rationed food, the abuse from guards, the "protection" that was anything but. It had been meant to instill fear of ending up in such a place, and it had worked.

When the program returned, Odinaka turned up the volume until it was clear to Ejem she had been dismissed.

Ejem decided that her first foray in her new cloth would be to visit Doreen in her shop. Doreen would know just what to say to ease the restless hurt brewing inside her. She may even know enough of Delilah's history to put Ejem's runaway suspicions to rest. Doreen had invited her to visit the bookstore many times—"You can't stay in here forever. Come. See what I've done. See what an unclaimed woman can build on her own."

Wearing self-cloth in the safety of Odinaka's building was one thing. Ejem dawdled in front of the mirror, studying the softness of her stomach, the firm legs she'd always been proud of, the droop of her breasts. She picked up the cloth and held it in front of her. Much better. She secured it in a simple style, mimicking as best as she could the draping and belting of the sophisticated women she'd encountered.

For the first time in her adult life, no one stared at her. When she gathered the courage to make eye contact with a man on the sidewalk and he inclined his head respectfully, she almost tripped in shock. It was no fluke. Everyone—men and women—treated her differently, most ignoring her as yet another body on the street. But when they did acknowledge her, their reactions were friendly. Ejem felt the protective hunch of her shoulders smooth itself out, as though permission had been granted to relax. She walked with a bounce in her step, every part of her that bounced along with it shielded by the cloth. Bound up in fabric, she was the freest she'd ever felt.

Ejem was so happy that when she saw a familiar face, she smiled and waved before she remembered that the bearer of the face had disowned their friendship some months ago. Chidinma gave a hesitant wave in return before she approached Ejem, smiling.

"You're covered! You're claimed! Turn around; let me see. Your wife-cloth is so fine. I'm upset you didn't invite me to the claiming ceremony."

The words were friendly but the tone was strained, their last exchange still echoing in the air.

"There wasn't a ceremony. There was nothing to invite you to."

Chidinma's smile faded. "You don't have to lie. I know I was awful to you; I'm sorry."

"No, really, there wasn't." Ejem leaned closer, yearning to confide, to restore their former intimacy. "It's self-cloth. I covered myself."

It took Chidinma a moment to absorb this. Then she bristled, pulling back any lingering affection. Her smile went waxy and polite.

"You must be very happy with your husband."

"Chidinma, I don't have a husband. I'm covering myself."

Chidinma's look turned so vicious that Ejem stepped back, bumping into a man who excused himself.

"Are you, now? A self-cloth, is it? Someone from a good family like yours? I don't believe it." Unlike Ejem, Chidinma didn't lower her voice, earning startled glances from passersby. Ejem shushed her.

"Oh, are you ashamed now? Did something you're not entirely proud of?"

When Ejem turned to leave, Chidinma snatched her by the cloth. Now she whispered, "You think you're covered, but you're still naked. No amount of expensive 'self-cloth'—how ridiculous! —will change that."

It was a spiteful and malicious thing to say, meant to hurt, and it did. Ejem tried to pull her cloth from her old friend's fist, but Chidinma didn't let go. She continued, her voice cracking with tears.

"You don't get to be covered without giving something up; you don't get to do that. It's not fair. After everything I did for you, it's not fair."

Chidinma cried openly now, and Ejem used the opportunity of her weakened grip to twist away, near tears herself.

It had been easy, Ejem thought, in the opulence of Odinaka's house, to forget that they were breaking laws. Easy too to clink glasses night after night. What had some woman given up so that Ejem could have this cloth? Was she a weaver by choice or indentured, deemed past her prime and burdened to earn the care of the state? The fabric felt itchy now, as though woven from rough wire.

Ejem hurried back the way she had come, to the safety of Odinaka's building. On the verge of panic, she fumbled with the keys to her apartment and let herself in. Once inside, she leaned against the door and slid to the floor, head to knees, catching her breath. She felt . . . something, which made her look around, and that's when she saw the osu woman standing in the corner. Her skin was light, almost blending into the dusky beige of the wall, her scar a gristly, keloided mass on the side of her head. She appeared to be Ejem's age or older. She held a bottle of cleaning solution and a rag. She was naked.

It was clear by the hunch of her shoulders and the wary look in her eye that it was not a nakedness she enjoyed. How long had it been since Ejem had carried that very look on her own face? How long since she'd felt shame so deep she'd nearly drowned in it?

The day she'd lost her father-cloth, she'd pleaded with her father, fought him as he'd attempted to rip the fabric away. Her mother had cried to her to bear it with some dignity, but Ejem had gone mindless. When her father had finally taken all of the cloth, uncurling her fingers to snatch even the frayed strip she'd held on to, Ejem had curled into herself, making a cover of her appendages. Each day since had been a management of this panic, swallowing it deep in her belly where it wouldn't erupt.

The osu woman nodded to Ejem, then slipped through a panel in the wall and disappeared. The panel slid back into place soundlessly, and when Ejem went to the wall she could feel no seam. She clawed at it, bending and breaking her nails, trying to force a way in. Finding no entry from her side, she pounded and called out, seeking a welcome.

MARTIN CAHILL

Godmeat

FROM *Lightspeed Magazine*

THE GODMEAT STANK of hibiscus and saltwater. Its noxious divinity threaded through the kitchen, the air itself feeling suddenly buoyant in its wake. If Hark closed his eyes, he could almost imagine himself on the beach where Spear had killed the Sea Mother: pale green water lapping at his feet, miles of white sand stretching into the distance, while pink blossoms bobbed in the surf. He could almost see Spear standing on top of the godthing, her weapon shimmering with the blue blood of the dying Beast.

Hark took in the cut of godmeat before him, shining a bloody pink against his dark skin, clean and ready for a dry rub of spices. Seven dishes he'd had the honor of crafting, and it still quickened his heart to handle the raw flesh of one of the Great Beasts; no other chef in all the Wild World could say they'd done it, and none could do it so well as Hark.

All he'd had to do for this opportunity was condemn the Wild World itself to die. But what was the annihilation of a world against the pursuit of culinary perfection? The question echoed in the back of Hark's mind, and like every time before, he ignored it.

Sprinkling a mélange of ochre, emerald, and golden spices onto his palm, Hark rubbed his hands together and sank them into the cut. On contact, desperate emotion shivered up his wrists; visions of waterfalls, lily pads, coastal storms, and ice floes rode on the dying whalesong of the godthing still inside the meat. Ever the professional, he paused; after the first few meals, he learned that the visions, no matter how strong, eventually subsided. When they did, he continued on with his work. The Hollowed would only wait so long for their next course.

Footsteps behind him dragged the shadowed taste of cloves, mint, and ash into the room. Hark rankled. "Put that out, Spear. Please. I've lived almost seventy years in perfect health. I am *not* going to die from your secondhand smoke."

She grunted, challenging as ever, but Hark wouldn't back down. She could smoke those wherever in the Wild World she pleased, but the kitchen was his kingdom and he'd be damned to let Kai'nese tobacco into it. After a moment he heard her crush the butt in the sink and felt her eyes on the back of his neck. "There's a carafe of peach and raspberry tea in the icebox if you're looking for something to fiddle with. This is going to take some time."

She pulled out the carafe and poured a glass. "Hollowed don't like to wait." She slurped tea with the delicacy of a street urchin in finishing school; Hark bit the inside of his cheek. Four years they'd been working together, and there were still some days he wanted to throw her into the ocean.

"They'll have to," he replied, tasting sand and seaweed in the back of his throat. He patted the thoroughly spiced cut of godmeat with admiration. "She was one of the oldest, and she'll take a *long* while to cook. To eat the Sea Mother raw would destroy them, their gullets breaking with storms, their blood boiling with salt." He turned to smile at her, his sun-sharp grin unwavering in the face of her sternness. "They'll let me take my time, or they'll simply drown in the air."

She shrugged, left her dirty glass on the counter, and walked out of the kitchen, weapons jangling against her hips.

Hark sighed, but didn't let her immaturity distract him from the meal. Turning back to the godmeat, he placed it with care inside a circle of salt, lily petals, and steel shavings and set a timer, one of those fussy new clockwork pieces from across the Spidered Sea.

As he reveled in the satisfactory ticking of the copper mechanism, a pressure grew behind his eyes. He didn't have time for this; there were side dishes to prepare. But he closed his eyes all the same.

In the darkness of his mind, a light grew. As his vision adjusted to the brightness, Hark stood before the Hollowed, seated in their gnarled thrones of wood, bone, and glass.

They numbered nine, and when they'd first approached him, they'd been little more than the idea of ghosts, fragile clouds pinned to a harsh sky. Now they were more than hale. Myriad

Hells, they were practically robust. Skin had yet to solidify on all of them; rich flashes of crimson muscle and webbed veins ran through them, and Hark did his best not to stare. But the past four years of divine consumption had invested in them a very true sense of existence, and they were beyond eager to cement themselves back onto reality.

Where they came from exactly, Hark didn't know, and he wasn't stupid enough to ask. They'd introduced him to Spear, who he assumed was in it for the same reasons he was, and sent them off into the Wild World.

They'd sworn fortune in success, torture in failure, and so far they hadn't backed down from either end of that promise. All it took in exchange was four years of murdering ancient godbeasts who kept the laws of reality in place, and serving them up for sumptuous dinner.

It only gnawed at Hark's conscience in the beginning; concerns fell away once he began to revel in the art of the meal. Pride always had a way of replacing fear throughout his life.

In the center sat their leader, jawline red and exposed. The Golden King opened his crimson mouth, and his breath was a dry, foul wind in the psychic space.

"Where is our meal, chef? We hunger for the Sea Mother." Every sound he made was a fat black fly tickling Hark's nose. He shivered, as he always did.

The other Hollowed murmured their agreement, and Hark couldn't stop his eyes from wandering across their thin bodies, their red muscles, their empty eye sockets: Mother of Knives, Fisher Knight, Father Flame, Hunter of Screams, Sister Rapture, the Visionary, Heart's Crown, and Cloudbreaker. Each claiming to be a god, each hungry to be filled up again with the divine potential they once possessed and usher in a new age of the Wild World, each a nightmare to behold.

But he'd be damned if he was cowed by a gathering of impatient, hungry patrons who wanted him to skip to the end simply because their bellies were rumbling. To Hark, it didn't matter if he was making a soup of fresh tomato, basil, and cream or a seared steak of the finest divine beast: he would serve when it was ready, and not a moment before.

He cleared his throat and folded his arms, staring into the

empty eye sockets of the Golden King in what he hoped was a humble but imperious manner.

"Look here, my lord. It has been four years since you hired Spear and me to produce for you all the divine ingredients necessary for your actualization in the physical world. And have I even *once,* even for but the breath of a *moment,* served any of you your meal before it was ready?" The Hollowed sat still as syrup, and Hark could feel very real sweat leaking into existence on his forehead. But he had to forge ahead; you couldn't very well stop churning the butter halfway through, could you?

"Your demands do not respect me. Your ignorance of the work I do continues to grate on my professionalism, and your aggression only demeans me as I work well beyond the methods of my culinary career in preparing that which you have asked of me." He took a deep breath as each of the Hollowed sat taller in their chair, their bones rattling with rage. "Please know that I have no intention of dishonoring any of you, your positions, or your needs, but you must remember that while I am mortal, the work I do is divine and needs the proper patience. Else you're wasting my time, Spear's time, and, most importantly, your time." He tried an old smirk on for size, one he used to give his line cooks when they would mouth off at him. "Or did you all think that you were immortal just yet?"

Their silence crawled over Hark. It would be insane for them to kill him, yes? Their contract was almost up, just one more after the Sea Mother, and—

Hark blinked, and found himself back in reality. A whisper in his ear, and a sensation like a wasp landing on the nape of his neck: *Get it done and* serve us.

Hark let out a shaky breath. His hands were gripping the marble counter with an intensity he reserved for cutting root vegetables. Then, a flat voice from the other room: "I told you they wouldn't be happy."

"Shut up, Spear." He snatched up a rag and mopped his brow.

A sizzling to his left interrupted his terror. He looked up to see that the steel shavings, the salt, and the lily leaves had burnt away to a fine pink powder that pulsed like morning light on ocean stillness.

He sighed with relief, happy to throw himself back into his

work. He lifted the cut of godmeat, scooped the bright powder into a glass vial, and went back to preparation. There were still hours to go before the Sea Mother was ready for consumption, but Hark didn't mind. This was his calling, and he answered it gladly, even if the Hollowed did not respect it.

He hummed a song to himself as he worked and tried to forget that the world was one meal closer to ending.

The Hollowed may have had the ability to act like spoiled children, but they truly knew how to appreciate a meal when it reached their table.

Spear and Hark stood at attention while each of the Hollowed took a fair portion of the Sea Mother's fillet; even from where he stood, Hark's mouth watered at the smell of the steak, his eyes drinking in the velvet line between rare and medium-rare, his nostrils screaming at the scent of woodsmoke, sea salt, and hibiscus that lingered around the meal like swaddling robes. But the Sea Mother was not for him, and though it tantalized every aspect of his appetite, to taste of the godbeast would drive him mad.

As one, the Hollowed feasted, savoring every morsel of the ancient goddess that graced their palates, the taste of ages caramelizing in their mouths like apple butter, every bite releasing torrents of rainwater and storm winds into their stomachs, the long history of the Sea Mother playing out like an orchestra between their teeth. Coils of white lightning arced between the Hollowed as they ate, and in their eye sockets pulsed the night-blue light of hurricanes.

When the meal was finished, Hark watched the Golden King work his now full jaw back and forth, skin the color of midnight fully drawn over it, taut. Only his eyes remained empty, the sockets flashing the blue of the deep, as the power of the Sea Mother ran through him.

"Visionary," he said, his voice booming like tidal waves crashing to the sand. "Tell me what you glimpse with the Sea Mother's gaze."

The Visionary's nine eye sockets, arranged in a diamond across his copper face, all glowed with the hue of the ocean, and he sucked in a strangled breath of glee. "Ships, I see them! Numbering twelve, bedecked with cannons and steel, usurping the gift of wind do they travel on the Haljredan Strait, to make war upon their neighbors."

The Golden King's grin was infectious. "Father Flame. Speak to me of the sky."

Father Flame's fingers burned with the trembling spark of barely held lightning. His gums glowed like newborn embers on a fire and lit his smile from behind. "The clouds are swollen with heat. Oh, how they wish to dance!"

One by one, the Golden King questioned his brethren. With every answer he received, he only laughed, until the echoes around Hark made him sick to his stomach. He and Spear had not moved an inch, and dared not turn from the exultation of the Hollowed.

The Golden King held up a fist as dense and sharp as coral. "Her power is ours. The Sea Mother lives on in us, and so does her strength." Hark could feel the Golden King warping the air in the room, increasing the pressure around them all in his corrupt joy. "Cloudbreaker! Pummel ships with hurricane winds. Father Flame! Strike coastlines alight with your lightning. Mother of Knives, corrode fisherman's steel with salt. Fisher Knight, encircle boats with sharks and squids." One by one, the Golden King commanded his brethren, smiling, as across the Wild World ships drowned, coasts were ravaged, cities were hammered by lightning, metal rusted away, and children were swept out to the deep.

The Golden King purred, satisfied, a lion among sheep. "Teach the Wild World that we are coming back."

Hark heard a rattling sound. Turning his head just so, he glimpsed Spear. She stood at attention, her ankles pressed together, her arms behind her back. Her eyes bored ahead with a focus Hark envied. But when he looked closer, he could see that she shook, ever so slightly, her knives and daggers trembling with her. Hark saw the tightness in her jaw, the muscles in her neck bulging, her eyes only just wider than normal, and he realized: she was afraid.

Finally, he thought. *Something I understand.*

"Chef. Attend." The Golden King's voice was a hook in Hark's lip, dragging him back to attention. "Do not for a moment think you may shirk focus simply because our contract is almost at an end."

Hark bowed slightly from the waist. "Of course, my lord."

"Delivered unto us have you eight Great Beasts of the Wild World. Through our veins flow their strength over its seas, its mountains, its creatures, its skies . . . ours to will, and to shape, and to crush."

Hark couldn't help but recount them, the Beasts he'd watched die, the dishes he'd made, had been *happy* to make. No other chef in all the Wild World had done what he had done. *I melted the Sunsword into a soup. I sliced open the heart of the Iron Hound and boiled it for a pudding. I cracked the ribs of the Mountain Worm and garnished them with flowers. I baked the head of the Firestag and broke its antlers over my knee. I grilled the Sea Mother's hide.* Hark felt proud, and wondered for a brief moment what else sat within him just then, the ghost of an emotion that did not wish to speak its name but whose shape he knew and feared. He stuffed it down inside, deep and away. Now was no time for introspection.

"Our contract is almost fulfilled, hunter. Our contract is almost up, chef. There is no doubt in your minds as to who we seek to eat for the very last, is there?" The Golden King's voice curdled hearts as it did milk, and Hark struggled to swallow the bile in his throat.

"The Messenger, my lord. The Great Beast of Death."

The Hollowed sat and nodded, smiling at each other like small children, eager to have dessert. "Once we have consumed death, then no longer will death have the chance to consume us. Not again. With our immortality secured, we shall release you both." The Golden King's eyes narrowed, as though finally finding prey. "Though how long you survive in this world we make, *that* will be a mystery."

Thank the dead Beasts for Spear, who filled the silence with a question. "The Messenger, then. Where does it speak now?"

The Golden King gestured to his siblings.

Cloudbreaker's halo caught the candlelight, and when she glanced toward the sky, her brow shone like a broken mirror. Her empty eye sockets glazed over with golden light, letting the power of the Sunsword hawk fill her. After a moment she spoke. "South and south again, across Lament's Rush and Once Mighty Drazbaadinmar, south, even further, pushing through the breast of Haddikstant and across the Iron Plains! The Messenger followed the scent of war horns and rattling sabers, drinking the carnage of clashing spears and skins. Now the Beast resides in the heart of the Ruined Lights, supping on the souls of the haunted wood."

Cloudbreaker's beatific smile did nothing to offset the sharpness of her teeth. "You'll find the Beast there, bloated on the blood and smoke of the Plains. I await your concoction, chef." Cloudbreaker snapped her jaws playfully.

The Golden King raised a hand. "Bring us death's head on a platter and you will both know riches and sweet reward, to be enjoyed in the beautiful moments before our return. Come back with anything less and you'll both know damnation. Are we clear?"

Spear jerked her head up, a sneer slicing her face. "I know how threats work. We'll get it done, and then you'll leave us alone." Spear grabbed Hark's arm and pulled him back with her, both of them tumbling out of the psychic space.

Hark broke his arm free of Spear's grip. "They've killed people for less, Spear!"

Spear glowered at him, unblinking. She spat on the floor and got to her feet. "And I've killed people for less than that. They don't scare me," she said, as though she wasn't just trembling before them. She started to walk toward the supply pantry, which doubled as her armory. "C'mon. Let's do this, then."

Hark grabbed a handkerchief from the counter and wiped away Spear's spittle before getting to his feet and following.

Thanks to reality-bending Persuasion Workers, the pantry was almost fifty feet deep, and on each wall, their tools; Hark had the right wall for his utensils and Spear had the left for her weapons. Already she was running her fingers across the steel that waited, tracing the edge of a sword, testing the heft of a flail. Hark stood at the other wall, his neuroses making his fingers itch. He always got antsy whenever Spear picked her weapons; it reminded him of the old days, when he'd smack wrists and crack knuckles, expecting perfection of the young charges in his restaurant as they learned to sharpen knives, learned which blade worked for which cut. That he didn't know anything of her tools made him anxious.

After a few moments Spear turned to face him, already done. She had her arms crossed and an eyebrow raised; with the sheer amount of weapons she'd strapped to her body, she resembled nothing less than a steel porcupine.

"Are you really going to need all of those?" Hark asked, regretting it immediately. She glowered, and he was reminded of just how little he knew of her. Neither of them were very friendly people, and whatever polite inquiry he made into her past she tamped down like a stray spark, as though a friendly question could make her catch fire. Though if he were honest with himself, if she bothered to ask him anything, he'd probably do the same.

"I was thinking of bringing nothing, but then I remembered

I'm hunting the Great Beast of Death, which has been around since the inception of the concept of the Wild World, so I reconsidered."

Hark scowled, running a hand across his stubbly scalp; shaving his dreadlocks cut down on how much gray he saw each day. "Fine, be a bitch. What do I care? After you murder this thing and I cook it into art, we'll be rid of each other."

At this point she'd normally shove past him, go to the rune in the foyer, and be gone, leaving him to prepare the recipe and side dishes until she returned with the Beast in tow. Instead she stood there and would not look away from his eyes, ringed as they were with wrinkles and creases. "What are you looking at?" he said, his heart turning stony and cold at the attention of such a hard-bitten woman.

She scowled, picking her nose and then moving the same finger behind her ear. "I'm looking."

Hark folded his arms and crouched his chin into his chest, embarrassed suddenly, and feeling oddly petulant. "For what? My coin purse, no doubt, you mongrel woman. I bet you'll never be satisfied, even after you've murdered the last Great Beast and are awash in gold and steel!"

Spear snorted, and then in a sudden motion took Hark around the shoulders and pulled him close, into a hug, tight; he could feel various weapons poking him in places he did not wish to be poked. "There it is! Oh, there it is, Hark. I see it now. Sometimes you hide it, but I know it's always there."

His heart leaping at the physical contact, he recoiled and shoved out of her embrace, almost knocking over a cart of bowls and utensils. "What in the Myriad Hells are you talking about? Are you drunk? Did you sneak into my wine cellar when I wasn't looking? I bet you did!"

She laughed again, higher, and Hark sensed a mania he did not like. Spear's eyes shone with a sinister light, and Hark began to fold in on himself as she advanced, her shadow falling across him. "I guess you could say I drank madness and developed a taste for it. It's easy to go mad when you have nothing left to live for." She sidled closer, leaning down until her hot breath danced by his ear. "I used to have *a lot* to live for. But the Hollowed saw to that: reached right through reality and burned it all down with everyone inside. So I'd rather just fucking work for them and die than try to pretend I have anything left to live for; let them crumble the world to cinders. My own world is already ash.

"But you?" she hissed. "I know all about you; I've read up on you. You don't want the world to end because you hate it. You don't even care about the world. You're just bored and beaten down. Bitter. Arrogant. Lonely. And the Hollowed gave you a challenge. Who cares if you help bring about the apocalypse? You'll have done something no one else has done. You'll be able to step on the necks of all those who told you that you'd fail."

Spear took a step back then. She smiled down at him, pity in her eyes. "That doesn't make you mad, just petty. And that makes you worse than me, Hark. You're far worse."

And then she laughed. It pierced Hark's heart as surely as an arrow. And she kept laughing. And her laughter followed her across the Wild World as she left the manor.

It lingered, wrapped itself around Hark like a noose, and pulled tight.

Hark's manor was in the seaport town of Awrant, just off the Spidered Sea, and with Spear's laughter echoing after him, he found himself bursting out into the bright spring day and lurching toward the water.

He would do this as a boy, fresh bruises from his aunt and uncle shivering into existence on his stomach, his shoulders, the back of the legs, where no one would think to look. And now, as then, Hark's feet stepped staccato, his whole body quaking with the aftermath of a beating, unseen, but his soul was already bruising over.

His manor nestled in a patch of gardens, tucked away from the main road but only a short distance from his once greatest triumph. Now, as he came upon the ruined shell of his old restaurant, he could barely look at it. Even passing it brought noxious memories to the surface like cold apples in water, bobbing and demanding attention. And just like the taxes he didn't pay, and like the codes he chose not to follow, and the workers whose plights he passed by, he chose not to see those memories. The restaurant died because not enough people loved it, he had reasoned to himself; it had not been his fault.

So he staggered past, ignoring the dark interior, the graffiti, and the smell of garbage that stroked his cheek. Fuck the restaurant, he thought desperately. It didn't want to live, so let it die. It wouldn't matter, not as long as he did his work.

He walked down Main Street, composing himself in front of the men and women and children going about their day. His chef whites gleamed in the late-afternoon sun, looking like raiment compared to the drab wear of the Awranti. His uncle was a naval scorpion, his aunt a jungle weaver, his parents unknown to him and better off that way. He would never wear anything to remind him of any of them again, and so he pushed himself forward with pride in standing out. Better to gleam like a bright blade than be smothered in the burlap crowd.

Children sang for alms on Viscounts Way, and he ignored them all. Let them work, if they were to earn a living. Through Dishra's Gift, the wide, sweeping park green and lush, ignoring the families as they ran and played, doing his best to ignore the longing for what he could've built with Fenli and never had the time for. If Hark looked closely, he could almost see Fenli waiting for him under the cherry trees, his poet's face long and sad. Hark shook his head then, sweat forming on his upper lip; Fenli wasn't here. He had moved on, to take up a fisherman's life with his husband in Albercari. Hark was alone.

Huffing, almost out of breath, his heart racing, he turned onto Sandrazi Road and made his way through the fashion district, scenting for the cologne of the sea on the wind. Salt, wet wood, and gull feathers. He was close; he had to hurry, his ghosts were gaining on him.

And then, past the stalls of crafts, textiles, and coffee shops before the port, he turned and saw the ocean. Something in him finally gave way. Endless, blue and green, the sun a dazzling orange lance thrown across the horizon, Hark forgot his age and ran, ran for the water. Down past the docks, past the Endless Empire war galleys and the Julaywi song ships, he ran out and past them, into the sand, past the sand, into the surf, past the surf, and into the water proper.

He pushed out, farther, farther. The water rose from ankles to knees to waist to chest, to nose. Hark, harried by Spear's laughter, the ghosts of his failures, the anger and arrogance of his youth, found himself up to his nose in the sea he had once loved and given up for the kitchen. The ocean did not let him live, and so he had been ordered to stop swimming. He felt it coming, a great peace that the sea always offered and which he had been aching for, for many years.

Except the sea-salt sting in his nose offended him, and the endless blur of water in his eyes brought him back to the Sea Mother, that godbeast he had as surely helped kill as Spear, and too quickly the water was too close and he was too deep, and it seemed at the thought that the entire sea lifted him up and away, and Hark's gut churned, and he retched into the water, emptying himself, sobbing.

As he stood there in the water, floating in the sea that was the home of his youth, standing amid his ruined lunch, gasping for air, he saw something slice through the sky. A flash of white against the bright blue, then gone. He blinked, rubbing at the saltwater tickling his eyes.

Again, a glimpse of white, then gone. Hark blinked, turned, tried to push himself on his toes, back toward land.

A third time he saw it, and then heard a string of curses in a high-pitched squeak. He followed the sound, the absurdity of it distracting him from his despair long enough to see a small girl on the shore, uttering every curse known across the Spider Coast and farther, holding in her delicate brown fingers a broken kite. White sailcloth bunched up in her hands, straddled by beams of thin wood, as she cursed at it for not working. Her mother stood behind her, laughing, but doing it quietly enough for the girl not to notice. All Hark could do was watch as, after a moment's chuckle, the mother came forward, knelt by her daughter, and slowly pointed out where things had gone wrong and how to make it better.

Hark's heart ached, knowing that in a few short days the Hollowed would be freed by his hand, and there would never be any chance to make it better.

It would be all his fault, just like everything in his life.

If he were not too stubborn to give up, he would have floated out to sea. But Hark was not one to give up, even his life. He had only given up on the world being good to him.

So he hurled himself out of the water and walked dripping wet back to his manor, to consign the world to death.

Salt. Pepper. A little butter. Sear both sides, and then let it cook in the oven for thirty minutes. Hark even prepared a small salad to be served with it, to keep his mind from the impending destruction of the world.

Spear never told him what the Messenger had looked like. A week and a half after she left to hunt, she reappeared, reached into her bag, and pulled out a dark, hot lump, fixing him with a cold fury in her eyes. "Go on, then," she had whispered. "Show the cruel world how great you are. Make a fillet of death."

She walked with him through psychic space until they reached the Hollowed's banquet table, where each of the nine soon-to-be-gods sat with slavering impatience. Hark made them wait as long as possible, though he couldn't articulate why. He poured a blood-red wine, a Trevaldi 491, aged on butterfly smoke and white chocolate. He served his salad, laden with berries, arugula, goat cheese, almond slices, and a dusting of volcanic ash. Finally he served out the portions of the Messenger's heart, small on the wide plates, encircled with a sauce of dark chocolate, coffee, and orange bitters.

The Golden King raised a glass of wine. The other Hollowed followed suit. "To Hark and Spear," the Golden King purred, a smile splitting his cracked lips. "Thanks to them, we'll soon walk the world. And in doing so, break it for our revenge. To the end of the Wild World and the start of a new one!"

The Hollowed cheered.

The Hollowed drank.

The Hollowed ate.

Hark stood with his feet together, his hands behind his back, and his eyes full of tears. Beside him, Spear did the same. He had to do something. He couldn't let them out into the world. He couldn't do anything, but he had to do something.

As one, they finished their plates, and Hark felt the edges of psychic space break open, unfurling like a languid rose. The Hollowed stood in the Wild World now, the Messenger acting as the final anchor to true reality. They stood in an antechamber just off the kitchen, and Hark yearned to go there, to hide from what he'd done. Already he could feel the tangle of power the Hollowed gave off, a massive surge of dominance over the laws of reality once held by the Great Beasts. He could taste war on the wind, feel the thrum of collapse in the soles of his feet, hear a hot sickness flooding through his blood.

But before he could do anything, the Golden King stepped forward, smiling, with a look of knowing in his empty eyes, those hollow sockets that had not filled for any of them, even in life anew.

"We thank you, chef. Your despondence, your dedication, and your own small cruelties made you the perfect vessel for our return. Like you, we were failed by the world we hoped to lead. Like you, we were cast out in the pursuit of our perfection. Like you, we hungered to fill the emptiness within us and show those in the world we were not what they thought we were. And now we have that chance to revenge upon them, to move in a way you have only wished to for so many years."

Hark's eyes went wide as the words sunk in.

They had not sought him for his talent.

They had chosen him because he was just like them: hollow.

The wall around his heart shattered then, with the roaring strength of a pounding tide. Hark fell to his aged knees and raised beseeching hands over his head.

"Wait! My lords! My ladies! My lieges, all, please hear me!" He could feel their searing gaze on him, but he dared not meet them. "To commemorate such a momentous occasion, I have . . . prepared something for you all; a small trifle, something special to cleanse your palates with before striding out into the Wild World. Please grant me a short time to prepare it and bring it to you all."

"Rise." Hark looked up.

Numbered nine and radiant all, the Hollowed watched him, smiling with a wicked edge.

The Golden King nodded. "There is the obeisance we've been waiting for. Go and bring us your treat, chef. You've earned some slight patience."

Hark bowed and turned on his heel. He felt Spear right behind him.

"What in the Myriad Hells are you doing?" she whispered, both of them pushing into the kitchen. Hark's heart pounded, though for the first time in four years he was utterly calm.

Hark looked around his kitchen, his kingdom, and smiled. It had been so good to him; in a world that had hurt him, his kitchen was an oasis he'd retreated to so many times. He ran his hands along the black-and-white marble counter, picking at small nicks in the cutting boards. He gazed out through the bay window by the fireplace and, there in the distance, the sea he so loved. He found himself walking toward the pantry and opening it with reverence.

Spear watched him in silence. She stood motionless as his hands glided along his wall of tools and found an ivory knife handle and, drawing it from its guard, a shining white blade.

It was a knife to be used only in certain procedures. Butterflying the heart of a cosmic whale. Slicing off shavings of psychotropic dark-matter mushrooms from the underverse. Cracking the shell of a Dwarf Star Turtle to consume the radiation inside.

It was a precise tool meant for precise actions.

Hark handed the hilt to Spear.

She took it, her face slack, her eyes dead. "What am I doing with this?"

He pursed his lips, thinking, and then wiped the corners of his eyes as the answer took hold of him and sudden tears threatened to fall. "It is too late to stop them, Spear. They are free, and I freed them. Every part of me is screaming to curl up and die, to let them run rampant. But . . ." Here he paused, the memory of his failed restaurant, his failed career, his failed family, ruin after ruin flashing before him. Then, a young girl on the beach, and learning that you can always try again, if you work to fix what went wrong. "That wouldn't be right."

He smiled at Spear, a genuine thing, and found he quite liked it. "Should this fail, then let it fail. But I'll not give up the world to die, even though I gave up on it long ago."

Spear spun the ivory knife back and forth, testing its weight, hefting its handle. She didn't offer an argument, just as Hark knew she wouldn't. She looked up at him, her eyes as cold and clear as a forest spring. "Where, then?"

Hark took her hand in his own. He lifted the knife's tip up to his right eye. All he could see through one eye was steel; through the other, Spear, steady as a stone and waiting. "Both, Spear. Please, make it quick."

She said nothing. Only nodded.

The pain that shattered through him was unlike anything he had ever felt. It demanded his full attention, and Hark writhed on the ground, screaming with all his broken heart. And when he thought he couldn't scream anymore, some new part of him discovered he could.

It was some time before he found consciousness, and when he did, it was a world of touch and taste and sound and patience. He found his feet, and a hand under his arm. Spear's husky, harsh voice was right next to him. "I have them, Hark. What am I doing with them?"

His voice was a whisper. "In my hand, please. I have it from here."

It was slower than he thought it would be, but the more than fifty years in his kitchen, his kingdom, had not left him. Sliding his hands along the counters, he inched his way to the cabinet of glasses. He found nine champagne flutes. There was an angry, thumping pain at the front of his skull, and there was wetness slipping down his face, and though it demanded all of his attention, Hark denied it.

He had work to do.

With Spear's assistance, he went to his old chopping block and, holding each eye just so, sliced them thinly, arraying them in the bottom of the flutes. She helped him pour a thick port wine into each glass, only guessing that the liquid was mulberry and pomegranate in color. And with Spear's guidance adorned a serving tray with the flutes and walked them toward the Hollowed.

They did not ask questions, because gods do not ask questions. They said nothing, only taking the flutes and toasting each other, the crystalline tinkling of glass on glass a strange music to Hark's ears. If they saw his ruined eyes, they did not care. They simply drank, and swallowed.

It was only a few moments before they began to scream.

Spear will tell him later that the looks on their faces made it worthwhile, as matter began to boil into their hollow sockets and eyes began to grow, eyes that looked so much like Hark's own. She will tell him of the dumbfounded looks on their faces, the way that rage battled with confusion, of how doubt, ever elusive in the face of such power, began to creep in.

At that moment, though, the Golden King screamed, "Chef! What is the meaning of this? What have you done to us?"

Hark's voice was knife-thin but cut through the newborn gods' screaming all the same. "You were right, my lord. We are the same. I have felt hollow myself for some time, and I would do anything to fill myself up with some purpose, even if it was destruction, pride, or power. I thought the world was evil because it did not understand me or work to make me happy. But I was also stubborn, arrogant, and foolish too, to think the world would come to my door and give itself to me. I did not learn from my mistakes, and so I lost it all. I blamed the world for that too. But the world doesn't deserve to die because of my small heart. And it doesn't deserve to wither under your gaze either, simply because you once tried to fix it and it rejected you. You all have a chance to make things right. If you may see things more clearly because of my eyes, see the joys or lessons or hopes I have witnessed, then I am happy to give them to you, and give this world a small chance at living on."

Silence, and the weight of nine pairs of his own eyes looked down upon him from thrones of wood, bone, and glass.

"We will remember this transgression, chef," the Golden King said, in a voice that could splinter mountains and freeze stars.

Hark chuckled, and found he liked it. "I should hope you do. I hope you never forget this day, or this meal. I hope it lingers in your hearts for centuries to come." Hark paused, lifted his chin, and stared up at the Hollowed with empty eyes. "We can do better. All of us."

Spear will tell him later how they all looked down on him, scowling, furious, righteous, and powerful. And then how, after a moment, their faces softened, their new eyes creased with concern, and how they all looked to each other, seeing each other truly for the first time in millennia, and how like smoke on the wind they faded from sight.

But all Hark heard in that moment was silence, and it wasn't until Spear took his elbow and whispered, "They're gone, Hark," that he collapsed to his knees, hyperventilating. His body wracked with sobs, and he didn't fight it. The world still spun on, and so he hoped beyond hope that he got through to them.

And when Spear asked him where he'd like to go, he didn't hesitate.

"To the sea, I think," he said, knowing he would be seen in his chef whites, his face a ruin, and not caring. "I think I crave some time by the sea, for as long as it's there."

Spear took him by the elbow, and together they made their way to the water, enjoying in silence every moment the world had not yet ended.

ADAM R. SHANNON

On the Day You Spend Forever with Your Dog

FROM *Apex Magazine*

WHEN THE DOG dies, she doesn't know she is dying. You shouldn't feel sorry for her. To her, life lasts forever.

Infants and dogs recognize the flow of time, but not their presence in it. Psychologists show two films to a child so young it cannot comprehend the difference between itself and the universe. In the first film, water pours from a pitcher into a glass. In the second, time is reversed: water spirals out of the glass to replenish the pitcher. The child will stare longer at the film that violates the rules of causality. She believes, without knowing she believes, that time goes one way.

She doesn't know that time pervades her very flesh, a dimension of her physical existence. She doesn't know that it will require her to die. She believes that time is progress. For a while you believe it too, and the mistake damages all your equations. It isn't until Jane dies that you reach the solution.

You don't know it yet, but there is a feeling of being inside time. It suffuses your awareness as thoroughly as your height and weight and position in space. It is as comforting as riding at a constant speed and in a constant direction, rocking to sleep on a train or in a car driven by someone you trust. When you go back in time, it hurts.

The first injection calms the dog. Her breathing slows, and she puts her head on your foot. It is an unexpected move, and a little unsettling. Jane has seldom wavered in her determination to watch over you. She watched when you went to the bathroom. She followed you without condemnation when you walked up the stairs, forgot why you were there, and immediately descended with her in tow. She watched today as you made the last batch of muffins. She kept an eye on your movements even as she licked the bowl. For you, it's the last time she will ever lick the bowl. For her, it's forever.

The sedative allows her to relax in her self-appointed duties. Her watchfulness fades and she looks past you.

Jane doesn't know about the drugs. She just transitions from what she was to what she becomes, as unaware of her own trajectory as she is of its destination.

The second injection places her in a profound sleep. She's unaware of anything happening to her, unable to feel pain. You touch her paws, stroke the black curve of her nails, but she does not withdraw.

"Don't leave me," you whisper, knowing the only reason you can ask is because she cannot understand. Her existence is a secret you can never tell her. If she ever learned, she would know she is dying.

The last injection stops her heart. It feels as if your heart stops too, ceasing its stuttering progress through space.

You shouldn't feel sorry for her. She lived forever.

When you first found her, Jane had a broken leg and a healing gash over the bony ridge of her pelvis. She had been hit by a car on New York Avenue at 4 a.m. and was picked up by the crew of a passing trash truck. It took two people to lift her into the cab for a trip to the emergency vet. She snapped weakly at their hands, furious at her pain.

The company fired the driver for diverting from his route. Sometimes you wonder what might have happened if that man had gone to the shelter and found her recovering in her bare metal cage. There are no alternate realities in which he took Jane home and she watched over him the way she watched over you. No timelines exist in which she settled beside him on the couch and watched him as he watched TV, in which she walked with him and watched everything for a chance to prove her love.

There's only one timeline. If you go back far enough and wait, you eventually find yourself exactly where you started.

You will go back anyway.

*

You like to joke that a time machine is theoretically possible but that the materials are in short supply. You must first construct a stable wormhole. This would require harnessing a daunting amount of energy and solving certain problems related to the production of exotic matter.

Assuming you can overcome this technological hurdle, you would then place one end of your wormhole on Earth—preferably in your lab, where no one can mess with it. Put the other end on a spaceship and accelerate it to near the speed of light. Relativistic effects will gradually induce time drift between the two openings. After one year at .9 times the speed of light, the end on your ship has traveled 1.294 years into the future, compared to the aperture that you left behind in your lab.

There are problems. You can only travel between the two ends of your fabricated wormhole. You will never travel back to observe World War II. Dinosaurs will never come roaring through your portal to wreak havoc on the modern world, scaly metaphors for fascism and the fall of an empire.

Also, you do not have a stable wormhole and no plausible means of creating it.

For a while your theories make you a star in the field. A few awards fall into your lap, and you believe the words engraved in the bases.

Then the accolades slip away and are redirected into the careers of colleagues with more plausible equations. Your lab space is reassigned to the nanoengineering unit, which filed actionable patents while you imagined flying about with a wormhole.

Eventually you wonder if only your dog still cares about you.

You abandon the time machine, encrypt your files, and drift between ideas. Jane watches and follows as you walk around the house in a bathrobe. She still limps a little, a physical recording of past trauma. She rolls on her back on the couch as you waste a few hours of your life on an old sitcom. She growls as you rub her belly. The deep menace in this sound sometimes frightens people who don't know that this is how she speaks her love.

She watches over you.

Then she struggles to get up, limping more noticeably, sensing that you're upset and wondering how she can protect you.

She brushes her gray muzzle against your face, watching you to know how she should feel. You pretend to be fine and call her a good girl. She is a good girl. Your misery comes from watching her body falter, from the inevitable progress toward a terrible decision, but she can't know that.

You're sitting on the kitchen floor next to her as she pushes her food bowl around the tiles. The fridge rises like a steel monolith at your back. It is a place for giants. You feel secure next to her on the cool floor. She bumps you with the food bowl and uses your weight to pin it down while she finishes her dinner. You pat her side, and she burps before lying down, slowly, against your hip. You've forgotten to make yourself dinner.

Then it's the day when she dies, although she doesn't know it.

No one watches over you now. You're free to spend nights in the lab, catching fitful naps under a desk, wondering what previous resident stuck their chewed gum in a line of Morse code under the rim. The gum is the record of passing time, the message that is the past.

Then you understand: no one moves through time. Time is merely a form of encryption, much like the files on your computer. The past is decoded; the future remains locked into a cypher. The present is merely a floating translation point between encoded and decoded information.

There is only one timeline, one message. You might want to change it—to save a planeload of doomed passengers or avert a war. But you're free of the burden of that power. When you go back, you're simply reencrypting the timestring. Your equations show, with almost total confidence, that you won't be able to change anything.

You're going back for one reason—to see your dog again.

When you go back in time, it hurts more than you thought possible. The universe presses its weight against you. Exploding molecules are welded back together. Healed wounds are torn open before ceasing to exist. Disentangled particles fall back under each other's painful influence.

Pages come in contact, stick, and knit back together. Your memories are stripped from you and scrambled into code.

When you go back, you don't know you've gone back. You

roll back the clock and experience your life again for the first time. You're yourself, just as you always were, and always will be forever. You're like Jane. You have no memory of the future. You just exist.

You walk past rows of metal cages—dogs clamoring for attention or turning in tight circles or huddling with their backs to the door. None of them are the dog you're looking for. You hear the deep resonance of her voice from two rows down. The shelter staff tells you that this dog is scheduled to be euthanized. No one has come to pick her up. She has tried to bite two handlers and has been labeled a threat. In honor of her unknown origins, they have named her Jane Dog. Her barks rise in amplitude, as if she's trying to catch up with someone who is walking away.

When you pass her cage, she leaps up against the wire mesh, breathes in your face, and watches you. Her flank is shaved over a ragged wound and her front leg is splinted. The staff member warns you to be careful. Jane's eyes are nearly level with yours, and in them is an unwavering sense of purpose.

You tell the staff all the right things. You understand that she is dangerous, that she will require time and training and patience and structure and socialization and still may always be in some way broken. You leave the building tethered to each other.

In three years you will watch the needle slide into the soft fur and cry uncontrollably, and struggle to remember life without her. You'll bury your face in the thick sable neck and feel more adrift than anyone has ever been in time.

It hurts the same amount every time, although you never remember the reencryptions from one to the next. You collapse eventualities like a tent being folded in on itself. You bend along your dimensions in bone-shearing recombinations.

Every time you return to the past is the first time. You have no memory of how many times you've gone back to be with her.

She loves the woods. Every breath is a painting: ochre splatter patterns of squirrels flashed through with bright blue glimpses of every dog who has peed on the scabby trunk of rotten oak. Green swirls of skunk sift through the trees.

You are tethered together in the woods when a man runs

around the bend in a trail, arms pumping, puffing with exertion. You startle. Jane feels the tremor through the leash, and you don't have time to pull her in close to your leg before the man runs past. She lunges, wrenching your shoulder with unexpected fury. The man pitches away and falls into the dead leaves. You're apologizing and stepping forward to help him up, but Jane is barking and pulling, and the man looks more terrified every time you step closer.

"Holy shit!" he yells. "Control your dog!"

The man's fear has transformed into anger. He's tugging at the leg of his shorts, and you see the fabric is ripped. You're apologizing and asking if he's all right. There is no blood, no wound. You part forever.

In two years the needle slides in and she's dead. She's dead and you're back again to where she's gone, your past decoded and painfully plain.

Did she always lunge for the man?

The memory feels fresh as a wound. Before you went back, did you remember the torn cloth in the man's hand, the angular wedge of exposed skin? Did Jane wrench your shoulder?

Perhaps it always happened this way. There is no denying the fact that you remember it. The other possibility is terrifying: that the timeline is softer and more subject to revision than you had theorized.

If you can alter the timestring, then maybe you can make things better. This is almost as terrifying a prospect as helplessness.

There's no way of knowing for sure. The lunge is coded into the universe now, a fossil pressed into stone. Somewhere out there, a man remembers the day he nearly was attacked.

What you are doing here suddenly feels strange and dangerous as theft. You walk the house alone. When you do laundry, trying to pretend that everything is normal, the lint trap is clean of dog hair, and you cry into the warm clothes.

So you go back again.

When you return, when the needle goes into the soft fur, she whines for a moment, her eyes going wide.

Did she always whine? Perhaps you just forgot it in the terror of those final moments with her. Or perhaps you've further damaged her.

*

There are techniques in cryptography that allow one party to demonstrate that a given piece of information is true without actually revealing the information to another party. These protocols can be used to verify the authenticity of encryption keys without disclosing the key.

Your perceptions are the result of progressive encryption. The message flows only one direction along the gradient, but you can use knowledge protocols to verify that one piece of information is true for the entire length of the information string.

You can't retain your memories when you travel back, but you can broadcast one crucial piece of information to yourself. There is only one message that can be transmitted, and it is that this is not the first time the string has been decoded.

You're watching television with Jane on the couch. Her paws are rough and warm. They smell like Fritos, although you have never eaten Fritos and subsequently found yourself thinking of dog paws. Some information flows only in a single direction.

The claws curve out of the soft fur over her pads. When you take a paw between your palms, she withdraws it, eyeing you for signs of intent to clip her nails. You take her paw again and rest it on your palm, and she watches with liquid brown eyes. Her front leg twitches, prepared to withdraw if the clippers appear.

"We're holding paws," you tell her.

There is something satisfying about annoying her just a little, seeing how much stupid behavior she'll put up with. Sometimes, sitting on the kitchen floor together, you throw your arms around the sable ruff of her neck and hug her. She tolerates it for a moment because it's you, and she knows you perform many meaningless actions. If someone else attempted this, she would probably bite their ear.

Then you remember, you're time traveling.

You know nothing more of the future than this simple fact: this is not the first time you've lived this moment. At some point in your coming life, you will discover a way to return to this body on the couch with Jane, armed with the alarming piece of information that this is not the first time you've been here.

You look around the room. There's an old episode of a sitcom on TV. Nothing here seems out of place. Why did you pick this moment? You wait, and nothing happens, except Jane rumbles a low growl and withdraws her leg. She stands up and moves further away on the couch. She's had enough of holding paws.

In a year you put your arm over her and bury your face against her neck. "Don't leave me," you whisper, knowing you could never ask this if she could understand. She whines when the needle goes in. You wait for another exasperated sigh, another breath. You put your hands over her soft, warm paws, caressing the rough pads, and she does not pull away.

Did she always growl on the couch when you held her paw?
   Did she always lunge at the man?
   Did she always whine when the needle went in?

Don't leave me, you said. But you were the one who left her. She reached the end of her timeline and stopped, while you went on without her. Her life was completely decoded, but you are still living inside the cypher. You should not feel sorry for her.

What would have happened if you'd never loved Jane? You would never have been in the woods the day she showed you she would fight for you. You would never have thought her warm paws smelled like Fritos. You would never have sat together on the kitchen floor, with Jane snuggled against your hip, and realized you weren't going to get up and make dinner if it meant leaving her.

What would happen if you went all the way back to before you ever met Jane in the shelter? What if the driver of the trash truck went into the shelter before you and walked out tethered to her, and she went home with him, and watched him on the sofa and the kitchen floor, and endured his silly hugs and attempts to hold paws and show his love in all the strange ways you must when you know someone will die but can never speak it?

What would have happened if you were never driving along New York Avenue at 4 a.m. and felt a thud?

You hurt her. If there's any way to go back and undo the hurt, you're going to try it.

You go back. You are driving on New York Avenue at 4 a.m. and feel a thud. You don't see anything in the rearview mirror. A week later you notice the dried blood on the bumper and go to the shelter, afraid of what you will find there.

She deserved better. She deserved never to meet you. You go back again.

You are driving on New York Avenue at 4 a.m. and you are time traveling. You don't know how you're aware of this, but at some point in the future you will devise a means of returning to this moment. There is a thud.

Three years later the needle goes in, and you ask her never to leave you.

Jane deserved better than you. You go back.

You are time traveling as you drive on New York Avenue at 4 a.m. There is a thud.

A week later she rears up and breathes in your face in the shelter and looks into your eyes, and you know that you would do anything to save her.

Three years later she is dying, and doesn't know she's dying. "Don't leave me," you whisper, knowing you can only say it because it's in a code she cannot understand.

Then you are time traveling and wondering if in every iteration you are harming her further because you can't let go.

You are time traveling. There is a thud. Again you feel the moment when you wrote the wound on her, inscribed the limp that lasted the rest of her life.

Still you go back.

There's no way to know how many times you've been here. Each iteration feels like the first: a painful crushing-together of unfolded possibilities, the encryption of treasured memories into gibberish. With each reversal of time, the love you felt for Jane diminishes like a failing light until you're in the shelter the moment before you saw her through the metal cage. Then it winks out entirely. The clocks move forward again, and it bursts into existence, the beginning of a new universe.

Always there is the thud, and always, three years later, the needle. And on this return—the first, or the thousandth—you understand that it's not your first day that has drawn you back but the last. Not the accident but the needle.

You will go back one final time.

You find a way to fold one additional piece of information into the message you broadcast along the timestring: this is the last decryption.

You don't go back to undo what you've done. You can't hurt or love her any more than you already have. There's comfort in that knowledge. You go back, just as you went back after the accident, to find her in the shelter.

You're time traveling. You don't know how you know, but at some point in the future you will invent time travel, and you've returned to this moment for a reason. But this is the last time.

You are driving on New York Avenue at 4 a.m. and feel a thud.

A week later you find dried blood on the bumper and you go to the shelter. The dogs clamor as you walk by the cages, but none of them are the one you're looking for. You hear Jane barking as if she is trying to catch someone who is walking away.

This is the last time you will be here. It's up to you to figure out why.

You stand outside her cage and she rears up to face you.

"Be careful," says the man from the shelter.

Jane's flank is shaved over a ragged wound and her front leg is splinted. Her brown eyes are calm and confident. She breathes in your face. You draw nearer.

Jane has been labeled as dangerous. She will need time and training and patience and love. You could fail her. She will never consider alternate timelines or wonder if she deserved better. She will never know when her last day comes.

This will be your only chance. The most important thing about this moment is not that it has never happened before but that it will never happen again.

In three years you will rest your hand in the soft ruff of her neck as the needle goes in, and she will relax under your hand, and you will let the moment go.

You touch her bandaged paw through the cage. She does not withdraw.

"I'll never leave you," you whisper, and you never do.

Contributors' Notes

Other Notable Science Fiction and
Fantasy Stories of 2018

Contributors' Notes

Nana Kwame Adjei-Brenyah is a writer from Spring Valley, New York. His first book, *Friday Black,* was chosen by Colson Whitehead as a National Book Foundation "5 Under 35" honoree and won the PEN/Jean Stein Book Award. He graduated from SUNY Albany and went on to receive his MFA from Syracuse University. He was the 2016–2017 Olive B. O'Connor Fellow in fiction at Colgate University. His work has appeared or is forthcoming in numerous publications, including *Guernica, Printers Row, Gravel, Esquire, The Paris Review, Longreads,* and others.

▪ "Through the Flash" was one of the most difficult stories I've had to write, and somehow in that difficulty I knew it was the piece that would complete my collection. I wondered what it would be like to have a young girl who had somehow traveled to the very bottom of evil, seen what was to be seen, and come back intact and ready to help, knowing there was nothing worthwhile in the pit. To get there I needed an event. I imagined a nuclear fallout. One so devastating the future might try to stop it. And what if in their changing of history a timeline was flung from the continuum and set to a loop? What were the possibilities there? This story offered a chance to play in that possibility, starting with Ama, a girl who is as bad as they come and also the best. It was fun to learn who she was: a reformed viscous monarch. Still, it was also very hard to get the story to stabilize in a way that was followable. Time is a quick looping circle and I had to find a way to make that clear. More importantly, I had to find ways to make it feel that even in a loop, even if everything every day is the same, there might be a chance for something better.

Lesley Nneka Arimah was born in the U.K. and grew up in Nigeria and wherever else her father was stationed for work. Her stories have appeared in *The New Yorker, Harper's Magazine, McSweeney's,* and *Granta* and have been honored with a National Magazine Award and an O. Henry Award. She has received support from the Elizabeth George Foundation and the MacDowell Colony and was selected for the National Book Foundation's "5 Under 35." Her debut collection, *What It Means When a Man Falls from the Sky,* won the 2017 Kirkus Prize and the 2017 New York Public Library Young Lions Fiction Award and was selected for Now Read This, the *PBS NewsHour–New York Times* book club, among other honors. Arimah is a 2019 United States Artists Fellow in Writing. She lives in Las Vegas and is working on a novel about you.

▪ I was surprised by how much harder this story was to write than other speculative fiction I'd written to that point. It was originally intended to be in my first collection, but I couldn't get it together to make the story work. With most of the speculative stories I'd written, there was a specific element of "magic," whether live hair babies or someone with the ability to remove grief, and those elements helped to drive the story forward. In this case the invention (forced nakedness) was a state of being, not a pro-pulsive element that provided any momentum. It didn't help that Ejem, the protagonist, didn't want anything tangible that I could send her after; she just knew she didn't want what other women had. This uncertainty led to a lot of narrative aimlessness, something I'm not used to, and I threw a lot of things at the story that wouldn't stick (A resistance! A revolution!). What finally grounded the story was lessening the scope to the everyday. It didn't need a big bang or a "final battle"; it was at its center a story about female friendship.

Martin Cahill is a writer working in Manhattan and living in Astoria, Queens. He is a graduate of the 2014 Clarion Writers' Workshop and a member of the New York City–based writing group Altered Fluid. He has had fiction published in *Fireside Fiction, Nightmare Magazine, Beneath Cease-less Skies, Shimmer Magazine,* and *Lightspeed Magazine.* Martin also writes nonfiction reviews, articles, and essays for *Book Riot, Tor.com,* the *B&N Sci-Fi and Fantasy Blog,* and *Strange Horizons.*

▪ Through every draft of Hark's story, he and the reader are immedi-ately confronted with the strange: a cut of godmeat stinking of hibiscus and saltwater. "Godmeat" takes the reader to a strange, fantastic world of gods, monsters, and magic and the many people living amid that chaos. It also offers a new perspective on this strange world: that of a chef. Bringing that grounded perspective in with Hark, seeing how he dealt with the fan-tastical, how he cooked and prepared the gods themselves, was one of my favorite parts of the story. But watching him navigate a world full of beings beyond him with only his innate talents was one thing; seeing him recog-nize the power and position he finds himself in was another. For someone who's never had power but who holds so much pain, Hark doesn't realize until too late what it is he's allowed himself to keep doing. When he fi-nally does see how his actions have put the world at risk, it breaks something in him and pushes him toward a potential chance at redemption.

"Godmeat," can be a story about many things: what addiction to power does to someone in pain, how you can't truly serve others without giving away a part of yourself, how redemption and change can come at any age, and much more. I hope readers get something out of the story they never realized they were looking for and enjoy this first, strange foray into the Wild World. Most of all I hope readers finish the story and find it hard to shake that first image and what it represents: the raw godmeat on the counter, stinking of hibiscus and saltwater, and the skilled, broken man who will cook it, only just becoming aware of what he's doing.

Adam-Troy Castro made his first nonfiction sale to *Spy* magazine in 1987. His twenty-six books to date include four Spider-Man novels, three novels about his profoundly damaged far-future murder investigator Andrea Cort, and six middle-grade novels about the dimension-spanning adventures of young Gustav Gloom. Adam's darker short fiction for grownups is highlighted by his most recent collection, *Her Husband's Hands and Other Stories*. Adam's works have won the Philip K. Dick Award and the Seiun Award (Japan) and have been nominated for eight Nebulas, three Stokers, two Hugos, and, internationally, the Ignotus (Spain), the Grand Prix de l'Imaginaire (France), and the Kurd Laßwitz (Germany). His latest release was the audio collection *Other Stories,* which features thirteen hours of his fiction, including the new stories "The Hour in Between" and "Big Stupe and the Buried Big Glowing Booger." Adam lives in Florida with his wife, Judi, and a trio of revolutionary cats.

▪ "Pitcher Plant" was initially called "The Intruder," but the editor said that this was awfully generic and I ultimately agreed. This title actually tells you more, though you won't know it until after you finish it. I could just as easily have used the metaphor of a roach motel, I guess.

The premise is one I've been toying with for some time, for a novel that has yet to gel and might never (or, conversely, might). If the novel ever shows up, it will not be an "expansion" of this premise but an entirely different creature, attached to this iteration only by the flimsiest of threads. Don't hold your breath.

I have been asked how this resolution of the tale would affect life as we know it. My sad answer is that the new normal would be beyond horrific. Think about it.

Nino Cipri is a queer and trans/nonbinary writer, editor, and educator. A former resident of Chicago, they are a graduate of the Clarion Writers' Workshop and the University of Kansas's MFA program. Nino's fiction and essays have been published in dozens of different venues. Their short story collection *Homesick* won the Dzanc Short Story Collection Prize, and their novella *Finna*—about queer heartbreak, working retail, and wormholes —will be published in 2020. Nino has also written plays, screenplays, and radio features; performed as a dancer, actor, and puppeteer; and worked as a stagehand, bookseller, bike mechanic, and labor organizer. One time an angry person on the Internet called Nino a verbal terrorist, which was pretty funny.

▪ My mom moved to an old farmhouse a couple years ago. To get there, you have to drive down a long, creepy dirt road, past an old graveyard, decrepit barns, and some sheep that are definitely up to no good. So this story started from a particular scene on that dirt road: two characters in a car, and one of them unintentionally starting to drive dangerously fast. Why? What was happening in that car? What were they talking about? The story spun out from what turned out to be a climactic scene. The beginning came easily, but the middle was a muddle. Maddie and Nita's many conversations sat in a notebook for a couple years until I left Chicago for grad school in Kansas. The feelings of being simultaneously homesick for a place and estranged from it leaked into the story—with some added monsters and creepiness, just to keep things fun. I originally planned to write "Dead Air" as an audio drama, but realized that formatting it as a transcription would create a fourth wall for some extra horror to break through. Not that it was easy. It took multiple drafts before I could strike the right balance between giving readers enough information to understand the story and keeping the found footage aesthetic and structure.

Phenderson Djèlí Clark is the author of the novellas *The Black God's Drums* and *The Haunting of Tram Car 015*. His short stories of speculative fiction have appeared in various online and print venues. He presently resides with his wife, infant daughters, and pet dragon in an Edwardian castle in New England, where he is also a historian of slavery and emancipation.

▪ In a Mount Vernon ledger book, nestled between payment for window repairs at George Washington's Alexandria home and compensation to a ship captain for imported Nankeen cloth, is a curious notation: "By Cash pd Negroes for 9 Teeth on Acct of Dr. Lemoire." Washington's dental problems are part of popular Americana. They weren't actually wooden (as folklore suggests) but instead made from numerous materials. And perhaps, based on this notation, the teeth of slaves. I wanted to write a story about those mysterious teeth and the lives of the enslaved who parted with them. When it comes to the voices of the marginalized, the historical record at times throws up vexing silences. This case was no exception. Who the enslaved were and their motives remain lost to us. But even if we can't know, we can still imagine. As the early African American writer Pauline Hopkins maintained, fiction can be utilized to illuminate the larger truths of our fractured past. So in this story I turned to the speculative: mixing bits of history with elements of the fantastic to try to root out those larger truths.

Hugo Award–winner **Sarah Gailey** is an internationally published writer of fiction and nonfiction. Their nonfiction has been published by *Mashable* and the *Boston Globe,* and they are a regular contributor to *Tor.com* and *B&N Sci-Fi and Fantasy Blog.* Their short fiction credits include *Fireside Fiction, Tor.com,* and *The Atlantic.* Their debut novella, *River of Teeth,* was published in 2017 and was a 2018 Hugo and Nebula Award finalist. Their adult novel debut, *Magic for Liars,* was published in 2019. You can find links to their work at www.sarahgailey.com; find them on social media @gaileyfrey.

▪ "STET" was a labor of spite. I wrote this story after a conversation in which someone professed skepticism at the ability of a writer of genre fiction to read literary fiction and explore form in a similar fashion to a "literary" writer. At the time I tried to engage them about the false distinction between literary fiction and genre fiction, but when I got home, I was still angry. I decided to write a piece that in form referenced some of my favorite literary fiction, told in footnotes that inject emotion into an otherwise dry piece. My partnership with *Fireside Fiction* in publishing this was what brought it to the level it is now, both in content and in form.

Daryl Gregory's most recent novel, *Spoonbenders,* was a Nebula, Locus, and World Fantasy Award finalist for 2018. His next novel will be coming out in 2020. Other recent works are the young adult novel *Harrison Squared* and the novella *We Are All Completely Fine,* which won the World Fantasy and Shirley Jackson Awards and was a finalist for the Nebula, Sturgeon, and Locus Awards. The SF novel *Afterparty* was an NPR and Kirkus Best Fiction Book of the Year and a finalist for the Lambda Literary Award. His other novels are the Crawford Award–winning *Pandemonium, The Devil's Alphabet,* and *Raising Stony Mayhall.* Many of his short stories are collected in *Unpossible and Other Stories* (a *Publishers Weekly* top five sci-fi/fantasy book of the year). His comics work includes *Legenderry: Green Hornet* and the *Planet of the Apes* and *Dracula: Company of Monsters* series (the latter cowritten with Kurt Busiek).

▪ Here's the metaphor I'm going with: stories are rivers fed by many streams. "Nine Last Days on Planet Earth" came from many different ideas flowing through my head over the years, and it's impossible to say which came first, or which gave rise to the others. It's the mixing that makes the story. Here's a short and incomplete list of influences—ready? Our civilization's failure to deal with global warming because we can't think in global timescales, or even generational ones. My grandmother's house in Tennessee. The unlikely tidiness of science fiction stories in which huge problems are identified and solved in the space of weeks or months. Love.

My trip to Colombia. My best friend in high school, who risked coming out to me. Richard O. Prum's book *The Evolution of Beauty,* which introduced me to bowerbirds and the arbitrariness of aesthetic choices. Inflatable car-lot air dancers. Love. The video game my son created in high school which featured Fibonacci sequences. A time-lapse video of a bean sprout reaching for a ladder. The wacky 1973 book *The Secret Life of Plants,* and Alanna Collen's considerably less wacky but more eye-opening book, *10% Human.* Andy Duncan's meteoric mnemonic. My aging parents. My divorce. My aging body. My children. Love.

Ada Hoffmann's debut novel, *The Outside,* was released in June 2019. She is also the author of the collection *Monsters in My Mind* and of dozens of speculative short stories and poems as well as the Autistic Book Party #own-voices review series. Her work has been longlisted for the BSFA Award for shorter fiction, the Rhysling Award, and the D Franklin Defying Dooms-day Award. Ada is a computer scientist at a university in eastern Ontario, Canada, where she teaches computers to be creative and undergraduates to think computationally about the human mind. She has also worked professionally as a church soprano, free food distributor, and token au-tistic person. Ada is bisexual, genderfluid, polyamorous, and mentally ill. She lives with her primary partner, Dave, her black cat, Ninja, and various other animals and people. You can find Ada online at ada-hoffmann.com, on Twitter at @xasymptote, or support her work on Patreon at patreon. com/ada_hoffmann.

▪ "Variations on a Theme from *Turandot*" began in 2010, when I saw a full production of *Turandot* for the first time. I was enchanted by the char-acters and the music but dismayed by more or less the entire third act. My first instinct was to write a fix-it fic, the kind of thing that could go up on Archive of Our Own (AO3). But the more I worked on sketching out my ideas, the more I realized that there were more layers to them. I needed Liù not just to grow a backbone but to realize she was in an opera and to enter something very timey-wimey and meta. The questions I was tackling with this fic were so big that in 2010 I couldn't quite work out where to start.

   In 2013 the story idea was still itching in my head. Having some time off school between degrees, I set aside a few weeks and dived into all of the *Turandot* scholarship I could find, as well as a musicological biography of Puccini. (I would recommend the paper "Turandot's Victory," by Jack M. Balkin, as a starting point.) This led me, finally, to a very clean-looking first draft.

   This was already the most careful planning and research I had ever put into a short story, but it was only the start of a long process of further revi-sion. With every personal rejection and rewrite request I found even more layers that needed to be added in, including the hesitant relationship between the two sopranos in the "real" world and all the characterization of the Prince, whose interiority I had been actively avoiding at first. I consider the finished story one of the finest things I've ever written.

N. K. Jemisin is the first author in the genre's history to win three consecutive best novel Hugo Awards, all for her Broken Earth trilogy. Her work has also won the Nebula, Locus, and Goodreads Choice Awards. Her speculative works range from fantasy to science fiction to the undefinable; her themes include resistance to oppression, the inseverability of the liminal, and the coolness of Stuff Blowing Up. She has been a reviewer for the *New York Times Book Review*, an instructor for the Clarion and Clarion West writing workshops, and a writer for the comic book *Green Lantern: Far Sector*. In her spare time she is a gamer and a gardener, and she is single-handedly responsible for saving the world from King Ozzymandias, her dangerously intelligent ginger cat, and his phenomenally destructive sidekick, Magpie. Her essays and fiction excerpts are available at nkjemisin.com.

▪ I wrote "The Storyteller's Replacement" to practice using a frame to tell a story, and to dig a little at the roots of modern English-language fantasy to see what I could learn from them. In particular I decided to see if I could tell a Grimm Brothers–esque fairy tale that suited my tastes better —you know, retaining the quintessential fucked-upness of the old tales but without the anti-Semitism, etc. What fascinates me about the Grimms' tales is how utterly amoral they are. Moralizing, certainly—but not moral. In the pursuit of their goals, Grimm heroes frequently do horrific things; their heroism is strictly in the eye of the beholder. So what the tales teach, when they're shared with children, is not only the societal morals being centered but also which morals a society considers disposable in the process. I wanted to explore that. (And I'm aware that there are entire fields of study devoted to deconstructing folklore like this, but I'm not a scholar. When I want to understand a thing, I write.)

After I wrote this story, though, I was sort of at a loss for what to do with it. It didn't seem to fit any of the SF/F markets out there, and I didn't feel like it was literary enough to try that route. I knew it was a good story. It was just doing its own thang, not slotting neatly into any particular kind of category. That happens sometimes. So I set it aside until a place appeared for it or until I could *make* a place for it—which happened when I published a short story collection. Nice to see my patience pay off!

Usman Malik is a Pakistani writer who divides his life between Florida and Lahore. He has won the Bram Stoker and British Fantasy Awards and been nominated for the Nebula, World Fantasy, and storySouth Million Writers Awards. His stories have been reprinted in several best-of-the-year anthologies. In his spare time Usman likes to run distance. You can find him on Twitter @usmantm.

▪ As a child I was fascinated by snakes. I used to dream about having a snake as a best friend—weird, I know, but you have to understand I grew up watching movies about shape-shifting serpents and reading stories about the *naag mani,* the subcontinental version of the philosopher's stone that the oldest and wisest of king cobras is said to possess. In 2013 I was crossing a rain-thrashed street in Florida when a black eastern racer sped past me, scaring the crap out of me (I didn't realize until later what the species was). That was when I finally decided to put my pen to paper.

The idea of the child bride and the nomads of Thal and Rajasthan came from my memories of Pakistan and my wonderment at what a relationship between a man who raises a girl to marry and his bound protégé must be like. I have known such families in Pakistani villages and small towns, and are those not the stories we must tell, no matter how unseemly?

The most challenging thing about this story was the voice. I had to get it just right, because the narrator is an addict and I had to make sure he would ramble but just enough not to impede the flow of the story. That took patience and a lot of time—commodities I find in short supply in my life these days.

Theodore McCombs is a 2017 graduate of the Clarion Science Fiction and Fantasy Writers' Workshop in San Diego. His stories have appeared in *Beneath Ceaseless Skies, Guernica, Lightspeed Magazine,* the *Magazine of Fantasy & Science Fiction,* and *Nightmare Magazine,* among others. He lives with his partner and his cat in San Diego.

▪ Peter Wilson's *Twentieth Century Hangings* suggested the formal conceit for this story—an execution registry, with the convicts' crimes, motives, and last words drily noted—and supplied the white-hot rage that powered me through the writing of it. Because of course, most of the original crimes were against women. The execution registry, with its radically compressive form, juxtaposes these atrocities with the pathos of the men's executions and their wretched life circumstances; that juxtaposition seemed important to writing about capital punishment and to writing about misogyny. Sometimes when male authors write violence against women, even when it's properly treated as horrific and wrong, there's a tinge of indulgence to it. The diabolical super-rapist and the foregone victim is still a fantasy of male power over women, even if that power is finally rejected or restrained. In "Six Hangings . . ." the men are hopelessly outclassed, their power limited and provisional, and yet their violence still does lasting, bitter harm. That seems truer to my experience.

The story's other major influence is Henry James's Boston. I'd just finished *The Portrait of a Lady,* which I loved—those wily purple sentences belong to a brilliant old queen—but in retrospect I was responding to *The Bostonians,* which I had long ago given up on, with its ugly satire of nineteenth-century suffragism. So I suppose one can look at this story as my weirdest, grisliest, tardiest hot take on *The Bostonians,* if that seems fun.

Seanan McGuire is the Hugo, Nebula, Campbell, and Alex Award–winning author of more than forty novels, starting with 2009's *Rosemary and Rue* and extending through this year's *The Unkindest Tide.* Seanan has written for the *Alien* and *Predator* franchises and has written comics for Marvel Comics, including *Kitty Pryde, Nightcrawler,* and *Ghost Spider.* Her short fiction has appeared in collections published around the world. Seanan doesn't sleep very much and can be bribed into sitting still with offerings of Disney memorabilia, horror movies, and cold Diet Dr Pepper. When not writing, she can be found at Disney parks and in that one haunted cornfield where all those people disappeared last October. Where the corn is, Seanan can be found. Seanan lives in the Pacific Northwest, where she shares an idiosyncratic old house with her abnormally large, fluffy cats and several axolotls and spends her days writing too many words, pretending to catch up on her email, and reading comic books.

▪ Everyone makes big assumptions about monsters. Including what does and does not deserve the label. As someone who's worked in wildlife rescue and conservation, I am far too aware that sometimes the difference between "monster" and "magnificent" is just a matter of having soft-looking fur and big dewy eyes. Charismatic megafauna gets all the good press, even when it isn't deserved.

"What Everyone Knows" came from the questions of how monsters are labeled and how many of the things we view as monstrous are simply natural behaviors of creatures that deserve to be left alone. I have big feelings about reptile rescue and conservation. Some of those big feelings leak out in this story.

Annalee Newitz is a science journalist who writes science fiction. Founder of the website *io9,* she is the author of *Scatter, Adapt, and Remember: How Humans Will Survive a Mass Extinction,* which was nominated for the L.A. Times Book Prize in science. Her first novel, *Autonomous,* won the Lambda Literary Award, and her latest novel is *The Future of Another Timeline.* She is currently at work on a nonfiction book about archaeology and ancient abandoned cities. She cohosts the sci-fi podcast *Our Opinions Are Correct* and writes regularly about science and tech for *New Scientist,* the *New York Times, Slate,* and other publications.

▪ I first started thinking about "When Robot and Crow Saved East St. Louis" while I was visiting an archaeological dig at Cahokia, an ancient indigenous city that's just outside East St. Louis. Though nobody is sure why it was abandoned, we know Cahokia probably had a population of over 30,000 people a millennium ago—making it bigger than Paris at the time. All that remains of it today are massive earthen mounds, one of which has a footprint the size of the Great Pyramid at Giza. It's huge, and you can still climb it today. The rest of the city lies under at least two feet of earth. I spent two summers in a row visiting the dig and talking to the archaeologists working on it, who told me a lot about how the city changed over the three to four hundred years it was occupied. Cities are not static; Cahokia went through many different configurations and political structures before the last urbanites left in the 1400s. East St. Louis is actually built on top of a Cahokian neighborhood, as is St. Louis. So there is an ancient metropolis buried under the modern cities in the area, and that got me thinking about what would be built on top of East St. Louis eventually. I think of this story as taking place at the very beginning of a new kind of world that might replace our own. And who knows? Maybe it will have more in common with Cahokia than it will with East St. Louis.

Silvia Park's stories have appeared in *Tor.com, Joyland Magazine,* and *The Margins (Transpacific Literary Project)* and won the 2018 Fiction Prize from *Sonora Review.* Silvia is a graduate of the NYU MFA program and the 2018 Clarion Science Fiction and Fantasy Writers' Workshop. She's working on a novel about robotics in postwar Korea.

▪ When the Asian American Writers' Workshop released a call for submissions on the theme of plastic, I knew how this story would end.

Last year I read a news article about the vaquita, a deathly endangered porpoise with a beatific smile. A rescue team of veterinarians hauled in a rare female in the hopes of saving the species, which has fewer than thirty left in the wild. Placed in a sea pen, she deteriorated rapidly. They rushed to release her back into the ocean, but by then it was too late.

There is something immensely poignant about our efforts to salvage what we've ruined and destroyed.

I wanted to apply this earnest, flawed lens to a mermaid species, who look so eerily human it's tempting to think we understand them. Written in a gaze that is all too limited, this is a story that mourns and scolds and celebrates our unceasing attempts at empathy, restitution, and conservation—even if it's too late.

Brenda Peynado has been awarded an O. Henry Prize, a Pushcart Prize, the *Chicago Tribune's* Nelson Algren Award, a Dana Award, a Fulbright Grant to the Dominican Republic, and other prizes. Her work appears or is forthcoming in *Tor.com, Lightspeed Magazine, The Georgia Review, The Sun, Southern Review, Kenyon Review Online, The Threepenny Review,* and other journals. She's currently writing a novel about the 1965 civil war in the

Dominican Republic and a girl who can tell all possible futures, and she teaches in the MFA program at the University of Central Florida.

▪ This story came out of me in a sleepless twenty-four hours, all in one go. This happens for me when the story comes from an emotional outcry. It started with a vision of deep longing and pain for a lost world—that was the first image of the story, all those dragonflies crying out when looking up at kites. That emotion, that irreparable sense of loss, gradually mixed with the yearning of the narrator.

After that it was the feeling of guilt and responsibility that the narrator had for atrocities she could never take back that took over the story. Some readers have paid attention most to the neo-Nazis in the story, but what I wanted to explore was white and white-passing guilt, complicity in acts of hatred and misunderstanding that we regret. The narrator keeps continuing to cause harm in ways that are less obvious than those of the neo-Nazis, which means they're easier for her not to acknowledge, easier for her to cloak under the guise of trying to right her wrongs. She wants to be forgiven so badly, but the easy way. I wanted to explore more than the black-and-white good and evil that is so easy to fall into when writing dystopias. Yes, the system has codified so much wrong, but so can human nature, our best intentions, our need to call ourselves good.

Kelly Robson is an award-winning short fiction writer. In 2018 her story "A Human Stain" won the Nebula Award for Best Novelette, and in 2016 her novella *Waters of Versailles* won the Aurora Award. She has also been a finalist for the Hugo, Nebula, World Fantasy, Theodore Sturgeon, John W. Campbell, and Sunburst Awards. In 2018 her time-travel adventure *Gods, Monsters, and the Lucky Peach* debuted to high critical praise. After twenty-two years in Vancouver, she and her wife, fellow SF writer A. M. Dellamonica, now live in downtown Toronto.

▪ "What Gentle Women Dare" was a hell of a hard story to write. It went through nine versions over three years, all starkly different, though they all dealt with Liverpool sex workers in the 1700s. What was the problem? Overambitiousness, mostly. I was trying to encompass the entire history of violence against women—it's what the story demanded.

Nothing worked until I—quite incoherently—whined about the story to my friend Dominik Parisien, coeditor of *Uncanny Magazine*'s "Disabled People Destroy Science Fiction" special issue. He said, "Why don't you think about 'The Screwfly Solution'?" James Tiptree, Jr., is a huge influence on my work, and it turns out that that suggestion was exactly what I needed to dig the story out of its hole.

Sofia Samatar is the author of the novels *A Stranger in Olondria* and *The Winged Histories*, the short story collection *Tender*, and *Monster Portraits*, a collaboration with her brother, the artist Del Samatar. Her work has received several honors, including the John W. Campbell Award, the British Fantasy Award, and the World Fantasy Award. She teaches African literature, Arabic literature, and speculative fiction at James Madison University.

• Of all the stories I've written, I find "Hard Mary" the spookiest. Like many disturbing things, it started out fun. One October night I was swapping stories with friends, and my husband's cousin, who was raised Amish, shared some superstitions about Old Christmas that she remembered from childhood. I immediately wanted to put this stuff into a story, and when I did, I stumbled, just like my characters, onto a robot. At this point I was having a great time imagining this near-future or alternate-future community, filling it with surnames from my own Amish and Mennonite family tree and exploring the ways such a group might incorporate a new technology, as well as questions of personhood for robots and women. But soon another, weirder question began to assert itself, and this was the question of character. I became fascinated by the human desire for the almost-human: the way we consistently impose a humanlike character on our toys, domestic animals, cell phones, and, of course, the characters we write. Since these characters are only *like* humans and not actual people, our moral obligation to them is fuzzy. We're often unmoved—even entertained—when bad things happen to them. This started to creep me out. I felt that when Lyddie, my main character (!), insisted that the robot was a person and not a machine, she was also defending herself. She was defending herself against me. Is it possible to see a literary character as kind of artificial intelligence? And if so, what do we owe them, and how should we treat them? In writing "Hard Mary," I felt a character turn and look at me.

Adam R. Shannon is a career firefighter/paramedic and fiction writer. His work has appeared in *Apex Magazine, Compelling Science Fiction, Every Day Fiction,* and other magazines and anthologies. "On the Day You Spend Forever with Your Dog" was included in *Locus Magazine*'s recommended reading list and was a finalist for the Sturgeon Award. Adam is a graduate of Clarion West 2017.

• I wrote this story at Clarion West in the summer of 2017. I had been planning a lighthearted piece with a dog as one of the characters. Then our dog Zeus became extremely ill, and we had to euthanize him. He was a gentle, deaf German shepherd with spinal problems; we had lowered our bed so he could get into it without falling. He understood a few hand-signed commands and liked to pretend he couldn't see us when he didn't feel like doing what we wanted. This story emerged like a cry of pain at his loss. A lot of people have said that it made them cry too—sometimes in places they didn't plan to shed tears, like on the bus to work—and I can only hope that reading it was cathartic for them.

It can be agonizing to love something, or someone, when you know your lifespan will likely exceed theirs, and worse yet to know that you will probably be the one to make their end-of-life decisions. I hope this story reminds people to hold tight to the moment of committing yourself to another creature, no matter how time and events conspire to make the endings painful.

LaShawn M. Wanak lives in Wisconsin with her husband and son. Her fiction, poetry, and essays have been published in *Tor.com, Fireside Fiction, FI-YAH,* and many others. She reviews books for *Lightspeed Magazine* and is a graduate of Viable Paradise. Writing stories keeps her sane. Also pie. Visit her blog at tbonecafe.wordpress.com.

▪ Back in 2015, I was struggling with a lot of things—grief over my miscarriage, turmoil at my day job, fear over the upcoming election. During this I discovered Sister Rosetta Tharpe and her gospel music, which I latched on to like a lifesaver. Her songs and exuberance made me want to dig deeper into the music of that time, so when I came across Memphis Minnie and her blues, I knew I had to get them in a story together.

This story allowed me to weather the storm of that turbulent time. I used it to wrestle with faith, to mourn over loss, and to speak when I couldn't raise my voice. It gave me a chance to honor my past through the rich history of the South Side of Chicago. It connected me to my African American heritage of using music to uplift, encourage, and fight injustice. And while I can't sing to save my life, writing this story became my own form of beautiful resistance.

Plus, come on. It's a story about black women saving the world with the power of voice and guitars. That. Is. *AWESOME.*

Other Notable Science Fiction and Fantasy Stories of 2018

Selected by John Joseph Adams

GREENBLATT, A. T.
And Yet. *Uncanny Magazine*, March/
April

HARN, DARBY
Princess Mine. *Strange Horizons*,
March
HARROW, ALIX E.
A Witch's Guide to Escape: A
Practical Compendium of
Portal Fantasies. *Apex Magazine*,
February
HEADLEY, MARIA DAHVANA
You Pretend Like You Never Met
Me, and I'll Pretend Like I Never
Met You. *Lightspeed Magazine*,
September
HILL, JOE
You Are Released. *Flight or Fright*, ed.
Stephen King and Bev Vincent
(Cemetery Dance)
HO, MILLIE
Hehua. *Fireside Fiction*, January
HUANG, S. L.
The Woman Who Destroyed Us.
Twelve Tomorrows, ed. Wade Roush
(MIT Press)

IRIARTE, JOSÉ PABLO
The Substance of My Lives, the
Accidents of Our Births. *Lightspeed
Magazine*, January

JEMISIN, N. K.
The Ones Who Stay and Fight.
How Long 'til Black Future Month?
(Orbit)
JOFFRE, RUTH
Nitrate Nocturnes. *Lightspeed
Magazine*, April
JONES, STEPHEN GRAHAM
Broken Record. *The Devil and the
Deep*, ed. Ellen Datlow (Night
Shade)

KERR, JAKE
Three Speeches About Billy Granger.
*Resist: Tales from a Future Worth
Fighting Against*, ed. Gary Whitta,
Christie Yant, and Hugh Howey
(Broad Reach)

LA FARGE, PAUL
The Adventure of You. *Welcome to
Dystopia*, ed. Gordon Van Gelder
(OR Books)
LAVALLE, VICTOR
Ark of Light. *Particulates*, ed.
Nalo Hopkinson (Dia Art
Foundation)
LEE, YOON HA
The Starship and the Temple Cat.
Beneath Ceaseless Skies,
February
LE GUIN, URSULA K.
Firelight. *The Paris Review*,
Summer
LIU, KEN
Byzantine Empathy. *Twelve
Tomorrows*, ed. Wade Roush
(MIT Press)

MCGUIRE, SEANAN
Swear Not by the Moon. *Infinity's
End*, ed. Jonathan Strahan
(Solaris)
MILLER, SAM J.
My Base Pair. *Analog Science Fiction &
Fact*, May/June
MORRIS, STEPHANIE MALIA
Bride Before You. *Nightmare
Magazine*, May/June

NEWITZ, ANNALEE
The Blue Fairy's Manifesto. *Robots vs.
Fairies*, ed. Dominik Parisien and
Navah Wolfe (Saga)
NICHOLS, RUSSELL
Con Con. *Terraform*, September

OKORAFOR, NNEDI
    The Heart of the Matter. *Twelve Tomorrows,* ed. Wade Roush (MIT Press)
OLUKOTUN, DEJI BRYCE
    The Levellers. *Welcome to Dystopia,* ed. Gordon Van Gelder (OR Books)
OWOMOYELA, AN
    The Hard Spot in the Glacier. *Mechanical Animals,* ed. Selena Chambers and Jason Heller (Hex)

PINSKER, SARAH
    The Court Magician. *Lightspeed Magazine,* January

RIVERA, LILLIAM
    Crave. *Nightmare Magazine,* March
ROBSON, KELLY
    Intervention. *Infinity's End,* ed. Jonathan Strahan (Solaris)
ROLON, NELSON
    Saudade. *FIYAH,* Autumn

SINGH, VANDANA
    Widdam. *The Magazine of Fantasy & Science Fiction,* January/February

VAUGHN, CARRIE
    The Huntsman and the Beast. *Asimov's Science Fiction,* September/October
    Where Would You Be Now? *Tor.com,* February

WASSERSTEIN, IZZY
    Unplaces: An Atlas of Non-Existence. *Clarkesworld Magazine,* March
WILBER, RICK
    Today Is Today. *Stonecoast Review,* no. 9
WILSON, DANIEL H.
    Bastion. *Resist: Tales from a Future Worth Fighting Against,* ed. Gary Whitta, Christie Yant, and Hugh Howey (Broad Reach)
    Blood Memory. *Guardian Angels and Other Monsters* (Vintage)
WISE, A. C.
    In the End, It Always Turns Out the Same. *The Dark,* June
WONG, ALYSSA
    All the Time We've Left to Spend. *Robots vs. Fairies,* ed. Dominik Parisien and Navah Wolfe (Saga)
    Olivia's Table. *A Thousand Beginnings and Endings,* ed. Elsie Chapman and Ellen Oh (Greenwillow)

YU, CHARLES
    America: The Ride. *Resist: Tales from a Future Worth Fighting Against,* ed. Gary Whitta, Christie Yant, and Hugh Howey (Broad Reach)
YU, E. LILY
    Music for the Underworld. *Terraform,* March
    The No-One Girl and the Flower of the Farther. *Clarkesworld Magazine,* March

THE BEST AMERICAN SERIES®

FIRST, BEST, AND BEST-SELLING

The Best American Comics

The Best American Essays

The Best American Food Writing

The Best American Mystery Stories

The Best American Nonrequired Reading

The Best American Science and Nature Writing

The Best American Science Fiction and Fantasy

The Best American Short Stories

The Best American Sports Writing

The Best American Travel Writing

Available in print and e-book wherever books are sold.

Visit our website: hmhbooks.com/series/best-american